For a split secon

At first his m

Mondrago must

He ripped out a no   stick
in a martial-arts grip,

Chantal's eyes had been following Landry's in the direction of Athens. Neither of them had seen it. Now they whirled around, wide-eyed.

"Stay here!" Jason commanded, and ran after Mondrago, who was already out of sight.

He scrambled up to the cleft and looked left and right. Mondrago was just vanishing from sight behind a boulder. Jason followed and caught up with him in a tiny glade where he stood, gripping his walking stick like the lethal weapon which, in his hands, it was. He was looking around intently and, it seemed, a little wildly.

"Gone?" Jason asked, approaching with a certain caution.

"Gone," Mondrago exhaled. He relaxed, and something guttered out in his eyes.

"Did you see what I saw?"

"Depends on what you saw, sir."

"I *think* I saw a short humanoid with wooly, goat-like legs and, possibly, horns."

"On the basis of a very brief glimpse, I confirm that. Doesn't seem likely that we'd both have the same hallucination, does it?"

"It's even less likely that we'd actually see something corresponding to the mythological descriptions of the god Pan."

SUNSET
OF THE
GODS

STEVE WHITE

SUNSET OF THE GODS

Copyright © 2013 by Steve White

A Baen Books Original

Baen Publishing Enterprises
P.O. Box 1403
Riverdale, NY 10471
www.baen.com

ISBN: 978-1-4767-3616-7

Cover art by Kurt Miller

Map by Randy Asplund

First Baen printing, January 2013

Distributed by Simon & Schuster
1230 Avenue of the Americas
New York, NY 10020

Library of Congress Cataloging-in-Publication Data
    2012035231

Printed in the United States of America

10 9 8 7 6 5 4 3 2 1

SUNSET
OF THE
GODS

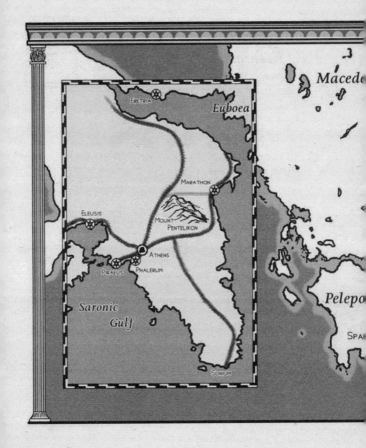

Thrace

AEGEAN

SEA

Euboea

Eretria

Plataea

Athens

Delos

Naxos

Samos

Sardis

Miletus

Lydia

Caria

CHAPTER ONE

EVEN ON OLD EARTH, nothing was forever unchanging, as Jason Thanou had better reason than most to know—not even on the island of Corfu, however much it might seem to drift down the centuries in a bubble of suspended time, lost in its own placid beauty.

For example, the Paliokastritsa Monastery had long ago ceased to be a monastery, and the golden and silver vessels were no longer brought there every August from the village Strinillas for the festival of the Transfiguration of Jesus Christ, by a road which had led laboriously up the monastery's hill between tall oak trees and through the smell of sage and rosemary. Now aircars swooped up to the summit, and the monastery had been converted into a resort, bringing visitors from all around Earth and far beyond it, who stared at the ancient chambers, a few of those visitors at least trying to comprehend what must have been felt by the cenobites who had lived out their lives of total commitment under the mosaic gaze of Christ Pantocrator.

They came, of course, for the incomparable location. From the monastery balcony, one could look out on the endlessness of Homer's wine-dark sea. Northward and southward stretched the coast, its beaches broken into a succession of coves by ridges clothed in olive and cypress trees and culminating in gigantic steep rocks like the one that the local people would still tell you was the petrified ship the Phaecians, once rulers of this island, had sent to bear Odysseus home to Ithaca and his faithful Penelope.

Now Jason stood on that balcony and wondered, not for the first time, what he was doing here.

He could have taken his richly deserved R&R in Australia, where the Temporal Regulatory Authority's great displacer stage was located . . . or, for that matter, anywhere on Earth. Or he could have gone directly back to his homeworld of Hesperia—his fondest desire, as he had been telling everyone who would listen. Instead he had come back to Greece . . . but only to this northwesternmost fringe of it, as though hesitating at the threshold of sights he had seen mere weeks ago. Weeks, that is, in terms of his own stream of consciousness, but four thousand years ago as the rest of the universe measured the passage of time.

There were places in Greece to which he was not yet prepared to go, and things on which he was not yet prepared to look. Not Crete, for example, and the ruins of Knossos, whose original grandeur he had seen before the frescoes had been painted. Not Athens, with its archaeological museum which held the golden death-mask

Heinrich Schliemann had called the Mask of Agamemnon, although Jason knew whose face it *really* was, for he had known that face when it was young and beardless. Certainly not Santorini, whose cataclysmic volcanic death he had witnessed in 1628 B.C. And most assuredly not Mycenae with its grave circles, for he knew to whom some of those bones belonged—and one female skeleton in particular. . . .

Unconsciously, his hand strayed as it so often did to his pocket and withdrew a small plastic case. As always, his guts clenched with apprehension as he opened it. Yes, the tiny metallic sphere, no larger than a small pea, was still there. He closed the case with an annoyed snap. He had seen the curious glances the compulsive habit had drawn from his fellow resort guests. The general curiosity had intensified when word had spread that he was a time traveler, around whose latest expedition into the past clustered some very odd rumors.

"Is it still there?" asked a familiar voice from behind him, speaking with the precise, consciously archaic diction Earth's intelligentsia liked to affect.

A sigh escaped Jason. "Yes, as you already know," he said before turning around to confront a gaunt, elderly man, darkly clad in a style of expensive fustiness—the uniform of Earth's academic establishment. "And what brings the Grand High Muckety-Muck of the Temporal Regulatory Authority here?"

Kyle Rutherford smiled and stroked his gray Vandyke. "What kind of attitude is that? I'd hoped to catch you before your departure for. . . . Oh, you know: that home planet of yours."

"Hesperia," Jason said through clenched teeth. "Psi 5 Aurigae III. As you are perfectly well aware," he added, although he knew better than to expect anyone of Rutherford's ilk to admit to being able to tell one colonial system from another. Knowledge of that sort was just so inexpressibly, crashingly vulgar in their rarefied world of arcane erudition. "And now that you've gotten all the irritating affectations out of your system, answer the question. *Why* were you so eager to catch me?"

"Well," said Rutherford, all innocence, "I naturally wanted to know if your convalescence is complete. I gather it is."

Jason gave a grudgingly civil nod. In earlier eras, what he had been through—breaking a foot, then being forced to walk on it for miles over Crete's mountainous terrain, and then having it traumatized anew—would have left him with a permanent limp at least. Nowadays, it was a matter of removing the affected portions and regenerating them. It had taken a certain amount of practice to break in the new segments, but no one seeing Jason now would have guessed he had ever been injured, much less that he had received that injury struggling ashore on the ruined shores of Crete after riding a tsunami.

The scars to his soul were something else.

"So," he heard Rutherford saying, "I imagine you plan to be returning to, ah, Hesperia without too much more ado, and resume your commission with the Colonial Rangers there."

"That's right. Those 'special circumstances' you invoked don't exactly apply any longer, do they?" Rutherford's expression told Jason that he was correct. He was free of the reactivation clause that had brought him unwillingly out of his early retirement from the Temporal Service, the Authority's enforcement arm. He excelled himself (so he thought) by not rubbing it in. Feeling indulgent, he even made an effort to be conciliatory. "Anyway, you're not going to need me—or anybody else—again for any expeditions into the remote past in this part of the world, are you?"

"Well . . . that's not altogether true."

"What?" Jason took a deep breath. "Look, Kyle, I'm only too well aware that the governing council of the Authority consists of snobbish, pompous, fatheaded old pedants." (*Like you*, he sternly commanded himself not to add.) "But surely not even they can be so stupid! Our expedition revealed that the Teloi aliens were active—dominant, in fact—on Earth in proto-historical times, when they had established themselves as 'gods' with the help of their advanced technology. The sights and sounds on my recorder implant corroborate my testimony beyond any possibility of a doubt. And even without that. . . ." Jason's hand strayed involuntarily toward his pocket before he could halt it.

"Rest assured that no one questions your findings, and that there are no plans to send any expeditions back to periods earlier than the Santorini explosion." Rutherford pursed his mouth. "The expense of such remote temporal displacements is ruinous anyway, given the energy expenditure required. You have no idea—"

"Actually, I do," Jason cut in rudely.

"Ahem! Yes, of course I realize you are not entirely unacquainted with these matters. Well, at any rate the council, despite your lack of respect for its members—which you've never made any attempt to conceal—is quite capable of seeing the potential hazards of any extratemporal intervention that might come in conflict with the Teloi. The consequences are incalculable, in fact."

"Then what *are* you talking about?"

"We are intensely interested in the role played in subsequent history by those Teloi who were *not* trapped in their artificial pocket universe when its dimensional interface device was destroyed—or 'imprisoned in Tartarus' as the later Greeks had it. The 'New Gods,' as I believe they were called."

"Also known as the Olympians," Jason nodded, remembering the face of Zeus.

"And by various other names elsewhere, all across the Indo-European zone," added Rutherford with a nod of his own. "They were worshiped, under their various names, for a very long time, well into recorded history, although naturally their actual manifestations grew less frequent. And as you learned, the Teloi had very long lifespans, although they could of course die from violence."

"So you want to look in on times when those 'manifestations' were believed to have taken place? Like the gods fighting for the two sides in the Trojan War?"

"The Trojan War. . . ." For a moment, Rutherford's face glowed with a fervor little less ecstatic than that which had once raised the stones of the monastery. Then the glow died and he shook his head sadly. "No. We cannot send an expedition back to observe an historic event unless we can pinpoint exactly when it took place. Dendrochronology and the distribution of wind-blown volcanic ash enabled us to narrow the Santorini explosion to autumn of 1628 B.C. But after all these centuries there is still no consensus as to the date of the Trojan War. It is pretty generally agreed that Eratosthenes' dating of 1184 B.C. is worthless, based as it was on an arbitrary length assigned to the generations in the genealogies of the Dorian royal families of Sparta. On the other hand—"

"Kyle. . . ."

"—the Parian Marble gave a precise date of June 5, 1209 B.C. for the sack, but it was based on astronomical computations which were even more questionable. Other calculations—"

"*Kyle.*"

"—were as early as 1334 B.C. in Doulis of Samos, or as late as 1135 B.C. in Ephorus, whereas—"

"*KYLE!*"

"Oh . . . yes, where was I? Well, suffice it to say that even the Classical Greeks couldn't agree on the date, and modern scholarship has done no better. Estimates range from 1250 to 1180 B.C., and are therefore effectively useless for our purposes. The same problem applies to the voyage of the Argonauts, the war of the Seven against Thebes, and other events remembered in the Greek myths. And, to repeat, the gods tended not to put in appearances in the full light of history. There is one exception, however." Rutherford paused portentously. "The Battle of Marathon."

"Huh?" All at once, Jason's interest awoke. It momentarily took his mind off the irritation he felt, as usual, around Rutherford. "You mean the one where the Athenians defeated the Persians? But that was much later—490 B.C., wasn't it?"

"August or September of 490 B.C., most probably the former," Rutherford nodded approvingly. The faint note of surprise underlying the approval made it less than altogether flattering. "By that period, it is difficult to know just how widespread *literal* belief in the Olympian gods was. And yet contemporary Greeks seem to have been firmly convinced that Pan—a minor god whose name is the root of the English 'panic'—intervened actively on behalf of the Athenians."

"I never encountered, or heard of, a Teloi who went by that name," said Jason dubiously.

"I know. Another difficulty is that Pan—unlike most Greek gods, who were visualized as idealized humans—was a hybrid figure with the legs and horns of a goat and exceptionally large . . . er, male sexual equipment."

"That doesn't sound like the Teloi," said Jason, recalling seven-to-eight-foot-tall humanoids with hair like a shimmering alloy of gold and silver, their pale-skinned faces long, narrow, and sharp-featured, with huge oblique eyes under brows which, like their high cheekbones, tilted upward. Those eyes' strangely opaque blue irises seemed to leak their color into the pale-blue "whites." The overall impression hovered uneasily between exotic beauty and disturbing alienness.

"Nevertheless," said Rutherford, "the matter is unquestionably worth looking into. And, aside from the definite timeframe involved, there are numerous other benefits. For one thing, the more recent date will result in a lesser energy requirement for the displacement."

"Well, yes. 490 B.C. is only—" (Jason did the mental arithmetic without the help of his computer implant) "—twenty-eight hundred and seventy years ago. Still, that's one hell of an 'only!' Compared to any expedition you'd ever sent out before ours—"

"Too true. But the importance of investigating Teloi involvement in historical times is such that we have been able to obtain authorization. It also helped that the Battle of Marathon is so inherently interesting. It was, after all, crucial to the survival of Western civilization. And there are a number of unanswered questions about it, quite aside from the Teloi. So we can kill two birds with one stone, as people say."

"Still, I don't imagine you'll be able to send a very large party." The titanic energy expenditure required for displacement was tied to two factors: the mass to be displaced, and the temporal "distance" it was to be sent into the past. This was why Jason had taken only two companions with him to the Bronze Age, by far the longest displacement ever attempted. Since the trade-off was inescapable, the Authority was constantly looking into ways to reduce the total energy requirement, and the researchers were ceaselessly holding out hope of eventual success, but to date the problem remained intractable. This, aside from sheer caution, was why no large items of equipment were ever sent back in time. Sending human bodies—with their clothing, and any items they could wear or carry on their persons, for reasons related to the esoteric physics of time travel—was expensive enough.

"True, the party will have to be a small one. But the appropriation is comparable to that for your last expedition. So we can send four people." Rutherford took on the aspect of one bestowing a great gift. "We want you—"

"—To be the mission leader," Jason finished for him.

"Even though this time you have to *ask* me to do it," he couldn't resist adding, for all his growing interest.

Rutherford spoke with what was clearly a great, if not supreme, effort. "I am aware that we have had our differences. And I own that I may have been a trifle high-handed on the last occasion. But surely you of all people, as discoverer of the Teloi element in the human past, can see the importance of investigating it further."

"Maybe. But why do you need me, specifically, to investigate it?"

"I should think it would be obvious. You are the nearest thing we have to a surviving Teloi expert." Jason was silent, as this was undeniable. Rutherford pressed his advantage. "Also, there is the perennial problem of inconspicuousness." Rutherford gazed at Jason, who knew he was gazing at wavy brown-black hair, dark brown eyes, light olive skin, and straight features.

Jason, despite his name, was no more "ethnically pure" than any other inhabitant of Hesperia or any other colony world. But by some fluke, the Hellenic contribution to his genes had reemerged to such an extent that he could pass as a Greek in any era of history. It also helped that he stood less than six feet, and therefore was not freakishly tall by most historical standards. It had always made him valuable to the Temporal Regulatory Authority, which was legally interdicted from using genetic nanoviruses to tailor its agents' appearance to fit various milieus in Earth's less-cosmopolitan past. The nightmare rule of the Transhuman movement had placed that sort of thing as far beyond the pale of acceptability as the Nazis had once placed anti-Semitism.

"If we were sending an expedition to northern Europe,"

Rutherford persisted, "I'd use Lundberg. Or to pre-Columbian America, Cardones. But for this part of Earth, you are the only suitable choice currently available, or at least the only one with your—" (another risibly obvious effort at being ingratiating) "—undeniable talents."

Jason turned around, leaned on the parapet, and looked out over the breathtaking panorama once again. "Are you sure you really want me? After my latest display of those 'talents.'"

Rutherford's face took on a compassionate expression he would never have permitted himself if Jason had been looking. "I understand. Up till now, you have taken understandable pride in never having lost a single member of any expedition you have led. And this time you returned from the past alone. But that was due to extraordinary and utterly unforeseeable circumstances. No one dreamed you would encounter what you did in the remote past. And no one blames you."

"But aside from that, aren't you afraid I might be just a little too . . . close to this?" Once again, Jason clenched his fist to prevent his hand from straying to his pocket.

Rutherford smiled, noticing the gesture. "If anything, I should think that what you know of Dr. Sadaka-Ramirez's fate would make you even *more* interested."

Deirdre, thought Jason, recalling his last glimpse of those green eyes as she had faded into the past. *Deirdre, from whom it is practically a statistical certainty that I myself am descended.*

He turned back to face Rutherford. "Well, I don't suppose it can do any harm to meet the other people you have lined up."

CHAPTER TWO

SEVEN DECADES EARLIER, Aaron Weintraub had held the key.

Before that, time travel had been merely a fictional device. That it could *never* be anything more than that had been as certain as any negative can ever be. Over and above its seemingly preposterous physics, the concept self-evidently violated the very logic of causality. The classic statement was the "Grandfather Paradox": what was to prevent a time traveler from killing his own young, childless grandfather? In which case, how could the time traveler have been born? And who, therefore, had killed the grandfather? No; this was one case in which the dread word *impossible* was pronounced without hesitation or doubt. Physicists and philosophers were at one about that. Reality protected itself.

Then Weintraub had embarked on a series of experiments to verify the existence of the temporal energy potential which he had postulated (to the near-unanimous hoots of his colleagues) as a necessary anchor to hold matter in time. If it existed, theory predicted that it could be manipulated. And Weintraub had proceeded to do precisely that. Subatomic particles had appeared in his device a few microseconds *before* the power was turned on and remained for a certain number of nanoseconds, and then vanished for the same number of nanoseconds *after* the switch was thrown. And nothing would ever be the same again.

But temporal energy potential had proven to be very resistant to manipulation. Subatomic particles sent back microseconds in time were the limit—and they only tolerated such unnatural treatment for nanoseconds before indignantly snapping back to their proper time. The physicists had heaved a qualified sigh of relief, the philosophers an unqualified one; Weintraub's discovery, however revolutionary in theory, was clearly devoid of practical applications, including the murder of grandfathers-to-be. Reality still protected itself.

Or so it had seemed for twenty years. Then Mariko Fujiwara had persuaded the by-then aged Weintraub that he had been traveling a dead-end road. Their joint experiments had confirmed her intuition: no energy expenditure could manipulate temporal energy potential to any significant degree; but a tremendous yet finite one, properly applied, could *cancel* it altogether, breaking the anchor chain, as it were, and setting an object adrift in time. That terrific energy surge sent the object three hundred years into the past before it became controllable. But beyond that it *was* controllable, and the object, living or otherwise, could be sent to a predetermined temporal point in the past. (*Not* the future, for temporal energy potential was in an absolute sense nonexistent beyond the constantly advancing wave-front known as "the present.") There the object would remain until its temporal energy potential was restored—very easy to do, for reasons relating to its already-known stubbornness. A temporal retrieval device that could be so miniaturized as to be easily surgically implantable, and that drew an insignificant amount of energy, sufficed to bring the object back to the location (relative to the planetary gravity field in question) from which it had been displaced, after a total elapsed time identical to that which it had spent in the past.

Neither Weintraub nor Fujiwara had been the kind of sociopath common in the fiction of the twentieth century, when science had first become scary: the "mad scientist" who would pursue his reckless experiments to the bitter end with fanatical if not suicidal perseverance, heedless of the consequences to himself or the world. They had recognized, and been duly terrified by, the mind-numbing potentialities of what they were doing. Moreover, they had been products of a society which had recoiled from the Transhumanist madness just as Europe had once recoiled from the seventeenth century's savage religious wars into the eighteenth century's mannered *ancien regime*. True to the twenty-fourth century's almost Confucian-like ethos, they had concluded that if reality no longer protected itself, someone else had to—preferably the bureaucratized intellectual elite committed to safeguarding the integrity of the human heritage that had almost been lost.

Thus the Temporal Regulatory Authority had been

born. The safest course would have been not to use the Fujiwara-Weintraub Temporal Displacer at all, but the temptation to settle history's controversies and resolve its mysteries by direct observation had been irresistible. So the Authority had been given exclusive jurisdiction of all extratemporal activity. Its legal monopoly had been confirmed by its possession of the only displacer in existence—an exclusiveness that hardly needed to be legislated, given the installation's colossal expense and power requirements, which placed it beyond the reach of any private individual or group. And even if some other organization *had* been able to build and operate such a thing, it could never have done so unnoticed, barring some as-yet-elusive breakthrough.

Then, as experience in time travel had accumulated, two realizations had dawned—the first one staggering in its implications, and the second one seeming to contradict the first.

The first was that the past could be changed.

The second was that reality still protected itself.

"There are no paradoxes," Jason stated firmly to his new team members. "There are no alternate worlds or branches of time either."

They sat in a briefing room deep in the Authority's town-sized installation in Western Australia's Great Sandy Desert, northwest of Lake Mackay—as far from population centers as it had been possible to put the displacer and its dedicated power plant, lest the latter's multiply redundant failsafe systems should ever prove inadequate. (As some wag had put it centuries earlier, "Mister Antimatter is *not* your friend.") Rutherford was also there, although he had thus far been uncharacteristically laconic, letting Jason conduct the orientation.

"But I don't understand," said Dr. Bryan Landry, with the thoughtfully perplexed look that came naturally to his mild, rather broad face. That face was gray-eyed and fairly light complexioned, and his straight hair was a prematurely graying brown. In short, he was not going to blend as well as the Authority—and Jason—preferred. But there was no help for it; all the available Mediterranean-looking experts in Classical Greek studies were disqualified by reason of age or health. The Authority sent no one back in time who was not up to the rigors of an extended stay under primitive conditions. Would-be time travelers had to be reasonably young and physically fit, and to pass a course in low-technology survival . . . and, for certain particularly blood-drenched milieus, a course in self-defense. It was a winnowing process that continued to elicit howls of "Discrimination!" from the groves of academe, but the Authority was adamant. When necessary, a cover story would be crafted around a team member's incongruous appearance. In the present case, their group would supposedly be from Macedon, where coloring and features like Landry's were less uncommon.

"You're not the only one who doesn't understand," Jason assured him. "Over the last half century, physicists and philosophers have joined the ranks of occupational groups—lawyers, for example—noted for drinking to excess."

Landry refused to be put off—Jason had already learned he could be stubborn in his mild-mannered professorial fashion. "Let me put it this way," he said, while reloading his briar pipe with his favorite brand of gengineered non-carcinogenic tobacco. (It was an indulgence he was going to have to do without in Classical Greece.) "I've done some background reading on the Authority's operations, and I know about your 'message drops.'"

"Yes," Jason nodded. "Putting a message on some very durable medium and concealing it in a prearranged place is the only way time travelers can communicate with the present."

"But if what I've read is true, such a message *isn't there* in its prearranged place before a period of time has passed in the present equal to the elapsed time the time travelers have spent in the past before placing it there."

"The 'linear present,' we call it," Jason interjected helpfully.

Landry looked even more perplexed. He puffed the pipe to life as though fueling his thought processes with tobacco. "Well then, suppose a time traveller, a day after his arrival in the early twentieth century, shot Hitler? By analogy, it would seem that those of us in the present day would continue for a day, until that point in the, uh, linear present, to live in a world whose history included Hitler and World War II and everything that flowed from them, and then suddenly, after that point . . ." He trailed to a bewildered halt.

Jason smiled. "Here's why your example doesn't apply. Those locations we use for our message drops are obscure ones where nothing is ever known to have happened. Hitler and World War II *did* happen. You can't go back and shoot Hitler—a favorite bit of time travel wish-fulfillment, by the way—for the simple reason that *we know he didn't get shot*. The past can be changed, but observed history can't."

"But *why* can't it?"

"No one knows. In fact, the question appears to be meaningless. All we do know is that something will prevent you from doing anything that creates any paradoxes."

Alexandre Mondrago spoke up. "This makes it seem like you have an awful lot of freedom when you're in the past, Commander." (He used Jason's rank in the Hesperian Colonial Rangers. The Temporal Service had no structured system of rank titles, and seniority was on an ad hoc basis; Jason was simply designated mission leader.) "Do anything you damned well want to do, because as long as you *can* do it, you know it won't do any harm." A white-toothed grin split his swarthy face. "Sounds like it could be a lot of fun."

Rutherford gave a pre-expostulation splutter. Jason waved him to silence while studying the Service man he wished he'd had more time to get to know.

Mondrago was shorter than Jason, lean but wide-shouldered and long-armed, with a nose that belonged on a larger face. People often wondered whether he was French or Italian. In fact, as Jason knew from his file, he was of Corsican descent—heir to a long and violent tradition. He had served as a professional soldier in a variety of capacities, but there was less and less use for his talents on today's Earth. So he had made himself a master of various styles of low-tech combat, eventually becoming so good that the Temporal Service had accepted his application despite certain reservations. This was to be his first extratemporal expedition. He was on it because what they were going into—while not quite bad enough to require the entire team to be combat trained—might involve a little more than Jason alone could handle, especially given the possibility of Teloi involvement. So, to assure the safety of the academics, Jason had been assigned a second Service man.

As a theoretical question of detached, intellectual interest, Jason wondered if he could take him.

"That's an attitude we don't encourage," Jason said. "And I'll tell you why. Before my last expedition, one of the team members asked me the same kind of question about shooting the young Hitler that Dr. Landry just did." *Deirdre*, flashed through his mind, and he stopped himself before he could reach for the little plastic case in his pocket. "I told her that if you tried it, the gun might jam. Or you might find out later that you'd shot the *wrong* little tramp. But here's a third possibility: maybe one of the hydrocarbon-burning ground cars they were starting to use in the early twentieth century would run you over while you were drawing a bead on him. You've heard that old saw about reality protecting itself? Well, reality doesn't give a damn *how* it protects itself. You might not want to be standing nearby when it's doing so. Clear?"

"Perfectly, sir." Mondrago's tone was more serious, but his eyes met Jason's unflinchingly.

"Furthermore," said Rutherford, no longer to be restrained, "there is the matter of elementary caution. Half a century's experience of time travel leads us to believe that what Commander Thanou has been telling you is true. But in the absence of absolute proof, we prefer to behave as though it is our responsibility to *make* it true. One example is the course of treatments you will soon be undergoing to cleanse your bodies of evolved disease microorganisms to which the people of the fifth century B.C. would have no more resistance than the Polynesians did to smallpox. We believe that reality helps those who help themselves. Or, at least, we dare not assume otherwise."

Chantal Frey spoke in the diffident, almost timid way Jason had learned was usual for her. "Is that why you've ruled out any expeditions to study the Teloi before 1628 B.C.?"

Jason studied her. The xenologist was a fellow colonial, from Arcadia, Zeta Draconis A II. He recalled that a tidelocked world of that binary system's red-dwarf secondary component held the enigmatic ruins of a long-dead race, which might help explain her interest in aliens. She was a youngish woman, certainly not a spectacular looker like Deirdre Sadaka-Ramirez (again he stopped his hand short of his pocket) but not altogether unattractive in a slender, intellectual-appearing way, with narrow, regular features and smooth dark-brown hair. Jason viewed her presence with a certain skepticism, doubting her ability to stand up under the various stresses of time travel. Granted, the Authority had certified her as up to it, but there was something about her—something besides her seeming physical fragility, a kind of weakness that went beyond that—that bothered him. He also wished she had some secondary skill to contribute, for if they did *not* encounter the Teloi, and the "Pan" legend proved to be just that, then an expert in alien life forms was going to be fairly useless.

At least, he thought (although he had no intention of

sharing the thought with her), her quiet personality should make her inconspicuous in the profoundly sexist society of Classical Athens, where the only assertive, articulate women were the *hetairai*—high-end whores/geishas whose unconventionality must have been a tinglingly irresistible turn-on for men accustomed to, and doubtless bored to distraction by, the "respectable" female products of the prevailing purdah.

"That certainly has something to do with it," Rutherford acknowledged. "That, and the ruinous expense of sending an expedition of useful size into the really distant past."

Landry looked troubled. "We've all heard something of these Teloi, and the rumors have been rather sensational, but it's all been awfully vague."

"We have been releasing the information with great caution, because of its revolutionary if not explosive nature. However, the three of you have a legitimate need to know more than the general public. As you recall, the Articles of Agreement you signed contain a clause requiring you to abide by all confidentiality restrictions applicable to information imparted to you. I trust you are clear on this—and on the legal penalties for violation." Rutherford paused. Jason reflected that Mondrago would be no problem—he understood security classifications. He sensed a hesitancy in the other two, and he understood why: they were academics, committed to the free flow of knowledge, and the whole concept of official secrecy was repugnant to them. But all three heads nodded.

"Very well. On that understanding, I'll ask Commander Thanou to give a brief summation of what he learned on his expedition to study the Santorini explosion."

"The Teloi," Jason began without preamble, "were an alien race of unknown origin. I say 'were' because we've found no trace of them in our present-day interstellar explorations. They were a very ancient race which had sought to genetically engineer itself into gods. They succeeded in making themselves effectively immortal, although not literally so, of course, and they could certainly die by violence. A side effect was a mentality incomprehensible to us—insane by our standards. Their chief drive became a need to find something to fill the eons of their empty, meaningless lives. About a hundred thousand years ago, one group arranged to maroon themselves on Earth, where they had discovered a species—*Homo erectus*—which by sheer coincidence was of a general physical form that could be molded by genetic engineering into a kind of sub-Teloi, useful as worshipers and as slaves."

Jason saw in their eyes that they knew where he was headed.

"Yes," he said, as gently as possible. "The Teloi created us. *Homo erectus* evolved by the natural course into *Homo neanderthalensis* in northern Eurasia, but the Teloi gengineered it into *Homo sapiens* in an area to the south, where northeastern Africa and southwestern Asia were then joined, in societies that were vast slave-pens."

"Now you understand why we have been reluctant to make this general knowledge," said Rutherford into the silence.

"We can be proud of our ancestors," Jason said firmly. "The Teloi didn't know what they'd created. The humans soon began to break free of their control, spreading across the planet, wiping out the Neanderthals and differentiating into the various racial stocks we know."

"How did you learn all this?" demanded Landry, puffing furiously.

"We learned it from Oannes, a member of another alien race. The Nagommo were hermaphroditic amphibians, extremely long-lived by our standards, who had been at war with the Teloi for a long time. One of their warships crash-landed in the Persian Gulf in the early fourth millennium B.C. The survivors, with a perseverance foreign to human psychology, continued to follow their basic mission statement, which was to fight the Teloi wherever possible, in any way possible. Stranded on Earth, this meant helping the humans in the area rebel, and teaching them the rudiments of civilization."

Landry almost choked on his pipe-smoke. "Oannes! Wasn't that the name, in Sumerian mythology, of a—"

"—Supernatural being, half fish and half man," Jason finished for him. "As rebellions spread, the Teloi tried to create a kind of super-stock of humans, using women as surrogate mothers of artificial embryos, to serve as proxy rulers. This was the origin of our legends of semi-divine Heroes." *One of whom I got to know*, he thought, remembering Perseus. "Once again, the Teloi blundered; their tame demigods were even less amenable to control than the general run of humans, and led still more rebellions.

"Eventually, the Teloi withdrew in disgust from the original civilized areas. By 1628 B.C., their area of activity stretched from western Europe to northern India, with a special focus in the Aegean."

"The Indo-European pantheon!" Landry blurted, scattering hot ashes on his shirt-front, which looked as though this had happened to it once or twice before.

Jason nodded. "Yes. We know them by many names from many places. In Greek mythology the older ones were the Titans, the first generation of gods—Cronus, Hyperion and the rest. The younger ones were the Olympians."

"But," Landry persisted, brushing off his shirt, "what happened to them? As I said, one hears some rather remarkable rumors about your expedition."

"Some rather remarkable things happened," said Jason mildly. "You see, the Teloi had an absolutely invulnerable refuge: an artificially generated 'pocket universe' with only one access interface, which was portable. We arranged for that interface to be obliterated in the Santorini explosion. The 'Titans' were permanently trapped in the pocket universe with most of their high-technology paraphernalia."

"Imprisoned in Tartarus by Zeus," Landry breathed.

"So the later Greeks thought. But it wasn't Zeus who did it. Oannes gave his life to make it possible." *The last of his race,* Jason recalled. *Not just on Earth but in the universe. Their war with the Teloi had proceeded to mutual annihilation. The Nagommo evidently won, but to do so they gengineered themselves into overspecialized subspecies . . . unsuccessfully, in the long run.*

I knew that, having seen the horror show that is the Nagommo home planet in our era, an endless vista of ruins inhabited by none but degenerate, deformed, sub-sentient travesties of what was once a great race—the race that unknowingly died to give us a future free of the Teloi. But

I never told him I knew it. I thought I was being merciful. Was I?

"One of my team members also gave his life," Jason continued. "A Dr. Sidney Nagel." *A conceited, opinionated, socially inept little twit . . . who taught me what courage is.*

"Wasn't there a third member of your expedition?" Mondrago asked.

Jason's features went immobile. "Dr. Deirdre Sadaka-Ramirez," he said expressionlessly. "She remained in the seventeenth century B.C."

They waited attentively for an explanation. None was forthcoming.

"Thank you, Commander Thanou," said Rutherford briskly. "Now you all know the background in general terms. During the next few days, you will be given more in-depth presentations, including video and auditory recordings of both the Teloi and the Nagommo."

Chantal Frey's eyes lit up with enthusiasm, which was immediately banked down by puzzlement. "But. . . . If you don't mind my asking, how were such recordings obtained? The Articles of Agreement were very explicit: we aren't allowed to carry any out-of-period equipment into the past."

"Good question," Mondrago nodded. "I'm new to the Service, but even I know about *that* restriction."

Jason and Rutherford exchanged a look. No words were needed to express their joint conclusion: these people had had about all they could handle for now.

"The answer will become clear in due course," said Rutherford smoothly. "In the meantime, I suggest you all get some rest. We have a busy day ahead of us tomorrow, including the implantation of your temporal retrieval devices."

Their faces reflected their distaste, which performed the distraction function Rutherford had intended.

CHAPTER THREE

THE FOLLOWING DAY, they underwent the biological cleansing process of which Rutherford had spoken—painless, but involving a certain degree of discomfort and indignity. In accordance with his usual policy, Rutherford also hastened them through something he had no desire to let them stew about.

"The temporal retrieval device, or TRD, is very tiny." He held up a metallic object no larger than a small pea. "It can be implanted anywhere; we generally prefer to use the inside of the upper left arm. It is a very simple in-out surgery."

Landry rubbed his itchy face (Rutherford had ordered all three of the men to start growing beards), scowled, and asked the question they always asked. "Do we *have* to have it implanted?"

"The Articles of Agreement you signed state that you consent to it."

"Yes, yes, I know. But is it *really* necessary?" Landry's uneasiness was reflected in Chantal Frey's face and, to a lesser extent, in Mondrago's. They had all grown up in post-Transhumanist society, and to them anything that blurred the line between man and machine was both illegal and flesh-crawlingly obscene.

"The Authority," Jason explained, "is responsible for getting you back to your proper time. Yes, we could build the TRD into some in-period object that you could carry. But then you might lose it, by inadvertence or theft. And with no TRD to restore your temporal energy potential, you'd be marooned in the fifth century B.C. permanently." He saw that he'd gotten through to them. "You *can't* lose something that's inside your flesh."

As was often the case, Chantal's voice was so quiet and hesitant as to be almost ignorable. "But . . . didn't you say that the third member of your expedition remained in the Bronze Age. How could that be, if—?"

"That was due to unforeseen circumstances, Dr. Frey." Jason's features and tone were carefully neutral. "The Teloi detected Dr. Sadaka-Ramirez's TRD and had it cut out of her."

Chantal's color didn't look particularly good.

"That sort of thing doesn't normally happen," Rutherford put in quickly. "In point of fact, that was the only time it has *ever* happened. At any rate, you now understand the importance of this procedure. And please be assured that the implant is a totally passive one, not involving any kind of direct neural interfacing." Their expressions combined relief with revulsion at the very concept. "The TRD activates at a predetermined moment, timed by atomic decay, at which moment you will find yourselves back on the displacer stage."

"And until that moment," said Jason, forestalling another question that always got asked, "there is no way to return to the present. You're going to be in the past for a fixed duration, come hell or high water. This accounts for the stringent health and fitness qualifications you had to meet, and the low-tech survival course you had to pass . . . and also for the non-liability clause the Authority has written into the Articles of Agreement."

"But," Landry persisted somewhat peevishly, "why can't you take along a . . . er, switch, or whatever, so you can activate the TRDs and bring us back if we find ourselves in difficulties?"

"Retrievals must be according to a rigid, entirely predictable schedule. That way, the Authority can assure that at the time you are due to return the displacer stage is clear of all other objects—objects with which you might otherwise find yourself sharing a volume of space." Jason smiled at his listeners' expressions. "Admittedly, the likelihood of this happening is small. But its consequences don't bear thinking about."

"One problem, Commander," said Mondrago. "We *don't* have inner atomic clocks. Isn't it going to be kind of startling when, to our eyes, the universe suddenly disappears without warning and is replaced by what we can see from the displacer stage?" From their expressions, it was clear that Landry and Chantal found the prospect unsettling to say the least.

Jason's eyes met Rutherford's. This could no longer be put off.

"It won't be without warning," said Jason. "I'll give you advance notice—not only to preserve your mental equilibrium, but also to make sure we vanish in private, so as not to alarm the locals."

"But how can *you* predict when the moment is going to be?" Mondrago persisted, in the tones of a man who was more than half sure he already knew the answer, at least in its broad essentials.

"My ability to do so relates to what I said before about recordings of the aliens we encountered in the Bronze Age Aegean. The fact of the matter is that I have an actual, neurally interfaced computer implant. Among other things—and this is almost the least of its functions—it provides me with a countdown to the time all our TRDs activate. It also has a recorder feature, spliced directly onto my optic and auditory nerves: whenever I activate that feature by mental command, it records everything I see or hear on media that can be accessed after I return to the present."

He studied their faces. Mondrago was taking it with equanimity—he had doubtless heard Service rumors about this sort of thing. The other two bore the excruciatingly embarrassed look of people who were too polite to reveal the prejudice they felt.

One of the human race's keys to survival is that human beings almost never carry any idea to its ultimate logical conclusion. There are, of course, exceptions: the Nazis and the Khmer Rouge come to mind. So it had been with the Transhuman movement, which, in the two or three generations it had ruled Earth before being swept away in fire and blood, had sought to exploit to the fullest the possibilities inherent in late-twenty-first-century cybertech and genetic engineering, splintering humanity into specialized castes serving an elite of supermen. The human psyche had never recovered from that abuse. The result had been the Human Integrity Act, which by now enjoyed the kind of quasi-sacred status the people of the old United States of America had accorded their Constitution. Any tampering with the human genome was forbidden. So was anything that blended human brains and nervous systems with computers. So was any application of nanotechnology that made nonlife difficult to distinguish from life. All of this had been seared into the human soul by the Transhumanists and their experiments upon themselves; legislation was almost superfluous.

"It has other useful—in fact, indispensable—features," Jason continued before the abhorrence could crystallize. "It gives me access to a great deal of information. For one thing, it can project directly onto my optic nerve a map of our surrounding area. We'll never be lost. And the recorder function is especially necessary in an era like the one we're going to, when paper and other such conveniences don't exist. Remember, what you bring back to the present, like what you take into the past, is limited to what you can carry—which, like the clothes you're wearing, is effectively part of the same 'object' as your body, as far as temporal energy potential is concerned." He saw that he had scored a point with the academics.

"So," Rutherford said briskly, "you can see why the Authority was able to make a case for the kind of limited exemption from the Human Integrity Act enjoyed by certain law enforcement agencies. And now, let us proceed to have the TRDs implanted—a very brief, practically painless procedure." He ushered Landry and Chantal out of the room. Jason was about to follow when Mondrago caught his eye.

"Question, Commander," he asked when the others were well out of earshot. "This computer implant of yours: as a fellow Temporal Service member, do I also get one?"

"No," Jason stated flatly. "That limited exemption Rutherford mentioned is *very* limited, and subject to constant scrutiny. We have to demonstrate a genuine need. As a practical matter, this means only the mission leader has one. You'll get one at such time as your seniority and experience qualify you for the mission leader function."

Mondrago looked thoughtful. "If you should buy it, sir, then as next senior Service member I'll be acting mission leader, and if so—"

"—You'll just have to get by without it. Sorry. We couldn't justify extending the exemption to cover potential acting mission leaders."

"Understood, sir." Mondrago's expression was unreadable.

"However," Jason continued, "as you've pointed out, you're a Service member, unlike Drs. Landry and Frey. So there's something you need to know and they don't. I'll take this opportunity to reveal it to you. Their TRDs—and yours—incorporate a passive, microminiaturized tracking device. Remember what I said about the map I can summon up? Well, the current locations of the three of you are going to appear on that map as little red dots."

"I can see how that might come in handy." Mondrago showed no sign of resentment.

"Extremely handy. Especially when a member of the expedition is lost or a prisoner." *And most especially when the TRD in question has been chopped out of its owner and we're trying to recover it.* Jason's hand strayed toward his pocket, but he was getting better about halting it. "Drs. Landry and Frey are having enough trouble accepting the necessity for any kind of implant. The fact that it has an additional function would only upset them unnecessarily. So you won't reveal it to them except with my permission. Clear?"

"Clear, sir."

"Good. Now let's get to the lab."

There followed the standard three-week orientation period . . . only in this case it lasted a little more than three weeks. The reason became apparent when Rutherford discussed the matter of language.

"The obvious pointlessness of sending people into the past unable to communicate in the target milieu," he declaimed, "enabled us to obtain yet another variance of the Human Integrity Act—a minor one. In the interest of practicality, the Ionic dialect of Classical Greek—the speech of Athens—will be imposed on the speech centers of your brains by direct neural induction. The process is harmless and non-invasive, although it can be disorienting, which is why our standard procedures call for rest and, if necessary, antidepressant drugs afterwards."

Landry was clearly unconcerned. In his excitement, he reflexively fumbled for the pipe that was no longer there. "Yes! Of course, this process won't enable us to speak the language like natives. But that works out perfectly, since we're supposedly from Macedon. Fifth century B.C. Greek was divided into four distinct dialects: Ionic, Doric to the south, Arcado-Cypriote (a survival of the old Mycenaean idiom) and North-West Greek. The last one—of which we'll supposedly be native speakers—was the most divergent. In fact, Athenian snobs affected to be unable to understand it at all."

Rutherford's intellectual forebears, Jason thought with a mental snigger.

"Our very thoughts," that worthy acknowledged with a gracious nod to Landry. "In this case, however, we will also be providing you with a *second* language, which you will find more difficult to assimilate: that of the Teloi."

Chantal—who clearly hadn't shared Landry's Classical Greek enthusiasms—now showed definite signs of interest at the prospect of learning a nonhuman tongue. "But how is this possible?"

"I was, for a time, a prisoner of the Teloi, Dr. Frey," Jason explained. He didn't elaborate. "In order to expedite interrogation, they rammed their language into my brain by a brute-force version of what you are going to be undergoing, with no chemical cushioning. The language's utterly alien structure didn't help either. Nevertheless, I came through the experience with about the level of comprehension that would be expected of a reasonably bright secondary-school graduate in a foreign language. By a reversal of the process, this was downloaded from me, and can now be provided to you—with great gentleness, of course. If we do encounter any surviving Teloi, you ought to be able to haltingly communicate with them . . . if the opportunity to do so should arise, and if you should want to."

Chantal, in her excitement, ignored the cautionary tone of Jason's last few words. With her and Landry both properly motivated, the team proceeded to the labs.

The rest of their linguistic preparation was relatively free of emotional hurdles, involving as it did conventional learning techniques supplemented by the kind of neuro-electronic "sleep teaching" technology that was an accepted part of their social background. They acquired a basic ability to read the Classical version of the Greek alphabet—unnecessary for Landry, who would be available to see them past any difficulties—for literacy was widespread among Greeks of their assumed social status. It was an accomplishment that Athenians would find impressive in natives of an ill-regarded place like Macedon, and would help offset the social stigma of such an origin.

Also, Rutherford drilled them in the Ionic Greek speech that had been impressed on their brains, assuring himself that they could actually converse in the language. This was more difficult for Chantal and Mondrago than for Landry, who already knew it as a written language, and Jason, for whom it fell somewhere between his own ancestral Demotic Greek and the harsh ancestor of Mycenaean Greek he had acquired for his last expedition.

For the Teloi tongue, Jason was of course the only one who could perform this training function. He took them through exercises, playing the role of a Teloi.

"Is something bothering you?" Landry asked him solicitously during one of these sessions. "A few times I've noticed—"

"No," replied Jason, more curtly than he had intended,

for in fact he *did* find this more disturbing than play-acting should have been, awakening memories that he'd thought he had suppressed, and other memories he'd forgotten— or never known in the first place—that he had. His annoyance with himself for feeling this way, and for taking it out on Landry, helped clear his mind of his distaste. "All right," he said briskly, "you next, Chantal."

She stepped forward eagerly, showing no signs of having shared Landry's observations. It was during this part of the training that she seemed to truly come alive, and this, too, disturbed Jason, for reasons he could not put his finger on.

CHAPTER FOUR

ORIENTATION OFTEN INVOLVED an actual jaunt to the target area, for purposes of familiarization. In this case, Rutherford deemed it unnecessary and possibly counterproductive, given almost twenty-nine hundred years' worth of changes. And in Landry's case—and, to a lesser extent, in Jason's—modern Greece was old hat anyway. Instead, he took them on virtual tours, enhanced by modern scholarship's best guesses as to what the landscape in question had looked like. Jason knew from experience that those guesses were sometimes surprisingly good . . . and sometimes not. He dared hope that the former was the case for the city of Athens, which had been the subject of centuries of dedicated and painstaking archaeological work.

They were also drilled in the historical background of the period—or at least Jason, Chantal, and Mondrago were. Given his academic credentials, Landry was an

39

integral part of the instructional staff, and quickly came to dominate it. For this, Jason eventually came to be grateful. Landry, a product of the same sort of social background as Rutherford, could be something of an irritating know-it-all at times. But he was a true teacher, not to be confused with an educational bureaucrat who held that title. In his introduction, he managed to clarify the labyrinthine complexities of fifth century B.C. geopolitics.

"To put it in the simplest possible terms—"

("Please do," Mondrago was heard to mutter.)

"—the Greek, and specifically Ionian, colonies on the Asiatic shore of the Aegean were loosely dominated by the kingdom of Lydia in the mid-sixth century B.C." Landry manipulated a remote, and a cursor ran over the area in question—the western fringe of what would much later become Turkey—on the map-display that covered the rear wall of the briefing room. "Then the Persians, under their first Great King Cyrus, conquered Lydia, including the Ionians. In order to keep the Ionian city-states under control, the Persians established tyrannies in them."

"They must have loved that," Modrago grimaced.

"Actually, that word doesn't have the blood-stained connotations it later acquired in English. A Classical Greek 'tyrant' was simply a man who ruled a city from outside the normal constitutional framework, with the support of one of the popular factions. The closest later-day parallel would be a North American big-city 'boss' of the late nineteenth and early twentieth centuries, although the position of Greek tyrant had more formal recognition than that."

"So he was well advised to take good care of his constituency," Jason opined.

"Precisely. But the tame tyrants of Ionia tended to lose sight of that because their other constituency—the one they *had* to keep happy—was the Great King of Persia."

"Why?" asked Chantal. "If their own people were behind them, couldn't they defy him?"

Landry gave her a look of rather supercilious annoyance, as though he considered the question naïve. Instead of answering it directly, he held up the remote and expanded the map to the east and south. And expanded it. And expanded it, until the peninsula of Greece and the entire Aegean basin had shrunk to kind of an afterthought at the upper left corner.

"The Persian Empire," he explained with almost patronizing care, "was the world's sole superpower. It had conquered the entire Near East and Egypt, as well as parts of Central Asia and the Indus Valley over here to the right of the map, in western India. It is believed to have had a population of at least sixteen million people, while Greece and the Aegean islands had, at most, two and a half million. Furthermore, it was not the result of gradual expansion over a span of centuries. Cyrus didn't begin his career of conquest until around 550 B.C. This unprecedented empire had burst on the world in a mere sixty years."

Mondrago studied the map intently. "How could the Persians possibly hold an empire that size together, at that technological level? I mean, infantry marching on foot. . . ."

"Yes. The Greeks were incredulous when they learned that the Persian capital of Susa was three months' march eastward from the Aegean shore. They would have been even more incredulous if they had known that the empire extended *another* three months' march beyond that."

"Then how—?"

"The Persians were the first empire-builders in history to recognize that communication was the key to control. They used a combination of fire beacons, mounted couriers using a system of highways with posting stations, and other techniques, including aural relay in mountainous regions."

"'Aural relay'?" queried Mondrago.

"Yes. They had men trained in breath control who could literally *shout* to each other across valleys and ravines where the acoustics were good, with lots of echoes, thus transmitting messages almost instantaneously across the right kind of terrain. By using all these various means the Great King was able to get information from the frontiers and send orders back in mere days, which seemed supernatural to the Greeks."

"I'm beginning to understand why the Ionian tyrants had to kowtow to him," Mondrago said seriously. "The *capo di tutti capi*."

"Yes. But by so kowtowing they were swimming against the tide of the Greeks' inveterate xenophobia, and thereby running the risk of alienating their own people. So their rule was always teetering on a knife-edge, and they were ready to jump either way: gain still greater favor with their master; or, failing that, go into rebellion out of sheer desperation.

"In 500 B.C. Histaeus, the tyrant of Miletus, the largest and richest of the Ionian cities, tried the first option. He himself was living at the Persian court in a kind of gilded hostage situation—they gave him the title 'Royal Table-Companion'—but through his nephew Aristagoras, who was standing in for him at Miletus, he offered to expedite a conquest of the Aegean island of Naxos, where he had contacts among the disgruntled aristocracy. As it turned out, Aristagoras made a total botch of the expedition. Rather than sit with folded hands and await the usual fate of Persian puppets who failed, Aristagoras reversed himself: he declared himself a convert to democracy of the kind Athens had had for the past eight years. He also called on the other Ionian cities to establish democracies and join Miletus in rebellion."

"The expression 'big brass ones' comes to mind," commented Jason.

"Indeed. The rebellion spread like wildfire through Ionia and beyond, and Aristagoras persuaded the Athenians to come to the aid of the new democracies. In 498 B.C. they sent an expeditionary force which marched inland and burned Sardis, the seat of Artaphernes, the local Persian satrap, or governor." Landry caused the cursor to flash on Sardis.

"Mission accomplished," Mondrago remarked drily.

"Not quite. The town was burned but the citadel held out and the Greeks were forced to retreat to the coast. On the way, they were cut to pieces by the Persian cavalry."

Mondrago looked perplexed. "I've studied the ancient Greek style of warfare, and I've always gotten the impression that the Persians had no answer to the hoplite, or heavy infantryman. That seems to be the pattern all the way up to Alexander the Great's conquest of the Persian Empire."

"One gets that impression because, as you've pointed out, the Greeks won in the end," Landry explained with a chuckle. "It's always the ultimate winner's successes that are remembered. It comes as a shocking surprise to most people that George Washington was soundly trounced whenever he came up against professional British troops in the kind of open-field set-piece battle they were organized and trained to fight. However, your point is well taken as applied to the phalanx of hoplites. When it could be brought to bear under the right conditions—head-to-head combat on a narrow front—it was indeed unstoppable by anything except another phalanx. But it was a rigid, inflexible formation, and the hoplites who comprised it, loaded down with fifty to seventy pounds of armor and weapons, were incapable of rapid maneuvering."

Landry manipulated his controls again. An image appeared on the screen, superimposed on the map. It showed a man who seemed to have stepped out of a Grecian vase-painting. He wore greaves on his lower legs, a cuirass with curving metal shoulder-plates, and a face-enclosing helmet with an impressive-looking but (to Jason's eye) impractical-seeming horsehair crest. He carried a large round shield and a spear a couple of feet longer than he was. At his side hung a leaf-shaped sword. The image represented modern scholarship's best reconstruction, which had turned out to be very much like those vase paintings after all.

"When hoplites armed and equipped like this couldn't form up, as in the retreat from Sardis, the Persian cavalry could ride circles around them and shoot them to pieces with arrows. In 479 B.C., that Persian cavalry nearly won the Battle of Plataea, before the Spartan phalanx could be effectively brought to bear. But the Persian style of warfare was, at bottom, a raiding style. The Greeks finally won by forcing decisive battles. Alexander became 'the Great' because he could catch his enemies between a phalanx and the heavy shock cavalry his father Phillip had invented—the most effective heavy shock cavalry the world would see before the advent of the stirrup. But the point is, we're going to be seeing the first of those decisive hoplite battles." Landry's eyes glowed with anticipation, then he shook himself and returned to his subject.

"At any rate, after the debacle of the retreat from Sardis, Athens withdrew into isolationism, leaving its Ionian allies to be brutally subjugated, a process that was completed by 494 B.C. with the destruction of Miletus. After which the Great King Darius decided it was time to punish those Greeks across the Aegean who had aided the rebels. In 491 B.C. his emissaries toured Greece demanding 'earth and water'—the tokens of submission. Athens and Sparta violated the diplomatic niceties by killing the emissaries, in the case of the Spartans by throwing them down a well, at whose bottom they were told they could find what they sought." Mondrago smothered a guffaw. Landry shot him a primly disapproving look before resuming.

"This was very bold, you see; the Persians had already established a satrapy in Thrace, to the north of the Aegean, and had an army there. But their accompanying fleet was wrecked by a storm, which made invasion from the north impractical. Instead, a new fleet was prepared—six hundred ships, including some specialized for transporting cavalry horses. It carried an army we believe numbered as many as 35,000 infantry and 1,000 cavalry—the Greeks later claimed it was hundreds of thousands, but they always believed in making a good story even better. It also carried

Hippias, the last tyrant of Athens, who had been working for the Persians since being deposed in 510 B.C. He was now over eighty years old, but still hoped to be restored to power. Instead of working its way north, the fleet island-hopped directly across the Aegean and took the city of Eretria on the island of Euboea, an Ionian ally, with the help of fifth columnists. They then burned it and enslaved the population . . . which was also meant to be the fate of Athens."

"Which brings us to your mission," said Rutherford, who had entered the room unnoticed. "You omitted one thing, Bryan: in 492 B.C King Alexander I of Macedon, who was reliable only as a weathervane, made his kingdom a Persian client-state. This is convenient for us, for your cover story is that you are Macedonians who opposed submission to Persia and are in exile as a consequence. This should assure you of a friendly reception in Athens—particularly from the man we intend for you to contact. But for now, I believe it is too late in the day to begin your detailed briefing on the Marathon campaign itself—which, at any rate, should be left to the end, so as to be as fresh as possible in your minds. Also, we have other matters to take up tomorrow."

CHAPTER FIVE

THEIR ORIENTATION INVOLVED a great many mundane things, such as their wardrobe.

The fabrics had to be authentic, of course—mostly wool, but also flax and the coarse animal-hair cloth called *sakkos*. But the Authority's specialists had a lot of practice at producing such things. The basic male garment—there was no such thing as underwear—was the tunic known as the *chiton*, fastened at both shoulders and tied at the waist with a girdle. Over this was worn the *himation*, a large rectangular woolen cloak draped around the left shoulder and back around under the right arm and across the front. Anything even remotely resembling trousers was regarded as hilariously effeminate, which was one reason why the Athenians had underestimated the Persians before their disastrous expedition in support of the Ionian rebels. By 490 B.C., of course, the trouser-wearers from the East were no longer quite so funny. The *chlamys*, or cold-weather cloak, shouldn't come into the picture in the time of year they were planning to spend in ancient Greece. As travelers from afar, they would be able to justify wearing sturdy boots rather than the more typical light sandals, and also the broad-brimmed felt hat, or *petasos*.

Chantal would wear an ankle-length linen tunic, held up by pins at the shoulders and at other points to form loose sleeves. Over this she would be expected to drape the *himation*, preferably wrapped around her head—or, alternatively, a head-scarf. Classical Athens was not all that unlike fundamentalist Islam where the status of women was concerned. At least she should be able to get away with light sandals rather than bare feet. Her hair was long enough to be pulled back with ribbons into the orthodox ponytail or bun.

The men would naturally not be lugging around the hoplite panoply. As Landry explained, even hoplites only burdened themselves with that load of armor and weapons a few minutes before taking their places in the phalanx for battle. And at any rate, Jason didn't expect to be doing that sort of fighting; still less did Mondrago, given his assumed social class, and least of all did Landry. There were no such things as professional soldiers in fifth century B.C. Greece, aside from the Spartans, who were considered freakish for the degree to which they specialized in war. Athenian hoplites were simply the male members of the property-owning classes of citizens, who could afford (and were expected) to equip themselves with the panoply. They were liable for military service from eighteen to sixty, and given Greece's chronic internecine wars they were likely to spend the majority of their summers that way. In between, training was minimal. In phalanx warfare, what counted was the steadfastness that held the shield-wall unbroken even in the shattering clash of spears. Those men weren't flashy martial artists, but theirs had been the collective courage in whose shelter Western civilization had survived infancy.

However, the team's supposed homeland of Macedon was a backwater which had retained the simple monarchy of the Bronze Age while the other Greek states had been evolving into civic societies. In fact, Macedon probably came closer in some ways to what Jason remembered from the seventeenth century B.C. Jason would pose as a minor nobleman, Mondrago as a disaffected former member of the "King's Companions," a Macedonian holdover of the Bronze Age war-band. As such it would be normal for them to carry swords. Rutherford let them choose their blades off the rack.

One day Jason was in the station's gym, putting himself through some exercises with the double-edged, slightly leaf-shaped cut-and-thrust sword he had chosen—the most typical Greek pattern of the period—when Mondrago walked in from the adjacent courtyard, wiping his brow. The Corsican was holding a very simple sling: a small leather pouch with two strings attached, one of which was looped over a finger and the other gripped by the thumb. The user then swung the sling around the head and sent the stone or lead bullet on its way, propelled by centrifugal force. Jason had never used one, although he knew it was the favorite missile weapon of the Classical Greeks, who had never made any secret of their disdain for archery.

"Can you really get any accuracy with that?" Jason asked.

"You'd be amazed, sir," Mondrago said, with a jauntiness bordering on insouciance. "It takes a lot of practice, but I've been getting some. I asked the shop to make me some in-period lead bullets. They swear these are very authentic." He took one from his pouch. It was oval, an inch long, and bore on its side the Greek words for "Take that!"

"I'll take their word for it," Jason laughed. "By the way, did you ever pick out your sword?"

"Yes, sir." Mondrago went to the sword rack and took down a weapon quite different from Jason's: a single-edged Spanish sword, or *falcata*, forward-curved for maximum efficiency at chopping, although it had an acute point for thrusting—a vicious-looking weapon somewhat resembling the *kukri*, or Gurkha knife, but longer and with a finger-guard. Like Jason's more conventional weapon it was iron—strictly speaking, extremely low-carbon steel—and made to authentic specifications, although very well made within those limits.

"I know it's a slightly eccentric choice where we're going," said Mondrago, as though anticipating an objection. "But it's pretty common there. I've seen it in Greek vase paintings. And I kind of like it." He gave Jason an appraising look and lifted one expressive eyebrow. "Would you like to see a demonstration, sir?"

"Sure." They went to another rack and took down the small round wooden shields carried by Classical Greek light troops, not the heavy, awkward things carried by hoplites in phalanxes. Then they went through a couple of passes. Mondrago was good, Jason had to admit, and the *falcata* was like an extension of his sinewy arm. Jason found himself on the defensive, barely able to interpose the shield between himself and Mondrago's chopping strokes, until he got into the rhythm of the thing and began to use his superior size and weight to push aggressively, forcing his way in to closer quarters.

Mondrago backed off and indicated the shield. "Even these light versions kind of slow you up. Want to try it without them, sir?"

"Fine. Let's get suited up." Without allowing an opportunity for any reckless suggestions, Jason turned and walked toward the locker room, leaving Mondrago no option but to follow.

They put on impact armor, flexible but with microscopic passive sensors that detected incoming blows and caused the electrically active nanotech fabric to go to steel-like rigidity at the instant of contact. The stuff was standard equipment for riot police and certain others . . . and regulation safety equipment for weapons practice. Then they returned to the exercise floor and went at it in earnest.

Mondrago now altered his technique, using the *falcata* almost like a long knife, holding it low and emphasizing the point. Again, Jason had to adjust, parrying a dizzying series of thrusts. Then, abruptly, Mondrago shifted again, chopping down. As Jason raised his sword to parry, Mondrago brought his right foot around in a sweeping *savate*-like move, knocking Jason's feet out from under him. He brought the *falcata* up and then down in another chop.

But Jason brought his sword around and up. At the moment the *falcata* hit the instantly rigid fabric at Jason's left shoulder in a blow that otherwise might well have severed his arm, Jason thrust upward into Mondrago's crotch. There was no impact armor there. Jason stopped the thrust with his sword-point less than an inch short.

For a moment their eyes met. Then, with a crooked smile, Mondrago extended a hand and helped Jason to his feet.

"Very good, sir," he said. "But then, I've heard stories about some of the stuff you did in the Bronze Age, on your last expedition."

"Probably exaggerated. You're good, too. Very good. But I imagine a ranged weapon like that sling would be more useful than a sword if we should happen get into any trouble with the Teloi."

"Yes . . . the Teloi." Mondrago's eyes took on a look Jason thought he could interpret . . . and that he wasn't sure he liked, in light of what he had learned of the Corsican's background.

"In that connection," he began, "I've naturally studied your record. . . ."

Mondrago went expressionless. "Yes, sir?"

"Oh . . . never mind." Jason decided not to pursue the matter, at least for now.

And maybe not at all, he thought. *There's no point in making an issue of something that I'm hoping will never* become *an issue.*

In addition to clothing and weapons, something else produced with careful attention to period detail was the money they would be carrying. It was a great convenience that money existed in this target milieu, unlike the Bronze Age, where Jason and his companions had had to carry a load of high-value trade goods, well-concealed (but stolen anyway, to Jason's still unabated annoyance). The coinage of the period was chaotic, with each city-state issuing its own, but all were widely accepted. They carried Athenian silver *oboloi*, six of which made a *drachma*, which would buy a tavern meal with wine, and four of which made a *stater*. Also, because it would be natural for people coming from Macedon, which had been under Persian influence for a couple of years, they carried Persian gold *darics* worth about twenty-five *drachmai*, showing the Great King drawing a bow.

"The street name for these coins was 'archers,' for obvious reasons," Landry told them. He chuckled. "In the next century, when the Persians finally learned that the way to neutralize the Greeks was to subsidize them to fight each other, one Great King quipped, 'It would seem that my best soldiers are my archers.'"

In addition to gear, they needed names. Jason could use his own given name. So could Mondrago; "Alexander" wasn't uncommon enough to make his being a namesake of his former king remarkable. There was nothing in Greek even close to the other two's names, so Rutherford let them choose from a list. Landry would go by Lydos, Chantal by Cleothera. In the relatively elementary society of Macedon, people generally had no second names, identifying themselves as "son/daughter of so-and-so" if necessary. Chantal would be a cousin of Jason's, under his protection and that of his follower Alexander. Landry would be a part-Thracian family retainer, son of freed slaves, educated in Athens years earlier before returning to Macedon, who had been "Cleothera's" tutor and was still in her service.

Rutherford lectured them on the timing of their expedition. "Traditionally, it was believed that the Battle of Marathon took place on September 12. But for this to make sense the Persian fleet would have had to spend an inordinate amount of time getting across the Aegean. Furthermore, it is based on the Spartan calendar, which may have been a month ahead of the Athenian. And finally, it rests on unrealistic assumptions about logistics—specifically, the ability of the Persians to keep an army of such size fed. So the weight of scholarly opinion has shifted steadily in favor of a date in August. This is one of the questions you will be able to settle.

"You will arrive in Attica on July 15, 490 B.C. This will give you time to establish yourselves in a position to observe events, and also to discover the answers to the various unsettled questions concerning the preliminaries to the battle. But this expedition does not involve the evaluation of long-term effects, so an extended stay will be unnecessary. You will only remain for sixty-five days, after which your TRDs will activate on September 18, almost a week after the battle's latest possible date, although no one really takes the September 12 dating seriously anymore."

Landry's disappointment at the brevity of their stay was palpable.

"The experience of temporal displacement," Rutherford continued, "is a profoundly unnatural one which can cause disorientation. We have learned that this effect is intensified—sometimes dangerously so—if it takes place in darkness. Therefore, despite our preference for minimizing the chances of local people witnessing the, ah, materialization, you will arrive not in the dead of night but just after daybreak. Commander Thanou, with his extensive experience, will recover first and will be able to assist the rest of you until the effect wears off.

"You will arrive on the road—the Sacred Way, it was called—from Athens to Eleusis, a little to the east of the latter. There should be no one about at dawn there."

"Eleusis!" Landry's eyes took on a dreamy look. "The central shrine of the Eleusinian Mysteries! The ancient Greeks believed that Hades, the God of the Dead, abducted Persephone, daughter of Demeter, the harvest-goddess, and the resulting compromise was how they explained the seasons. A cave at Eleusis was believed to be the actual site where Hades emerged from the underworld and returned Persephone to her mother." He seemed to do a quick mental calculation, and his dreaminess turned to excitement. "Kyle, couldn't we stay for just a *little* longer? The ceremonies—about which we have very few hard facts, as the initiates were forbidden to speak of what they had experienced—took place just slightly after your return date, with the procession from Athens the thirteen miles to Eleusis, where—"

"—Where the initiates went through a series of purification rites for which they had been carefully and secretly prepared," Rutherford reminded him gently. "What, exactly, would you plan to do?" Landry looked crestfallen. "No, Bryan. With only one displacer stage in existence, our schedules are, of necessity, inflexible, as Commander Thanou has long since explained. And we have to draw the line somewhere. There would always be just one more enigma you'd want to unravel.

"You will proceed directly to Athens, where you should arrive in the afternoon. Commander Thanou, using the resources provided by his computer implant, will have no difficulty guiding you. He can neurally access a map showing all the main thoroughfares. I doubt very much if a complete map of ancient Athens *ever* existed, and if it had, it would have resembled a plate of spaghetti; most of the city was a maze of narrow pathways, lanes, and alleys. But you are going to be seeking hospitality from an individual whose area of residence is known. He is a prominent public figure, so once you are in that area, minimal inquiries should suffice to locate his house. And your politics should assure you a welcome there, as he is a leading advocate of resistance to Persian aggression." Rutherford looked annoyed. "Or rather, he *was*. Tenses are such a problem when discussing time travel!"

The rest of their orientation passed rapidly, and toward its end Rutherford allowed them a day of relaxation. On the last evening before displacement, Jason found himself at the bar of the station's lounge. As he ordered the last Scotch and soda he would have for two and a half months, he heard a familiar quiet voice behind him.

"Commander Thanou? May I join you for a moment?"

"Of course, Dr. Frey. But please call me 'Jason.' And may I call you 'Chantal'?"

"Certainly . . . Jason. We're going to be working together closely for some time."

They found a table and he ordered Chablis for her. She took a couple of sips as though to fortify herself.

"I've been hoping to speak to you privately," she began, "but the opportunity never seems to have arisen.

You see . . . I can't help being fascinated by that neurally interfaced implant inside your head."

"Fascinated? Most people are repelled by the concept."

"I know. I'd be less than honest if I didn't say *I* was, just a little, at first. But at the same time there's something exciting about it—the way it almost takes you beyond the ordinary human experience. I mean . . . what's it *like*?"

"There's really nothing transcendent about it. It's very utilitarian—just an extremely convenient way of accessing information in various forms and recording sensory impressions. That's as far as exemptions from the Human Integrity Act ever go, even in cases like ours where there's clearly a legitimate need." Jason laughed grimly. "Anything more is altogether too reminiscent of the Transhuman movement for most people's taste."

"Yes, I know. And of course they did many terrible things. And yet . . . I sometimes wonder if we're right to automatically reject all their goals. Surely there must have been some power in their ideals, at least at first, before the movement took power and grew corrupt. Perhaps some of the things they sought could be made to benefit the human race without resorting to their extreme methods."

Jason gave her an appraising look and ran over in his mind what he knew of her people's history.

They had been among those who had left Earth on slower-than-light colony ships in the early days of the Transhuman movement's rise to power, fleeing what they could see coming. The bulk of colonizers had gone to the nearer stars. The settlers of Arcadia, however, wishing to exile themselves even *more* irrevocably, had dared the thirty-five-light-year voyage to Zeta Draconis, most of that time spent in suspended animation. They had awakened to find that the second planet of that binary system's Sol-like primary component was a hospitable world, fully deserving of the name they had bestowed on it. And there they had remained in the utter isolation they had sought.

Meanwhile the near-Earth colonists had returned to Earth on the wings of the negative-mass drive they had invented, blowing in like a fresh wind that had begun the toppling of the Transhumanist regime. Only *afterwards* had the main body of the human race reestablished contact with Arcadia.

Thus, Jason reflected, this woman came of a society that had opted out of history and avoided the entire titanic, blood-drenched drama. Now, of course, in this day of faster-than-light travel, the Arcadians had reentered the mainstream of human society and subscribed to its dominant ethos. But perhaps they—and she—could not be expected to feel exactly the same thing the rest of humanity felt at the sound of the word "Transhuman."

"You won't find many people who'll agree with you," he said mildly.

"I know," she acknowledged. "And I'm not even sure *I* agree with it, if you know what I mean. It *certainly* isn't something I feel strongly about. I just can't help wondering." She fell silent, and remained so for a few moments before speaking up again.

"Com . . . Jason, I hope you won't mind if I ask you another question."

"Go right ahead. As you pointed out, we're going to be working together. We shouldn't have any secrets."

She took another sip and laughed nervously. "One thing

I almost wish you *had* kept a secret: what happened to Dr. Sadaka-Ramirez's TRD." She shivered.

"Please don't let that prey on your mind. Rutherford was telling the truth when he said it doesn't generally happen, and that in fact it had *never* happened before. People of past eras have no way to detect implanted TRDs. It was her misfortune that the Teloi did." Jason halted his hand almost before it began to stray.

"And now we're going in search of the Teloi. . . ."

"The surviving Teloi, if any," he corrected. "If we do encounter them, they'll be in a far less powerful position than they were in the Bronze Age. Furthermore, this time their existence won't take us by surprise."

"I keep telling myself that. But there's something I'm puzzled about. Why couldn't she have been rescued?"

"Rescued?"

"Yes. It seems as though it would be possible—at great expense, admittedly—to send a second expedition back to the time just after your departure, carrying a new TRD for her, timed the same as those of the expedition members."

"Temporal energy potential doesn't work that way. You're linked to the time from which you come. Such a TRD would have returned to the time from which we brought it—but *she* wouldn't have, because she didn't come from that time." Jason took a long pull on his Scotch and soda. "And besides, you misunderstand. She didn't remain because she had to. We succeeded in retrieving her TRD. The self-sacrifice of Dr. Nagel, our third member, made that possible. She could have held it in her hand and returned. But she chose to stay."

"Why?" Chantal's question was barely audible.

"Very simple: she fell in love." Jason laughed shortly. "You know the old cliché about the hero getting the girl. Well, in this case the Hero did. Remember what I was telling you about the origin of demigods? She got herself a prime specimen: Perseus. Yes," he added as Chantal's eyes grew round, "*that* Perseus. One of the female skeletons Schliemann found in the shaft graves at Mycenae must have been her."

"I suppose he never knew what she had given up for him," Chantal whispered.

"You know, I never thought of it from that angle. But then, I'm not a woman."

"So," Chantal said after a thoughtful silence, "when you came back, I suppose her TRD appeared on the displacer stage with you . . . as did Dr. Nagel's corpse."

"Neither. Dr. Nagel's remains, TRD and all, were taken inside the Teloi pocket universe just before its access portal was atomized. And as for Dr. Sadaka-Ramirez's TRD. . . . Remember I mentioned that I spent time as a prisoner in the pocket universe? We all did—and she spent more time there than Dr. Nagel and I. And the Teloi kept the time-rate there slower than in the outside universe—it helped them seem immortal to their human worshipers. And the atomic timers of the TRDs. . . ." Jason saw that she had grasped it. He grimaced. "I was the first time traveler in the history of the Temporal Regulatory Authority to return behind schedule. I don't mind telling you I was nervous about appearing on the displacer stage at an unforeseeable moment! Fortunately, Rutherford had gone to great lengths to keep the stage clear."

Chantal wore a look of intense concentration. "If, as you

say, Dr. Sadaka-Ramirez was in the pocket universe longer than you—"

"Precisely. At some completely unpredictable time, her TRD will be found on the floor of the displacer stage."

Chantal looked at him very thoughtfully. "I've noticed that whenever this subject comes up you have a habit of reaching for something in your pocket."

"You are extremely observant. Just before my displacement back to the present she burned her last bridges by giving me her TRD." Jason brought out the little plastic case and opened it, revealing the tiny sphere. "Still there, I see."

"But sometime you'll open the case and it won't be. It will be on the displacer stage. And you'll have a kind of closure."

"You're as perceptive as you are observant—uncomfortably perceptive, in fact. Not that I'm complaining. It will be a highly useful quality where we're going." He regarded her with new eyes. "This isn't the most tactful thing to say, Chantal, but I think I may have underestimated you."

"People sometimes do."

"I've had my doubts about your ability to hold up under the conditions we're going to be experiencing," he told her bluntly. "I've also had doubts about your usefulness. But to some extent, that last has been wishful thinking on my part."

"I don't understand."

"Then let me put it this way. I hope your specialized field of knowledge will turn out to be irrelevant to our mission. In other words, I hope we'll find that by 490 B.C.

every last Teloi on Earth is dead and only remembered in myth. You'd probably consider them fascinating. I consider them abominations."

"You're very forthright. Actually, the same sort of doubts about what I can contribute have been worrying me. If you get your wish about the Teloi, I'll try to make myself as useful as possible, and not be a burden."

"I can't ask for more than that. And every member of an expedition is always needed. You can never foresee everything that's going to come up, and you never know what talents and abilities are going to come in handy."

"Thank you for the reassurance."

"Not at all. Let's have another round. By the way, have you ever tried any authentic Greek wine in the present day?"

"No, I haven't."

"Well, you'd better drink as much of that Chablis as you can while you've got the chance."

The day came, and they entered the vast dome that held the thirty-foot-diameter displacer stage, surrounded by concentric circles of control consoles and instrument panels. Rutherford gave each of them the handshake he always bestowed before withdrawing to the glassed-in mezzanine that held the control center. As he turned to go and the others climbed onto the stage, Jason spoke. "Uh, Kyle, I'd like you to keep something for me."

"I rather thought you might." Rutherford took the plastic case that would have been very hard to explain in the fifth century B.C.

Jason took his place on the stage and waited.

CHAPTER SIX

NO ONE HAD EVER SUCCEEDED in putting the sensation of temporal displacement into words. Words are artifacts of human language, and this was something outside the realm of natural human experience.

There was nothing spectacular about it—except, of course, from the standpoint of the people in the dome, to whose eyes the four of them instantaneously vanished with a very faint *pop* as the air rushed in to fill the volume they had occupied. As far as they themselves were concerned, there were no such striking visual effects. There was only a dreamlike wavering of reality, as though the dome and the universe itself were receding from their ken in some indescribable fashion. And, as though awakening from that dream, they were left with no clear recollection of having departed from the dome and no sensation of time having passed. Instead, crowding out the dream-memories, as the waking world will, was the dirt road they stood on, with the rising sun just clearing a ridge of hills and spreading its bronze illumination across the body of water that lay close to their right and the island of Salamis that could be glimpsed across that gulf. There was no one else in sight.

As predicted, Jason recovered from the disorientation first. Mondrago wasn't too far behind him. The other two both pronounced themselves ready to travel not too long thereafter.

"All right," said Jason, "let's cover as much ground as possible as early as possible. It's going to get hot later, at this time of year." As they hitched up the sacks holding their belongings and set their faces eastward toward the sun, Landry cast a wistful look over his shoulder at the barely visible hump of the acropolis of Eleusis to the west.

"Maybe we can find time for a side trip later, Bryan," Jason consoled him.

They proceeded along the Sacred Way with the aid of their four-and-a-half-foot walking sticks, skirting the Bay of Eleusis, as the sun rose higher into the Attic sky whose extraordinary brilliance and clarity had been remarked on by thousands of years of visitors, even during the Hydrocarbon Age when Greece had been afflicted by smog. Looking about him, Jason could see that the deforestation of Greece was well advanced since he had seen it in the seventeenth century B.C. Presently the road curved leftward, turning inland and leading over the scrub-covered ridge of Mount Aigaleos, which they ascended in the growing heat. They reached the crest, turned a corner, and to the southeast Attica lay spread out before them, bathed in the morning sun. In the distance—a little over five miles as the crow flew, with the sun almost directly behind it—was the city itself. Like every Greek *polis*, it clustered around the craggy prominence of its acropolis, or high fortified city . . . except that this one would forever be known simply as *the* Acropolis. It wasn't crowned by the Parthenon yet, but Jason knew what he was looking at, and what it meant.

He let Landry pause and stare for a few moments.

As those moments slid by, the sun rose just a trifle higher, and its rays moved to strike a certain cleft in the rocks. For a split second, Jason got a glimpse of—

At first his mind refused to accept it.

Mondrago must have been looking in same direction. He ripped out a non-verbal roar, grasped his walking stick in a martial-arts grip, and sprinted for the cleft.

Chantal's eyes had been following Landry's in the direction of Athens. Neither of them had seen it. Now they whirled around, wide-eyed.

"Stay here!" Jason commanded, and ran after Mondrago, who was already out of sight.

He scrambled up to the cleft and looked left and right. Mondrago was just vanishing from sight behind a boulder. Jason followed and caught up with him in a tiny glade where he stood, gripping his walking stick like the lethal weapon which, in his hands, it was. He was looking around intently and, it seemed, a little wildly.

"Gone?" Jason asked, approaching with a certain caution.

"Gone," Mondrago exhaled. He relaxed, and something guttered out in his eyes.

"Did you see what I saw?"

"Depends on what you saw, sir."

"I *think* I saw a short humanoid with wooly, goat-like legs and, possibly, horns."

"On the basis of a very brief glimpse, I confirm that. Doesn't seem likely that we'd both have the same hallucination, does it?"

"It's even less likely that we'd actually see something corresponding to the mythological descriptions of the god Pan."

"I don't know, sir. You saw some actual Greek gods on your last trip into the past—or at least some actual aliens masquerading as gods."

Jason shook his head. "Even if any of the Teloi are still around eleven and a half centuries after I encountered them, what we saw was definitely not one of them. It also bore no resemblance to any nonhuman race known to us in our era. And speaking of nonhuman races . . . I couldn't help noticing your reaction to this particular nonhuman."

Mondrago's face took on the carefully neutral look of one being questioned by an officer. "I was startled, sir."

"No doubt. But what I saw went a little beyond startlement." Jason sighed to himself. This could no longer be put off. He should, he now realized, have brought it up that day in the exercise room. But his hopes had led him to avoid the issue. He paused and chose his words with care. "As I mentioned to you once before, I studied your record during our orientation period. Among other things, I learned that you served with Shahanian's Irregulars in the Newhome Pacification."

"I did, sir," Mondrago said stiffly. His expression grew even more noncommittal.

As far back as the end of the twentieth century, the end

of the Cold War had led to a proliferation of PMCs, or "private military companies" like Executive Outcomes and L-3 MPRI, offering customized military expertise to anyone who could pay. This had proven to be a harbinger of the future. The need of fledgling extrasolar colonies for emergency military aid had soon outstripped the response capabilities of the chronically underfunded armed services, leading to a revival of the "free companies" of Earth's history, although in a strictly regulated form. The need arose in large part from the recurring failure of human colonists to recognize until too late that a new planetary home was already occupied by a sentient race, simply because that race lacked all the obvious indicia of civilization. Civilization, it had turned out, was a statistical freak. Tool-using intelligence, however, was not. Neither was the capacity to feel resentment at the environmental disruption that even the most minimal terraforming unavoidably caused.

Newhome, DM-37 10500 III, had been a case in point. The autochthones had been physically formidable to a degree that was exceptional for tool-users: steel-muscled hexapods whose three pairs of limbs could all be used as legs, propelling their quarter-ton mass faster than a cheetah. The forward pair could also be used as arms, the middle pair as relatively clumsy ones. The saberlike claws, the whiplike tail, and the tusklike fangs were, on some basic level, more frightening than the proficiency that the beings had acquired with captured and copied firearms. The colony had survived, thanks to imported professional soldiers who had inculcated the natives with a certain respect for the human race. But it had been too close for comfort, and an accommodation had been worked out under which human developments were restricted to geographically and ecologically distinct enclaves. By all accounts, the natives were now avid customers for the products of human civilization, and would soon be as peaceable and corrupted as one could wish.

During the fighting, though. . . .

"I've read some pretty harrowing accounts of that fighting," said Jason. "Some of them were almost unbelievably so."

"You can believe them, sir."

"You say that like a man who knows whereof he speaks. And I seem to recall a couple of comments in your record. . . ."

Mondrago's features remained immobile, and his eyes stared fixedly ahead. But they burned. "They used a captured M-47 AAM launcher to shoot down one of our transport skimmers. Some of the men survived and were taken, including a couple of friends of mine. We did a search-and-rescue sweep and found them . . . or what was left of them. I won't try to describe what had been done to them. Another time, we were a little too late responding to a distress call from a terraforming station. These weren't soldiers like my friends. There were women and children— although you could barely tell. We made those filthy alien vermin pay the next time we hit one of their villages."

A quaver had crept into Mondrago's tightly controlled voice by the time it reached the word *alien*.

"Yes," Jason nodded. "All this was touched on in those comments I mentioned. There were other comments in later stages of your career, whenever your duties brought you into contact with nonhumans. Never enough to actually get you in trouble, but. . . ." Jason met Mondrago's eyes squarely. "There's always been a possibility that we'd encounter aliens on this expedition. On the basis of what's just happened, I'd say that possibility has to be upgraded to a strong probability. Are you going to be able to handle that in a disciplined manner?"

The fire had gone out in Mondrago's eyes, and the stiffness had melted from his expression. He spoke with his usual insouciance, something short of insolence. "I was under the impression that protecting this party from aliens was what I was here for, sir."

"Wrong! You're here to protect the party from whatever I tell you to protect it from. And I have no intention of provoking any unnecessary conflicts with anybody, human or otherwise. That's not our purpose." Jason spoke quietly, but Mondrago unconsciously came to something resembling a position of attention. "Compared to some of the outfits you've served in, I'm sure the Temporal Service seems like a mildly well-supervised excursion agency. But you've read the Articles, including the provisions concerning the authority of a mission leader."

"I have, sir."

"Good, because it's not just boilerplate. Let me explain a little history to you. On Earth, about five and a half centuries before our time, a sailing ship or a military unit overseas was effectively out of communication with its home base. The commander therefore had to be granted a very high degree of authority to act on his own initiative— and to enforce discipline. Then electronic communications came in, and brought with them—"

"Micromanagement."

"No argument. But now the pendulum has swung back. With no such thing as faster-than-light 'radio,' messages have to be sent on ships, and a captain in the Deep Space Fleet is about as much on his own as a wet-navy skipper before they had the telegraph, and his legal status reflects that. With us, it's even more extreme. The 'message-drop' system gives us a not-very-satisfactory way to send information to our own time, but there's absolutely no way we can get information—or instructions—*back*. The Temporal Service may look like a loose-jointed quasimilitary organization, with no formal rank structure and everybody on a first-name basis, but in the crunch, a mission leader has legal enforcement powers that Captain Bligh would have envied. And I *will* have my orders obeyed, even if they cause you trouble because of the way you feel about aliens. Is that clear?"

"Yes, sir."

"I thought it would be. You're military, and you understand the necessity for this. The civilian members of extratemporal expeditions can't be expected to, and we prefer not to rub their noses in it unless it's absolutely necessary, which it usually isn't." Deciding that he had struck the right balance, Jason turned away. "Now let's get back to Drs. Landry and Frey. They're probably getting worried."

The two academics did in fact look jittery, but they still waited by the roadway. *Thank God*, Jason breathed inwardly. *They're the kind that can follow orders.* He'd had altogether too much experience with the other kind.

"What happened?" asked Landry, not unreasonably.

Jason never kept secrets from expedition members unless he had to. He forthrightly described what he and Mondrago both believed they had seen and had tried unsuccessfully to catch. His listeners' excitement— Landry's at the possible grain of truth in a Greek myth, Chantal's at a possible unsuspected nonhuman race—was palpable. He firmly squelched it.

"For now we're going to have to file this away under the heading of 'unexplained mysteries, to be deferred until later.' And we won't mention this incident to any of the locals. Clear? Now let's get going."

They descended into the rocky lowlands of Attica and walked on along the dusty road, past clumps of marjoram and thyme, and asphodel-covered meadows. They began to encounter people, but no one took any particular notice of them, save for an occasional glance occasioned by the oddity of a woman traveling abroad. But Chantal had wrapped her *himation* modestly around her head and face, so no one looked scandalized.

In this era long before automobiles, there could be little "sprawl." Besides which, there was something to be said for living within the protection of the walls. So the city was sharply defined. Landry had mentioned that historical demographers estimated its population at this time at a little over seven thousand, and that of the entire *polis* or city-state of Attica as maybe a hundred and fifty thousand counting slaves and resident foreigners.

"Athens was almost the only 'city-state' that really was one," he explained as they approached the walls. "Most of them were almost completely rural, with a little *asty*, or town, of not more than two or three thousand at the center of the *agros*, or countryside. So 'city-state' is a completely misleading translation of *polis*."

"Then why did the term become so well established?" inquired Chantal.

"Because we historians have always fixated on Athens, which was atypical to the point of being *sui generis*. It became—or 'will become,' I suppose I should say—even more atypical after the Persian Wars in the Periclean era, as the capital of an empire of 'allied' states, with a previously unheard-of population of over thirty thousand for the city itself and maybe as many as half a million for the entire *polis*."

They entered Athens through the Dipylon Gate, whose fortifications lacked the moat and forward defenses that would be added later, after this era's thoroughly unimpressive wall had been destroyed by the Persians in 480 B.C. and afterwards rebuilt. The man they were seeking was destined to be the driving force behind that rebuilding, and much else besides.

They passed through the labyrinthine alleys of the malodorous potters' quarter known as the Ceramicus, although in truth it was as noted for its cheap whores as for its ceramics. A number of the former were in evidence, or at least the women they saw had to be assumed to be such, for Athens's sixth-century B.C. lawgiver Solon (one of the most consummate misogynists ever to draw breath, according to Landry) had laid it down that any woman seen in public alone was presumed to be a prostitute. Only the direction-finding feature of Jason's computer implant enabled them to find their way through that maze, for they knew in general that their destination was south—and, unfortunately, downwind—of the Ceramicus, away from the potteries and whorehouses but near the Hangman's Gate outside of which was the dumping ground for the bodies of executed criminals and suicides. And the streets (by courtesy so called) still teemed with dogs, goats, pigs, and their fleas.

In addition to all the actual stenches, Jason detected a psychic one—that of fear. He had been in cities living under the threat of invasion before.

As they traversed the winding, unpaved, filth-encrusted alleyways, Jason frequently glanced at his followers. He knew from experience the difficulty twenty-fourth-century people had in adjusting to the urban aromas of antiquity, and those aromas were a particularly ripe combination in this part of Athens. Mondrago looked stoical, and the other two seemed to be holding up reasonably well.

"What made him decide to live in *this* area?" asked Chantal. Her tone implied that there *must* be more desirable neighborhoods.

"Politics," Landry chuckled. "He's of aristocratic birth, though not from a politically prominent family. But his pitch is to the poorer elements, so he moved here from the family estates so he could be closer to his constituency. It was also a good location for an attorney—yes, he was the first man in history to parley a legal practice into a political career. And finally, it's within walking distance of the Agora, where all the political and legal business is conducted. As far as we know, he's still living here now even though three years ago he was elected Eponymous Archon—the head of state for a year."

"A year? Then what's he doing now?" Chantal wondered.

"It is believed that at the time of Marathon he was *strategos*, or general, of his *phyle*, or tribe, called the Leontis. You must understand, this is an elective office. Every year each of the ten tribes into which the Athenian citizenry is divided elects a *strategos*, who can be reelected an unlimited number of times. The official commander-in-chief is the *polemarch*, or War Archon, who is elected by the whole citizen body."

"More lack of military professionalism," Mondrago commented with a sniff.

Political prominence naturally made him easy to find. Jason's first inquiry—which incidentally confirmed that they could make themselves understood in the Ionic dialect—yielded directions to a house larger than any of those nearby. It looked like it had been extended as its owner's political prominence had waxed. Still, it had the same basic look as all the others: built of plaster-covered mud brick, with rooms organized around three sides of a small courtyard, the fourth side facing the street with the main door in its wall. All the larger windows faced inward to overlook the courtyard; only narrow slits faced the street. From within came the sound of flute and cithara music.

Jason was wondering if it would be good form to knock on the door when a sound of voices came from around a corner of the street. A small group appeared, clustered around a man in his mid-thirties to whom they were talking animatedly. Never mind sandals and chitons; Jason knew political networking when he saw it.

But he only had eyes for the man at the center of the group. It wasn't every day that he gazed on someone to whom Western civilization at least arguably owed its survival.

Besides the conventionally idealized sculptures of the man they sought, Jason had seen a later Roman bust which was believed to have been a copy of one done from life. Now he realized that belief was correct, as he stared at the solid, powerful, thick-chested build, the blunt features, the massive jaw covered by a beard as dense and black and close-cropped as the head hair. The overpowering impression was one of unsubtle strength. That impression, Jason knew, was completely false, at least as far as the lack of subtlety was concerned.

The hangers-on departed, and Jason took the opportunity to approach. "Rejoice," he said, giving the conventional general-purpose greeting. He immediately found himself on the receiving end of a politician's smile, over which eyes of a very intense brown-black studied him. He launched into the stock story of their lives. "So," he concluded, "we departed Macedon because we could not live with our king's willingness to grovel before trousered barbarians. We were told that, as enemies of the Great King of Persia, we could hope for hospitality from the *strategos* who lives in this house."

The smile widened into something a little more genuine. "Well, Fortune has smiled on you, for you have found him. I am Themistocles."

CHAPTER SEVEN

THE COURTYARD WAS COBBLESTONED, as was typical of the better class of houses. As they entered it through the door in the street-side wall, they saw the duo that was the source of the music they had heard.

"It's not always easy getting Eupatrids to come to an address like this," said Themistocles in the tone of one anticipating an oft-asked question. The word he used was best translated as "the well-bred"—the monumentally snobbish Athenian aristocracy's term for itself. "So I like to invite the most popular musicians to use my house for rehearsal." He sounded ebulliently pleased with himself for his own cleverness. Jason had a feeling that he not infrequently sounded that way.

Themistocles led the way through the courtyard, with its surrounding portico which supported a balcony of the second-story women's quarters, to a doorway leading to the kind of reception room Jason's orientation had led him to expect. It was a small room—almost all Classical Greek rooms were—with an elaborate black and white pebble mosaic floor. The walls were painted in a singularly handsome pattern, with a baseboard in white-lined black and the main wall above in dark red. Themistocles motioned to servants to bring in the chairs and stools which, in sparsely furnished Athenian homes, were constantly moved from room to room as needed. Like everything else the Classical Greeks made, their furniture was beautiful.

The slaves also brought wine. It was the resinated wine that unkind non-Greeks all through history compared, unfavorably, to turpentine. In this case it tasted like turpentine-flavored water, for as custom dictated the wine was diluted. It was easy to understand why alcoholism had not been a widespread social problem in ancient Greece.

"You are most kind, *strategos*," said Jason, "to extend your hospitality to refugees." The word he used actually implied even more, for a Greek without a *polis* was in a very real sense a non-person, without an identity. *And not registered voters in Athens*, he left unsaid.

Themistocles gave an indulgent hand-wave. "Who am I to quibble about background? My mother Abrotonon was a Thracian." He bestowed a smile on Lydos/Landry.

"Ah," said Landry. "So your mother was not . . . that is, we had heard stories that a Carian—" He shut up under a surreptitious glare from Jason. *He's already told us all we need to know, Bryan*, his glare said.

It was the answer to yet another question. They had hoped that this version of Themistocles's parentage would prove to be the correct one, as it would give their host a certain sense of kinship with them. A second theory had held that his mother had been a Carian woman from Halicarnassus named Euterpe. Either way, there was no doubt that his aristocratic descent on his father's side had not saved him from being a youthful outsider in the maniacally exclusive society of Athens.

"In the old days," Themistocles continued, confirming Jason's unspoken assumption, "that was enough to deny me citizenship. We lived in Cynosarges, the immigrant district outside the city walls, when I was a boy. But then, eighteen years ago, came the reforms of Cleisthenes. The Pisistratid tyranny was overthrown, and the law changed."

"As I understand it, *strategos*," Landry ventured cautiously, with a nervous side-glance at Jason, "the need to fill out the numbers of the tribes into which Cleisthenes divided the Athenian people also helped extend the citizenship."

"No doubt about it," Themistocles nodded. "That was one of Cleisthenes's masterstrokes. Faction-fighting among the Eupatrid dynasties had brought Athens to the edge of ruin and opened the way for the tyranny of Pisistratus and his sons. His solution was to simply sweep away all the old family and clan identities by dividing Attica into ten tribes, made up of demes scattered all over. He even made people take their second names from those demes." He chuckled. "One of the demes was named after the Boutads, one of the grandest of all the aristocratic families. Instead of sharing it with every goatherd in the deme they gave themselves a new name: the *Authentic* Boutads!"

They all laughed. Actually, Jason had already heard the story from Landry, who'd said it reminded him of an incident in the history of his native North America, where vaporing beyond description had erupted in Boston around the turn of the twentieth century when a certain unpronounceable Eastern European immigrant had taken it into his head to shorten his name to "Cabot." It was good to have another anecdote verified. So far, this was proving to be one of those expeditions whose findings tended to confirm orthodox expectations.

Except, of course, for a certain sighting on the Sacred Way near the crest of Mount Aigaleos. . . .

"But," Themistocles continued, sobering, "it worked. For the first time, everyone—regardless of birth or wealth—could speak and vote in the Assembly. Athens became the first true *demokratia*."

Jason and Landry exchanged a look, for it hadn't been certain that this word—meaning a state in which power, or *kratos*, was invested in the people, or *demos*—had actually been in use this early.

"You have no idea what it was like," Themistocles continued. "Under the tyrants, we Athenians had never amounted to very much. Suddenly we behaved like heroes. Enemies from Sparta and Thebes and Chalcis descended on us like vultures, thinking we'd be easy prey—and we defeated them all!"

Actually, internal dissention—probably incited by Cleisthenes' bribery—stopped the Spartans, Jason mentally corrected, recalling his orientation. But for a fact, the Athenians had seemed transformed overnight by their democratic revolution. Themistocles's next words helped him understand why.

"So a whole new world of opportunities had been

opened up for me and others like me—there seemed no limits any more. When I reached the required age of thirty, my ancestry through my father made me eligible to run for Archon." Jason nodded, recalling that even though every citizen could vote only the upper classes could run for high office. "I could never have dreamed of such a thing before!"

Which, of course, gave you a very intense and personal commitment to the new order, thought Jason.

A servant entered and signaled to Themistocles, who excused himself. They were left to themselves for a few minutes, and Jason motioned them to silence, bestowing a special cautionary look on Landry. Presently their host returned, looking a little preoccupied.

"That was Euboulos, a shipbuilder," Themistocles explained. "I needed to talk with him. He's been offering to support me in the Assembly, in exchange for my influence in sending certain contracts his way in the future."

"When you were running for Archon," Landry prompted, "did you not argue for a new harbor, and expansion of the fleet?" Jason kept his features immobile, for this would be well known enough to make the question legitimate.

"Expansion of the fleet?" Themistocles snorted. "We have practically none to expand! Seventy triremes! And if we did, where would we base it—that miserable open bay at Phalerum? It's absurd! We can't even protect our shipping from the flea-bitten pirates who infest the island of Aegina, only fifteen miles south of Salamis and squatting across our trade routes! And that's the least of the threats we face. That very year, the Persians wiped out the Ionian fleet at Lade, after which they sacked Miletus and ended the rebellion."

"Wasn't the Ionians' defeat at Lade the result of the desertion of the ships from Samos, who wanted to doom their traditional commercial rivals in Miletus?"

"You're very well informed, Lydos." Jason held his breath, but Themistocles continued, for this was obviously a pet subject. "Yes, that's the curse the gods seem to have laid on us Greeks: we can never unite. Show us a common enemy, and all that most Greeks can see is an opportunity to betray some other Greek to him, for private gain or to avenge some age-old slight." He gave the exasperated sigh of a brilliant man forced to work with short-sighted fools while pretending to respect them. "Well, anyway, as Archon I was able to get work started on a new seaport for Athens at Piraeus, just to the east of Phalerum. That's the place!"

"Isn't Piraeus two miles farther from Athens than Phalerum is?" asked Jason, mentally calling up the glowing map that seemed to float a few inches in front of his eyes.

"A small price to pay! That easily defensible rocky headland offers *three* natural harbors. It allows space for our merchant fleet to grow, as it's been growing along with all the rest of our economy now that people know they can work for their own betterment without fear of having all they own taken from them by a tyrant. It will also provide a base for the war-fleet we need . . . if I can ever persuade the Assembly that we *do* need it, and if we can ever find the money to pay for it. That's the prospect I keep holding out to Euboulos and others like him."

Themistocles paused, brooding for a moment. Looking at him, Jason reviewed in his mind the things he knew but could not reveal: that in seven years a rich lode of silver would be discovered at Laurium, near the southern tip of Attica; and that under Themistocles's urging the Assembly would excel itself, spending the windfall on the fleet of triremes that, three years later in 480 B.C., would (with the help of Themistocles's genius for adroit disinformation) win at Salamis the victory on which the future of this planet and a great many others rested.

All at once, the full realization of just who it was whose watered wine he was drinking truly hit Jason.

Landry interrupted their host's thoughts. "We have heard that there were other issues as well . . . such as the impending trial of Miltiades the Younger."

"Ah, yes," said Themistocles, animated once more. "As you probably know, being from the North, the elder Miltiades was a member of a Eupatrid family called the Philaids who was forced out of Athens sixty years ago because he opposed the tyranny of Pisistratus. He founded a colony in the Thracian Chersonese." (*The Gallipoli Peninsula*, Jason translated automatically.) "He died childless, and his step-nephew Miltiades the Younger ruled the colony as a tyrant. He joined the Ionian revolt and fought heroically, capturing the islands of Lemnos and Imbros in the name of Athens. When the revolt collapsed, he fled to Athens. And what did the Assembly do when the most renowned Persian-fighter of them all landed at Phalerum and offered his services? Put him in prison for the crime of tyranny in the Chersonese!" Themistocles gave another sigh of utter weariness and frustration.

"Fortunately, his trial was scheduled after that year's election. As Archon, I was able to exert some small influence on the proceedings."

I'll just bet you were! It was, thought Jason, yet another reason why that election had been one of the most crucial ever held in all history. Aloud: "Yes, we'd heard that he was triumphantly acquitted, and has now been elected one of the ten *strategoi*."

"True. We need him now, in light of the current situation. Speaking of which. . . ." With an air of getting down to business, Themistocles proceeded to ask them a rapid-fire series of very shrewd questions about the state of affairs in Macedon, now a Persian satellite. Drawing on their orientation, they were able to give very specific answers. As heirs to centuries of painstaking historical research, they knew far more about Macedon, Thrace and adjacent areas in the early fifth century B.C. than contemporary Athenians did. Themistocles was clearly impressed.

"Yes," he finally said, leaning back. "You've been very informative. That obligates me to help you in any way I can—which is my inclination anyway, since you obviously hold the same views I do on appeasement of the Persians. The first need is to get you established as *metoikoi*."

Resident non-citizens, Jason translated: accepted in polite society and not without certain civil rights, but unable to vote, own land, or marry citizens—and at the same time liable for military service. For Classical Greeks, *polis* identification was everything. As *metoikoi* they would at least have a recognized status in Athens.

"You'll also need a place to stay," Themistocles

continued. "I know people who have accommodations to let. I assume. . . ." His voice trailed off. As an aristocrat— at least on his father's side—he naturally could not bring up so crass a subject as ability to pay.

"Of course, *strategos*," said Jason, earning a smile of approval from Themistocles for his ability—surprising in a hick from the north—to grasp what had been left unspoken. "We are indebted to you for your help in arranging all this."

"And," Mondrago spoke up, "we doubt whatever information we have been able to provide will be useful enough to repay your kindness, now that the main Persian threat is no longer from the north."

"No, it isn't." Themistocles's brooding look was back, but now it held a new undertone of discouragement. They didn't break into his black study with matters of common knowledge.

The natural approach for the Great King Darius to take in chastising the Athenians for their support of the Ionian rebels had been a southward advance from his satrapy of Thrace through his new client-state of Macedon. But such a strategy required the support of a fleet working its way around the northern end of the Aegean—a fleet that had been wrecked in a storm off Mount Athos. Then Mardonius, the swashbuckling Persian general in command of the northern front, had buckled one swash too many and gotten himself seriously wounded in an attack on some mountain tribe of goat-stealers.

So the Great King had adopted a new strategy—an unsettlingly original one.

"When the newly assembled Persian fleet of six hundred

ships departed from Cilicia earlier this year," said Themistocles, speaking more to himself than to them, "nobody was too alarmed at first. Surely, everyone thought, it must be headed north, to follow the coast around the Aegean. That was the way it had always been done. But then, once past the ruins of Miletus and through the strait between Mount Mycale and the island of Samos, it turned *westward*, straight out across the open sea from island to island! First they obliterated Naxos and enslaved the population. Then they stopped at Delos, the sacred birthplace of Apollo and Artemis, and their commanders Artaphernes and Datis—he's the real commander; Artaphernes is just a blue-blooded Persian figurehead that they had to have because Datis is a Mede—put on a hypocritical display of respect for Apollo. This, after the Persians had burned Apollo's oracle at Didyma and plundered his bronze statue! Maybe some Greeks will actually be stupid enough to be taken in by it."

Carrot and stick, thought Jason.

"Do you know what that smooth-tongued snake Datis had the nerve to tell them on Delos?" Jason could have sworn Themistocles' indignant tone held just a touch of professional envy. "He actually claimed with a straight face that the Ionian rebels hadn't been worshiping the *true* Apollo at Didyma, but rather a kind of imposter: one of the *daiva*, the Persian demons or false gods or whatever. What a gigantic load of goat shit!"

Themistocles, Jason reflected, was even more right than he knew. As Landry had explained during their orientation, Datis' propaganda line was nonsense in terms of Zoroastrian dualistic theology. Just as Ahura Mazda, the supreme god of truth and light, had his counterpart in Ahriman, god of lies and darkness, so his six emanations, the *amesha spenta* or "beneficent immortals," had dark shadows in the form of the *daiva*. A Zoroastrian priest would have gagged on the idea of Apollo—one of the *daiva* himself, according to them—having such a shadow. But the Greeks of Delos hadn't been up to speed on such subtleties, and with the Persian army occupying their island they hadn't been disposed to dispute the point.

"I understand the Persians have Hippias with them," said Landry.

Themistocles gave him a sharp look. "You really are *very* well informed, Lydos."

Jason shot Landry a warning glance, for once again he was displaying an implausible level of knowledge. "We heard people in the streets saying so," he explained quickly.

"Well, it's true. The last tyrant of Athens, chased out twenty years ago, has been a faithful toady of the Great King ever since. And now the doddering old bastard has convinced himself that if he betrays Athens to them the Persians will restore him as tyrant. Ha! He's a fool as well as a traitor. They'll just use him as a source of information."

"And," Jason suggested, "maybe for any contacts he still has within the city." The term *fifth column* would of course mean nothing to Themistocles.

"Yes." Themistocles grew very grim. "And even if there aren't really any of his fellow traitors within the walls, the suspicion that there *may* be some aristocratic faction ready to open the gates from the inside poisons our air." He shook his head. "Ah, well, it's just one more reason why we're lucky to have Miltiades. I only hope that he was right in talking the Assembly into trying and executing the Persian ambassadors that came last year demanding earth and water." He was clearly worried that Athens, at Miltiades' urging, had forfeited the moral high ground.

"If possible," Landry said diffidently, "we'd like to meet him, having heard so much about him."

"Hmm. Yes, I think that could be arranged. I'll see what I can do. But for now, you're welcome to stay here tonight."

As they got up, murmuring their thanks, Jason spoke up, hoping his interest sounded only casual. "Oh, by the way, we've heard certain odd rumors on our journey. Have there been any incidents of . . . well, of people claiming to have seen manifestations of the gods?"

Themistocles gave him a look which he could not interpret. It was never easy to know just how literally the people of pre-scientific societies really took their gods. One of the few things of which the Classical Greeks were intolerant was atheism . . . strictly speaking, *asebia*, or failure to worship the gods. It was the crime for which Socrates would be sentenced to drink hemlock eight decades from now. But what was the real gravamen of the offense: impiety, or a dereliction of civic duty? Jason knew he had to tread very warily.

"No, not that I've heard of," said Themistocles after a pause. "Why do you ask?"

"Oh, only curious," said Jason hastily. They made their exit as soon as was gracefully possible.

CHAPTER EIGHT

THIS WAS NOT THEIR ACROPOLIS.

The serene perfection of the Parthenon, the inspired eccentricity of the Erechtheum, and all the rest lay half a century and more in the future, when Pericles would loot the treasury of the League of Delos—Athens's subordinate "allies"—to build them, replacing the temples the Persians had burned in 480 B.C. Now, ten years before that, even those earlier temples were for the most part nonexistent.

Seven centuries earlier, the five-hundred-foot-high crag had been the citadel of a semi-barbaric Bronze Age king like those of Jason's recent acquaintance. That age-old megaron had long since vanished, for starting three generations ago, the Eupatrid clans had cluttered the summit with private building projects, competing with each other in the efflorescence of gaudily painted statuary, culminating with the large, flamboyant "Bluebeard Temple" reared by the supremely rarefied Eupatrid family of the Alcmaeonids for its own glorification and the overshadowing of its rivals, the Boutads (who hadn't become "authentic" yet). But even such monuments to aristocratic self-importance had not robbed these precincts of their sacredness, for here was the olive tree, believed to be immortal, that Athena herself had granted to the city, besting Poseidon in the matter of gifts and winning the Athenians' special worship. (Jason wondered if some Teloi power-struggle lay behind the legend). And the old, shabby temple of Athena Polias held an archaic olive-wood statue of the goddess believed to be a self-portrait, fallen from the sky.

Jason and his companions shouldn't have been seeing any of this, as the crest of the Acropolis was supposedly barred to all but native-born Athenians. But it was becoming more and more apparent that a lot of exclusionary legislation was honored more in the breach than in the observance, in this state without a nit-picking bureaucracy. And besides, they were friends of Themistocles. So Landry had gotten his wish and they now walked among all the schlock that would eventually be swept away by Persian fire or Athenian urban renewal or both. Jason dutifully recorded it all through his implant simply by looking at it, knowing how interested Rutherford would be.

As far as he was concerned, the most edifying thing about the Acropolis at this stage of its history was the view from it. To the west was Mount Aigaleos, scene of the unexplained sighting that still rankled in Jason's mind. To the south was the bay of Phalerum, Athens's port whose inadequacy was such an insistent bee in Themistocles's entirely metaphorical bonnet. To the northeast was the marble-quarry-scarred Mount Pentelikon, beyond which lay the beach and horse-breeding plains of Marathon. Two roads led there, one to the north and one to the south of the mountain—roads which were going to acquire a vital strategic significance in the next few weeks.

Closer than any of these things—almost directly below to the southeast, in fact, within the city itself—was what looked like an unfinished construction site. Which, in fact, was precisely what it was: the longest-unfinished construction site in history.

When Pisistratus had taken power as tyrant in 560 B.C., all the competitive building on the Acropolis had come to an end; *grands projets* were only to be for the glorification of the tyranny. And his sons and successors, Hippias and Hipparchus, had had a perfect opportunity, given that the Athenians had been so remiss as to neglect to raise a temple to Zeus, the king of the gods. In a precinct traditionally sacred to Zeus, they had begun work on a temple of truly Pharaonic grandiosity. It had been uncompleted in 510 B.C. when the tyranny had been overthrown and Hippias sent into exile. Afterwards, the new democracy had neither finished it nor torn it down. Instead, they had simply left it standing, half-finished, as a mute testament to the tyrants' megalomaniacal folly. And so it would stand until the second century A.D., when the Roman Emperor Hadrian would deign to complete it.

Jason, who had known Zeus personally, tried to imagine just how that second, generation Teloi would have taken all this.

He touched Landry's shoulder. "Let's go, Bryan. It's

time to meet Miltiades down in the Agora." The historian reluctantly complied.

The four of them turned away, toward the gates, past the immense bronze four-horse chariot placed by the democracy in this one-time aristocratic showcase as a monument to its victories over those who had tried to strangle it in its cradle. They proceeded on down the great ramp and through the crumbling old wall that still marked the outline of the Bronze Age lower town. There they turnēd right and followed the Panathenaic Way, past the temple enclosure of the Eleusinium on their right, from which the procession to Eleusis for the Mysteries would depart in October. After the next intersection, on the left, was the fountain-house where the women of Athens came in the morning to collect water—one of the tyrants' more useful projects. Then, beyond that, the Agora opened out to their left.

It had been called the Square of Pisistratus, after the tyrant who had cleared it. Like the fountain-house, and unlike the temple of Zeus, this was something the democracy could use. In fact, it had needed such a gathering-place for its public business. So the detritus of the tyranny had been cleared away and replaced by public buildings like the Bouleuterion where the *boule* that prepared the agenda for the popular assembly met, and the circular Tholos where its members ate at public expense. Emphasizing the political change was the bronze statue of two men, heroically nude, with drawn swords—Aristogiton and Harmodius, "the tyrannicides," who had killed Hippias's brother and co-tyrant Hipparchus, and died for it.

As they passed that statue, in the center of the Agora, Landry provided an amused elucidation. "They were homosexual lovers. Hipparchus took a shine to Harmodius and tried to use his political power to have his way with him. Eventually he pushed the two of them just a little too far. They decided their only way out was to murder him."

"And for this they put up a statue of you in this city?" Mondrago wondered.

"Well, the new democracy needed all the heroes it could get," Landry explained. Jason, who had visited the late twentieth and early twenty-first centuries, recalled the word *spin*.

They continued on, through the noisy merchants' stalls. The shady plane trees that featured in so many artists' impressions of the Agora still lay in the future, waiting to be planted after the Persians' retreat in 480 B.C. Jason would have welcomed them, on this sunny late-July afternoon. He paused for an instant under a merchant's striped awning and looked at the crowd. There was a subtle difference from what one would expect in such a marketplace—an unmistakable undercurrent of tension. This was, unmistakably, a city under threat.

One head stood above the general run. The man's exceptional height was the first thing that attracted Jason's attention. What held his eyes was that, unlike most of the people who made up the Agora's sweaty, dusty, entirely ordinary bustle, this man looked the way Classical Greeks were supposed to look, complete with the straight, high-bridged nose and regular features. The longer Jason looked, though, there was something about him that wasn't specifically Greek at all, but was ethnically unidentifiable.

Unlike most mature men in this setting, he had no beard, and in fact looked like he had very little facial hair to grow.

Jason took all this in as the man passed them in the opposite direction, headed toward the Panathenaic Way. He thought the man's eyes—large, golden-brown—met his own for a fraction of a second, but he couldn't be sure. Then he felt a tug on the shoulder of his *chiton*.

"Jason," said Chantal, in as close to a whisper as she could come and still make herself heard. "That tall man who just passed us—I saw something under his *himation*. I just got a quick glimpse . . . but it was something that didn't belong in this time."

"Huh?" Jason stared at her. "What was it?"

"I don't know. I probably wouldn't have been able to identify it even if I'd seen it for longer than a fraction of a second. But it was some kind of . . . device. And it had an unmistakable high-technology look."

"Chantal, this is impossible! We're the only time travellers in the here and now—and even if we weren't, nobody is ever allowed to bring advanced equipment. And while that man may look a little out of the ordinary, there's no possibility that he's a Teloi. You must have imagined something."

Chantal took on a look of quiet stubbornness. "You once told me that I'm very observant. You might as well take advantage of that quality." A trace of bitterness entered her voice. "It's the only thing about me that's been any use so far."

Jason chewed his lower lip and looked behind them. The man's wavy dark-gold head could still be seen above the generality. He reached a decision and turned to Mondrago.

"Alexandre, follow that man. Don't reveal yourself, and don't take any action. Just find out where he's going, then come back and report. We'll be over there near the Tholos."

"Right." Mondrago set out, blending into the throng. The rest of them continued toward the Kolonus Agoraeus, the low hill bordering the Agora on the west, with a small temple of Hephaestus at its top and the civic buildings grouped at its foot. To their left was the Heliaia, or law court: simply a walled enclosure where the enormous juries of Athens—typically five hundred and one members—could gather. Just to the left of the Tholos, a street struck off to the southwest, passing another walled quadrangle: the Strategion, headquarters of the Athenian army.

Landry was staring raptly at a small building—a workshop of some kind, it seemed—tucked into an angle of a low wall across the street from the Tholos, near a stone that marked the boundary of the Agora. "What is it?" Jason asked him.

Landry seemed to come out of a trance. "Oh . . . sorry. But that building there . . . I don't know who's occupying it now, but a couple of generations from now it will be the house and shop of Simon the shoemaker." Seeing that this meant nothing to Jason, he elaborated. "It's the place Socrates will use for discussions with his pupils—like Plato and Xenophon."

"Oh," was all Jason said. Inwardly, he was experiencing an increasingly frequent tingle: a sense of just exactly where he was, and what it meant . . . and what would have been lost had the men of Athens not stood firm at Marathon.

Up the street from the Strategion came a group of men, as Jason had been told to expect around this time of day: the *strategoi*, the annually elected generals of the ten tribes, who advised the War-Archon. Jason recognized the latter from descriptions he'd heard. Callimachus was older than most of the *strategoi*, a dignified, strongly built gentleman, bald and with a neat gray beard, wearing a worried expression that looked to be chronic. Themistocles walked behind him.

At Callimachus' side, and talking to him with quiet intensity, was one of the few *strategoi* of his own age. This was a man of middle size, lean and wiry, obviously very well preserved for his age, which Jason knew to be about sixty. He still had all his hair, and it was still mostly a very dark auburn, darker than the still visible reddish shade of his graying beard.

The group began to break up, with Callimachus shuffling off as though stooped under the burden of his responsibilities. Jason wondered if he remembered how to smile. Themistocles led the man who had been expostulating to Callimachus to meet them.

"These are the nobles from Macedon I mentioned, Miltiades." He performed introductions, then excused himself. Jason explained that "Alexander" was currently indisposed.

"I would be, too, if I shared the name of that lickspittle king!" Miltiades gave a patently bogus glare, then laughed. He showed no sign of being scandalized at the presence of a woman in the group, which Jason had hoped would be the case given his background in the wild and wooly frontier of Thrace, where he had married Hegesipyle, the daughter of the Thracian King Olorus. He asked them a series of rapid-fire questions concerning the current state of affairs in those parts, which they were able to answer as they had answered Themistocles.

"We hope we have been of assistance to you, *strategos*," Jason said afterwards. "And we are grateful to you for taking the time to talk to us. We know how much you have had to concern you, ever since . . . well, the news from Naxos and Delos."

"Yes," said Miltiades grimly. He swept his hand in a gesture that took in the Agora crowd. "Can't you feel the suspense as we wait to hear where Datis and his fleet will strike next? And just think: the whole thing could have been avoided if only the Ionians had listened to me twenty-three years ago!"

"You mean," Landry queried, "the matter of the Great King's bridge of boats across the Danube?"

"Yes! Darius, puffed up from his conquests in India, had led his great cumbersome army into Scythia. Of course he couldn't catch the Scythian horsemen, who harried him so mercilessly he was lucky to escape." (*Ancestors of the Cossacks*, thought Jason, remembering what he knew of Darius's invasion of the Ukraine in 513 B.C.) "He'd ordered his subject Greek tyrants—including me—to build that bridge, and await his return before the horrible winter of that land set in. I proposed to the others that we destroy the bridge and leave him stranded north of the river, to either freeze or be feathered with Scythian arrows. We would have been free! But that crawling toad Histaeus, tyrant of

Miletus, persuaded the others that my plan was too bold, too risky. So the bridge remained, and the tyrants welcomed back their master."

"Including you," Landry ventured.

"Of course. Do you take me for a fool? Yes, I groveled with the best of them. But later I joined the rebellion Histaeus instigated through his nephew Aristagoras." Miltiades's scowl lightened as though at a pleasant recollection. "The only good outcome was what happened to Histaeus after the rebellion had been crushed. He had the effrontery to demand that the Persian satrap send him to Susa to appeal to his old friend the Great King! The satrap complied—by sending his head there, pickled and packed in salt."

"There was one other good outcome," Landry demurred. "You yourself escaped."

"Yes—twice. First from the Persians, and then from the Athenian Assembly after arriving here! This, even though after capturing the islands of Lemnos and Imbros from the Persians I gave them to Athens! I have Themistocles to thank for my acquittal. I'll never forget that, even though he and I don't agree on everything."

"Like the fact that you persuaded the Assembly to execute the Persian emissaries who came demanding submission last year," Chantal suggested diffidently. "He mentioned that he had reservations about that." Even Miltiades looked slightly taken aback at a woman speaking up unbidden, but after a slight pause he continued.

"A lot of people discovered that they have reservations, after the fact. They said the person of an ambassador is sacred, and that we'd brought down the disfavor of the gods on ourselves." Miltiades's scowl was back at full intensity. "They just don't understand. In a city like this, so traditionally riven by the feuds of aristocratic cliques, so uncertain of its new democracy that hasn't had time to acquire habitual loyalties. . . ." Miltiades seemed to have difficulty putting it into words. In this land with so few rivers worthy of the name, there was no metaphor of burning bridges. "We needed to make our rejection irrevocable, by taking a dramatic step that left us with no alternative but to resist. Besides which, as a practical matter, it aligned us unbreakably with Sparta, which had killed the emissaries without even the formality of a trial."

Jason was silent, remembering the twentieth-century debate over the pros and cons of the Allies' "unconditional surrender" policy in World War II—a debate which hadn't entirely died down among historians even in the twenty-fourth century. Miltiades had argued the Athenians into something like a mirror image of that: unconditional defiance.

"Can Sparta truly be relied on?" asked Landry, probing again for an historical insight.

"If Cleomenes were still alive, I'd be sure of it," said Miltiades, referring to one of the Spartan kings, of whom there were always two. "Yes, I know, he was an enemy of the democracy in its earlier days—tried to force us to take Hippias back as tyrant! But . . . well. . . ." Fifth-century B.C. Ionic Greek also didn't have anything about politics making strange bedfellows. "Lately, he was as staunch an enemy of Persia as any. And four years ago he did us all a favor by crushing Argos, which was threatening to stab us all in the

back by joining the Persians at the Battle of Sepeia."
Miltiades chuckled. "He attacked them by surprise on the
third night of a seven-day truce. When someone asked him
about it, he said he'd sworn to the truce for seven days but
hadn't said anything about nights! And then when the
Argive survivors retreated into the sacred grove of Argos,
he ordered his helots to pile brush around the grove and
burn it."

"How horrible!" exclaimed Chantal.

"Exactly. Burning a sacred grove was just one more
affront to the gods, added to the Spartans' throwing the
Persian emissaries down a well. And of course the gods
wouldn't be fooled by that trick of having the helots light
the fire; they knew who gave the order." Clearly, Miltiades
was more concerned with the trees than with the Argives.
"But that was Cleomenes for you. An unscrupulous
conniver, to be sure, but *our* unscrupulous conniver.
However, he finally outsmarted himself. He bribed the
Oracle of Delphi to pronounce his co-king Demaratus
illegitimate, so he could bring in that pliable little rat-
fucker Leotychides in Demaratus' place. When the story
came out, Cleomenes was killed—pay no attention to that
goat shit about suicide. Too bad. But his successor, who'd
married his daughter Gorgo, may have promise. Young
fellow named Leonidas."

Leonidas, thought Jason, and the familiar tingle took
him once again. *Leonidas, who ten years from now will
lead three hundred Spartans to Thermopylae, where they
will leave their bones under a tomb inscribed with
"Stranger, go tell the Spartans that we keep the ground
they bade us hold," and sear into the very soul of Western*

civilization a standard against which every subsequent generation of Western men must measure themselves.

"And now you must excuse me," said Miltiades. "I have people to talk to, people to persuade of what we must do when—not if—the Persians come. And the debate has already begun in the Assembly." Landry restrained himself with an effort as they said their farewells. He would, Jason suspected, have sold his soul for the opportunity to observe the Assembly, but they all knew it was out of the question for resident foreigners like themselves.

As Miltiades receded into the Agora crowd, Mondrago reappeared. "I followed that man as ordered, sir," he reported crisply. "He went back in the direction of the Acropolis, and through the gate in that old wall at the base—but not up the ramp to the summit. Instead, he turned left when nobody was looking and skirted the side of the hill—pretty rough footing, I can tell you. He scrambled partway up the side, past some really old-looking shrines or whatever."

"The sides of the hill," Landry interjected, "especially the northern side, were riddled with tiny shrines, some of them of Bronze Age vintage, in Classical times. In fact, come to think of it, there was a shrine to Pan in a grotto there. Although," he continued, sounding puzzled, "it's always been believed that that shrine was established *after* the Battle of Marathon."

"Well," Mondrago resumed, clearly uninterested, "he vanished into one of those shrines. I expected him to reappear soon—it seemed barely large enough for him to take a leak in! But he never came back out. I thought I ought to get back here and report."

"You did right." Jason turned to Landry and Chantal. "You two get back to our rented house. Alexandre and I are going to look into this."

CHAPTER NINE

IT WAS LATE AFTERNOON when Jason and Modrago passed through the gate at the base of the Acropolis ramp, and there was almost no one about. So they turned unnoticed to the left and began to scramble along the steep, craggy northern side of the Acropolis.

Looming above them to the right were the walls that surrounded the summit. Below to the left spread the sea of small, tile-roofed buildings and winding alleys that was Athens. They had eyes for neither, for it was all they could do to keep their footing on the crumbling ancient pathways that clung to the almost cliff-like face.

Here and there, they passed the mouths of shallow caves holding the worn-down remnants of shrines carved into the hill in ages past, often holding barely recognizable statues which must surely predate written history.

Jason knew full well that humans were quite capable of imagining gods for themselves without the help of the

Teloi—the entire religious history of humanity outside the Indo-European zone bore witness to that. So he didn't know how many of these Bronze Age sculptures represented the alien "gods" and how many reflected images that had arisen from the subsoil of the human population's own psyche. All he knew was that these shrines, sacred to the forgotten deities of a forgotten people, belonged to a different world from the bustling city below or the self-conscious monuments above. Child of a raw new world, he had always found Old Earth's accumulated layers of ancientness oppressive—almost sinister. Now he had passed into a realm of ancientness beyond ancientness, and the tininess of his own lifespan shook him.

"This is the one," he heard Mondrago say.

It was much like the others, little more than a rough indentation in the hillside. Inside and to the left was one of the crude sculptures, in a roughly hewn-out niche with an opening to the sky. It got no direct sunlight, here on the north side of the Acropolis, but there was enough illumination to make out the statue's outlines. With a little imagination, it was possible to see a goat-legged man.

"He's gone," said Mondrago.

"Gone from *where*?" Jason demanded irritably, waving his hand at the little cavern, which hardly deserved the name; it was barely deep enough for a man to stand up inside. "Are you sure this is the right shrine?"

"Of course I'm sure!"

"But he could barely have squeezed in here, much less remained for a long time."

"I tell you, this is where I left him!" Mondrago angrily

slammed the rocky rear wall of the cavern with his fist for emphasis.

With a very faint humming sound, a segment of the rough stone surface, seemingly indistinguishable from the rest, slowly swung inward as though on hinges.

For a moment the two men simply stared at each other, speechless in the face of the impossibly out-of-place.

"I must have hit exactly the right spot," Mondrago finally said, in an uncharacteristically small voice.

Jason shook his head slowly. No one in the twenty-fourth century had any inkling of anything like this under the Acropolis. "This has to be the work of the Teloi."

"Why? Chantal said she saw high-tech equipment on a *human*."

"I know what Chantal said. But she had to be mistaken. The Authority doesn't allow it. *Ever*."

Mondrago's brown face screwed itself into a look of intense concentration. "Look, ours is the only expedition that's ever been sent to this era, right? So if there *are* other time travelers around here, they must have come from *our* future."

Jason shook his head. "The Authority has a fixed policy against sending multiple expeditions to the same time and place, where they could run into each other. God knows what paradoxes *that* could lead to!"

"But you told us—"

"—That there are no paradoxes. Right. But I also told you that we don't go out of our way to *invite* paradoxes, because the harder we push, the harder reality is apt to push back—maybe so hard as to be lethal."

"Yes, I know, that's another fixed policy. But think about

it: maybe sometime in our future, the Authority's policies will change. Maybe the Authority itself will change . . . or even cease to exist."

Jason was silent. This had of course been considered, for it was obviously not impossible that it could happen in the unforeseeable scope of the twenty-fourth century's future. But while no one had ever denied the possibility, no one ever seemed to think about it very much either. Its implications didn't bear thinking about; the mind reeled from the potential consequences of unregulated *laissez-faire* time travel. And as more and more expeditions had returned from the past and reported no indication of other time travellers from further in the future, the thought had receded to the back of people's minds. Everyone had settled into the comfortable assumption that, for whatever reason, the restrictions imposed by the Temporal Regulatory Authority and the Temporal Precautionary Act under which it operated must be forever immutable.

"Anyway," said Mondrago, interrupting his thoughts, "why are we standing here speculating? Let's investigate this."

Jason eyed the opening dubiously. "We're unarmed."

"No, we're not." Mondrago lifted his *himation*, which he was wearing hanging from his left shoulder and draped around despite the late-July heat, and the *chiton* under it. He had contrived a heavy cloth sheath with leather strings, by which his short Spanish *falcata* was strapped tightly to his left thigh.

Jason frowned. Going armed was not customary in Athens, and the sword would have taken some explaining if anyone had spotted it. But this was no time to raise the issue. He peered through the doorway, which admitted enough light to reveal a flight of shallow steps carved in the stone, leading downward into the gloom.

"We'll see how far we can get before the light gives out," said Jason. As they passed through the doorway, he looked for whatever machinery had opened it, but it was concealed beyond his ability to find it in the dimness.

They descended the steps, and as their eyes accustomed themselves, they saw they were in what appeared to be a small, natural cave from whose opposite side a tunnel had been dug. At the tunnel's far end was a faint glow.

"My God," whispered Mondrago. "How far under the Acropolis does this extend?"

"Shhh!" Jason motioned him to silence. Straining their ears, they detected a murmur of voices from the tunnel.

Without waiting for orders, Mondrago drew his sword.

They advanced into the tunnel, in which Mondrago could just barely stand up straight and Jason had to stoop slightly. The sides were too smooth and even to be entirely the work of nature. But it was crude excavation, and Jason began to think that humans of the Bronze Age or earlier were responsible for the basic work, to which the Teloi had later added high-tech touches like the door.

The glow grew brighter as they approached, and they could smell the aroma of burning oil lamps. The sound resolved itself into voices joined in a kind of low chant—a dark, weird, unmelodious drone that was somehow repellent. Jason was wondering if it was bringing to the surface of his consciousness certain memories from the Bronze Age that he had no desire to recall.

Nearing the tunnel's end, they flattened themselves against opposite walls in shadow and cautiously peered through the opening. In the light of the lamps they saw a large, roughly circular cavern, clearly of natural origin but shaped by human tools as the tunnel had been shaped. Its floor had been flattened and smoothed, and it was crowded with figures in nondescript local clothes, who were producing the chanting. Those people—they were humans—were arrayed in a half-circle, focused on an idol on a rough dais toward the rear of the cavern and somewhat to the left. It was a crude idol similar to the one in the outside shrine, but in better condition as consequence of being sheltered, and therefore more readily recognizable, even in the dim flickering lamplight, as representing the Pan of mythology.

But Jason's attention was riveted on the tall man standing behind the idol—the man they had seen in the Agora. He stood with arms folded, not joining in the chanting but surveying the chanters. His eyes looked down on them with a cold remoteness reflected in the set of his thin lips. It was an expression too far removed from the merely human to be arrogant. He did not sneer, any more than a man sneers at dogs.

He's definitely no Teloi, thought Jason, *but he could scarcely seem any less human if he was one.*

Abruptly, the man unfolded his arms and spread them wide. The chant instantly ceased, leaving a palpably expectant hush.

Then the man spoke. His voice was a rich, deep baritone. But there was more to it than that. Below the level of audibility there was something that compelled one to listen to it, to the exclusion of every other sound, and to believe what it said in defiance of all critical faculties. Jason wondered if certain otherwise inexplicable historical figures as disparate as Joan of Arc and Adolph Hitler had possessed the same quality.

"Rejoice!" he said. "The time is at hand—the time you have been promised. And this time was chosen for a reason. Your god knew that this would be the time when your city would stand in its greatest danger. Even now, the barbarians close in on Athens! Everyone knows it! Nothing your leaders can do will save you from death, your sons from being gelded, your daughters from being raped, and all your children from being enslaved and scattered like dust among the rabble of slaves all across the vastness of Persia. And after another generation, no one will remember that the Athenians ever existed!"

A low moan of utter desolation filled the cavern.

"But your god will save Athens!" The extraordinary voice rose like a clarion. "Your devotion is enough to cause him to withhold his righteous anger against this city for its failure to worship him. He will cause the barbarians to go mad with fear, as he has the power to do, and they will flee, howling, to their ships!"

A rapturous sound arose from the worshipers.

"Afterwards, Athens will erect a proper shrine out there on the north slope where our poor shrine now is, and offer sacrifice to him every year. But," he continued, and his voice dropped, "no one must ever know of the secret doorway to this, the god's *true* shrine. For you and your successors will continue as you always have to be the custodians of his innermost mysteries. And every few generations, at the prophesied times, the god's promise to you will be kept, as it has been before."

The air of the cavern was now thick with breathless anticipation.

"Such a time is now come, as was foretold to your ancestors. I and my companions are only the heralds. Now there comes among you . . . *the Great God Pan!*"

Without warning, some well-concealed lighting fixture in the wall behind the idol—and hence at about ten o'clock, from Jason's perspective—activated, and a harsh glare flooded the cavern. The worshipers' eyes, which had been focused on the idol, were dazzled. But Jason's, viewing it from an angle, were not. So he was able to discern, in the glare, the idol sinking into the floor with a practically inaudible hum, leaving a hatchway through which a living being emerged—a being at which Jason's mind reeled. But he didn't doubt his sanity, for it was inarguably the figure he had briefly glimpsed on the slopes of Mount Aigaleos.

The artificial light—supernatural to the worshippers in the cavern—faded to a relatively dim glow. In that glow stood revealed an outrage against nature, with the legs of a goat and the upper body of a brown-skinned, hirsute, muscular man—very definitely a man, for it was grotesquely male, almost ridiculously so. The head was that of a man—broad, snub-nosed, full-lipped, with thick, curly hair and beard of a dark reddish brown. From amid that hair grew a pair of horns.

An ecstatic, almost orgasmic moan gusted from the worshipers.

The tall man from the Agora turned toward the apparition with the air of a magician who had produced a rabbit from a hat. The motion caused him to face the tunnel opening.

It belatedly occurred to Jason that the opening where he and Mondrago had crouched in shadows was no longer shadowed.

The classically handsome face of the speaker contorted into a mask of rage. "Intruders!" he bellowed. "Seize them!"

"Run!" Jason yelled to Mondrago as the worshipers began to emerge from shock. They ran back along the tunnel, as fast as its cramped confines permitted.

That slight head start enabled them to reach the steps ahead of their frantic pursuers—who then caught up as they struggled up the steps. Jason felt his legs grappled from behind and below. He wrenched one leg free and kicked backwards, feeling facial bone and cartilage crunch under his hard-driven heel. Momentarily free, he ascended the rest of the way to the area just inside the tantalizingly open doorway, where there was more room. Mondrago was already there. Jason saw him spring backwards after delivering a slicing sideways lunge with his Spanish sword that ripped through a pursuer's throat and sent him silently to the floor, his head flopping loosely on a neck that had been severed to the spinal column. Jason recognized the Afghan fighting technique, but he had only a split second to admire Mondrago's mastery of it before a crush of bodies from behind bore him to the floor and a shattering impact to his head caused the universe to explode into a shower of stars and then go dark.

CHAPTER TEN

JASON AWOKE to a nauseatingly painful headache. He didn't want to open his eyes, but to fail to do so was out of the question. He parted his eyelids very cautiously.

The light sent fresh pain stabbing through his head, but it was not quite as bad as he had feared—he could sense that it was dim interior lighting. Lying on his back as he was, all he could make out was a completely nondescript ceiling. He slowly turned his head to the left.

He found himself looking into a pair of brown eyes, somehow like the eyes of an animal, but not quite, for they held something that no animal would ever know. Those eyes looked out at him from under bushy brows of the same dark russet color as the curly hair and beard that framed a face whose expression he could not interpret. The head lowered to look more closely at him, a motion which caused the horns to dip.

Unconsciousness mercifully took him again.

✠ ✠ ✠

When he awoke again his head was clear. Another difference was that he was sitting up, in a chair to which he was tied. One of the first things he noticed in the light of the oil lamps as his eyes darted around the small, windowless room was that Mondrago was similarly seated and bound to his right, although he was only just stirring from unconsciousness. He also saw a man in local garb walking out the door, holding a hypospray injector by which he and Mondrago had presumably been awakened.

But mostly he noticed that now he was looking into a human face. Human . . . but inhumanly perfect.

It was the man they had seen in the Agora and in the inexplicable cavern under the Acropolis. Now he sat at his ease in a chair of local manufacture. His wavy hair was an unmistakable shade: a unique kind of blond-black, like an alloy of gold and iron. His eyes were large and luminous, the color of amber. His lips were full without being thick. There was no indentation between his brow and the bridge of his ruler-straight nose.

"Well," he said in his strangely compelling voice, "what are we to do with you?" He spoke in twenty-fourth century Standard International English.

Jason made himself blink with incomprehension before swallowing to moisten his dry throat and speaking in indignant Greek. "What is this barbarian babble? Who are you? And how dare you hold us prisoner? I am a nobleman of Macedon, and this is my retainer. And we are friends of the *strategos* Themistocles! Release us at once or it will go hard on you."

The perfect lips quirked in a momentary smile. "It's no

use. Our instruments detected the energy surge your arrival produced. It was just by chance that we happened to be in the vicinity at the time, between Athens and Eleusis." The man gave an irritated headshake. "And it was an *unfortunate* chance that you happened to spot Pan. It's all your fault, you know. We would have preferred to simply avoid you and let you return to your own time, blissfully ignorant. We still wish we could have. If only you hadn't meddled—!"

Jason had almost stopped listening after the word *instruments*, for he suddenly recalled what Chantal thought she had seen, and what he had definitely seen in the shrine on the Acropolis north slope. "Who the hell *are* you?" he blurted, all thoughts of dissimulation forgotten. "You're brought advanced technology back in time! That is flatly contrary to the regulations of the Temporal Regulatory Authority, besides being a felony under the Revised Temporal Precautionary Act of 2364."

This time the full lips formed a smirk. "We don't concern ourselves with either."

Jason stared at him. "You must be from our future."

"Evidently not, since we didn't know you were going to be here in this time-period. If we had known, it would have made things awkward for us, as this expedition is essential to us but, like you, we make it a point to avoid creating possibilities for different time travelers to encounter each other. That's one rule of the Authority which we follow— an uncharacteristically sensible one. We would have had to go to great lengths to avoid attracting your attention."

"But if you're not from our future, how can you be here? The Authority certainly didn't send you."

Another smirk. "We have our own arrangements."

"You keep saying 'we.' Will you kindly answer my question and tell me who you are? What's your *name*, for God's sake?"

For an instant the man seemed to weigh the pros and cons of revealing the information. Then he smiled as though pleasurably anticipating the effect his answer would have.

"I am Franco, Category Five, Seventy-Sixth Degree."

Jason stared. "But that's a—"

"Yes. I am a genetically upgraded agent of the Transhuman Dispensation."

"What are you trying to put over on us?" demanded Mondrago, now fully awake. "The Transhuman movement was wiped out a generation before Weintraub discovered temporal energy potential."

"So you Pugs think." From history lessons, Jason recognized the Transhumanist acronym for *products of uncontrolled genetics*—their term for the human race in its natural form. "You truly believe you successfully stood in the way of evolutionary destiny. You merely delayed it. Our inner circles withdrew into concealment, in various hidden places all around Earth and the Solar System, where we have secretly continued our great work."

"Too bad," remarked Jason. "We really did think the universe had been cleansed of the Transhuman abomination."

Franco leaned forward, and his amber eyes glowed as though fervor burned like a flame behind them. "It is you who are the abomination: a form of life that has outlived its time but refuses out of mere parochialism and nostalgia to step aside and get out of the way of its successors. Humanity is clinging to its primordial state—a race of randomly evolved apes—when for centuries it has had the technology to transform itself into a consciously, rationally self-created race of gods—"

"—And monsters." Jacob shook his head irritably. "Why am I wasting my breath talking to you? I have no idea who you really are, but you're obviously a liar in addition to being a raving lunatic. The fact that you're here and now proves that. The Authority has never sent any diehard Transhumanist fanatics into the past, and it never will."

Franco took on an infuriatingly complacent look. "Who said anything about the Authority?"

"Talk sense! The Authority operates the only temporal displacer in existence."

"So it pleases the Authority to think. Shortly after Weintraub's initial experiments, we stole his data—it was pathetically easy, and we were *very* interested in its potentialities. Our research ran parallel to, but in advance of, Fujiwara's. She and Weintraub were brilliant, for Pugs, but they followed several false trails. The result was a 'brute force' approach to temporal displacement, requiring a titanic installation and a lavish expenditure of energy. We soon spotted the flaws in their mathematics. *Our* displacer is relatively compact and energy-efficient, and therefore concealable."

"Are you saying," said Jason, thunderstruck, "that there are *two* displacers on Earth in our era?" He wanted to believe it was a lie, because it removed the foundations of his accustomed structure of assumptions. But, try as he might, he could see no other way to account for the presence of unauthorized time travelers with proscribed equipment.

"Only since the Authority's came into operation," said Franco, amused. "Ours was the first. We'll probably build more, as the one we have is getting somewhat overworked. As I mentioned, we have been intensely interested in time travel ever since Weintraub demonstrated that it was a theoretical possibility."

"Why? I've never heard that the Transhumanists had any interest in historical research."

"We don't." Once again Franco leaned forward avidly. "We look to the future, not the past. We don't want to study history. We want to change it."

For a heartbeat or two, Jason stared openmouthed. Then he burst out laughing.

"Now I *know* you're a lunatic!" he finally gasped. "History *can't* be changed! But please don't let me stop you. I hope you try—I really do. In fact, I hope you try very, very hard!"

"I never said we thought we could change *observed* history. But have you ever considered how much of the human past is unobserved and unrecorded? There are vast empty stretches of territory and time in which we are constantly changing the past, filling up those stretches with what will, in the end, turn out to have been humanity's secret history—a history inevitably leading to our eventual triumph at a date which . . . I don't believe I'll reveal to you. We call it, simply, *The Day*."

"And how, precisely, are you doing that?" Jason inquired, unable to keep a reluctant and horrified fascination out of his voice. In one corner of his mind, he wondered why Franco was telling him all this. Probably the Transhumanist simply felt a need for someone besides his own underlings to brag to. Jason had known enough blowhards, in his own time and others, to be able to recognize the type.

Of course, there was another, more unsettling explanation: Franco thought his revelations could do no possible harm because he had no intention of letting his listeners live.

"We have various techniques. For example, we plant genetic flaws in the unmodified human population by infecting populations with gengineered retroviruses, which by The Day will have rendered those populations vulnerable to a biochemical warfare using tailored proteins or polysaccharides. Another approach is to plant retroactive plagues, spreading mutagens whose genetic time-clocks result in the poisoning of certain vital food supplies on The Day. And there are even more subtle 'time bombs' that we plant, some of a purely psychological nature."

"But," said Jason with an incredulous headshake, "things like that would be extremely long-term, and require repeated visits to various eras in succession." Inwardly, he fought to hold at bay an obscene vision of Earth as a rotten apple, seemingly sound on the outside but a writhing mass of worms inside the skin, waiting to break through it.

"To repeat, our temporal displacement technology is less expensive than yours by orders of magnitude. We are therefore less constrained in how far into the past we can go, and how often. This is particularly helpful in my own work: the establishment of cults and secret societies, which we nurture over the centuries by repeated visits from the same, seemingly ageless agent at prophesied times. At those times the agent foretells the next visit, dazzles the faithful with technological 'magic,' and gives them enough foreknowledge of the future to confirm the succeeding generations in their faith. As the ages pass and the scientific worldview takes hold, we will begin to reveal the truth to them. By then their loyalty will be practically hereditary, and we will offer them suitable rewards in the new order."

"A promise which naturally won't be kept," Mondrago stated rather than asked.

"Naturally. Promises to Pugs mean nothing. By the time The Day arrives, Earth will be riddled with such cadres, not knowing of each other's existence. Like all our other projects, it will not contradict recorded history. But recorded history will turn out to have been a mere ornamental façade, behind which *real* history has been building all along toward a Transhumanist future."

"And," Jason said slowly, "I imagine it helps to no end when you have some kind of pre-existing cult to build on." He wanted to keep Franco talking as long as possible, revealing as much information as possible.

"You're surprisingly perceptive. Yes, my first appearance in this region was in the late Bronze Age—the thirteenth century B.C. Pan, you see, is a very ancient god. And, since we are not limited by the irrational restrictions you labor under, my genetic code was resequenced by nanotechnological means, altering my appearance to godlike standards, as you've doubtless noticed."

"Actually I hadn't."

Franco's eyes narrowed a few microns and chilled a few degrees, but otherwise he showed no reaction to Jason's jab.

"At the same time," Jason went on, "it must limit you that you can't send any of your radically specialized—and unhuman-looking—gengineered castes back in time. Nor can you send those of your servitors with blatantly obvious bionics. They couldn't exactly blend, could they?"

"It is a handicap," Franco acknowledged. "But this was one of those cases in which we were able to make use of recorded history, rather than merely avoiding it. We knew, of course, of the later belief that Pan had intervened at Marathon. It was the perfect opportunity to reinforce our cult's fervor."

"And, of course, you've been able to show them their god Pan in the flesh. Another of your gene-twisted obscenities, of course—although I didn't realize that even you were able to produce anything so grotesquely divergent from the human norm."

"We're not, at least not without great difficulty. We had help. You see, in the course of my earlier visits to Greece, we acquired allies." Before Franco could elaborate, a door opened and a handsome but relatively nondescript man came in and whispered to him. He nodded, said "Bring him in," and turned back to Jason with a dazzling smile. "By a most fortunate coincidence, the leader of those allies is here now." He stood up and, to Jason's amazement, went to his knees.

"Greetings, Lord," he said, oozing a reverence that would not have deceived a child. But it seemed to satisfy the figure who entered, bending low to get through the door and unable to stand up straight without brushing his gold-shot silvery hair against the ceiling. His huge, disturbingly alien eyes stared at Jason, empty of recognition.

"Hi," said Jason in the Teloi tongue, eliciting a satisfyingly startled reaction from Franco. "It's been a long time. Well, actually it hasn't been all that long for me. But for you it's been almost eleven hundred and forty years."

Zeus looked puzzled.

CHAPTER ELEVEN

"YOU SEEM SOMEHOW FAMILIAR," said the Teloi, with a frown, stroking the beard he shared with some but not all males of his race. His deep voice held the indefinably disturbing quality Jason remembered.

"Let me refresh your memory," said Jason. "Do you recall your 'son' Perseus? It was at the time Santorini—or Kalliste, as it was called then—exploded. Surely you must remember that." While waiting for a reply, he glanced around and saw that Mondrago was staring, wide-eyed, in spite of having seen video imagery of the Teloi.

"Oh, yes," Zeus finally nodded, a little vaguely. "Perseus was one of the superior strain that we created for the purpose of leading the ordinary human masses into a proper state of submission to their creators. They were a great disappointment to us, from Gilgamesh on. But Perseus was better than most. He kept his word and established my worship at Mycenae after I had imprisoned the Old Gods forever."

Wait a minute! thought Jason, speechless. *What's this? You imprisoned them?*

"And now I remember you," Zeus continued. "You were one of the time travelers who appeared around that time. You were of some assistance to me." He turned to Franco. "He must be spared, for I pay my debts to mortals."

He's gone senile, Jason realized. *He really believes it. He thinks he really is a god. And he's forgotten how the senior Teloi got permanently trapped in their pocket universe. The myths and legends that his human worshipers have woven around what happened have become more real for him than the truth.*

And why should I be surprised? For almost eleven and a half centuries he and his faction of younger-generation Teloi—the ones who didn't get trapped—have been stranded on low-technology Earth without their extradimensional hidey-hole and with none of their advanced technology except what they happened to have with them when Santorini blew up and their tame human empire based on Crete was wrecked by the tsunami and other side effects. All that time, they've been running a bluff with the aid of whatever flashy displays of techno-magic they could manage.

All things considered, I suppose it's surprising he's retained any vestige of sanity at all.

Franco broke into his thoughts. "So you already know about the Teloi?"

Jason saw no point in evasion or denials. "We encountered them on an expedition to observe the Santorini explosion."

"Ah, yes . . . that expedition had departed from the

twenty-fourth century shortly before we did. So you must be Jason Thanou. I hadn't realized we had such a distinguished guest. By the time we encountered the Teloi, four centuries after you did, they had forgotten about you."

"But now I remember," Zeus broke in. "Yes, you were useful to me. And now new time travelers have arrived." He indicated Franco, who inclined his head graciously. "And they too recognize true divinity—not to be confused with a silly legend like 'Pan'! We helped them produce a living image of that legend, with which to gull the local human cattle, who deserve no better. In exchange, they will help restore my worship to this disrespectful city!"

"What?" Jason managed.

Zeus's voice had been steadily rising. Now he was almost raving. "Yes! Athens has sought the patronage of my daughter Athena, while neglecting me!" Familial affection, Jason recalled, was not a trait of the vastly long-lived Teloi, who produced children but rarely. In fact, the being Oannes who had told Jason the story of the Teloi on Earth had been of the opinion that their second generation, including Zeus, were infertile. Jason wondered if, in his increasing dementia, Zeus had come to believe the local mythology's version of his relationship to Athena. "At least the tyrant Hippias, son of Pisistratus, began building a suitable temple to me. But then the Athenians drove him out and failed to complete it. Instead they have left it standing unfinished, as though wishing to flaunt their impiety!

"But now, thanks to Franco—a member of an improved human stock called the *Transhumans* who have returned to the worship of us, the true gods, as he assures me—matters will be set right. The Persians are coming, and bringing Hippias back with them. Franco will enable them to win the coming battle, conquer Athens, and restore Hippias as tyrant. And then Hippias will put the Athenians to work completing his great temple, thus atoning for their ingratitude to me!"

Behind Zeus and out of the Teloi's range of vision, Jason saw Franco smile.

"What has this Transhumanist pimp been telling you about time travel?" Mondrago suddenly burst out. "He's lying. It doesn't work that way. History is fixed—and it says that the Athenians are going to kick the Persian army's ass up between the ears and then pull it out through the nose!"

"And even if Franco could prevent that," Jason added, "he wouldn't, because it's precisely what he's promised his cult of Pan-worshipers is going to happen, thanks to their 'god.'"

"Lies!" Zeus was truly raving now. He loomed up, standing as straight as he could, shaking with the extremity of his passion. His right hand grasped Jason's throat with choking force, half-lifting him from the chair. "All lies! Franco warned me to expect this. He told me you would be jealous of him as a more highly evolved form of life."

"Can't you see?" croaked Jason desperately. "He's just using you—making a fool of you!"

"No! He is my true worshiper. It is all clear to me now. But," Zeus continued, with the abrupt tone-change of the insane, "you served me well, long ago. Franco, this man and his follower must be spared." He released Jason, who sagged back down in his bonds, gasping for breath.

"Yes, Lord," said Franco smoothly. Zeus gave a vague

nod, and departed. As he stooped to get through the door, there was, in spite of everything, a quality about him that could only be called pathetic.

"You heard him," Jason wheezed to Franco through his bruised throat. "About not killing us, that is."

"He'll get over it." Franco's smile was charming. He shook his head with what Jason would have sworn was sincere regret. "We really would have preferred to just let you complete your studies and go home, ignorant of us. As it is. . . ."

"If you cut our TRDs out—TRDs that nobody in this era is supposed to be able to detect—and we don't reappear in our time on schedule, a lot of questions are going to be asked. The Authority isn't stupid, you know." Jason wasn't absolutely certain of the last part, but saw no useful purpose to be served by sharing his skepticism with Franco.

"Oh, we won't do that. We'll simply kill you in some acceptably 'in-period' way, and your corpses will appear on the Authority's displacer stage. Very sad. But we all know that human history is a violent place."

Without moving his head, Jason turned his eyes as far to the right as he dared and met Mondrago's. The latter nodded imperceptibly. He understood. Chantal and Landry, about whom the Transhumanists might be ignorant, must not be mentioned.

Franco seemed to read his mind, or at least read the byplay correctly. "And as for the other two members of your party, we will deal with them in due course. Oh, yes, we know about them. Since capturing you, we have brought certain intelligence sources to bear, and we've learned about Themistocles' Macedonian guests, and where they are lodging now." His eyes took on the unfocused look of one sending a command via direct neural induction through an implant communicator of a sort prohibited even to someone in Jason's position, involving as it did a proscribed melding of mind and computer.

Taking advantage of Franco's distraction, Jason mentally activated his map-display, with its red dots representing the party's TRDs. Chantal and Landry were still at the house. He forced himself not to let his relief show.

Presently, four of Franco's underlings entered the room. "Take them back to separate cells," he ordered.

The goons cut Jason's and Mondrago's bonds with unemotional efficiency and hoisted them to their feet. It took some hoisting, for they were horribly stiff, and Jason realized for the first time how hungry he was—they must have been unconscious for at least the better part of a day. As they were being led out of the room, a sudden impulse made Jason twist out of the grip of one of his two handlers and turn to face Franco. He had no time to try and understand his own motivations—what was the point of arguing with a Transhumanist?—but he looked into those large, perfectly shaped amber eyes and waved his one free hand at the door through which Zeus had passed.

"That thing that just left this room is the inevitable end product of the Transhuman movement's vision of humanity's future! Is that really what you want?"

Franco's face showed no resentment or anger, or anything at all except the certitude of the true ideologue. "Oh, no. You're wrong. Don't confuse us with the Teloi. We won't repeat their mistakes. Remember what you said earlier about gods and monsters? The Teloi sought to turn themselves into gods. They neglected the monsters. We won't."

The goons tightened their grip and marched the two prisoners through the door, into a corridor even more dimly lit than the room they had departed. As they proceeded, a short figure appeared from a side corridor to the right.

It took a heartbeat for it to register on Jason's mind, as his eyes met the brown ones of Pan. From Mondrago's direction, he heard a non-verbal growl.

Without consciously formulating a plan, he used a basic release technique: he went limp, ceasing to resist the two men holding him. By an instinctive reaction, they relaxed their grip.

With a Judo-like wrenching motion he freed himself and forced his still-stiff muscles to propel him forward. He grasped the startled Pan from behind, locking one arm around the hirsute throat. With his other hand, he grasped one of the horns. He took the creature halfway to the floor and pressed his right leg behind the creature's knees to prevent a backward kick of its cloven hooves.

"If you cry out," he snapped at the guards, "I'll break his neck. And then where will your 'god' be?"

He was betting that the guards didn't have implant communicators like Franco's. He recognized their sort from history disks. They were nondescript-looking, low-grade Transhumanists, doubtless with high but very specialized intelligence and little initiative. His intuition seemed to be paying off, for they stood seemingly paralyzed with indecision.

"I'll also break his neck," he continued, pressing his advantage, "if you don't release my companion."

They released Mondrago, who hurried to join Jason behind Pan.

"Don't hurt me."

It took a second for Jason to realize the voice was Pan's. It had an odd timbre to it, and was unexpectedly high-pitched, and it was difficult to sort out the emotions behind it. But he found himself thinking it was an undeniable—if odd—*human* voice. And it was pleading.

"I won't hurt you if you do as you're told," Jason said. "Show us to the nearest exit from this building."

With Jason still holding him in the same potentially neck-snapping grip, Pan moved in a cautious sidewise gait back along the corridor from which he had emerged. The four guards followed closely but cautiously, making no moves that might precipitate the death of the god the cult-worshipers expected. The corridor was a very short one, terminating in a door.

And here Jason faced a dilemma. They couldn't take Pan with them out into the city, where he would have been conspicuous to say the least.

"Kill it now!" hissed Mondrago, seeming to read his mind. "We don't need it as a hostage anymore—they won't be able to pursue us once we're outside in public. Kill it just before we bolt out the door. And that will be the end of their little scheme for a cult of the 'Great God Pan'."

"No," Jason heard himself saying. "We're not murderers."

If telepathy had been a reality, Mondrago's searing contempt could have been no more obvious. "'Murderers'?

This thing isn't human. It isn't even a decent animal. It's just a filthy, obscene mutant! Have you gone soft in the head?"

"We don't kill any sentient being without a reason! Remember that. And get ready to move . . . *now.*" With a sudden movement, Jason thrust Pan back into the narrow corridor. The four guards rushed, but got in each other's way in the confined space even before stumbling over Pan. Jason and Mondrago hit the door with their shoulders. It burst open, and they were out, into one of the crooked streets of Athens.

While running, Jason summoned up his map-display and saw that the red dots of his and Mondrago's TRDs were in the area south of the Agora, on the terraced lower slopes of the Areopagus hill—the vicinity of their rented house, where the dots of Chantal's and Landry's TRDs still glowed reassuringly.

Good! Jason thought as they sprinted through the winding, uneven alleyways. *Even in this maze, it won't take us long to find it. We'll get Chantal and Landry out of it before Franco can "deal with them in due course" . . . and find a new address.*

There were no such things as apartment blocks in fifth-century B.C. Athens. But there were blocks of houses—as many as six houses. Their quarters were in such a block. All the houses had the inward-looking design of Athenian residences, organized around miniscule courtyards and having upstairs rooms. A narrow street-front door in the mud-brick wall gave access to the courtyard.

It was ajar.

Off to the left, out of the corner of his eye, Jason barely

glimpsed a figure hurrying around a corner of the block, seeming to push another figure ahead. He was about to investigate when he heard shouting from within, in Landry's voice. Without waiting for Mondrago, he plunged through the open door.

The shouting was coming from one of the small rooms opening off the courtyard. Jason rushed in, to see one of the goon-class Transhumanists grasping Landry by on arm and holding a dagger in his other hand.

Without thinking, Jason sprang forward, reaching out to seize the wrist of the dagger arm.

With the strength of desperation, Landry broke the Transhumanist's grip and rushed frantically forward. He succeeded only in tripping himself and Jason. The Transhumanist grasped him from behind, under the chin, and brought his dagger-edge across the historian's throat. With a gurgling shriek, Landry fell across Jason. Mondrago, desperately trying to get into the room, stumbled over the fallen body. The Transhumanist, with the quickness of his unnatural kind, shoved him aside and plunged out the door.

Mondrago got to his feet and gave chase. By the time Jason could get out from under the body atop him, it was too late. That which had been Bryan Landry, Ph.D., lay in a pool of blood and excreta, his slit throat like a ghastly, grinning second mouth—an 'in-period' death.

Of Chantal Frey there was no sign. Jason checked his map-display again. It was unchanged, still showing both Landry's and Chantal's TRDs right here.

Mondrago returned. "The bastard got away," he gasped. "Where's Chantal?"

"She ought to be here." Jason began to look around frantically.

"Look," Mondrago said expressionlessly, pointing at the floor in a corner of the room. The small smear of blood was barely noticeable. So was the tiny metallic sphere that had been cut out of Chantal's arm.

Jason clamped calmness down on himself. "They can't have gotten too far with her. Let's go!"

As they reemerged onto the street, they heard a roar of voices from the direction of the Agora, like a disturbed sea with an undertow of terror. People were running along the street, wild-eyed.

Jason grabbed one such passerby. "What has happened?" he demanded. "What's going on?"

"You haven't heard? The news has just arrived. The Persians have sacked Eretria! Burned it to the ground and enslaved the people!"

Eretria, thought Jason, frantically summoning up information from his implant. *The one Greek city, other than Athens, that aided the Ionian rebels and therefore was marked for destruction by the Great King. Located on the island of Euboea, just across a narrow strait from Attica— within sight of Attica at its narrowest point, in fact.*

"The Eretrians resisted," the man went on. No Greek could resist recounting a story. "For five days they defended their walls. But then they were betrayed. Two members of an aristocratic faction sold out, opened the gates, and let the Persians in."

Uh-huh! thought Jason, remembering what Themistocles had said. *That's all the Athenians need to hear at this point.*

"And they'll be here next!" The man must have suddenly

remembered just how close Eretria was, for he grew wild-eyed and fled.

Jason consulted his implant for the calendar. It was still late July.

Well, I suppose we've settled the question of whether the Battle of Marathon took place in August or September. Kyle Rutherford will be interested.

It didn't seem terribly important at the moment.

CHAPTER TWELVE

THERE WAS NO SIGN OF CHANTAL. And no one was in a position to help find her, under the circumstances in which Athens now found itself.

"It's a shame about Lydos," Themistocles said distractedly as they hurried across the Agora. "I was glad to have the body taken care of, and of course I'll do what I can to find the murderer later. And I wish I could help organize a search for Cleothera. But now there's no time. The Assembly is about to bring the question of our strategy against the Persians to a final vote."

Jason saw that the Agora crowd was moving steadily southwestward, in the direction of the Pnyx hill where the *Ekklesia*, or Assembly of all citizens, had met since the establishment of the democracy. They were being herded in that direction by the exotically costumed "Scythian" police force of Athens. Some of these men were really Scythians; most were merely dressed up to resemble those famously fearsome barbarians from north of the Black Sea. But all were public slaves, and Jason had a feeling they relished any opportunity to ram it to the free citizens. This was such an opportunity, as they advanced through the Agora toward the Pnyx in a line, holding a long rope daubed with red powder. Any citizen found outside the meeting area with red marks on his clothing was fined. Athenian democracy was not just participatory; it was compulsory.

"Miltiades mentioned that the debate had been going on even before the news from Eretria," Jason remarked.

"Yes, and now we no longer have the luxury of time. A little time, true: the north coast of Attica, just across the strait from Eretria, is too rugged for a landing. They have to sail back down the strait. But we can't afford to let the debate drag on any further. The Assembly has got to act now and approve Miltiades's proposal."

"What proposal is that?" asked Jason, who already knew.

"The Eretrians made a big mistake: they took shelter within their walls and let the Persians land and deploy unopposed. A lot of fools in the Assembly want us to repeat that mistake. Miltiades—and he's got Callimachus and most of the *strategoi* behind him—argues that we should march out and meet them. And," Themistocles added grimly, "it's not as though there was much question about where they're going to land."

"Where is that?"

"Marathon. After they leave the strait and turn south, it's just around the headland. It's a wide, sheltered bay with room to draw up even a fleet the size of theirs. And beyond the beach is a flat plain that's always been horse-breeding country—perfect terrain for their cavalry. And not one but two roads lead from there to Athens, one north and one south of Mount Pentelikon." Themistocles looked grim. "They'll know all this—that traitorous dotard Hippias will have told them. Oh, yes, they'll be landing there any day now."

A man passed them. Jason recalled having seen him among the *strategoi*. He was about forty, tall for this milieu—taller than Jason, in fact—and distinguished-looking, with smooth deep-brown hair and a neatly sculpted beard of the same color, with a reddish undertone. His expression was one of studied seriousness, and he moved with a kind of self-conscious dignity, as though very aware of having an image to uphold. He and Themistocles locked eyes. *If looks could kill*, Jason thought, *there'd be two corpses in the Agora*. But they exchanged a glacially polite nod, and the tall man moved on in his grave way, nose in the air.

"Aristides," Themistocles told them with a scowl. "*Strategos* of the Antiochis tribe, as I am of the Leontis. He knows as well as I do that Miltiades is right. But, knowing him, he may argue against Miltiades just because I'm for him."

"So the two of you are political opponents?" Once again, Jason knew the answer full well but hoped to draw Themistocles out. He succeeded beyond his expectations. Clearly, Aristides was a subject on which Themistocles would expound to anyone who would listen.

"That pompous hypocrite! He poses as a model of old-fashioned, countrified virtue, preening himself on never accepting bribes while implying that I do!" Jason noted that, for all his indignation, Themistocles didn't actually deny it. "Ha! He doesn't *need* bribes—he's got a large estate outside Phalerum, and a whole network of rich relatives. But that doesn't stop him from letting his sycophants go around calling him 'Aristides the Just.' In fact, he cultivates the title." Themistocles looked like he wanted to gag. "Ah, well. Here we must part. Come see me afterwards and I'll tell you what happened."

Jason would have given a lot to have heard the debate on the Pnyx—arguably one of the most crucial in history—and he knew Landry would have given even more, a thought which caused him to feel a twinge like an emotional nerve pain. But it was, of course, as impossible as ever. One of the defining features of the Athenian version of democracy was its single-minded exclusivity. Only voting citizens were allowed in the Assembly. As *metoikoi*, or resident foreigners, he and Mondrago were no more likely to be admitted than women and slaves. They said their farewells and turned away, looking around them as they went for any sign of Chantal—or of any of the Transhumanists they had seen. As usual, there was none. As they walked through the now practically deserted Agora, Jason chuckled, despite his bleak mood.

"What's so funny?" asked Mondrago.

"Aristides the Just. I was remembering a story Bryan told me." As he spoke Landry's name, Jason found himself unable for a moment to continue. He would, he knew, be a long time coming to terms with the fact that a member of an expedition he led was now dead—at least one, for God knew what had happened to Chantal. And Landry had died, not in an act of heroic self-sacrifice like Sidney

Nagel's, but butchered by murderous enemies in Jason's very presence. And Jason hadn't saved him. Knowing he couldn't let himself dwell on his oppressive sense of failure, he resumed briskly.

"You see, the Athenian constitution provides for something called 'ostracism.' That doesn't mean what it will later come to mean in English. It means that they hold a kind of election where everybody can write someone's name on a potsherd, called an *ostrakon,* and if your name appears on over six thousand potsherds you're exiled for ten years."

Mondrago whistled. "Pretty harsh."

"It's not quite as bad as it sounds. The exile's property isn't confiscated. It's just a way of temporarily removing individuals who are felt to be getting too big for the britches they haven't got, for the health of the democracy. Sometimes it's the only way of breaking irreconcilable deadlocks. Anyway, at the present time, it's never been used. The first ostracism won't happen until 487 B.C. And then, in 482 B.C., Aristides will be ostracized. It will be a kind of referendum on Themistocles's naval policy, of which Aristides is a die-hard opponent. As a result, Athens will have the fleet it needs to defeat the Persians at Salamis in 480 B.C. when the *big* invasion comes. That's what I meant about breaking deadlocks."

"But what's the funny story?"

"During the election, an illiterate voter walks up to Aristides, not knowing who he is, and asks him to write the name 'Aristides' on a potsherd for him. Aristides asks him why—has Aristides ever done him any injury? Does he know of any wrongdoing Aristides has done? 'No,' the man replies, 'it's just that I'm so sick and tired of hearing him called Aristides the Just all the time!'"

Mondrago guffawed. "I'm with him!"

"It gets better. Aristides, without another word, goes ahead and complies with the man's request."

"Maybe at that point he decides there are worse things than exile from Athens and its politics."

Jason smiled wryly. "And then, in 470 B.C., Themistocles will be ostracized."

"*What?* Themistocles? After saving this city's bacon at Salamis?"

"Precisely the problem. By then the Athenians will have gotten just so sick and tired of him being so insufferably right all the time. Anyway, he'll go to Susa and end his life as a valued advisor of the Great King of Persia. Many people in our era are shocked to learn that. They find it crushingly disillusioning and disappointing—a colossal let-down."

"Not me. This self-opinionated, back-biting town doesn't deserve him." Mondrago shook his head and looked around at Athens. "I'm beginning to think I'd be willing to write my own name on one of those potsherds."

Jason said nothing, for now that he had told the story, his dreary inward refrain—*I've lost a team member*—was back in full force. The fact that they were, for the second time, unable to witness the Athenian Assembly in session made it worse, for he knew how unendurably frustrated Landry would have been.

It got even worse as they walked along, parallel to the South Stoa. It wasn't the long open-fronted building, with offices for governmental market inspectors, which would one day give its name to the Stoics, philosophers who would declaim in its colonnaded shade. That wouldn't be built until the late fifth century B.C. But Landry had been delighted to discover that an earlier version—just a long portico, really, fulfilling some of the same functions but never suspected by the archaeologists—existed in 490 B.C. He had insisted that Jason look at it and thereby record it. The recollection caused Jason another jag of emotional pain. He found himself compulsively glancing backward over his right shoulder, in the direction of the Pnyx.

I'm frustrated too, he suddenly realized. *Not as much as Bryan would be, of course. But still . . . considering the importance of what's going on there today. . . .*

Abruptly, he halted, and a sudden wild resolve drove the depression from his mind.

"Alexandre," he stated firmly, "we're going to that Assembly!"

Mondrago stared at him, goggle-eyed. "Uh . . . we haven't exactly been invited."

"Who said anything about invitations?" asked Jason with a grim smile.

"Sir, are you trying to get us in trouble—and jeopardize the mission?" Mondrago pointed back in the direction they had come, where the police had by now rounded up the last of the stragglers. "Those guys in the odd costumes don't strike me as having much of a sense of humor."

"We're not going that way, back through the Agora." Jason consulted his map-display of Athens. It confirmed his hunch. "There's a roundabout alternate route, where nobody ought to be just now. We'll work our way around to the side of the Pnyx."

"Won't somebody there notice us?"

"I have a feeling that everyone will be so focused on the debate that two extra men will be able to slip in unobserved. We'll have to keep our mouths shut, of course, and not draw attention to ourselves. And we probably won't be able to stay too long. But the outcome of this Assembly session is a matter of recorded history, so nothing we do should cause any harm."

"So you're always telling me, sir: no paradoxes. But you've also told me that there's no predicting what will happen to prevent paradoxes, and that whatever it is might be hazardous to your health." Mondrago's tone was respectful but determined, and Jason had to respect him for sticking to his guns. "If this debate is as important to observed history as you say, then reality, or fate, or . . . God, or whatever, might be even less particular about it than usual this time."

"I can't deny the hazards. And of course we won't be able to appreciate what we see and hear to anything like the extent Bryan could have. But my implant will record it all. It will be priceless data for historians, when we return. It's what Bryan would have wanted. We owe it to him." All at once, Jason could no longer meet the other's eyes. "Or rather, *I* owe it to him."

Mondrago's face wore an expression Jason had never seen, or expected to see, on it. "*You* didn't kill him, sir. Those Transhumanist vermin did. Now it's up us to get home with the information we've got on them, so that maybe they can be made to pay!"

Every word of which, Jason admitted to himself, was demonstrably true. Only. . . .

"I may not have killed him, but I didn't prevent it either—any more than I prevented Chantal's abduction. It may not make sense to feel that way, but I'm stuck with it. And I need to do this. If you don't want to come, I won't order you to. You can go back to the house and wait for me."

"Hell, somebody's got to keep you out of trouble," said Mondrago gruffly. "I've been doing it for officers for years."

"You'll pay for that," said Jason with a grin. "Let's go!"

They hurried on to the eastern end of the South Stoa. There, between the Stoa and the fountain-house, stairs ascended to a street that ran parallel to the Stoa, behind it and at a higher level. Here they turned right and followed the raised street a short distance, with the upper parts of the Stoa's rear elevation to their right. To their left were the low, white-plastered walls that enclosed the rear yards of the houses clustering on the lower slopes of the Areopagus hill. At the first break in those walls, they turned left onto an upward-sloping alley.

So far, it was the same route they would have taken to return to their quarters, now haunted by the ghost of Bryan Landry. But instead of taking the next turn, Jason led the way straight ahead, further up the slope. The houses began to thin out. As Jason had foretold, hardly anyone was about.

Beyond the houses, they worked their way to the right, scrambling around the middle Areopagus slopes toward the hill's northern side. Down to their right, they looked over the sea of tiled roofs to the southwest of the Agora. Ahead rose the Pnyx, their destination, from which a sound of distant voices could be heard.

Reaching the valley between the two hills, they came

among more houses. Here, too, the steep, narrow streets were practically deserted. There was, Jason reflected, something to be said for Athenian society's domestic seclusion of women, at least from the standpoint of one trying to get around unnoticed. Starting up the Pnyx, they passed between houses cut so deeply into the hillside that their rear rooms were semi-basements. Then they were on the undeveloped slopes, and began scrambling to the left and upward. The sounds of the thousands of men gathered ahead grew louder.

CHAPTER THIRTEEN

IN THE COURSE OF THEIR ORIENTATION, Jason had learned that the *Ekklesia,* or Assembly of all Athenian citizens, had originally been held in the Agora. After the overthrow of the tyrants the new democratic regime had decided to move it to the Pnyx, and a great workforce had been employed carving a fitting meeting place out of that hill's rocky slopes, a project that had only been completed fifteen years previously.

He also knew that in 403 B.C. the Athenians would erect a truly impressive artificial platform on the Pnyx, earthen but supported by a massive stone retaining wall set against the northwestern slope, with concentric semicircles of seats sloping downward in a theater-like way to a speaker's dais backed up against the higher slope that rose on the southeast side. Jason had seen a holographic image of that platform, based on the archaeologists' deductions, and he was very glad that it still lay eighty-seven years in the future. The only way to its top would be two steep and rather narrow stairways on the northwest side, rising from the twin termini of the road leading up from the Agora, along which the citizens were driven. With such limited access, there would have been no way a pair of *metoikoi* interlopers could have gotten past the vigilance of the police. That very consideration, Jason suspected, would at least unconsciously go into the design—an architectural expression of Athenian exclusivity.

But in 490 B.C. no such platform and no such stairways existed. The meeting-place was a shallow depression sunk into the slope. Thus it was possible to approach unnoticed, climbing the slope to the rim of the "bowl." That rim was lined with the backs of standing figures, for the rough-hewn seating only accommodated five thousand and the Assembly's quorum was six thousand. But everyone's attention was riveted on the speaker's platform below. No one noticed the two figures ascending the slope from behind and insinuating their way into the overflow crowd. Jason and Mondrago worked their way forward as inconspicuously as possible and reached the rim, just above the highest seats. They looked out over the packed amphitheater-like womb of democracy.

I'm getting all this for the historians, Bryan, thought Jason, activating his implant's recorder function. He held no belief that Landry could hear him or would ever know. But he himself knew. That was enough.

He ran over in his mind what he knew of the Assembly. Each of the ten tribes presided for one-tenth of the year— the *prytany,* or "presidency." Normally, meetings were on the average every nine days, to consider legislation proposed by the *boule,* or "Council," of fifty members from each tribe, selected by lot for a one-year term. But emergency sessions, of which this was emphatically one, could be called. Any citizen—not just those of the upper classes, as had previously been the case—could speak, but in practice only trained speakers did so. Voting was by a simple show of hands.

Looking toward the speaker's platform, stage to the amphitheater, Jason saw that the elite got the best seats. There were gathered the nine *archontes*, or administrative officers, and the ten *astynomoi*, or magistrates, all chosen by lot. In the same favored area were the ten elected tribal *strategoi*. He could pick out Themistocles' jet-black head and Miltiades' graying-auburn one.

There was, Jason thought, more than a quorum here today—hardly surprising under the circumstances. And the orientation of the meeting-place was such that the participants got an unrivaled view. For Jason, on the upper rim, the panorama was especially breathtaking. To the right rose the acropolis in all its awesomeness. Below spread the city, and beyond that the plain of Attica. In the distance Mount Pentelikon could be glimpsed, and the two roads to Marathon.

I can see why they moved the meeting-place here, Jason thought. Unlike the people of other Greek city-states, who invented fanciful foundation legends of heroic migrations and divine descent, the Athenians believed themselves to be autochthonous, sprung from the soil of the corner of Greece they inhabited, as much a part of the landscape as the vineyards and the olive trees and the very rocks. Up here, looking out over that landscape, it was hard for them to forget that.

The day's debate had begun while he and Mondrago had followed their indirect route, and was obviously well under way. And Themistocles had indicated that, after days of discussion, both sides were down to summations of their arguments. That seemed to be the case at present. A speaker was holding forth even now, untypically portly for this society, and evidently a Eupatrid, judging from his obviously imported himation, dyed Phoenician purple and lined with gold figurings. "We all know the Persians will have us hopelessly outnumbered. I have it on good authority that their army numbers *two hundred thousand men!*"

There was a collective gasp.

"I heard *six* hundred thousand!" somebody yelled from the seats. A shudder ran through the throng, accompanied by moans.

"Shit!" Mondrago muttered in Jason's ear. "How many men do these people think each of Datis's six hundred ships can carry, over and above its own crew?"

"Not to mention supplies," Jason whispered back, nodding. "What would all those men be eating? Each other?" He motioned Mondrago to silence, so as not to interfere with the audio pickup.

"And," the speaker continued, "They are bringing their cavalry!" A hush settled over the crowd. The memory of the retreat from Sardis was all too fresh among these people, many of whom had lost relatives to the arrows and javelins of the Persian horsemen. "And no Greek army has ever defeated them in open battle! We have no choice. We cannot submit and expect mercy—not after. . . ." He left the thought unspoken and glared in the direction of the *strategoi,* and specifically at Miltiades, who had advocated the trial and execution of the Persian envoys. "No. We must remain inside our walls and place our trust in the gods!"

"Like the Eretrians did?" came a coarse jeer. A commotion erupted. Jason recalled being told that the Assembly was a tough audience.

The presiding officer, chosen from the current *prytany*, called for order and sought for the next speaker to recognize. Miltiades stood up. A respectful silence gradually descended, for everyone knew his background.

"The last speaker," he began, "has addressed you with an eloquence I cannot hope to emulate, for I am only a rough, simple soldier who has spent his years fighting the Persians while *he* has perfected his oratorical skills." A titter arose from the audience, with outright laughs rising like whitecaps above it. The Eupatrid turned as purple as his himation. "Nor do I need to, for he has set forth, far more persuasively than I could have, the arguments for marching forth and confronting the Persians in the field!"

A flabbergasted hubbub arose. Miltiades raised his hands to silence it.

"Yes, the Persians are coming in overwhelming force, and are bringing their cavalry. And after the last few days' debates, we are all agreed that they will probably land at Marathon." Miltiades pointed theatrically toward the distant outline of Mount Pentelikon. "From there, two roads lead around that mountain to this city. If the Persians seize even one of those roads, their horsemen will have the freedom of the plain all the way across Attica!" He let the breathless silence last a couple of seconds. "*But*, if we can get there in time and deploy across those roadways, we can pen them up in their beachhead where the cavalry will have no room for maneuver."

Miltiades paused, and someone else got the attention of the presiding officer, clearly seeking leave to answer him. While that byplay was in progress, the Assembly seemed to lose focus as discussions began everywhere. Jason could sense a trend, which doubtless had been building up gradually over the last few days' debates, in Miltiades' favor. Nearby, among the standing-room crowd, one man's voice rose above the rest as he addressed those around him. "Miltiades is right! Let's all of us speak out in support of him when someone stands to argue with him."

"Right!" agreed someone else. "All of us. . . ." He looked around, and his eyes narrowed as they rested on Jason and Mondrago.

Uh-oh, Jason thought. *I knew this was bound to happen sooner or later. These men naturally clump together in tribal groups, and they all know each other—Aristotle considered that a basic precondition of democratic government. Any outsiders are bound to stand out. They've been fixated on the speakers so far. But now—*

"Who—?" the man began.

Time to fight fire with fire, Jason decided. "Who's that?" he shouted, pointing off to the side. Heads swiveled in that direction, and a commotion spread—a commotion that, Jason saw, was disrupting the new speaker's opening remarks. But that was all he stayed to see. He grasped Mondrago's arm, and while everyone's attention was distracted, they slipped back and scrambled back down the slope, working their way back the way they had come.

When they were back on the slopes of the Areopagus

and could afford to relax their haste a little, Mondrago finally spoke. "Remember that speaker you threw off his stride, there at the end?"

"Yes."

"Well . . . what if he *hadn't* been thrown off his stride? He might have been more effective, and talked the Assembly out of approving Miltiades' strategy."

Jason gave him a sharp look. It was the sort of unexpected thing Mondrago occasionally came out with. And it was one of the questions that gave the Authority headaches.

"I suppose," he finally said, "that if what I did influenced the outcome, it *always* influenced the outcome, if you know what I mean. In other words, it was always part of history. That's just what we have to assume."

Mondrago said nothing more, and neither did Jason, because he was still brooding over their enforced early exit from the Pnyx. *God, but I wish I could have stayed to the end!* he thought in his frustration. He consoled himself with the thought that Themistocles had promised them a recap that evening.

Themistocles looked drained but triumphant. He took a swig of wine with less water in it than usual. "We won! I have to admit, that canting prig Aristides came around in the end, even though some of his usual allies advanced strong arguments that we should squat inside the walls and settle in for a siege. The same arguments we've been hearing for days. But Miltiades was brilliant. He stood the whole argument on its head and turned the fear of the Persian cavalry to his own advantage."

"And, as Miltiades has more experience fighting the Persians than anyone else, his opinion naturally commanded respect," Jason nodded.

"Naturally. But nobody ever mentioned aloud what was really at the back of everyone's mind. It was too touchy a subject to raise in the Assembly." Themistocles smiled rather grimly. "The Eretrians didn't contest the Persians' landing, but withdrew inside their walls to resist. And all it took was two traitors to open the gates from inside. And now Eretria is a smoldering heap of rubble." He took a pull on his almost-neat wine. "In this city, with all its irreconcilable factions and aristocratic family feuds brought to a boil under the pressure of a siege, what are the chances that *no one* would accept Persian gold or take revenge for some old slight or seek to curry favor with the new rulers? Ha! I doubt if we'd last the five days that Eretria did before somebody betrayed us."

"Still, Miltiades's strategy seems to carry risks of its own," Jason prompted.

"Oh, yes. That nonsense about hundreds of thousands is just old women's rubbish, of course, but the fact remains that the Persian army is going to number several times the nine or ten thousand we can put in the field." (*Thirty-five thousand or so, by modern estimates, Bryan told us,* Jason thought. *Rutherford wants us to confirm that. All at once, like so many of Rutherford's priorities, it doesn't seem quite so important any more.*) "So if we're to have any hope of victory we're going to have to commit every man we have—which means that Athens itself will be left defenseless." Themistocles tossed off the last of the wine. "Ah, well, it's irrevocable now. By solemn resolution of the Athenian people, we will march as soon as the beacon-fire atop Mount Pentelikon is seen, confirming that the Persians have landed."

"Not before that?" inquired Mondrago with a frown. "If you could get there earlier, and secure the beach—"

"No. That was something even Miltiades had to concede. We can't be *absolutely* certain the Persians will land at Marathon, even though everything points to it. No, we have to wait until it's confirmed. Then we'll march, with every available man. Speaking of which," Themistocles continued without a break, "about your own military obligation. . . ."

"Yes, *Strategos*?" Jason had been waiting for this. One of the peculiarities of the Athenian system was that *metoikoi*, while denied practically all political rights, were liable for military service. "We naturally expect to serve the city that has so generously taken us in, as *ekdromoi*." The term referred to light-armed infantry, not very numerous and with a marginal role. The hoplites who made up the phalanx were members of the three uppermost property-owning classes, who could afford a panoply of armor and weapons costing seventy-five to a hundred drachmas, which was what a skilled worker could expect to make in three months. Jason was fairly confident that his and Mondrago's broad-spectrum expertise with low-tech weapons should enable them to function as hoplites, but that wasn't what they were here for. As skirmishers, around the fringes of the battle, they should be able to observe with minimal risk. More importantly, now, they would be in a position to watch for Transhumanist intervention.

"Ordinarily, that would be true," Themistocles nodded. "And in fact it *is* true in your case, Alexander. Coming from Macedon, you ought to be familiar with *that* kind of fighting." The remark held a note of unconscious condescension. The Thracians whom "Alexander" would naturally have fought were noted for hit-and-run skirmishing by light infantry called *peltastes*. It was looked down on by the southern Greeks, for whom *real* warfare meant the head-on clash of phalanxes composed of the Right Kind of People—which, Landry had speculated, was why the role of light troops at Marathon had always been ignored by historians. "But you, Jason, as a Macedonian nobleman . . . well, it would hardly be fitting for you not to take your place in the phalanx."

Jason groaned inwardly. He hadn't thought of this. He should have, for it went to the heart of the paradox of Classical Athens. Politically, it had the most radically democratic constitution in human history, a record it continued to hold in the twenty-fourth century. Socially, it was class-conscious to a degree that might have seemed just a bit much in Victorian England.

"Ah . . . *Strategos*, I have no armor, and no weapons other than my sword, and am in no position to supply myself with them." There was, Jason knew, no such thing as "government issue."

"Don't worry about a thing," Themistocles said expansively. "Remember, over the last twenty years, we Athenians have captured a lot of equipment in our victories over the Thebans and Chalcians. Most of it has been put on the market—a good thing, as it's reduced the prices and enabled more of our men to afford it. But there's a reserve of equipment, to be supplied at public expense to the sons of men who've met an honorable death in battle." Jason knew of the custom. He had wondered how the distribution was organized. Themistocles proceeded to enlighten him. "As *strategos* of the Leontis tribe, I have control of a portion of that reserve, for our people." He winked broadly. "I've always felt I have a certain latitude in exercising my discretion with regard to that portion."

No doubt, thought Jason drily. Aloud: "But, *Strategos*, I belong to no Athenian tribe." This, he knew, was an important point. The phalanx was organized by tribes, for the Greeks understood something that had eluded various bureaucrats throughout history. Men do not face the pain, death, and simple horror of combat for nationalistic abstractions, and they assuredly do not do it because some politician has made a speech. They do it for the other men in their unit. Never—not even in a Roman legion or in a regiment of the old British army—had this been more true than in a phalanx, where every man depended on the others, for if one man's cowardice broke the shield-line, all were dead. In the Roman legion or the British regiment, such solidarity was instilled by discipline, training, and unit traditions. In a phalanx it was inherent; the men to either side of you were men of your tribe, known to you from childhood and linked to you by kinship ties. To break ranks in their sight was unthinkable.

"Don't worry, Jason," Themistocles assured him, growing serious. "You'll stand with the Leontis tribe. I know it's a little irregular." (*Not that you've ever let that stop you*, Jason thought.) "But I'll tell those men that you have reason to hate these Persians who made slaves of your people and a puppet of your king. They'll know you can be relied on."

I hope they're right, Jason thought bleakly.

CHAPTER FOURTEEN

JASON LIFTED the little white-ground ceramic vase called a *lekythos*. It held the ashes of Bryan Landry.

Themistocles had arranged the cremation—an acceptable though non-compulsory rite. They had placed the traditional coins over the eyes—a tip for Charon, the ferryman who would convey the spirit across the River Styx into Hades. Due to their ambivalent status in Athens, and the general social disruption, they had been able to short-circuit the customary preliminaries of anointing the body with oils and wrapping it in waxed cloths. Nor, for the same reasons, were they under any pressure to have the *lekythos* interred in the Ceramicus beyond the wall. Jason intended to have it with him when their TRDs activated. Naturally Landry's own TRD—indestructible by mere fire—now lay, invisibly small, in the ashes at the bottom of the cremation oven and would appear on the displacer stage.

So would Chantal Frey's TRD. Jason had left it with

Themistocles for safekeeping, concealed in melted wax at the bottom of one of the small *pyxides*, or cosmetics-holding covered jars, that were among her possessions. Jason was grimly determined that it would arrive in the twenty-fourth century clutched in her living hand.

The second expedition in a row when I've gotten somebody killed, he thought, knowing how unreasonable the self-reproach was but unable to dismiss it. *It's getting to be a habit.*

It wasn't the only thing preying on Jason's mind. Whether or not any of them got back alive, the Authority *had* to be made aware that a Transhumanist underground was operating an unlawful temporal displacer. His plan had been to hire a local bronzesmith to hammer a message—unreadable by anyone of this milieu—onto a thin sheet of bronze, which he would deposit in this expedition's message drop, located on the slopes of Mount Pentelikon. But he'd had no opportunity. Besides, in Athens's current miasma of fear and paranoia, what was obviously writing in an unknown language and alphabet would surely draw suspicion onto the head of a foreigner like himself.

"It's time," he heard Mondrago say. He nodded. The great beacon-fire atop Mount Pentelikon had been sighted, confirming that the Persians were landing at Marathon.

They stepped out into the early morning coolness that unfortunately wouldn't last, and moved toward the Agora with all the other mustering men. Athens' unique economy, with over half of its wheat supplies imported and stored in granaries, had made it possible to concentrate the army at a central location rather than having to call men in from farms all over Attica. This, in turn, made the strategy of a rapid response to the Persian landing possible. Slaves carried the armor and weapons; the miserably uncomfortable fifty-to-seventy-pound hoplite panoply was intended to be donned no sooner before battle than was absolutely necessary, especially in the August heat. Of course, *ekdromoi* like Mondrago marched in their own lighter equipage of small round shields, leather shirts, slings, and two javelins, with light helmets hanging from the waist for travel.

As they descended the steps between the South Stoa and the fountain house and entered the Agora, Jason searched for the Leontis muster, hoping to spot Themistocles among the throngs. As he stood looking around, an older man approached him.

"You're Jason, the man from Macedon, aren't you? Rejoice! I'm Callicles, of the Leontis tribe. The *strategos* Themistocles—he's done a good turn or two for my family—asked me to look you up and sort of give you any help you may need, since you're new here."

Which, Jason thought, was damned nice of Themistocles. In the not-exactly-open society of the Athenian tribes, having a buddy in the ranks would help an outsider like himself to no end. He studied Callicles with interest. He already knew that hoplites were liable for active duty up to sixty, with no concessions of any kind to their age, and Callicles was fifty if he was a day—a much riper age than it was in Jason's world. But he looked like a tough old bird.

"Thanks," Jason said. "I know I'll be grateful to have you around, not being a member of the Leontis tribe at all."

"Don't worry about it," Callicles reassured him. "Themistocles told us about you. He explained that you're a well-born soldier in your own country." *Not a tradesman like most* metoikoi *in Athens*, was left unsaid. "Some of the men's sense of humor may be a little rough around the edges, I grant you. But nobody will really give you a hard time. Come on. We're over here." As he turned and led Jason toward his fellows of the Leontis, he spoke to Mondrago over his shoulder, as an afterthought. "The *ekdromoi* are over there," he said shortly.

Jason saw Mondrago make a gesture in the direction of Callicles' back—a gesture he suspected was a very old one in Corsica.

They joined the Leontis ranks, and Callicles greeted various fellow veterans of numerous campaigns in defense of the Athenian democracy. As he did, Jason noticed a knot of older men off to the side, surrounding a much younger man wearing only a loincloth and a headband. They seemed to be giving him last-minute instructions. A gooseflesh-raising thought occurred to Jason: *Could that possibly be . . . ?* Moved by a sudden impulse, he turned to Callicles. "Who is that young man over there?"

"Pheidippides. You wouldn't know about him, not being from Athens. He's the best runner we've got. We're sending him to Sparta to ask for their help." Callicles spat expressively and rubbed his grizzled beard. "Small chance, if you ask me. But even the Spartans ought to be smart enough to see that they're next, after throwing those Persian emissaries down a well."

Jason stared, and brought up information from his implant. Pheidippides was in his late teens or early twenties, tall and long-legged, with barely an ounce of body fat overlaying muscles that were long and flowing rather than massive and knotted. He looked like what he was: one of the greatest long-distance runners the human species would ever produce. For he would run the one hundred and forty miles of rough, winding, hilly roads to Sparta in two days—something a few athletes would duplicate starting in the late twentieth century, wearing high-tech running shoes and served by numerous watering stations. Then he would turn around and return to Athens in the same incredible time. And then he would fight in the Battle of Marathon. And then—if legend was to be believed—he would carry the news of victory the twenty-six miles to Athens in full armor, with an urgency that caused him to fall dead after gasping, "Rejoice! We conquer!" The last part had given rise to the Marathon race of the modern Olympic games (whose runners were not required to wear armor), but modern historians had been inclined to pooh-pooh it, asserting that Pheidippides's run to Sparta had become confused in popular imagination with the Athenian hoplites' rapid march back to Athens from Marathon after the battle. Rutherford wanted them to settle the question.

But there was another story that was somewhat more relevant to their present situation. On his return run from Sparta to Athens, on the heights just this side of Tegea, Pheidippides would afterwards swear that the god Pan had appeared, greeted him by name, and asked why the Athenians did not worship him, promising to aid them in the coming battle if they would do so henceforth. Historians had naturally written this off as an exhaustion-induced hallucination. It was, Jason reflected, an assumption they might just have to rethink.

He was, however, puzzled about one thing: how was

Franco going to get his pet "god" to the Tegea heights, roughly two thirds of the way to Sparta, for the occasion? Even assuming that they had already departed, travel by daylight would be out of the question, as Pan was not exactly inconspicuous.

But then there was no time to dwell on the matter further, for Themistocles was bawling orders and the roughly nine hundred strong muster of the Leontis tribe was shaking itself into marching order. Jason consulted his implant's calendar function. It was August 5.

The optic display read August 7 as Jason leaned on the camp's earthen defensive barrier, still drenched with sweat under the early afternoon August sun even though he was now out of his armor, and gazed out over the plain of Marathon.

He had always regarded himself—accurately—as being in excellent physical condition. It had been fortunate that he was, for the hoplites had marched from Athens to Marathon at a pace he was surprised that Callicles and the rest of the older men could sustain. Hoplites, he was learning, were very, very tough—especially the hoplites of Athens, who had been at war more or less continuously in defense of their fledgling democracy for almost twenty years. These men might not be professional soldiers—unlike the Spartans, they had day jobs, normally in agriculture, the only really respectable occupation for men of their class—but all of them except the very youngest were seasoned veterans.

They had arrived in time, while the Persians were still organizing themselves on their beachhead, amid the

inevitable chaos of all amphibious landings. They had
deployed across the two roads to Athens in a strong
defensive position, facing northeast from rising ground
with the higher wooded slopes of Mount Agriliki behind
them and a temple of Heracles with its sacred grove
shielding their right flank. Callimachus and Miltiades—
who seemed to function as unofficial chief of staff *cum*
operations officer, not that either term existed in this era—
had set them to work establishing a fortified camp. From
there they could look out across a scene that Jason was sure
caused these men, brought up on Homer, to imagine what
the defenders of Troy must have witnessed.

The beach curved away to the northeast, where the bay
was sheltered by a rocky promontory called the "Dog's
Tail." For miles, that beach was black with six hundred
ships hauled up on the sand. About half of these were
triremes—fighting galleys that could have overwhelmed
Athens's seventy-trireme fleet had the Athenians been
suicidal enough to commit it. The rest were transports of
various kinds, including fifty specialized ones that carried
twenty horses each. The almost fifty thousand rowers and
other sailors stayed on or near the ships. Just inland from
the base of the promontory was a marsh. Between it and
the Athenian position stretched a flat, barren plain,
hemmed in by hills and divided into northern and southern
halves by the Chardra, a stream mislabeled a river. To the
southwest of the marsh, just inland from the narrow sandy
beach, was the vast Persian camp, three miles from where
Jason stood, pullulating with thousands and thousands of
outlandishly clad invaders. Jason's practiced eye confirmed
the modern estimate of their numbers, which meant the

Athenians were outnumbered about three to one, even counting their light troops (which almost nobody ever did) and the addition of almost a thousand hoplites who had arrived, to vociferous cheers, from the small city-state of Plataea—its entire levy. It wasn't a large reinforcement, but it was the only help the Athenians were to get, and Landry had mentioned that Athenian gratitude to the Plataeans would endure for generations.

Then a stalemate had commenced. Something like a ritual had been established. The Greeks would form up their line in the morning, with light troops like Mondrago carrying forward *abittis* cut from the trees on the slopes to shield the phalanx's flanks. The Persians would also form up, and their dread cavalry would ride forth in their colorful trousered costumes, perform show-off caracoles, and shout taunts—the language was incomprehensible, but the tone was unmistakable—at the Greeks, who had no archers to respond. It was, of course, intended to draw the Greeks out, off the high ground and onto the plain. The Greeks would not rise to the bait; and the Persians, armed for raiding and not for shock tactics, would not venture to charge uphill against the shield line. And thus another day's morning ceremonies would conclude.

Jason became aware of Mondrago at his side. The Corsican was bathed in sweat even though he hadn't been encased in hoplite armor. "This is ox shit," he said with feeling.

"You look tired," said Jason solicitously.

"Tired? You'd be tired too. All you hoplites have to do is go through this morning charade, then sit on your asses the rest of the day while we *ekdromoi* go out on patrol!"

My God! thought Jason. *Is Athenian class consciousness getting to him?*

"But," Mondrago continued, calming down a little, "I'm sure Callimachus and Miltiades are happy as clams at high tide."

"How so?" asked Jason, who thought precisely the same thing but was curious to see if Mondrago had come to the same conclusion by the same path.

Mondrago waved an arm in the direction of the Persians. "They can't sit here forever. The food supplies for that horde must be getting used up fast, and they've been trying to gather some locally. Remember what I said about going out on patrol? At least I've been getting some practice with my sling. We've been going out into the hills to keep them from foraging—us and the horsemen."

"Horsemen?"

"Yes. Athens does have a tiny cavalry force, you know. It's largely ceremonial. Nobody around here even claims it would be close to being a match for the Persian cavalry even if the numbers were equal."

"I know." Jason recalled the Panathenaic frieze, and the flowing artistry of its procession of splendidly mounted young men—magnificent, but somehow not seeming very combat-ready. And that frieze had been from the Parthenon, as completed in 437 B.C. He somehow suspected that the current generation of Athenian cavalry, more than half a century earlier, would be even less impressive in battle.

"Still," Mondrago grudgingly admitted, "they've got heart. And they're good enough to help us cut up foraging parties. I can guarantee you the Persians are still consuming the supplies they brought with them."

"Logistics," Jason nodded. "It's the most important part of war, and the part that historians and novelists are most likely to forget."

"Something they're even more likely to forget about than food is what comes out the other end," said Mondrago with a nasty grin. "Can you imagine what that camp must be like, with that many men crammed into it? Ours is bad enough!"

Jason gave a grimace of agreement. With the exception of the as-yet-unborn Roman legions, camp sanitation had not been the strong suit of ancient armies. He, with his experience of past eras, and Mondrago with his military background, could endure it—barely.

"Right," Jason said. "No large army in this era can sit encamped in one place for long. It's only a matter of time—and not much of it—before disease, the real killer in ancient warfare, is going to hit, starting with intestinal ailments."

"And then they'll have tens of thousands of men with diarrhea packed in there." Even Mondrago, hardly the most fastidious of men, shuddered at the thought. "No doubt about it: time is on our side. Hence this miserable standoff we're in. Why should Callimachus seek battle when he can just watch the Persian army rot?"

"Besides," Jason reminded him, "Callimachus expects the Spartans to come. Why rush things when you're waiting to be reinforced by an army of full-time professional killers?" He was about to say something else, when, at the outermost left-hand corner of his field of vision, a tiny blue light began blinking for attention.

At first it didn't even register on Jason. His implant had

a number of standard features which had often come in handy in the Hesperian Colonial Rangers but which were irrelevant in past eras of history. He therefore never used them on extratemporal expeditions, and it was easy to forget they were there. So it took him a heartbeat or two to remember this one, from his time with the Hesperian Colonial Rangers, when it had been useful to have a sensor that detected the space-distorting effects of grav-repulsion technology. In retrospect, he could have used it in the Bronze Age; but, as he recalled, the Teloi "chariots" had always been upon him before such use had occurred to him.

Now, however, that blinking light told him that an aircar or some such vehicle was being used in the near vicinity.

Mondrago seemed to notice his distracted look. "What—?"

"Quiet!" Jason concentrated furiously, attaining the mental focus necessary for direct neural activation of the sensor's directional feature. He had barely done so before the blue light winked out.

"Something to do with your implant, right?" said Mondrago after a moment of silence.

Jason took a deep breath. "Yes. Somebody around here is operating a grav vehicle."

This got Mondrago's undivided attention. "The Teloi?"

"Presumably. But whoever it is, they just switched it off—" he turned to the left and pointed to the hill to the northwest "—up there, on Mount Kotroni."

Mondrago's gaze followed his pointing finger. It wasn't really a mountain, at seven hundred and eighty feet. Like the rest of the hills defining the plain of Marathon, it was forested in this era. "We've got to check this out."

"No, *I've* got to check it out. My implant will enable me to zero in on it if it's reactivated. I'm going up there." He instinctively reached for his waist and confirmed that he still had his leaf-shaped sword.

Mondrago looked around. "I have a feeling these guys don't exactly approve of people going AWOL. Least of all now."

"So you have to stay here and cover for me. If anybody wonders where I am, make up some excuse."

"Like what?"

Jason started to try to think of one . . . and then came to the realization that he trusted Mondrago fully to handle it on his own. And, in fact, the further realization that he was glad to have the Corsican at his back in general.

"You'll think of something." Without waiting for a reply to this gem of brilliance, Jason turned away and headed for the camp's eastern perimeter. At least everyone seemed too relieved to be out of armor to notice him.

CHAPTER FIFTEEN

IN THE EARLY AFTERNOON AUGUST HEAT, Jason was grateful for the shade of the foliage as he scrambled up the slopes of Mount Kotroni.

As he neared the crest, a level clearing opened out before him. At that moment, the tiny blue light began flashing again.

He looked around and saw nothing where the sensor assured him he should. But experience-honed instinct caused him to take cover behind a boulder and take a fighting grip on his short sword. No sooner had he done so when he heard a faint, whining hum. And he saw dust swirling upward from the clearing, as though from the ground-pressure effect of grav repulsion.

Above the ground, now that he knew what to look for, he recognized the shimmering effect of a refraction field, which achieved invisibility by disrupting the frequencies of light and causing them to "bend" or "slip" around the field and whatever was within it. It was cutting-edge technology in Jason's world.

And I never saw the Teloi using it, he thought, puzzled.

Then the dust settled, and the field evidently was switched off, for an aircar appeared out of nowhere, settling to the ground—and Jason's puzzlement turned to shock.

It was a small model, little more than a flying platform with a transparent bubble and two seats, for the pilot and one passenger. This one held only the pilot—a human, who proceeded to raise the canopy and emerge. And it was not one of the overdecorated, somehow Art Deco-reminiscent Teloi designs Jason remembered. He recognized it as a Roszmenko-Krishnamurti model, a few years old as his own consciousness measured time.

Until this instant, he had been able to tell himself that Franco's claims of radically superior time-travel technology were mere braggadocio, or perhaps an attempt at disinformation. Now he knew he could no longer take shelter in that comfortable assumption. The Transhumanists had temporally displaced this aircar— along with all their personnel and God knew what else—almost twenty-nine centuries. The Authority couldn't have done that without an appropriation request that would have precipitated an all-out political crisis. The Transhumanists had done it using a displacer so compact, and drawing so little power, that it could be concealed somewhere on Earth's surface.

Rutherford has *to be told about this!* He cursed himself for not having somehow managed to leave word at the message-drop on Mount Pentelikon.

The pilot stepped to the ground and, with his back to Jason, fumbled for a hand communicator. Jason suddenly realized that, after the man reported in, his own window of opportunity to take any action would vanish. Without pausing for further thought, he bunched his legs and launched himself over the boulder.

It was fairly artless. Jason hit the totally surprised Transhumanist from behind, smashed him over prone. His sword-holding right arm went around the man's neck, while his left hand grasped his left wrist and pulled that arm up behind his back.

But this Transhumanist was one of the genetic upgrades designed for, among other things, strength. His free right arm went up behind Jason's neck while his legs sent both of them surging upwards until he had Jason practically piggy-back. Then, with a further surge, he threw Jason over his right shoulder.

Jason's trained reflexes took over for him. He kept his grip on his sword, and hit the ground in a roll which brought him back up to his feet even as he whirled to face his enemy. The Transhumanist was already rushing him, hands outstretched in what Jason recognized as one of the positions of combat karate.

Jason's options suddenly became very simple. He had hoped to take the man alive, but he had no desire to have blade-stiffened hands smash through his rib cage and pull out his lungs. With a twisting motion, he evaded those hands while driving his sword into the Transhumanist's midriff. Then he dropped to his knees, wrenched the sword point-upward inside the guts in which it was lodged, and rammed it straight up. Blood gushed from the

Transhumanist's mouth as he fell to his knees and toppled forward, pulling the sword out of Jason's hand by his sheer weight.

Jason retrieved his sword, wiped off the blade, and used the pommel to smash the communicator the Transhumanist had never had a chance to use. Then he examined the aircar. It was, as he had thought, a standard model aside from the decidedly non-standard invisibility field. He activated its nav computer and brought up its last departure point on the tiny map display.

It was a point in the heights just east of Tegea, just over ninety miles to the southeast as the crow or the aircar flies.

Just about where Pheidippides swore that Pan appeared to him, came the thought, bringing with it a flash of understanding.

Jason summoned up his implant's clock display. He really needed to be getting back to camp. But at the aircar's best speed he could cover the distance in less than half an hour. And this had to be looked into.

He had neither time nor tools to bury the Transhumanist's body, but he didn't want to leave it to be found. With difficulty, he hauled it into the passenger seat and tied a heavy stone to it. Then he set the computer to retrace its last course, lowered the canopy, activated the invisibility field, and took to the air.

Jason's route took him over Mount Pentelikon and just north of Athens, but he was in no mood to appreciate the view, and at any rate the outside world appeared in blurry shades of gray when viewed from inside the field. He flew on into the dim-appearing afternoon sun. Soon he was over the island of Salamis, and the waters where ten years from now the navy that was now only a gleam in Themistocles' eye would scatter the fleets of Xerxes. Then the waters of the Saronic Gulf were beneath him. He stopped, hovered only twenty feet above the waves, and made certain there were no boats nearby whose crews might have noticed a body appear out of nowhere in midair and fall into the sea. He raised the canopy and pushed his deceased passenger out.

Resuming his flight, Jason went feet-dry over the Argolid. He did not permit himself to glance to the right, toward Mycenae and the bones that lay buried there. Instead, he spent the few remaining minutes of flight wondering just what the aircar had been doing landing on Mount Kotroni. No answer came to him, and none would now be forthcoming from the former pilot.

Approaching the end of the route, Jason resumed manual control of the aircar. Zooming the map display to its largest scale, he narrowed the landing site down to a flat area on a ridge overlooking the road from Sparta. He set the aircar down as gently as possible, to minimize the telltale dust-swirl. After satisfying himself that there was no one about, he deactivated the invisibility field and stepped out and walked to the edge of the ridge.

Looking cautiously down, he could see the winding road. On a lower level of the ridge, two humans were observing the road from concealment. Above them, but slightly lower than Jason, Pan crouched behind a boulder.

To Jason's right was a smooth, gentle slope which allowed easy access to Pan's position. He slipped very quietly down the slope, taking advantage of the fact that he was facing the sun and therefore casting his shadow behind him. He worked his way close behind the obviously preoccupied Pan and, with an adder-sudden movement, his left arm went around the being's neck, forcing the chin up. With his right arm, he pressed the edge of his sword against the exposed throat. It wasn't much of an edge—these swords were primarily for thrusting—but it would do.

"Quiet!" he hissed. The two Transhumanists below, their attention riveted on the road, hadn't noticed. "Don't make a sound."

Pan remained rigid but did not struggle. "What are you going to do with me?" he whispered.

Which, Jason realized, was a very good question. He hadn't formulated a plan, and when he thought about it he wondered why he hadn't simply killed Pan outright. Arguably, it would be the rational course—at least Mondrago would have so argued.

"What are you here for?" he whispered back, temporizing.

"I'm waiting for the Athenian runner who is returning from Sparta. He should be passing here soon. I am to accost him and ask him why the Athenians fail to honor me, and promise to aid them nevertheless in the coming battle by causing the Persians to flee in terror. And at the height of the battle, I am to appear to the Athenians, so they will believe they owe me their victory."

"And are you going to do it."

"I must!" The whisper held a quavering squeak. "I have been ordered to."

"Do you always follow orders?"

"I have no choice!" For an instant Pan's voice rose almost to a full squeak. Jason pressed his sword-edge harder against the hairy throat, and Pan subsided into a dull whisper. "You don't know what it's like!"

"You mean they torture you?"

"They don't need to. My entire existence is torture! Only they have the power to deaden it."

"I don't understand."

"How could you? Franco and his people came to this country fifteen years ago and persuaded the Teloi to help them create me, knowing this was the year they would need me to be available. They used . . . medicines to make me mature faster," Pan explained, coming as close as fifth-century B.C. Greek could to the concept of artificial growth accelerants. "They needed the help of the Teloi to do all this."

Jason nodded unconsciously. Of all the perversities forbidden by the Human Integrity Act, species modification—genetic tinkering which introduced genes not native to the original human genome—was the ultimate obscenity. The Transhumanists, of course, had had no compunctions about it. But even they had never developed it to the level that must have been required to create a thing like Pan. Evidently, though, they and the Teloi together had been equal to the task.

"But," Pan continued, still struggling with the limits of the language, "the parts of me that are not human could not be made to really *fit*. And my forced growth made it worse. Almost everything I do, especially walking, is unendurable . . . or would be without the medicines they constantly give me."

Again, Jason understood. It was one of the reasons species modification was regarded as such a unique abomination. The human organism was a totality. It was not designed to support, say, a digitigrade walking posture. Pan was a living mass of incompatibilities—a biological *wrongness*. And applying growth accelerants to such a ramshackle skeleton must have made it even worse, especially considering that the Transhumans and their Teloi allies probably hadn't bothered with any of the usual precautions.

Yes, Pan would never be free of pain, or at least discomfort, for a second of his waking life—and how would he ever sleep?—without chemical analgesia. He surely would have long since escaped into madness had it not been for the drugs that only his creators could supply . . . or withhold.

Now Jason understood how they controlled him. And from what he had heard in Pan's whisper, he dimly sensed how much the twisted being must hate them.

Killing Pan now would be the merciful thing to do as well as the expedient one.

Only, thought Jason as his grip tightened on the sword-hilt, *he might be a valuable source of information on the Transhumanists.*

"Listen," he said, improvising, "you can get away from them. You can get help from the Temporal Regulatory Authority." Of necessity, he said the last three words in English.

"How?" whispered Pan in a tone of dull scorn.

"Well. . . ." This was no time for a lecture on the physics of time travel, even had it been possible in the language.

"After I return to my own time, I'll come back to this time with soldiers to kill those two men down there—it can be a few minutes after this point in time, in fact—and I'll bring with me the medicines you need." Once Rutherford knew what was at stake, Jason was sure he could get an appropriation for such an expedition, and a waiver of the rules to allow him to bring back a substantial supply of advanced medications.

"Can you take me to your time?"

"No." Jason found he could not lie. "You are of this era. There can be no travel forward in time."

"But *you* travel forward in time!"

"No." How to explain temporal energy potential? "I only return to the time from which I came, and where I belong. You belong here, and must remain here. But we can free you from your dependence on Franco and the Teloi."

Afterwards, Jason was always certain that Pan wavered for a heartbeat before stiffening convulsively. "No! I can't trust you! They created the agony that is my life, and only they can grant surcease from it. I must do as I am told."

At that moment, before Jason could reply, one of the Transhumanists below—from whom Jason had never entirely taken his eyes—rose to his feet and gestured at the road from Sparta. In the distance was a tiny, running figure.

The sight of that figure—Pheidippides, returning with the news that the Spartans would be delayed—distracted Jason for a fraction of a second, causing him to lower his sword. That was enough. With the strength of desperation, Pan broke free of him and scrambled recklessly downhill despite Jason's efforts to catch him by his caprine legs.

Jason could only watch, cursing under his breath, as he joined the Transhumanists.

He really ought, Jason knew, to return to his aircar while the Transhumanists' attention was riveted on the road and get back to Marathon. But curiosity held him. He compromised with caution by ducking behind the boulder and watching as Pheidippides reached a point almost directly below. He saw one of the Transhumanists manipulate a remote control unit. A concealed device by the side of the road erupted into a flash of light and a thunderclap of sound. With a cry, the runner staggered and fell to his knees. While his eyes were still dazzled, one of the Transhumanists shoved Pan forward and up into plain sight. When Pheidippides could see again, the "god" stood on the ridge looking down at him.

"Pheidippides of Athens," said Pan in more-in-sorrow-than-in-anger tones, "why have the Athenians failed to worship me?"

Pheidippides groveled in the dust of the road. "We do, Great God, we do," he stammered frantically.

"No. My sacred grotto on the slope of the Acropolis is neglected, save by a few. The smoke of sacrifice does not rise from my altar there."

"We will neglect you no longer, Great God. I swear it! After I tell what I have seen, we will make amends. We will offer sacrifice."

"It is well. Continue on your journey, and assure the Athenians of my affection for their city. Tell them also that I know the peril in which Athens now stands, and that I mean to come to its aid very soon, because I trust that your promise to me will be kept."

Pheidippides looked timidly up. "Aid us how, Great God?" he dared ask.

"You know, Pheidippides, the power I possess to arouse unreasoning fear in men," Pan replied obliquely. "Now go, and complete your errand, and bear my words to the Athenians!"

The hidden Transhumanist touched his remote again, and the bogus thunder and lightning sent Pheidippides flat on his face with a wail. Pan scurried back to join his two handlers. After a few moments, Pheidippides cautiously looked up and rose to his feet. Still blinking, he cast nervous glances all around. Then a slow smile awoke on the young face—a smile of serenely confident hope, the kind of smile rarely seen among Athenians these days. The smile broadened into a grin as he resumed his run.

The Transhumanists crouched, preparing to leave as soon as the runner was out of sight, and Jason dared delay no longer. He retraced his steps, flung himself into the aircar, reactivated the invisibility field, and set his course back to the clearing on Mount Kotroni, overlooking the Greek camp on the plain of Marathon.

Once in the air, he had leisure to reflect wryly. *Of course I didn't kill Pan. History says Pheidippides claimed to have met him on the road.*

Only . . . if I had killed him, then maybe Pheidippides would have hallucinated him anyway, as historians think he did.

He shook his head and flew on, with the westering sun behind him.

CHAPTER SIXTEEN

MOUNT AGRILIKI ROSE TWO THOUSAND FEET to the southwest of the plain of Marathon, with the Athenian camp backed up against its lower slopes. Jason found a clear ledge about halfway to the summit and shielded from the view of those below. He doubted if the Transhumanists had a means of locating it when it was powered down. Of course they might have installed some kind of beacon that had enabled them to track its flight, but concealing the aircar was worth a try. He might well want to use it again, and what Rutherford didn't know wouldn't cause him to have a stroke.

He scrambled down the forested slope in the late-afternoon shadows. He slipped into the camp without difficulty, as nobody was being particularly careful about guarding its mountain-protected rear when the Persians were bottled up on the plain.

Mondrago, who had not been required to account for Jason's absence, greeted him with relief. They found a relatively private spot toward the rear of the camp and Jason recounted his story.

"It would be nice to think you stranded them there on that ridge in the Peloponnese," Mondrago remarked when Jason was finished. "I can't believe the Transhumanists could have displaced more than one aircar almost twenty-nine hundred years into the past."

Jason shook his head dourly. "They must be able to call in Teloi aircars, even if those are restricted to flying at night because they lack invisibility fields. In fact, they must be using them already. The aircar I took can only carry two, and I saw four: the pilot I killed, two more on the Tegea heights, and Pan."

"And that nauseating little mutant is still alive!" said Mondrago venomously. The look he gave Jason was accusing.

"I'm still hoping to turn him. I've told you how much he resents his own existence."

"He should. And I'll bet it's not just the things you told me about." Mondrago grinned nastily. "That gigantic dong of his must have been designed for nothing but show. It probably hurts him to piss."

"I hadn't thought of that," Jason admitted with a grimace.

"So what's the plan?"

"I'm just going to have to improvise. Remember, they'll be bringing him here before the battle—come to think of it, that must have been what their aircar was doing on Mount Kotroni, scouting out a suitable landing spot. Maybe that will be my chance."

"You say they're going to have him appear here so he

can take credit for spreading panic among the Persians. That sounds like they're planning to create the panic themselves. I can think of ways that might be possible."

"So can I," nodded Jason. Such effects could be achieved in ways involving focused ultrasonic waves affecting the human nervous system, sent along a laser guide-beam. And the Teloi might have other techniques.

"Well, then, sir," Mondrago continued, his tone changing to one of formal seriousness, "has it occurred to you that maybe this is why the Greeks end up winning the battle?"

"You mean, that the Transhumanist intervention has *always* been part of history? That *it's* the reason Western civilization survives?" Jason knew his voice probably reflected his unwillingness to believe it.

"Can you rule out the possibility? And if it's true, and if our theories about time travel are correct, you won't be able to undo it. Something will prevent you—maybe something lethal. And if those theories *aren't* correct. . . ." Mondrago left the thought dangling.

Jason drew a deep breath. "Remember when we were at the Athenian Assembly? This is sort of the opposite side of the coin from that. Once again, I don't deny that there are risks involved. But if the opportunity presents itself, I plan to try again to offer Pan our help in exchange for his cooperation."

Mondrago looked disgusted.

Pheidippedes half-ran and half-staggered into the camp the following night. He had paused only briefly at Athens to impart the news he now brought to the army. In the immemorial way of armies everywhere, Rumor Central promptly conveyed that news to everyone.

"Carneia!" old Callicles snorted, with his patented eloquent spit. "The Spartans are celebrating Carneia, their holy festival—quite a big festival, I've heard—and they can't march until the moon is full!"

Mondrago shared his feelings. "Greatest warriors in history!" he muttered to Jason in an English aside. "More like the greatest party animals!"

"Mark my words," Callicles continued, "if that bastard Cleomenes was still running things in Sparta, he wouldn't let any stupid 'period of peace' stop him. But now he's dead, and the Spartans are shitting in their chitons with fear that they may have offended the gods by throwing those Persian emissaries down that well, not to mention burning that sacred grove at Argos. So they're being very careful to observe their religious holidays—and never mind that we Athenians get butt-fucked by the Persians while they're doing it!"

A pair of men passed within earshot, heading toward the tents of the Aiantis tribe. One of them paused. In the light of the campfires, Jason saw he appeared to be in his mid-thirties, beginning to go prematurely bald. "But," he called out to Callicles, "if they set out at the full moon and march as fast as Pheippides says they promise to, shouldn't they be here in a week? Surely we can hold the Persians at bay that long."

Jason expected a scornful reply accompanied by another expressive spit. But Callicles's "Maybe you're right" was no worse than grudging. He sounded as though he knew the man, at least by reputation.

"Come on!" the man's companion called. "We're already late."

"Coming, Cynegeirus." The man waved to them and hurried on.

"Who was that?" asked Jason.

"Fellow named Aeschylus, from Eleusis," said Callicles. "Writes plays."

Jason stared at the retreating back of the man who was to become Greece's greatest dramatist—but whose epitaph would say nothing about that, only that he had fought at Marathon. And the familiar tingle took him.

"You've heard of this guy?" Mondrago asked him.

Jason nodded. "In our era he's going to be known as the Father of Tragedy."

"He seemed pretty cheerful to me."

"He may not be quite as much so after what is going to happen to the man with him—his brother Cynegeirus." Jason shook himself, recalling what Landry had told him. In the final phase of the battle, on the beach, Aeschylus would watch as Cynegeirus had a hand chopped off as he tried to grab the stem of an escaping Persian ship, a wound from which he would subsequently die. "I've got to go. The generals must be meeting now to decide where we go from here, and I want to get that meeting on my recorder—there have always been a lot of unanswered questions about it."

"They're going to just let anybody listen in?" Mondrago sounded scandalized by such sloppy security.

"Maybe not. But I'll never know if I don't try." And Jason slipped away through the camp.

Security almost lived down to Mondrago's expectations—indeed, it was a barely understood concept in this place and time. In the heat of the August night, Callimachus and the ten *strategoi* were meeting under an open tent. Herodotus had claimed that command of the army had been rotated among those ten tribal generals, one on each day, and that as the day of battle had approached the others had handed command over to Miltiades on their allotted days. Mondrago had scoffed at that, declaring roundly that no army could or would have tried to function under such a nonsensical system. He had turned out to be right. Their initial impression—that Callimachus the war archon was in actual as well as honorary command, assisted by Miltiades as *primus inter pares* among the *strategoi*—had proven to be correct. Mondrago, whose sole intellectual interest was military history, had mentioned the names "Hindenburg" and "Ludendorff."

Jason had a great deal of experience at making himself inconspicuous. He now brought all the subtle techniques he had learned to bear as he moved among the campfires and approached the open tent. He saw Pheidippides walking groggily away from that tent, where he must have finished rendering his formal report and would now doubtless collapse into a very long sleep that no one would begrudge him. Jason continued on in his unobtrusive way toward that tent and its murmur of voices, working his way inward until he could see the figures within, illuminated by flickering torchlight, and his implant's recorder function could pick up the voices.

"You heard Pheidippides," said someone Jason didn't recognize. "All we have to do is hold out until the Spartans arrive: seven days if they keep their promise, and he's convinced they will."

"And there's no reason why we can't keep this stalemate going that long," said someone else. "All we have to do is stay here, in this fortified camp on ground of our choosing."

A murmur of agreement arose from what seemed to be a clear majority of the generals. The murmur rose to a pious pitch when one voice added, "And remember, according to Pheidippides we have Pan's promise of assistance!"

Miltiades rose to his feet, the torchlight glinting from the remnants of red in his beard. The self-convincing murmur gradually subsided. All the *strategoi* were veterans of wars against the enemies of Athenian democracy— *Greek* enemies. But Miltiades knew the Persian way of war from inside and outside, and they all appreciated that fact.

"We can't just sit here behind our earthworks and wait for the Spartans," he said as soon as he had absolute silence. "The Persians have spies and well-paid traitors everywhere. Anything we know, we must assume *they* know. So don't you suppose they're taking account of Spartan schedules themselves?"

The silence took on an inaudible but perceptible quality of uneasiness. "Military intelligence" was still a barely understood concept among the Greeks, and there was something sinister, almost uncanny about it. But the Persians were the first people in history to recognize that information was the key to control. And Miltiades knew the Persians.

"Furthermore," Miltiades continued, "Datis is running out of time. Even on half rations, his food stores can't last more than a few days. I know we've seen some coming and going of ships, bringing in supplies from islands under

Persian control. But with harvest season coming on, even those supplies must be running low. Before the Spartans arrive, and before his army starves, Datis is going to have to try a new strategy."

"What strategy?" someone demanded. "What can he do? He can't attack us here in this position."

"What he can do," explained Miltiades patiently, "is embark his army and sail around Cape Sunium and land at Phalerum, with nothing between them and Athens, leaving us still sitting here, looking stupid."

A shocked silence fell. None of these men, Jason was certain, were under any illusions as to the likelihood that the undefended city wouldn't contain a single fifth columnist to open the gates as the gates of Eretria had been opened.

"When they begin to embark," Miltiades resumed into the silence, "We will have no choice. We will have to advance onto the plain and attack."

If possible, the silence deepened into still profounder levels of shock as the *strategoi* contemplated the prospect of doing exactly what Datis had been hoping they would do.

"But," said Miltiades before anyone could protest, "that will be our opportunity. Think how difficult an operation that embarkation will be for them—especially because they'll want to break camp at night, to conceal it from us. And the hardest part will be getting the cavalry aboard. Whenever they've loaded horses aboard ships before, they were able to use the docks in Ionia and at Eretria; they didn't have to get them up gangplanks on a beach in shallow water. They'll have to do that first, before daybreak.

If we can strike them at exactly the right time, they'll be without their cavalry, and off balance. We've never had such a chance! And we'll never have it again!"

"But," protested Thrasylaos, *strategos* of the Aiantis tribe to which Callimachus himself belonged, "we'll need to know in advance when they're preparing to depart."

Even at a distance, Jason could see Miltiades' teeth flash in a grin. "The Persians aren't the only ones with spies. They have a lot of Ionian conscripts over there, and among them are some old associates of mine from the rebellion. I still have contacts among them. They and I have arrangements for meeting and exchanging information, over there in the Grove of Heracles." Miltiades raised a hand to hush the hubbub. "That's all you need to know at present."

"But," Thrasylaos persisted, although his voice was that of a man who was wavering, "if we advance out onto the plain, they'll be able to outflank us, with their superior numbers." An uneasy murmur of agreement arose, for a phalanx was always terrifyingly vulnerable to flank attacks. "And they'll have their archers," he added, in a tone that held a mixture of conventional disdain—the Greeks had always looked on archery as the unmanly expedient of such dubious heroes as Prince Paris of Troy—and healthy apprehension.

Callimachus rose to his feet. His bald scalp gleamed in the torchlight, but he looked younger than he had when Jason had first seen him in the Agora, for he no longer had the stooped, careworn look. He now exuded calm confidence.

"We will prevent them from outflanking us," he

explained, "by lengthening our line. To accomplish this, our center—the Leontis and Antiochis tribes—will form up four men deep." He gave Themistocles and Aristides, the generals of the two tribes in question, a meaningful look. "The right and left wings will be eight deep as usual."

Themistocles and Aristides looked at each other, their mutual detestation for once in abeyance as they considered the implications of this order.

"*Polemarch*," said Themistocles respectfully, "we have observed over the past several days that the Persian center is always the strongest part of their formation." There was no fear in his voice. He was merely inviting his commander's attention to certain facts, with scrupulous correctness.

Aristides amazed everyone present by nodding in agreement. "It's where the Medes and the Persians themselves are concentrated, and the Saka from the east—the best troops they've got."

Miltiades answered him. "Yes. That's the standard Persian formation, with their weaker troops—levies from all over the empire—on the wings. And that's precisely why we're making our wings stronger."

Callimachus quieted the hubbub that arose. "You'll all understand why soon, for I mean to explain my plan to you so you can tell your men what to expect. And as for Thrasylaos' other point, about their archers. . . ." For the first time, Jason saw Callimachus smile. "Well, we'll just have to give them the least possible time to shoot their arrows!"

Out of the corner of his eye, Jason noticed men beginning to take notice of him. Reluctantly, he moved on, carefully projecting the casual air of a man who had paused for no particular reason. Given the reputation of the Persians for espionage, he couldn't risk any suspicious behavior.

And besides, he had a very good idea what Callimachus was about to say.

CHAPTER SEVENTEEN

ANOTHER DAY OF DEADLOCK WENT BY, and then another, and another.

The ritualistic morning confrontations continued, and Jason saw what Callimachus and Miltiades meant about the Persian formation. The Medes and Persians and their eastern ethnic relatives, the Saka, were massed in the center, with archers behind the protecting lines of infantry carrying wicker shields and armed with short spears and the short swords known as *akenakes*. Here as well were the lightly clad horse archers, and cavalry armed with spears and—alone among the Persian army—wearing bronze helmets. It was a typical Persian array, except that, having had to cross the sea, it contained a lower percentage of horsemen than was normal. And, just as typically, it was flanked by polyglot masses of troops from all over the empire, visibly less smart about getting into formation each morning and staying there in the baking August sun.

"Rabble," sniffed Mondrago with reference to the latter troops, late in the afternoon.

"Don't be too sure," Jason cautioned. "Remember, this army has spent six years crushing the Ionian rebels and conquering Thrace. They're veterans, and all that experience fighting and training together has probably given them about as high a degree of operational integration as is possible for such a multiethnic force. And they have a tradition of victory—they've never been defeated." He looked around to make sure no one was observing them. "Anyway, I need to get going."

Jason inconspicuously gathered up the fruits of his surreptitious labor over the past two nights. Mondrago looked at the small satchel dubiously.

"Do you really think these things are going to last over twenty-eight hundred years?"

"Why not? Archaeologists dig them up all the time." Jason took out one of the ceramic potsherds he had been collecting and inscribing with his report. Only a small amount of the English lettering would fit on each one, but he had numbered them; Rutherford should have no trouble puzzling them out when they appeared at the message drop.

"So now I'm going to have to cover for you again," Mondrago grumbled.

"Well," said Jason reasonably, "I have to be the one to go. Would you be able to find the message drop on Mount Pentelikon?"

"I know, I know. You're the one with the map spliced into his optic nerve." This clearly didn't sweeten it for Mondrago.

"I'm still going to need daylight, though. So I'd better get going now."

Jason slipped out of back of the camp and made his way up Mount Agriliki to the ledge where he had left the Transhumanists' aircar. It was still there, to his relief; the Transhumanists evidently had no way of locating it. He took it aloft and made his invisible way to Mount Pentelikon, rising over thirty-five hundred feet a few miles to the southwest.

Before their departure from the twenty-fourth century, he had taken a virtual tour of the mountain, and his implant had been programmed to project a tiny white dot on his neurally activated map display where an overhanging rocky ledge sheltered the spot that had been chosen as a message drop.

At this moment, in the linear present of the year 2380, it was empty. In a few minutes, Jason's potsherds would be there, to be discovered in the course of the next of the inspections of the site. But no one would be there at the precise instant of the linear present when Jason put them there. Something would prevent it. He suppressed the eerie feeling that always took him at moments like these.

He cruised about in search of a place where the aircar could rest concealed from any goatherds who might be about, finally settling for a kind of small glen. Save for being more extensively forested, all was as it would be in his era. He hefted his satchel and set off on a narrow path leading around the mountainside toward his destination. Turning a corner, he saw the flat top of the ledge under whose far end was the message drop, a few feet below.

But he had eyes for none of that, for he was not alone.

Ahead of him stood Franco, Category Five, Seventy-Sixth
Degree, and one of his strong-arm men . . . and Chantal
Frey.

For a heartbeat the tableau held, as they all stood in
shocked surprise. Then the low-ranking Transhumanist
sprang into action, as he was genetically predisposed to,
whipping out a short sword and lunging toward Jason.

Jason dropped his satchel and let his trained reflexes
react for him as he took advantage of the tendency of a
lunge to put the swordsman slightly off balance. Twisting
aside to his left and gripping the wrist of his assailant's
sword-arm, he pulled the man forward while bringing his
right knee up, hard, into his midriff. The wind whooshed
out of him as Jason pulled him forward, continuing the
lunge, and his grip on the sword-hilt weakened enough for
Jason to twist it out of his hand as he fell.

Jason whirled toward Franco, who was too far away for
a thrust. He knew he had only a few seconds before the
swordsman recovered. His sword wasn't designed for
throwing, but it would have to do. He drew it back. . . .

With an almost invisibly quick motion, Franco grabbed
Chantal in his left arm, swung her in front of him as a shield
and, with his right hand, put a dagger to her throat.

"Drop the sword or she dies," he said emotionlessly, in
his strangely compelling voice. Chantal's eyes were huge
in her frozen face.

A measurable segment of time passed before Jason let
the sword slip from his fingers and hit the flat rock ledge
with a clang. The guard retrieved it, and Franco released
Chantal. She took a step toward Jason.

"I'm sorry, Jason." She seemed barely able to form

words, and her features seemed about to dissolve in a maelstrom of conflicting emotions.

"It wasn't your fault," he said dully. But then he looked into those enormous eyes, and began to understand what he was seeing in them.

No, he thought as a horrible doubt began to dawn.

Then she stepped back and stood beside Franco, half-leaning against his side as he put an arm around her shoulders.

"No," said Jason, aloud this time but almost inaudibly.

"Yes," said Franco with a smile. "This works out very well. When she returns to her own time she'll be able to explain how you and the others met your unfortunate end."

"Returns to her own time? Haven't you made that impossible?" Jason jerked his chin in the direction of Chantal's left arm, which still had a bandage around it. She seemed to seek refuge deeper in the crook of Franco's arm. "Why did you do that, by the way? Just sheer, random sadism?"

"Oh, we had to, in order to keep you from being able to track her whereabouts. Oh, yes, we know about your brain implant, and the passive tracking devices incorporated in the other team members' TRDs." Franco pursed his lips and made a mocking *tsk-tsk* sound. "Whatever happened to your precious 'Human Integrity Act'?"

"You never told me about that, Jason," Chantal said with a kind of weak resentment in her voice. She snuggled even closer to Franco. "*He* did!"

"Chantal," said Jason, still struggling with his bewilderment, "don't you understand? He's made it impossible for you to return to your own time. You'll have to spend the rest of your life in this era!"

"Oh, no," Franco denied, shaking his head, before Chantal could speak. "Now that we have you, and while that thug of yours is otherwise occupied at Marathon, we'll find her TRD."

"You're lying, as usual. Why would you want to do that?"

"You'll learn in a moment. But, to resume, it must be at your house in Athens or, more likely, the house of your friend Themistocles." Jason tried to keep his features immobile and not confirm Franco's supposition. From the latter's expression, he saw that he had failed. "We'll retrieve it—sonic stunners will take care of his servants, and we have sensors that can detect it. We also have some field dermal regeneration equipment among our first-aid supplies. It will be a simple matter to re-implant it in her arm and restore the tissue."

"That will never get past a careful examination."

"But why should there be such an examination? There will be no reason for anyone to suspect her. At the same time, there will be a tendency to want to spare the single survivor of the expedition any further distress."

"So there will. It's called ordinary human decency."

"Yes—an obsolete concept that continues to serve a useful purpose simply because we have always been able to exploit it. She'll be welcomed back with open arms after she arrives accompanied by her companions' corpses, and receive a great deal of sympathy for the harrowing experience she has been through. She will therefore be in an excellent position to be a useful agent of ours."

Jason shook his head as though to clear it of a fog of unreality. "Chantal . . . *why*?"

"Jason . . . I'm sorry. I know what you're thinking. But he's made me understand—made me see things clearly for the first time. Remember our conversation in the lounge the night before our departure? I'd always wondered, but now, thanks to him, I *know*. Our society is trying to stand in the way of destiny—the destiny that the Transhumanists represent. It's . . . it's as though we're like the Persians at Marathon, unconsciously fighting to prevent a better world from being born. The human race can transcend itself, become something *better*."

"Chantal, I can't believe I'm hearing this claptrap! Surely you can't believe it—not after he murdered Bryan and did *that* to you!" Jason pointed at her left arm.

A convulsive shudder went through her. "He's explained to me that they never intended to kill Bryan. They were just going to take him as a hostage, like me. You *forced* them to kill him, by interfering. And as for me . . . he had to do that. He didn't know yet that he could trust me. He had no choice. But he truly regretted it—he's told me so." She looked up into Franco's face.

Jason saw the look she gave Franco, and Franco's smile. And all at once he understood.

A plain, shy, insecure girl, he thought. *Attracted to the study of aliens because she's always found them easier to cope with than her fellow humans—especially the male ones. And suddenly, at a time of special vulnerability, she's exposed to a man whose genes were tailored to maximize his charisma. He must have really turned on the charm, and the flattery. . . .*

"Chantal," he burst out desperately, "can't you see he's just using you? He's lying to you. He's not capable of love. And even if he was . . . to him you're nothing but a Pug!"

Jason's consciousness exploded into a spasm of sickening pain as the guard punched him from behind, hard, in the right kidney. He fell to his knees, gasping. When he finally looked up he saw Franco examining the contents of the satchel he had dropped.

"Very ingenious," said Franco, holding up one of the laboriously inscribed potsherds. He dropped it on the ground, and poured all the others out to join it. Then, with his foot, he crushed them into fragments.

"Chantal told us your message drop was up here on this mountain," he explained. "But of course she didn't know the exact location. We have patrolled the area periodically in the hope of encountering you. But it was just good fortune that we happened to be up here today on . . . other matters."

"You still don't know the message drop's exact location," Jason reminded him.

"No. But it would be useful to us—we could leave whatever messages we want, to be found by your superiors. That—and also the location of the aircar you stole—is information we will now obtain from you."

"You can try."

"And succeed. I don't have access to any high-tech means of torture, but I won't need them. To tell you the truth, I've always considered them overelaborate. Come, Chantal," Franco said offhandedly, turning on his heel and striding off without waiting for her. "And," he called out over his shoulder to the guard, "bring him."

Chantal, her face still working as though she was on the verge of an emotional collapse and her body moving as though it could barely remain upright, turned slowly and followed Franco like a sleepwalker. Jason, responding to a prod by the guard's sword, fell in behind her.

They were walking along the ledge when Chantal abruptly swayed, lost her balance, and began to crumple to the flat rock, near its edge.

The guard automatically reached out past Jason to catch and steady her. But his position was awkward, and she continued to fall, pulling him down.

Jason had only a split second to react, and he was not in a good position to do it. The best he could manage was a kick that caught the guard in his ribs and sent him sprawling over the ledge to the ground a few feet below. He bellowed in rage, but kept his grip on his sword and sprang back to his feet almost immediately. From up ahead, Franco was roaring with rage and running back toward them. All Jason could do was spin around and, without even a backward glance at Chantal, sprinted for his aircar.

He was around the bend in the path and in the aircar before his pursuers could see it. He activated the invisibility field just before the guard, with Franco behind him, came around the cliffside. In the murky grayness of the outside world, they looked around in bewilderment. Jason smiled grimly as he took off, blowing a satisfying amount of dust into their faces.

Once in the air, he released a long-pent-up breath, sank back into the seat cushion, and tried to sort out his swirling thoughts.

She looked like she was fighting off a nervous breakdown, he told himself. *It was just a lucky break that she collapsed when she did.*

Or . . . was that a deliberate stunt on her part, to let me escape?

I may never know.

Back in the camp that night, in the light of the full moon that had enabled him to scramble down the now-familiar slope of Mount Agriliki from his concealed aircar, Jason related the story to Mondrago, who muttered something about the Stockholm Syndrome. "And now," he concluded, "I've got to get back to Athens, go to Themistocles' house, and retrieve that jar containing Chantal's TRD."

"Back to Athens? Now? Are you crazy?" Mondrago shook his head. "It's just lucky you got back here no later than you did."

"What are you talking about?"

"Haven't you noticed all the commotion around here?" Jason hadn't, in his emotional uproar. "Well," Mondrago continued, "it seems that after sunset some unusual noises were heard from the direction of the Persian camp. Then, just before you got here, there were some comings and goings in and out of the Grove of Heracles over there to our right."

"Miltiades' Ionian spies!"

"Good guess. Anyway, there hasn't been any official announcement but the word has spread: the Persians are beginning their embarkation, starting with the cavalry. And we're going out there to attack them at dawn."

Jason hadn't looked at his calendar display in a while—

he'd had other things on his mind. Now he did. It was August 11.

The Battle of Marathon would take place on August 12, as Rutherford had assumed on the basis of an increasing consensus among historians starting in the early twenty-first century. Kyle would doubtless be interested. Jason, at the moment, didn't give a damn.

CHAPTER EIGHTEEN

NO ONE GOT MUCH SLEEP THAT NIGHT, under the light of the full moon that meant the Spartans were starting to march. The slaves were kept busy burnishing the shields and armor, the generals went over the plan repeatedly as they moved among their tribes with whatever pre-battle encouragement they could give . . . and everyone could hear the distant tramping of tens of thousands of feet as the Persians moved forward onto the plain, and the more distant sounds of the embarking cavalry.

The Greeks were not great breakfast eaters—a crust of bread dipped in honey or wine, at most—but before the afternoon battles that were customary in their interminable internecine wars they were wont to take a midmorning "combat brunch" including enough wine to dull fear. Not this time. This army mustered before dawn, sorting itself out into the tribal groupings. There was surprisingly little confusion, given that the light was limited now that the full moon had passed.

"At least we won't have to fight in the heat," old Callicles philosophized grumpily.

Jason, standing beside the elderly hoplite with the rest of the Leontis tribe, saw Aeschylus and his brother Cynegeirus, hurrying to the right flank to join the Aiantis. The playwright waved to Callicles—he must, Jason thought, have a good memory for faces. Then, with the help of slaves and each other, they began the task of donning the panoply that was never put on any earlier than necessary before battle, such was its miserable discomfort.

The greaves were the least bad: rather elegant bronze sheaths that protected the legs from kneecap to ankle, so thin as to be flexible and so well shaped that they needed no straps—they were simply "snapped on," with the edges nearly meeting behind the calves. But despite their felt inner linings they were apt to chafe with the movement of the legs and lose their snug fit. They were put on first, while the hoplite could still stoop over.

Next, over his chiton, came that which prevented him from stooping: a bronze corselet of front and back segments, laced at the sides and connected over the shoulders by curved plates. Jason had been given a choice from Themeistocles' stock and had found one that seemed to fit him reasonably well—an absolute necessity. But the weight and inflexibility of the thing, and its efficiency as a heat-collector in the August sun, made him understand why later generations of hoplites in the Peloponnesian Wars would abandon it in favor of a cuirass made from layers of linen. Feeling his chiton already begin to grow sweat-soaked even before sunrise, he decided he didn't need to worry about the Persians; heat prostration would get him first. The skirt of leather strips hanging from the lower edge was the only protection the groin had.

Even more uncomfortable was the bronze "Corinthian" helmet, covering the neck and with cheek pieces and nose guard, practically encasing the entire head and face. It had no interior webbing or other suspension, only a soft leather lining; its five-pound weight rested on the neck and head. Jason now understood why hoplites grew their hair as long and thick as possible, despite the problem of lice, and he wondered what it must be like for older, balding men. With no real cushion between helmet and cranium, blows to the head—such as those dealt by the axes favored by the Persians' Saka troops—were often fatal. And, of course, the heat and stuffiness inside such a bronze pot were stifling. Given all this, it was easy to understand why Classical Greek art usually showed the helmet propped back on the head; it was worn this way until the last possible moment before battle, at which time it was finally lowered over the face. At this point, the hoplite became semi-deaf (there were no ear-holes) and able to see only directly ahead. But, Jason reflected, in a phalanx that was really the only direction you needed to see. And it occurred to him that this was one more bit of cement for a phalanx's unique degree of unit cohesion. A hoplite need not worry about his blind zones as long as the formation held; but alone, he was locked into a world of terrifying isolation.

At least, Jason consoled himself, his helmet was not one of those with a horsehair crest, intended to make the wearer look taller and more fearsome but adding to the helmet's weight and awkwardness. He had made sure to draw one of the plain, crestless versions, whose smooth curved surface would have a better chance of deflecting a Saka axe.

Then the slave handed Jason his most important piece of defensive equipment: the shield, or *hoplon*, that gave the hoplite his name. It was circular, three feet in diameter, made of hardwood covered with a thin sheet of bronze that didn't add much to its protective strength but which, when highly polished as it was now, could dazzle the enemy. Its handgrip (*antilabe*) and arm grip (*porpax*) distributed its weight along the entire left forearm, making it usable. But there was no getting around the fact that the thing weighed sixteen pounds, and was damned awkward. Fortunately, its radical concavity made it possible to rest most of its weight on the left shoulder. Of course, carried that way, the *hoplon* couldn't possibly protect the right side of the man carrying it. For that, he was utterly dependent on the man to his right in the formation keeping *his* sixteen-pound shield up. Again, solidarity was survival.

Finally, Jason was handed his primary offensive weapon, far more important than the short leaf-shaped sword at his side: a seven-and-a-half-foot thrusting spear, carried shouldered while the phalanx was advancing, then held underhand for the final change, but afterwards generally gripped overhand for stabbing. It was made of ash with an iron spearhead and, at the other end, a bronze butt spike. The latter was useful because the spear, only an inch thick, often shattered against hardwood shields and bronze armor in the thunderous clash of two phalanxes; a man deprived of his spearhead could reverse what was left of the spear and stab with the spike. Also, the ranks behind, still carrying their spears upright, could jab downward into any enemy wounded lying at their feet as the phalanx advanced.

Speaking of feet, there was one thing Jason could not understand, and never would. The human foot, as he knew from painful experience on his last extratemporal expedition, was a vulnerable thing composed of numerous small and easily-broken bones. Hoplites went into brutal, stamping, stomping battles with nothing on their feet but sandals. Why men already wearing and carrying fifty to seventy pounds of bronze, wood, iron, and leather didn't go one step further and avail themselves of the fairly sturdy boots their society was quite capable of producing was a mystery he was never to solve. He had, with careful casualness, put the question to Callicles, and had gotten a blank look for his pains. Evidently, it was just the way things were done—which, as Jason already knew, was more often than not the answer to questions about the seemingly irrational practices of preindustrial societies.

Finally the outfitting was done. Jason looked at Callicles and knew that what he saw mirrored how he himself looked. *Dressed to kill*, he thought.

Themistocles moved among the Leontis, telling dirty jokes, calling men by name and asking how their children were, recalling various men's former heroisms, and generally being Themistocles. The fact that he was here told Jason that the customary sacrifices had been offered to the gods by the generals, and that the omens had proven favorable. Now the order was given, and in the first glimmerings of dawn the hoplites moved through gaps in the defensive earthworks and took up their positions in accordance with the plan on which everyone had been repeatedly briefed over the past few days. There was little talk, and most of that was in whispers, as older men offered advice and encouragement to newbies.

Themistoicles positioned himself in the front line, of course, as Aristides was doing in the Antiochis front rank to their immediate right. There, they and the other tribes' *strategoi* would fight as ordinary hoplites, which was precisely what they would revert to being after their tenures in office expired. Very few Classical Greek generals who held repeated commands died in bed; when phalanxes clashed, the commander of the defeated side was almost invariably killed, as were not a few victorious commanders. The idea of a general standing safely on a hill in the rear and issuing commands was utterly foreign to these men. The concept of "leading from the front" went without saying, and it was one more layer of psychic cement for the phalanx. Jason knew that Callimachus was taking up a similar position on the right flank, the traditional place for the war archon, among his own Aiantis tribe. The Plataeans were on the left. Only Miltiades, in his capacity of "chief of staff," was somewhere around the center, overseeing the big picture.

According to Herodotus, Jason told himself, *a hundred and ninety-two Athenians and eleven Plataeans get killed today, out of a total of ten thousand. Pretty good odds against being one of those two hundred and three.*

The sun cleared the hills of Euboea, visible in the distance across the water to the east, and for the first time the panorama on the plain was visible, with the dense masses of the enemy, and, beyond that, their camp, which must be mostly broken down by now. Along the curving beach, it could be seen that the Persians had gotten most of their ships into the water during the night, but the activity swirling around them suggested that the loading of the horses—obviously in progress, since very few cavalry were visible in the Persian formation—was still incomplete.

Jason stared at the Persian line, just under a mile away. Then he looked left and right at their own formation. *Let's see*, ran his automatic thought processes, *ten thousand hoplites, of whom two thousand in the center are arrayed four ranks deep and the rest eight ranks deep. . . . That makes a front line of fifteen hundred. Assuming each man has a total of three feet of space, that's a front forty-five hundred feet long, plus a little more to allow for spaces between the tribes. It looks like the Persian front is very little longer than that, and, our right is sheltered by the Grove of Heracles. But their formation is a hell of a lot deeper, with maybe thirty thousand men packed into it.*

He became aware that all the muttering and whispering in the ranks had ceased. Everyone was staring fixedly at the outlandishly costumed horde a mile across the plain, and especially at the center, directly ahead of them—the core, or *spada*, of the enemy array, ethnic Iranians all, and veteran soldiers. This was the army that had, in a mere two generations, conquered all the known world to the east, and beyond into the fabulous reaches of India. The army that had crushed the Lydians, the Babylonians, the Elamites, the Egyptians, and all the rest of the seemingly eternal ancient civilizations and ground their rubble into a new universal empire. The army that no Greeks had ever defeated in pitched battle.

It was, Jason thought, understandable that he could feel

a kind of collective shudder run through the tight formation. He also caught a whiff of an unmistakable aroma. From his expression, Callicles also recognized it.

"Always some who do it about now," he chuckled. "I've never done *that*, but I've occasionally been known to let the water run down my legs." The old hoplite's voice held no embarrassment, and no condemnation of the men who were voiding themselves. Fear was nothing to be ashamed of. The only shame was in failing to hold the all-important line. A hoplite could feel as much natural fear as he wanted, as long as he overcame it enough to keep formation.

Themistocles took a few steps forward and turned to face his men. He didn't shout, or even seem to speak loudly, but his voice carried. He pointed with his spear at the Persian multitude.

"Men of Leontis! These barbarians stand on Attic soil, where they do not belong—the soil from which *you* are sprung." A murmur of agreement ran through the ranks, for as Jason knew, this was no mere figure of speech to these men, with their literal belief that they were the autochthonous race of this land, unconquered for all time. "They are here to carry out their Great King's command: after killing you they are to castrate your sons and scatter your daughters in slavery all across his vast mongrel empire, as they have scattered so many conquered peoples. Thus your bloodlines are to be extirpated and Athens itself forgotten."

A paralyzing silence held the phalanx. But Themistocles knew what he was doing. He allowed the silence to hold for only a couple of heartbeats before resuming.

"Yes, this is the most terrible fear that any Greek can

imagine. But by being here, you have chosen to come face to face with that fear, and defy it, and thereby conquer it. You have chosen to prevent the obliteration of your families and your *polis*. You can make these choices because you are free men, not slaves. That freedom to choose gives you a power that the Persians will never know, for there are no free men among them, only slaves and slavemasters. It is a power that is new in the world—a power that you are going to unleash here, today, on this plain. And after you do, the world will never be the same again."

Themistocles fell abruptly silent and resumed his place in the line. There was no cheering or boisterousness, just a grim, steady determination which settled over the formation like a cloak.

Orders were passed. The Corinthian helmets were lowered into position, and the hoplites ceased to be individuals and became faceless automata. *Rutherford will bitch about the limited input my recorder implant has to work with,* Jason thought, looking through his tiny eye-slits. *To hell with him.* With a shuffling of feet and a clanging together of shield rims, the phalanx locked itself into rigidity.

In unison, ten thousand voices began to sing the holy paean.

Greek music—all ancient music, really—had rhythm and melodies, but no harmonies. That was true even of the instrumental music, and still more so of the singing. This was more of a chant. It sounded eerie inside Jason's helmet. He followed along as best he could, not that anyone could make out any individual voice.

Trumpets sounded, reverberating inside the bronze helmets. In accordance with the plan they all knew, the phalanx advanced, at a walk at first. Then, after just a few steps, double time. The air began to fill with dust as all those thousands of feet pounded the dry ground of summer, and the bronze-against-bronze clatter of jostling armor rose to a clanging roar.

Jason, peering through his helmet's eye-holes, became aware of something. Unable to see more than a small range of vision, barely able to hear at all, he was dependent on the *feel* of the shoulder-to-shoulder phalanx around him: the pressure and the pushing and the shoving. It became clear why every man drew courage from all the others, and why all were caught up in an irresistible compulsion to advance, ever forward.

He was also beginning to understand why men in their forties, fifties, and occasionally even sixties were to be found in the phalanx alongside those in their twenties. They weren't expected to hold up under the kind of endless campaigning endured in the trenches of World War I or the jungles of Southeast Asia or the high desert of Iota Persei II. Hoplite warfare wasn't like that. The whole point was to avoid ruinous protracted war between city-states by deciding matters in one brutal afternoon. The toil and the fighting and the bloodshed were concentrated and distilled into a single decisive clash of appalling violence but short duration. Callicles and his ilk could handle that. It also explained why men were able and willing to endure the awkwardness and discomfort of the hoplite panoply: they didn't have to do so for long.

They were getting closer, and up ahead Jason saw that

the Persians were starting, rather belatedly, to firm up their formation. At first they must have been unable to believe what they were seeing: the Greeks, with no archers, were actually coming out onto the plain and attacking three times their number. And then the rapid Greek advance had left them with less time than they had thought they had. But there was no panic. These were veterans. Now the spear-bearing infantry were forming up in front and grounding their wicker shields to form a palisade, while thousands and thousands of archers massed behind them, ready to release a sky-darkening sleet of arrows that would decimate the crazy Greeks, after which the infantry (and the few horsemen in the formation) would advance and slaughter the disorganized remnant. Such were the standard Persian tactics, and no army in the known world had ever stood before them.

Then the trumpets gave another signal. At what Jason estimated was a distance of six hundred yards from the Persian front, the double-time became a fast trot.

Herodotus had said the Athenian hoplites had run the entire distance of almost a mile, a unique event. Historians had hooted at that, flatly denying that men so equipped could have done it and been fit to fight afterwards. But, in the surge of adrenaline now singing through their veins, Jason didn't doubt that for the rest of their lives these men would remember what they were doing as a run. And those skeptical historians had overlooked one thing: hoplites trained, in the task-specific way of all successful exercise programs, to run in armor. In fact, one Olympic event was a foot-race whose contestants wore armor and carried shields. No, these men couldn't sprint a mile. But they could cover ground at a pace that few athletes of any other era, however well-conditioned, could have matched carrying the particular burden they carried. Jason only hoped he'd be able to keep up.

At the same time they began to trot, they began to scream their war-cry: a terrifying *alleeee!* calculated to fray the nerves of any who heard it. The ululation rose even above the clattering of shields. Jason recalled what a colleague who had observed the American Civil War had once told him about the "Rebel yell." Between that and the cacophony of moving armor, the noise reverberating inside Jason's bronze helmet was deafening.

The air was filling with the dust kicked up by ten thousand pairs of trotting feet, the August sun was getting hotter, and breath was coming in painful gasps. No one cared. They were all half-crazed now, and their trot covered the ground much faster than Persian tactical calculations allowed for. Blinking the sweat out of his eyes, Jason thought he could see frantic movement in the Persian formation up ahead.

Then, at a distance of two hundred yards, the war-cry rose to a collective nerve-shattering scream . . . and the trot became a run.

It was more than a run. It became, in the insanity of the moment, almost a race, as the phalanx thundered down on the now visibly rattled Persians.

Now the Persian archers let fly, and thousands upon thousands of arrows arched overhead with a *whoosh* like a rushing of wind and plunged downward. But most of them missed entirely, for the speed of the running attack had thrown the archers' timing off. And of those that hit, most were ineffective. Jason heard and felt them clattering off his shield and helmet. The advance did not slow, and the formation did not waver. If anything, it picked up speed. Exhaustion didn't matter anymore; adrenaline was irrelevant. These ten thousand screaming madmen were carried forward on a tide of sheer impatience to start killing these barbarians who had come to destroy their world and everything that gave their lives meaning.

Now, with a collective crash, the spears of the first two ranks were brought down into an overhand position and leveled.

The Persian archers scrambled to reload. But there was no longer any time for that.

Even through his helmet, Jason could hear new screams. They came from up ahead, and they were screams of panic, for the Persians now knew that these bronze killing machines in human form were not going to stop. Jason could see that horrified realization in the faces of the infantry just ahead. They were instinctively flinching backward, their shield-palisade dissolving.

Now, then, let's see, thought Jason in the calm, detached corner of his mind that was still running calculations even in these final seconds. *Ten thousand men, weighing an average of maybe a hundred and fifty pounds and carrying an average of maybe sixty pounds of weapons and armor. That comes to. . . .*

Over a thousand tons of bronze and hardwood and bone and muscle, bristling with iron spearpoints and moving at the velocity of a sprint, smashed into the Persian army.

CHAPTER NINETEEN

JASON HAD WITNESSED the Fourth Crusade's sack of Constantinople. He had seen the ghastly bloodbaths of the Thirty Years' War. He was no stranger to the brutal madness of battle waged with weapons driven by human muscle at face-to-face range amid the stench of sweat and blood and shit. But none of that had really prepared him for the crashing impact of a running phalanx.

In all the other low-tech clashes he had experienced, there had always been a last second instinctive flinching, an avoidance of an actual full-tilt collision. But hoplites were trained to smash straight in, rocking the opposing phalanx back and hopefully opening up tears in its shield-line, after which the battle would cease to be a battle and become a slaughter. The result of such a collision was one for which Jason doubted his generalized expertise in low-technology combat would have prepared him: a thunderclap of din and violence as the two phalanxes came together, the pressure of the rear ranks forcing the front rank ever forward into a nightmarish thunderclap of shields bashed against shields, of thousands of splintering spears.

But not this time. The front rank of the Persian army was simply pulverized as the thrusting spears went through wicker shields and quilted cloth and occasional armor of loosely hanging metal scales to punch into bodies. The phalanx ground on, trampling the shield palisade and seeking out the even less well-protected archers.

Jason drove his spear into the midriff of a Persian, looking into the man's terrified eyes and smelling his shit as the spearhead ripped through flesh, muscle, and guts before coming up against the spine. Yanking the spear out of the squalling Persian, he came to a realization that was simultaneously dawning on the Greeks all up and down the line: *their spears weren't breaking.* This time they weren't up against another phalanx. There were no hardwood shields and bronze breastplates for the spears to break against. A rectangular Persian wicker shield, made by threading sticks through a wet framework of leather, might as well not have been there when a hoplite thrust his iron-headed ash spear through it. So the spear could be used again . . . and again . . . and again.

The front ranks pushed on. Now the unbroken spears were being used overhand, for stabbing. Jason felt his sandaled feet almost slip in blood and entrails, and heard a scream as he stepped on a wounded Persian. He reversed the spear and slammed the butt-spike down into the terrified face, through the eye-socket into the brain, and jerked it out jellied and bloodied. He couldn't let himself think about it. But the next time he stepped on a screaming man he moved on, and heard the scream abruptly cease behind him. One of the men in the rear ranks must have brought his spear's butt-spike down.

In the midst of the crushing press of armored men, forging ahead through a welter of gore and a din of endless screams, Jason could see nothing of what was happening elsewhere on the field. He could only advance, thrusting again and again, through the abattoir that was the battlefield of Marathon. But he knew that the Greek flanks, eight ranks deep and facing second-rate troops, were advancing more rapidly than they were here in the center, where a formation only four deep faced a massive concentration of Persians and Saka. Soon the enemy flanks would give way entirely and flee in howling panic, seeking the safety of their ships. The Greek flanks would follow . . . but only for a hundred yards or so.

This, Jason knew, would be the crucial moment. And it would disprove what a small but persistent school of revisionists had been claiming ever since around the turn of the twenty-first century: that the Athenians had fought Marathon as a disorganized mob. None of those revisionist historians, Mondrago had remarked archly, had ever commanded infantry in combat. If they had, they might have spared themselves the embarrassment of making such a silly assertion, for they would have known that no disorganized mob could possibly do what the Greek flanks were about to do. First of all, they would halt their pursuit of a routed enemy on a trumpet-signal, leaving the light troops, or *thetes*, to harry the Persians along. And then they would pivot their formations ninety degrees, facing inward toward the center from left and right.

Even as Jason was thinking about it, he realized that their own advance in the center had halted, as the massive Persian numbers began to tell. He even had a split second to wonder at the courage of the Persian and Saka elite troops they faced here, for they were pushing back against the terrifying, spear-jabbing front line of the phalanx, forcing it back by the sheer weight of their mass of human flesh. The tide began to turn against the Athenian center.

Time lost its meaning. The sun was rising in the sky, and in the midst of heat and exhaustion and thirst the men of the Leontis and Antiochis tribes fought on, giving ground stubbornly, their thin line bending back but not breaking. From behind, their tribes' *thetes*, including Mondrago, kept up a supporting rain of javelins and sling-stones. They could do so over the heads of the hoplites because the withdrawal was now slightly uphill.

Jason's spear had finally broken, and the stump of it had been knocked out of his hand before he could reverse it and use the butt-spike. He frantically drew his short sword as the crush of enemy troops, sensing victory, pressed the Greek center further back. Now the Athenians were backing up into the wooded terrain in front of and to the right of their camp. That terrain had been their friend over the past days, screening their right flank from the Persian cavalry; now it turned traitor, causing the phalanx to begin to lose its cohesion. Now it was individual fighting, more a brawl than a battle, and the awkward *hoplon*, intended as an interlocking component of the phalanx rather than an individual defense, was almost more hindrance than help.

Jason saw a huge Saka—instantly recognizable as such by the distinctive pointed hat they wore—break free of the press and turn toward him, swinging his battle-axe in a powerful downward cut. Jason managed to raise his heavy shield in time to block it, but the hard-driven axe, striking off-center, knocked the *hoplon* aside. With a roar, the Saka recovered and brought his axe around for a second blow before Jason could get the sixteen-pound shield back in line. Jason raised his sword to parry the cut, deflecting the axe's arc, but it struck his helmet a glancing blow that caused stars to explode in his eyes. He instinctively whipped the sword around and drove it into the Saka's midriff, a vicious twisting thrust that brought a rope of entrails out with it when he withdrew the blade.

As the Saka sank, groaning, to the ground, Jason looked around him, cursing the helmet's limited field of vision. To his left, he saw Callicles, using the butt-spiked stump of his broken spear to fend off an *akenake*-wielding Persian. But exhaustion was finally beginning to tell, and the old hoplite was slowing. With a visible effort, he raised his shield to counter what turned out to be a feint. The Persian rushed in under it and brought his short sword upward, driving into Callicles' groin. Callicles shrieked. The Persian heaved the *akenake* out and stabbed again.

Jason lunged, swinging his *hoplon* around like a weapon. Its edge caught the Persian on the back of the neck, smashing his face into Callicles' shield, crushing his nose and breaking his teeth. Before the Persian could recover from the stunning impact and pain, Jason raised his sword and chopped down where neck met shoulder. Blood sprayed. The Persian and Callicles collapsed together, their blood mingling. It was all the same color.

At that moment, Jason became aware of a sea-change

in the battle. He must, he thought, not have heard the second trumpet call. For now the Persian center, so exultant mere minutes ago, was dissolving in consternation. A deafening cacophony of shouts and clashing weapons and armor to left and right told Jason why. The victorious Greek flanks, having wheeled inward in a way impossible for any but veteran troops well-briefed on a prearranged plan, were crunching into the Persian center, which was now boxed in on three sides. The Leontis and Antiochis men of the Greek center were now advancing again as the screaming Persians and Saka fled for their lives in the only direction left open to them, having had their fill of the horror, the sheer awfulness, of hoplite warfare. But as always in warfare at this technological level, running for one's life was precisely the wrong thing to do, for fleeing men could not protect themselves. The Athenians of the center went in pursuit, cutting them down in the ever-shrinking killing ground as the flanks pressed in from the sides. Jason was left behind.

He sank to his knees, feeling in his left temple the pressure from a dent the Saka's axe stroke had made in his helmet. He laid down his sword and shield, pulled the helmet off, threw it away, and took great gulping breaths now that he was free of its stifling confines. He also looked around, relishing the full field of vision. The slope was littered with the dead and dying, a wrack left behind as the roaring tide of battle receded. Otherwise, he was alone.

Now's my chance to get away, go up this hill to the aircar, get back to Athens and retrieve Chantal's TRD from Themistocles' house—assuming that Franco and his merry men haven't already beaten us to it, he told himself. *First,*

I have to find Alexandre. He forced his brain, still numb from what he had just experienced, to start forming the mental command that would bring up a map of the locality complete with TRD locations. . . .

At that moment, he saw out of the corner of his eye that he wasn't alone after all. A hoplite, still fully armed and equipped, was coming toward him at a trot, his face hidden by one of the crested Corinthian helmets.

Who is that? he wondered, looking at the inhuman facelessness of the Corinthian helmet. *And what's he in such a hurry for?*

"Rejoice!" he called out, one fifth-century B.C. Greek to another.

Instead of replying, the hoplite brought his spear up overhand and stabbed with it. For some infinitesimal fraction of a second, Jason clearly saw the spearpoint coming toward his unprotected face.

Jason's paralysis broke. He scooped up his shield and, with no time to get his arm through the *porpax* arm-grip, he awkwardly grabbed the shield by the hand-grip and the left edge and shoved it up and out as he surged to his feet.

The iron point, driven by all the strength of his onrushing assailant, punched through the shield's thin bronze covering and the hardwood beneath, protruding from the inner surface inches from Jason's arm. Jason twisted the shield sharply to the side, and the spear-shaft broke. Before the attacker could reverse it and use the butt-spike, Jason shoved the shield forward against him, pushing with his entire weight, bowling the man over. Taking advantage of the momentary respite, he scrambled backwards and retrieved the sword he had laid on the ground. At the same time, he frantically tried, using his left arm alone, to grip his shield properly. Clumsy and burdensome as the sixteen-pound *hoplon* was, it was all he had.

But the man had gotten to his feet with remarkable speed for one wearing hoplite armor, and was carrying his shield very easily—he must, Jason thought, be very strong, to be able to use the *hoplon* for personal defense. He swung the remainder of his spear-shaft almost like a mace and struck the rim of Jason's shield just as Jason was still trying to correct his grip, sending it flying. The spear-shaft also went flying, and the attacker whipped out his sword and rushed in. Jason knew himself for a dead man, for he stood no chance in a sword fight, shieldless and helmetless.

Only . . . at least I can see, *without that damned helmet!*

It was the only card he had to play. He lunged forward, evading the sword-slash and moving into the attacker's right-hand blind zone.

Even with these short blades, it was too close for swordplay. But taking advantage of his instant of invisibility, Jason got his right arm under the attacker's from behind and, holding both their sword-arms locked into temporary uselessness, used his free left hand to grab the man's helmet by its crest and wrench it off.

At appreciably the same instant, the attacker brought his clumsy shield sharply back, smashing its rim into Jason's left rib cage. The breastplate prevented it from breaking any ribs, but the impact caused Jason to lose his grip and the man flung him away. He landed supine, and a sandaled foot came painfully down on his right wrist, pinning his sword-arm to the ground.

Jason had time to look up into his assailant's face. It was one of the unpleasantly similar faces of Franco's gene-enhanced underlings. Jason recognized him as Landry's killer. The man raised his sword. . . .

There was an odd and unpleasant sound, which seemed compounded of those usually characterized as *whack* and *crunch*. The Transhumanist's face went abruptly expressionless, and blood began to seep from a small round hole in the exact center of his forehead. His raised sword fell to the ground, and he followed it there with a clang of armor as his legs crumpled.

Jason looked behind him. Mondrago held the sling that had sent its little lead pellet into the Transhumanist's brain.

"You really *do* know how to use that thing," Jason remarked, inadequately.

"You helped by getting his helmet off," Mondrago grinned, helping Jason to his feet. He glanced at the body. "So I suppose his job was to provide us with an 'in-period death.'"

For a moment they stood and looked to the northeast over the plain of Marathon, where the battle was roaring along toward the Persian ships. Jason knew what was happening up there. Datis, the Persian commander, had managed to get enough of a new line formed to hold the Greek light troops. But when the re-formed phalanx— moving slowly this time, for there were limits to the endurance even of hoplites—arrived, a final, desperate battle would rage. The Persians would hold the narrow beach long enough for all but seven of their ships to get away. But many of them would be driven into the great marsh behind their camp, and the sixty-four hundred

Persian dead that would be counted after the battle didn't even count the ones drowned there.

Still, the surviving Persians, including the dread cavalry that had embarked before the battle, would be at sea, and the way around Cape Sunium, to Phalerum and undefended Athens, lay open to them. And at the same moment that horrifying realization dawned on the Greeks, they would see a signal, like the sun reflected from a polished shield, flash atop Mount Pentelikon—surely the work of the traitors whom everyone feared lurked amid Athens' labyrinthine political factions.

So the weary victors would send a runner to assure the city that the victory had been won. And then they would set out for Athens, leaving the Antiochis tribe to guard the captured loot of the Persian camp. (Apparently only Aristides "the Just" was trusted with that particular assignment, and Jason had to admit that he himself wouldn't necessarily have trusted Themistocles with it.) These men who had just fought a battle would march, in full armor, the twenty-six miles back to Athens, starting at ten in the morning and arriving at Phalerum by late afternoon, barely in time. And the Persian fleet would sail away.

And as a result of all the sickening butchery on this plain Western civilization would live, to one day give humankind—for the first time—an economic system that allowed for at least the possibility of prosperity, a legal system that allowed for at least the possibility of justice, and a governmental system that allowed for at least the possibility of individual liberty . . . including the liberty of free scientific inquiry that would lead to the stars.

Rutherford wanted us to find out if there's any truth to the tradition that the runner is none other than Pheidippides, and that he drops dead after delivering his message, Jason recalled, *or if historians have been right to ridicule it . . . just as they've ridiculed the idea of the hoplites running to the attack. He also wanted us to find out the truth about the "shield signal" from Mount Pentelikon, because the mystery of that was never solved.*

Too bad, Kyle. We don't exactly have time for any of that at the moment.

"Come on," he told Mondrago as he discarded his breastplate and greaves and tried to discard his exhaustion with them. "Let's go. The aircar is concealed about halfway up here on Mount Agriliki. We'll take it to Athens and—maybe—make it to Themistocles' house and get that jar containing Chantal's TRD before Franco does."

They ascended the wooded slope behind the Greek camp, the sounds of shouts and screams and clashing weapons diminishing as the battle moved on. Jason concentrated on retracing his steps to the clearing. As a result, he almost missed the flicker of motion among the shadow-dappled underbrush.

"What?" Mondrago exclaimed, and bounded toward the barely-glimpsed movement. A figure broke cover and skittered frantically away.

It was Pan.

CHAPTER TWENTY

MONDRAGO SCRAMBLED UPHILL and plunged forward, catching the fleeing Pan around the legs. A backward kick of cloven hooves caused him to lose his grip and yelp with pain.

But the split second that kick took enabled Jason to catch up. Avoiding the goatish legs, he landed atop Pan's thrashing back, wrapping his left arm around the throat and gripping one of the horns with his right hand. The hybrid being was immobilized, and the force of his struggles confirmed an impression Jason had gotten when grappling with Pan before: that his muscularity was deceptive, or perhaps the word was "decorative." He didn't seem very strong, and there was an odd but unmistakable feeling of artificial fragility about him.

Mondrago got to his feet and drew the dagger that was part of standard *thetes* equipment. "I'll kill the miserable little—!"

"As you were! I want information, not a corpse." Mondrago subsided, and Jason addressed Pan, with a jerk on the horn for emphasis but a slight relaxation of the throat-hold. "Talk! What are you doing here? And how did you get up here anyway?"

"I came in a Teloi aircar," rasped Pan in his squeaky voice, through a still-constricted throat. "The Transhumanists have to use them, since you stole the only one they brought with them."

"Doesn't that limit their mobility, having to use aircars with no invisibility fields?"

"Yes. Franco's fury is terrible. But they have no choice. I came with one of his men, who was sent to kill the two of you. We were dropped off here on Mount Agriliki because of its location; the killer could slip down unnoticed behind the Greek center as it was being forced back. He ordered me to wait here."

And of course you had to obey, thought Jason. The Transhumanists had no need to worry that their "god" would run away and cut himself off from the drugs that made his existence endurable.

"Afterwards," Pan continued, "I am to be picked up and taken to Mount Kotroni." He pointed northward, to the left of the plain. "Franco has a machine set up there, which he is very shortly going to use to induce uncontrollable fear in the Persians when they form their second line, protecting the departing ships."

Jason called up his map-display; it made sense.

"That will have to be very soon," he said, listening to the distant battle-sounds.

"Yes. They'll be here for me any minute now. I am to

show myself on the slope, so the Greeks can see me. The Persians' panic—" (Pan did not smile) "—will be attributed to me."

Well, well, thought Jason, *so that was what their aircar was doing on Mount Kotroni when I took it. They were scouting out a good location.*

"Afterwards," Pan went on, "we are to return to Athens in the Teloi aircar. Even traveling cautiously to avoid being observed, we will arrive there in not many minutes—long before any runner that can be sent from here. I will appear to my worshippers in the cave under the Acropolis and tell them of the victory before anyone else in Athens knows. The Teloi will signal from Mount Pentelikon the instant the battle is over."

"Aha!" Mondrago burst out. "So that's the famous 'shield signal' that everybody has always wondered about."

"Right," Jason nodded. "The Greeks will think it's traitors signaling to the Persian fleet, even though the meaning and purpose of such a signal will be hard to understand, and afterwards no treason will ever be proved. But now we know what it's really for: to let Franco & Co. know exactly when they can proceed with the ceremony. It'll make it even more of a belief-strengthening miracle for the true believers when their god appears to them and tells them about the battle just as it's ending. A very precisely choreographed operation all around."

"And one which we're now in a position to abort!" said Mondrago wolfishly. "You've gotten your information out of him. Now let me kill him."

Pan stiffened with fear.

"No!" said Jason, without really knowing why.

"Why not? Franco will have egg on his face when the 'god' doesn't show up as promised."

Which, Jason was forced to admit to himself, made sense. Only. . . .

All at once, it came to him. He wondered why he hadn't thought of it before. But of course he *had* thought of it before, when he had last spoken to Pan on the Tegea heights above the road from Sparta.

"Listen, Pan," he said hurriedly. "We've got to go. I just need to know one thing: do you know how to pilot the Teloi aircars that the Transhumanists are using?"

"Why, yes." Pan seemed puzzled, as did Mondrago. "They taught me how, in case I should ever need to do it when alone." He didn't need to add that he could always be relied on to go to the destination he was ordered. In light of that utter reliability, it made perfect sense that the Transhumanists would have availed themselves of the flexibility of training him to pilot himself. But Jason had had to be sure.

"Good. Now, if I let you live, I know you've got to stay and do as Franco tells you . . . and I know why. But I'm going to do it anyway."

Mondrago began to splutter, inarticulate with outrage. Jason shushed him.

"I'm going to leave you here. But I'm going to stop the Transhumanists from using you as they intend to, over there on Mount Kotroni. And afterwards I'm going to take you to Athens."

"How will you accomplish all this?" Pan asked in a tone of dead incredulity, too hopeless even to sneer.

"Good question," muttered Mondrago.

"Never mind that for now. Just remember what I told you before about getting help for you, and freeing you from your dependence on the Transhumanists and the Teloi? Well, I swear to you that I'll do exactly that, in exchange for your cooperation."

"Cooperation in what?" The high-pitched voice was no longer entirely lifeless, for a flicker of eagerness had awakened in it.

"I'll want you to appear to the cult members and tell them that you're no god, and that the Transhumanists are some kind of evil supernatural beings—I'll leave the details to you—who've duped them. Do you agree to my terms?"

"If you do indeed take me to Athens, and protect me from Franco and the others, I'll do as you ask."

"Good." At that moment, the tiny blue light began to flash that told Jason a grav repulsion vehicle was approaching. In this era, when such vehicles weren't supposed to exist, it could mean only one thing. "The Teloi aircar is coming for you. We have to go. Remember what I said." He got to his feet and motioned the still visibly thunderstruck Mondrago to follow him. Mondrago looked at Pan, and then at his dagger, with obvious longing, but he obeyed.

The two men hastily ascended the short remaining distance, flung themselves into the Transhumanist aircar, and engaged the invisibility field. As they went aloft they saw, in the ghostly grayish world viewed through the field, an open-topped Teloi aircar flying low for concealment.

"Well," said Mondrago with a gust of released breath, "here they come to take Pan over to Mount Kotroni so he can put on his little performance—and there's not a damned thing we can do about it about it now. What, exactly, was the purpose of all those lies you told him?"

"I wasn't lying," said Jason distractedly as he set a course for Athens. "I meant every word."

"*What?* But how—?"

Jason turned to meet Mondrago's eyes, and all the distraction was gone. When he spoke, the bullwhip crack of command was in his voice. "At the present time, you have no need to know that. For now, you will simply follow orders. And any more borderline insubordination on your part will go into my report. *Is that clear?*"

Mondrago came to as close to a position of attention as the aircar's cramped passenger seat permitted. "Yes, sir!" he said with a new snap.

"Good." Jason allowed his expression to soften into a smile. "Oh, and by the way, thanks for saving my life. That also will be in my report."

With no need to conceal the movements of a vehicle that was, in the present milieu, supernatural, they were at Athens in minutes and were able to pick a landing spot with care.

While he was doing it, Jason spared a moment to consult his map display. The red dot that marked Chantal's TRD was still at Themistocles' house. He ordered his weary body not to go weak with relief. Now, no matter what happened to him and Mondrago, he would be able to scupper Franco's plan to use Chantal as a mole.

There was a small clear area just within the city wall near the "Hangman's Gate." Jason settled the aircar gently down and made sure no one was in sight. Leaving

Mondrago to keep the power on, Jason got out with the invisibility field still activated. To an observer, he would have seemed to step into existence from nowhere. Fortunately, there were no observers. He hastened through the narrow alleys, encountering no one, for all the women and old men and children who currently occupied Athens were either keeping to their homes or milling uneasily about the Agora, waiting for news.

Reaching Themistocles' house, Jason pounded on the door. The slave who opened it gasped at the sight of him—either from recognition or from sheer horror at the apparition, encrusted with dust and gore. This was no time for subtlety. While the slave was still goggling, Jason jabbed him in the solar plexus just hard enough to double him over, then wrapped an arm around his throat in a choke-hold that induced prompt unconsciousness. Then he rushed into the house, sending maidservants fleeing screaming as he went to the storeroom where he had left "Cleothera's" possessions. The jar was still where he had left it. He opened it to confirm the presence of the TRD, then ran from the house and retraced his steps to the open area and the carefully-memorized location of the aircar.

"Got it!" he told Mondrago as he took the aircar aloft. "We beat Franco to it."

"He probably thought he had plenty of time and no need to hurry," Mondrago opined. "Now he's going to be shitting rivets."

"Maybe." Jason frowned. "We've got to get out of Attica—and not just because the Transhumanists are going to be hunting for us. Themistocles is going to think we're deserters—and if the house slaves recognized me, he's going to think I'm a thief as well. I hate that."

"So do I. I like Themistocles. I'm glad he survives the battle."

"Not everyone does. Callimachus, for example, dies in the final battle on the beach, by the Persian ships, transfixed by so many spears he's propped up and can't fall to the ground."

"Shit." Mondrago shook his head at the thought of the gallant old war archon, to whom history would never accord as much credit for the victory as he deserved. "At least Miltiades lives, right?"

"Right—but he probably would have been better off getting killed." Seeing Mondrago's puzzled stare, Jason explained. "Later this year, the Athenians will give him command of their fleet, and he'll take it around the Aegean on an expedition against islands that collaborated with the Persians. At Paros, though, he'll be defeated and badly wounded in the leg. On his return to Athens, his political rivals, the Alcmaeonid family, will smell blood. They'll put him on trial and hit him with a fine of fifty talents—an impossibly large sum—as an alternative to execution. But by then he'll have gotten gangrene in his wound, and will die shortly after the trial."

"Shit!" Mondrago repeated, but in a very different tone. "So these people are going to do *that* to the man who, along with Callimachus, masterminded the victory of Marathon for them. And you told me how they're going to ostracize Themistocles after he does the same thing for them at Salamis when the Persians come back ten years from now. And I seem to recall something about making Socrates drink hemlock." He looked down at the receding maze of Athens. "Tell me again about how these are supposed to be the *good* guys!"

Jason was silent for a moment. When he spoke, it was to himself as much as to Mondrago. "Infants are awkward and messy—even the ones who end up growing into worthwhile adults. Democracy in Athens in this era is awkward and messy. But it had to survive this day. Otherwise, the world we come from could never have been." He fell silent again, then spoke briskly. "Anyway we're going to have to lay low for a month and six days, and as I said, we've made Attica too hot to hold us now, even if there weren't Transhumanists running around in it looking for us. We'll need to go somewhere else."

Mondrago held his peace about the promises Jason had made to Pan concerning the events of this very day, here in Attica. "Where?" was all he said.

Jason smiled. "Well, I remember a place I hid out once before."

He set a course for the island of Crete.

The shepherds and goatherds around Mount Ida now spoke the Doric dialect of Greek instead of a Hittite-Luwian language, and Jason noticed the occasional iron tool among them. Otherwise, they were exactly as he remembered their ancestors in 1628 B.C.

He had brought the aircar over Crete and across the Tallaion Mountains (as the Kouloukounas range was called in this era) and along the Mylopotamas Valley to the upland plain of Nidha, with the snow-capped mass of Ida looming up eight thousand feet above sea level. At least this time he hadn't had to struggle, lamed by a broken foot, over all that dramatic terrain. A slow circle of Mount Ida had revealed the well-remembered cave, under a looming shelf of rock, where he and Deirdre Sadaka-Ramirez had sheltered.

He had cut off the invisibility field as he had brought the aircar in for a landing on the nearest piece of level ground he could find, allowing any locals who happened to be around a glimpse of it. Rutherford, he knew, would have had heart failure. But among a profoundly illiterate population like this, any tales would die out after a couple of centuries at most, and never be believed by anyone in the greater world outside this totally ignored backwater of an island. And a little supernatural cachet wouldn't hurt.

And so it had proved. They had taken up residence in the cave, believed by some to have been the nursery of the infant Zeus. It, too, was much as he remembered, although this time it didn't lie under a sky polluted with the ashes of Santorini in the aftermath of the most cataclysmic volcanic explosion in history. After a while the locals had timidly sought them out. A series of hints, haltingly delivered through the barrier of dialect differences, had persuaded them to supply the uncanny pair of strangers with cheese and wine (by courtesy so called) and certain other items, while keeping their presence a secret lest the displeasure of certain baleful deities be called down on the whole region. Jason and Mondrago had certain skills—first aid, for example—that enabled them to repay the favors and in the process acquire even more prestige. And they were both experts in wilderness survival, who quickly improvised bows with which to hunt the wild goats. They passed late August and early September with no great difficulty.

As September 18 approached, Jason programmed a fairly complex navigational command into the autopilot of the Transhumanists' aircar. He sent it looping, pilotless, in a circle that brought it around to the opposite side of Mount Ida . . . and then, with all the acceleration it could pile on, directly into the mountainside. After his return, any investigators the Authority might find it worthwhile to send to that mountainside might find a few bits of wreckage that hadn't been there before.

Through it all, Mondrago remained stoically silent on the subject Jason had ruled off limits.

Finally the time came when they stood (it seemed undignified to arrive on the displacer stage sitting on one's butt) awaiting retrieval. Jason held the little jar stolen from Themistocles' house tightly in his hand. The digital countdown projected onto Jason's optic nerve wound down. It was nearing zero when Mondrago finally blurted, "Sir, I just don't get it!"

"What don't you get?"

"You know what I mean. If there's one thing I've learned about you, it's that you're a man of your word. And you told me that you meant what you said to Pan. But all the things you said you were going to prevent—the performances on Mount Kotroni and under the Acropolis—happened over a month ago, back in Attica. So you didn't keep your promise."

"Didn't I?" Jason grinned. "Aren't you forgetting something?"

"What, sir?"

"We're time travellers!"

Mondrago's bug-eyed stare of realization was the last thing Jason saw before the indescribable unreality of temporal transition took them.

CHAPTER TWENTY-ONE

AS ALWAYS, the glare of electric lighting in the great dome was blinding after instantaneous transition from a relatively dim setting—and practically all settings in past ages were relatively dim. It made the disorientation of temporal displacement even worse, affecting even an old hand like Jason. Between the blindness and the dizziness, it was a moment before he became aware of the hubbub among the people behind the ranks of control panels. They had been expecting four people to appear on the stage, not two.

Blinking the stroboscopic stars out of his eyes, Jason saw Mondrago shamefacedly getting to his feet. "Don't worry," he assured him. "Everybody loses his balance the first time." Looking around the floor of the stage, he spotted Landry's TRD, covered with the ashes of the crematory furnace. Then he saw Kyle Rutherford advancing toward the stage, his face a question mark.

"Dr. Landry was killed," said Jason, pointing at the tiny,

ashy sphere on the floor. He offered no further explanation. Rutherford restrained himself from demanding one.

"And Dr. Frey . . . ?"

"She remained in the target milieu. Her TRD is in here." Jason held out the ceramic vase.

Rutherford stared wide-eyed. Jason had a pretty good idea what he was thinking, after his own last extratemporal expedition. He recalled the words of a probably mythical twentieth century figure with the unlikely name of Yogi Berra: "*Déjà vu* all over again."

"Yes, it was cut out of her," he said, answering Rutherford's unspoken question.

Rutherford went pale. "The Teloi?"

"No . . . or at least not principally. There are a lot of things you need to know—things that can't be made public. Can we go somewhere for an informal preliminary debriefing?"

"Yes . . . yes, of course." Rutherford started to lead them away, then paused. "But from your choice of words, do I gather that Dr. Frey was alive when you last saw her?"

"Yes. I left her in the fifth century B.C. still alive. And . . ." Jason paused, and his face took on a look that caused Rutherford to flinch backwards. "And *this* time I'm going to get her back!"

Reducing Rutherford to a state of inarticulate shock had long been an ambition of Jason's. Now he had achieved it . . . and the circumstances made it impossible for him to enjoy it.

They sat in Rutherford's private office. It was more austerely furnished than the one in Athens that he preferred whenever he didn't need to be in Australia, but like that one it held a display case containing items brought back from the past. And here, also, the prize exhibit was a sword—in this case, a seemingly undistinguished medieval hand-and-a-half sword. A teenaged French peasant girl who believed the saints had told her to liberate her people and crown her Dauphin had found it buried behind the altar of the church of Saint Catherine of Fierbois in 1429 and carried it to the relief of Orleans. More to the point, the office contained the necessary equipment for playing the sights and sounds recorded on the tiny disc Jason had removed from his implant through an equally tiny slot in his skull, concealed by a flap of artificial skin. They had corroborated a story Rutherford clearly didn't want to believe.

Now Jason and Mondrago—uncharacteristically subdued, unaccustomed as he was to such surroundings—waited while Rutherford shook his head, slowly and repeatedly as though in a semi-daze. Jason wasn't sure which revelation had hit the old boy hardest: that a surviving Transhumanist underground still existed, or that they were operating an illicit temporal displacer on a higher technological level than the Authority's, or that they were taking high technology equipment into the past, or the objectives for which they were using their displacer. Now he sat amid the rubble of his well-ordered world.

"One thing in our favor," Jason concluded, trying to end on a positive note. "The Transhumanists are limited to sending their varieties that look more or less like normal humans—that's the only sort we saw—back in time. Their more extreme species variations would be pretty conspicuous in past eras, not to mention the cyborg warriors with grossly obvious bionic parts."

"But," said Mondrago, spoiling the effect Jason had intended, "there's no reason they can't have all of those on Earth in the present day, in the various concealed strongholds Franco bragged about." They all shuddered inwardly, as members of their culture always did at the thought of the grotesque and unnatural abominations the Transhuman movement had spawned, all of which were believed to have been extirpated a century before.

Rutherford gave his head a final shake, this time a decisive one. "This is terrible! It must be stopped! The potential consequences of what you have discovered are simply incalculable."

"Agreed," Jason nodded. "But the Authority can't handle it alone."

"I know." Rutherford's voice was desolate. The prospect of having to compromise the Authority's sacrosanct status as an independent agency was one more blow. "We shall have to involve the government's law enforcement agencies. Earth must be combed from pole to pole. This illegal displacer must be found!"

"Easier said than done," Jason cautioned. "Remember, they didn't steal the Authority's technology; they developed it themselves from Weintraub's original work, in a superior form. It won't be like searching for an installation the size of this one. *Their* displacer is compact enough to be hidden, and so energy-efficient that they could send a fairly numerous party equipped with an aircar twenty-nine hundred years back using a concealable power source."

This time a low moan escaped Rutherford. "And in the

meantime," he said in a dead voice, "we have no idea where to look for their various schemes of temporal subversion. You said the Transhumanists you encountered were from a time slightly earlier than the present—"

"Yes, Franco let that slip."

"—but we don't know how long they have been pursuing their nefarious program, nor how much further into our future they will be continuing to send expeditions back, nor where and when those expeditions will go. Our field of investigation is impossibly large. And we don't know where to begin!"

"Not altogether true. We know exactly what one of their schemes is: the Pan cult. And we know exactly how to scupper it." Before Rutherford could speak, Jason leaned forward and spoke with grim, tightly controlled urgency. "I propose that you send me and Alexandre and a couple of other combat-trained Service men back to the moment after I left Pan, the point of arrival to be Mount Kotroni, where they were about to take him."

"But . . . but . . . you and Mondrago were already there," stammered Rutherford, scandalized. "So you and your own earlier selves will be present simultaneously!" What Jason was proposing violated one of the most basic policies of the Authority.

"Once there," Jason continued, ignoring the interruption, "we'll stop them from using high-tech means to induce panic in the Persians while staging an appearance by Pan. Then, as per my agreement with Pan, we'll take him to Athens where he'll tell the cultists that they've been played for suckers. Of course," he added as an afterthought, "we'll need certain rather special equipment and supplies." He launched into a list. As he proceeded, Rutherford experienced more and more difficulty breathing, and by the time he was done the older man seemed on the verge of a stroke.

Rutherford gradually regained the power of speech. "But the expense! The illegality! The. . . ." He pulled himself together. "You realize, of course, that while I have a great deal of discretion as regards the Temporal Service's ordinary operations, I could not possibly take it upon myself to authorize anything like this. The entire governing council of the Authority will have to consider your proposal."

"Bring 'em on."

If Mondrago had seemed uncomfortable in Rutherford's private sanctum, he was positively fidgeting in the understatedly ornate conference room that held a quorum—indeed, almost the entirety—of the council, sitting around a long table with him and Jason at one end and Rutherford at the other.

The councilors had been summoned from around the planet to Australia—a summons sent under conditions of maximum security, for it had included the essential elements of Jason's findings. Since their arrival they had seen and heard the supporting evidence, and no one was inclined to doubt those findings. Not that there had ever been any serious doubt, given Jason's well-known reputation for competence, despite his equally well-known reputation as a wise-ass.

His proposal, however, was something else.

Helene de Tredville, a small woman of almost ninety

standard years with white hair pulled tightly back into a severe bun, stared down the table at him. "So, Commander Thanou, do I understand that you want us to let you take modern weapons back to the fifth century B.C.?"

"Modern weapons and *medical supplies*?" Alistair Kung's voice—unexpectedly high-pitched, coming from such an overweight body—rose to a squeak on the last two words.

"Yes to both. Actually, I'd also considered asking you to send back an aircar with an invisibility field." Jason knew it was wicked to relish the signs of incipient cardiac arrest around the table. He relished it anyway. "Fortunately, Pan knows how to pilot the Teloi aircars, so we can use one of those, even though the lack of invisibility technology will be inconvenient. But as for modern weapons . . . the Transhumanists surely have them, and we can hardly be expected to go up against them with in-period swords and spears."

"But the medical supplies," Kung began, only to be silenced by Jason's expression. All the flippancy slid away, revealing what lay beneath it.

"I promised Pan that if he did as I ask I would free him from his dependency on his Transhumanist and Teloi masters. I keep my promises. Since we've been back, I've had a chance to confer with medical specialists and ascertain precisely what he needs. We can take back a supply that will, quite frankly, last him as long as a twisted organism like him is likely to live. I intend to leave him the Teloi aircar and advise him to go somewhere out-of-the-way—maybe the part of Crete where Alexandre and I hid." A ghost of Jason's trademark raffish smile reawoke. "He can start a 'cult' of his own there to assure his safety. In a historyless place like fifth-century B.C. Crete, it won't cause any problems."

"But," dithered Alcide Martiletto with a flutter of slender wrists, "it's all so *improper!* We'd have to violate our own rules and protocols in just *so* many ways!"

"Desperate times call for desperate measures," Jason philosophized drily. Then, doing his best to make it seem an afterthought, he added, "There's one additional benefit. We can rescue Dr. Chantal Frey."

"What?" Jadoukh Kubischev leaned forward. Unlike the frankly corpulent Kung, he could be described with minimal charity as "well-fleshed." And in his case, the flesh was held up by a substantial bone structure. "Whatever are you talking about, Commander? You know perfectly well that this is impossible. The TRD restores the temporal energy potential of a person or other object, causing it to return to the time from whence it came. Dr. Frey's TRD was separated from her and came back with you. Even if you were to take an extra TRD with you and give it to her to hold, it would be inseparably linked to the linear present of the time from which it made transition—as is she. It would return to its own linear present, but she would not. This is axiomatic." He shook his head with a force that set his wattles jiggling. "No. That is the end of it. She is permanently stranded in Classical Greece."

"And besides," Martiletto honked, "by your own account, the bitch turned traitor!"

"No!" Jason took a deep breath and forced himself to keep his tone deferential. "I was there, and I ask you to believe me when I say she was . . . conflicted, and that I can win her back." He turned to Kubischev. "And as for how . . . well, you all know the rule of thumb for bringing objects back with you when retrieved. The restored temporal energy potential, in a manner still imperfectly understood, seems to encompass not just your clothing but any objects you can conveniently carry, and therefore such objects require no separate TRDs of their own. Dr. Frey is a slightly built woman, and I'm a reasonably strong man. Yes," he continued hurriedly, before the murmur around the table could coalesce into flabbergasted rejection, "I know, it's never been tried with a human before. But I know of no theoretical objection to it."

From the far end of the table, Rutherford studied him shrewdly. "So *that* was what you meant about 'getting her back.' This, despite the fact that the Transhumanists were planning to send her back as an infiltrator—a scheme which was prevented only by your recovery of her TRD before they could re-implant it, and which must have had at least her passive acquiescence. Jason, are you certain that, after your last extratemporal expedition, this isn't a matter of . . . working out guilt over what happened to Deirdre Sadaka-Ramirez?"

Once again, Jason recalled the Yogi Berra quote. He decided the humor wouldn't be appreciated here. He kept silent, fearing that anything he could say might damage his credibility even more than Rutherford had.

"However," Rutherford continued, addressing the meeting at large, "that is really immaterial. Whatever deep-seated feelings and motivations may lie behind Commander Thanou's proposal, the fact remains that he is *right*. This is the only point we presently know of where the Transhumanists' plans can be attacked—their only current point of vulnerability. We must exploit it. For one thing, we may be able to acquire valuable intelligence about the Transhumanist underground in the course of the operation."

"Maybe from Dr. Frey, if she can in fact be turned and brought back for debriefing," Mondrago ventured.

"Yes," Jason nodded. "Franco must have spilled *something* to her in the course of their . . . relationship." He trusted himself to say nothing more. He was coping with the unaccustomed—not to say unimaginable— sensation of feeling gratitude to Rutherford.

"An excellent point," nodded Rutherford.

"But the expense!" wailed Martiletto. "We just sent one expedition of four persons back nearly three millennia. Now you want us to send another!"

"The Authority has fairly substantial contingency reserve funds," said Jason, refraining from commenting on the council's notorious stinginess in spending them. "If this isn't an extraordinary emergency, I don't know what is."

"It would require extensive preparation," said Kubischev, wavering.

"Of course," agreed Jason. "But that doesn't matter. What counts is not the time we depart from, but the time we arrive in the target milieu."

"Quite true," said Rutherford with another nod, this time a brisk subject-closing one. "If there is no further discussion, I call for a vote."

CHAPTER TWENTY-TWO

THE TEMPORAL REGULATORY AUTHORITY solemnly maintained that its enforcement arm was not even quasi-military in nature. And, for a fact, the Temporal Service had never been noted for military punctilio. Nevertheless, the two new members of the team rose to their feet into something resembling the position of attention when Mondrago called out "Attention on deck!" and Jason entered the briefing room. They knew his reputation in the Service, and that he held the permanent rank of Commander in the Hesperian Colonial Rangers, not exactly an ill-regarded outfit.

"As you were," he said, studying the two as they resumed their seats. Like every officer who has ever led troops into battle, he would have liked to have had more of them. But he hadn't dared to press his luck by demanding that more than four people be displaced such a vast—and correspondingly expensive—temporal "distance." And he had to admit that, on short notice, it had been hard enough to find even two combat-trained people, not otherwise occupied, who possessed the particular qualifications required, including the ability to blend in fifth-century B.C. Greece. He didn't really expect them to have to do any blending, but Rutherford had been adamant.

It was that very difficulty in finding suitable people that had led Jason to accept a woman, despite his misgivings in light of the social milieu into which they would be displaced. And he couldn't quarrel with Pauline Da Cunha's combat record—in fact, on further reflection he'd decided he was lucky to have her after all. She was wiry, deceptively small, and dark enough to require a cover story as a Hellenized native of Caria in Asia Minor.

Adam Logan was of average size (hence on the large side, where they were going) and unobtrusively muscular, with nondescript features and medium-brown hair and eyes. He was sufficiently unremarkable-looking to pass in a wide range of Caucasian-inhabited historical settings, which made him valuable to the Service. His quiet competence made him even more valuable.

"By now," Jason began, "you've gone through all the preliminary procedures, including your microbiological 'cleansing' and the acquisition of the appropriate dialect of ancient Greek through direct neural induction." Jason didn't really expect them to be doing any hobnobbing with the locals on this expedition; it was just something else Rutherford had insisted on. "You have also received extensive orientation on the target milieu in general terms. This is in the nature of your actual mission briefing.

"You both volunteered on the strength of the highly

classified information that was offered to you, including the involvement of the Teloi aliens. So you know that this mission is not our usual escort duty—nursemaiding teams of researchers. In fact, it's unique in the history of the Service. This time we're going up against illegal time travelers—a surviving cadre of Transhumanists, in fact."

"That last part helped induce us to volunteer, sir," said Da Cunha. Logan's expression confirmed it.

"I know. I'm sure there would have been no lack of volunteers if we had put out a general call for them. We didn't, partly due to security considerations but mostly because we could only use people with certain qualifications. We're almost certainly going to be facing modern weapons, so we've obtained special permission to use such weapons ourselves. And you two are experts with those as well as with the various low-technology weapons we in the Service normally take with us into the past."

"What kind of firepower are we going to be dealing with, sir?" asked Da Cunha, who clearly did the talking for this duo. "We've heard that you had some run-ins with these, uh, Teloi when you were in the Bronze Age."

"The Teloi use rather low-powered neural paralyzers, designed to resemble heads—'Heads of the Hydra' they're called—when dealing with the primitive local humans. For serious work, they have weapon-grade lasers; the only ones I saw were pistol-sized, so I can't say whether or not they have anything heavier. As for the Transhumanists, I simply don't know. I never encountered any of their stuff—I got the impression that they preferred to use the local stuff whenever possible, thus minimizing the chances of having some awkward explaining to do. But since they have no scruples about taking modern equipment, up to and including an aircar, back in time, we dare not assume that they didn't take modern arms as well."

Da Cunha spoke up again. "What about us, sir? We *do* have scruples. Surely we've had to give some thought to avoiding the possibility of our weapons being observed."

That's an understatement, thought Jason, recalling Rutherford's jitters. "You are correct. A bit of forced-draft engineering was required. I had a hand in the design myself." He reached out an arm, and Mondrago handed him what appeared to be a four-foot walking stick of the sort typically used by the ancient Greeks, perhaps a trifle stouter than most such sticks.

"You will note a row of small knobs along the shaft, about a foot from one end, appearing to be natural bumps on the wood. If you depress the forward one. . . ." He did so, and the far end of the "stick" flipped open and folded out into a set of focusing lenses about three inches in diameter.

"The basic mechanism is that of the standard Takashima laser carbine, but miniaturized and redesigned to fit into this shape. Like the standard Takashima, it functions in two modes: 'kill' and 'stun.' In the former mode, it is a weapon-grade laser; in the latter, the laser is powered down to a guide beam to ionize the air, along which an electrical charge is carried. These functions are activated by pressing the second and third knobs respectively. The fourth knob back is the actual trigger. The fifth knob activates a harmless visible-light setting, which may be useful as we're going to be spending part of our time underground. Finally, the energy cells that provide power are fed in through this slot, opened by pressing the sixth knob. We are under orders to retrieve all ejected cells and bring them back with us." Jason ignored his listeners' expressions on hearing this, hardly the kind of order a combat infantryman wants to hear.

"As you know," he continued, "even the standard Takashima is not a battlefield weapon; you wouldn't want to take it up against opposition in powered combat armor. That is doubly true of this little improvisation, given the amount of power we've had to sacrifice on the altar of inconspicuousness. But it ought to be adequate for our needs, as any action we see should be at very short ranges."

Da Cunha looked thoughtful. "The stunner setting ought to work particularly well on this mission. For one thing, Greece has a dry climate; as we all know, the electrical charge does stupid things in rain or even high humidity. And as we also know, metal armor conducts the charge and actually attracts it."

"Agreed, with the caveat that our targets almost certainly won't be wearing armor. However," Jason continued, and his expression turned more chilling than he knew, "in the absence of orders to the contrary, your weapons should be permanently set on 'kill.' Remember, it's impossible for us to bring back prisoners for interrogation, however much I'd like to. There are two exceptions to this, which I'll get to in a few minutes."

Jason turned toward the rear wall of the room and touched a remote-control unit. Part of the wall flickered and became a screen displaying a map of the Marathon plain. He indicated Mount Kotroni, to the northwest of the plain. "We will materialize here, a few minutes after the point in time—precisely ascertainable thanks to my recorder implant—when Alexandre and I left Pan on Mount Agriliki." His listeners' looks of distaste at the mention of Pan were unmistakable, though quickly smoothed over. Their orientation had included imagery of the artificially engendered hybrid being. "At that time, the Transhumanists were on their way in a Teloi aircar to take him to Mount Kotroni, overlooking the current phase of the Battle of Marathon." He touched more controls, and color-coded battle lines appeared. "The Persians will have hastily formed a new line, adjacent to their camp, to shield the embarkation of their ships. As the Greeks—advancing slowly at this point—approach this line, the Transhumanists' plan to induce panic in the Persians by means of a sonic projector—a technique which, as we know, is useless against modern countermeasures, but which ought to serve this purpose—while having Pan appear on the slopes about here." He zoomed in on Kotroni and used a cursor to indicate its eastern slopes. "Our point of appearance will be here, so we can arrive unobserved by them. The element of surprise should be total." The cursor moved a third of the way around the peak, westward, to a level area on the opposite slope.

"We will proceed around behind them and kill all Transhumanists present. I want to emphasize that Pan must not be killed or even stunned, for he is essential to the next phase of the operation. He knows how to pilot the Teloi aircar—I ascertained that before making an agreement with him. In exchange for the pharmaceutical supplies we are bringing, he will take us to Athens in the aircar, which must be a model capable of carrying several passengers, given the use the Transhumanists were making of it. There we will make our way to the cavern under the Acropolis, where more Transhumanists—probably including their leader—and the members of the cult of which you learned in your orientation will be awaiting Pan. Here we will have to play it by ear: the Transhumanists must be neutralized with as few manifestations of out-of-period technology as possible. And Pan will tell the cultists that he's not really a god and that the Transhumanists are evil supernatural beings who have been deceiving them."

"That might not be easy, sir," said Logan slowly. "The ancient Greeks didn't have 'devils' or 'demons', and none of their gods were either purely good or purely evil. They were just a kind of super-powerful immortal humans."

"Very astute," said Jason with a sharp look. Evidently there was more to Logan than met the eye, or the ear. Rutherford had raised the same objection. "That's why I told Pan to use his imagination. But while awaiting retrieval on Crete I had time to think about it some more. In particular, I thought about a line of theological propaganda that the Persian commander Datis used on the Greek island of Delos on his way to Athens. There's no point in going into the details at this time, as it would sound like mumbo-jumbo to you. As a matter of fact, it *is* mumbo-jumbo. But since my return, after consultation with Rutherford and various experts on the period, I think it may work. It doesn't really fit into the conventional Greek version of metaphysics, but maybe Pan's word will carry weight anyway. As always, flexibility and adaptability are going to have to be our watchwords.

"At any rate, afterwards we will use the small gravitically

focused explosive charge we're taking with us to seal the tunnel without doing any damage to the buildings above. The cavern will be gone, but the historically attested grotto sacred to Pan on the north slope of the Acropolis will remain. The Athenians will continue to offer annual sacrifices to Pan there, as history says they did, but the Transhumanists' twisted cult will be aborted.

"Now, there's one other matter—the second of the two 'exceptions' I mentioned in connection with weapon settings. At some point in this operation, it is highly probable that we will encounter Dr. Chantal Frey, a member of my prior expedition to this milieu. As you know from your orientation, she had her TRD surgically removed and may have defected to the Transhumanists." Jason said this in a very even tone of voice, and he noted his listeners' carefully neutral expressions at his choice of words. "She must not, under any circumstances, be killed. It is permissible, if the situation seems to warrant it, to stun her. I intend to bring her back with us, willingly or otherwise, by actual physical carriage just as we have always brought various items back. It is a method that has never been tried before with a human or any other living organism. In fact, the idea of doing so has never occurred to anyone before, doubtless because we're so accustomed to thinking exclusively in terms of our standard procedures. But I am advised that it is within the bounds of theoretical possibility.

"Now, as to your TRDs. You're probably wondering why they haven't been implanted yet. The reason is that they've only just become available. They are a new model, hastily developed and rushed into production for this mission.

They are somewhat larger than the standard models, but the implantation will still be a minor operation. Unlike all TRDs up until now, these are not set to activate at a pre-set moment. Instead, they are designed to activate on command. The command is transmitted through my brain implant. I will decide when we are to be retrieved."

Da Cunha and Logan stared, for this was beyond unprecedented. "But how will anyone here know when to expect us?" Da Cunha asked.

"They won't." Jason permitted himself a wintery smile. "This, as we all know, would normally be out of the question due to 'traffic control' considerations on the displacer stage. Which, of course, is why TRDs like these have never been developed before; no one could imagine a use for them. But that issue won't arise this time, because the stage will be kept clear until we return. Which, in turn, won't be much of a problem because this is going to be the briefest extratemporal expedition in the entire history of the Authority. A couple of hours, if that, ought to be long enough for us to accomplish this mission, if it can be accomplished at all. And every additional minute we spend in the fifth century B.C. is just one additional chance for some kind of screw-up.

"Finally, Alexandre here is my second in command. This is due to his familiarity with the target milieu, despite his junior status in the Service. If either of you has a problem with this, now's the time to get it off your chest." Total silence answered him. "Very well. If there are no further questions, you are dismissed. We'll have further briefings, and opportunities to practice with these rather unique versions of the Takashima, at a later time."

As they filed out of the room, Mondrago lingered. "Sir, may I have a word?"

"Sure. What's on your mind?"

"Well, sir, about the 'all you can conveniently carry' rule on which you're basing your plan to bring Dr. Frey back to our time in the linear present. . . ." Mondrago trailed to a halt, looking uncharacteristically abashed.

"Yes?" Jason prompted. "What's the matter? You don't think it will work?"

"I'm sure I'm not qualified to say, sir," replied Mondrago, armoring himself in military formality. "If the experts say it will, I believe them. It just occurs to me that at the same time you're doing it . . . well, Pan is a fairly small being, and if it works at all I ought to be able to do the same with him."

Jason stared. "Are you saying you've decided you want to rescue Pan?"

"No, sir!" said Mondrago, a little too emphatically. "I'm just thinking that he might be a useful intelligence source, if we could bring him back for debriefing."

"I see." Jason carefully kept his face expressionless. "You know, you may have a point. I hadn't thought my idea out to its logical conclusion. I was thinking exclusively in terms of using it for Dr. Frey, because this is her proper time. But on reflection, that shouldn't matter; we're always bringing inanimate objects with us from their own periods in the past this way, and they stay here. Otherwise Rutherford wouldn't be able to keep that sword and the other souvenirs in his display case! And the experts keep telling me that whether the object is living or nonliving shouldn't matter. I'll tell you what: if the opportunity presents itself, without jeopardizing the success of the mission, I'll let you make the attempt. Good enough?"

"Yes, sir."

The time came, and the four of them filed onto the displacer stage with their "walking sticks." They also carried in-period daggers. Logan and Mondrago also carried the kind of satchels that ancient Greeks normally carried when going on lengthy walking journeys. The former contained the explosive charge; the latter the medical supplies for Pan, just in case Mondrago's idea didn't work. All of them carried, in the usual sort of waist-tied wallets, a supply of the energy cells for which they were strictly accountable.

Rutherford met them at the edge of the stage for the traditional handshake. On this occasion it seemed overlaid with a new grimness. In the past there had sometimes been a possibility that Rutherford was sending time travelers into battle; this time it was a certainty. As mission leader, Jason was the last to shake hands. But at the last moment he paused.

"Ah, Kyle . . . what with one thing and another, I haven't gotten around to asking you. But . . .?"

Rutherford's eyes met his. "Yes. It's still there."

Jason nodded. No more needed to be said. He mounted the stage.

CHAPTER TWENTY-THREE

THEY WERE ALL EXPERIENCED, so the disorientation didn't hit them too hard when the dome surrounding the displacer stage faded into oblivion as though it had never been and they stood on a ledge in Mount Kotroni's shadow.

Still, there was a moment when they would have been helpless had there been any hostiles present—assuming, of course, that those hostiles hadn't been stunned into immobility by their appearance out of thin air. It was why Jason had chosen the side of the hill opposite the side from which the Transhumanists would be overlooking the plain of Marathon, their attention riveted on the battle below and to the east.

That fixation couldn't be counted on, though, and the all-important element of surprise had to be preserved. Using the Service's standard hand signals, Jason motioned the others to follow him to the right. They silently worked their way around the hill's southern slopes, emerging into the morning sun. Jason spared an instant for a glance to the south, where the taller Mount Agrliki loomed beyond the Greek camp, defining the southeast end of the plain. Mere minutes ago, he thought with a sudden chill, his own three-months-younger self had left those slopes and was now flying his invisible aircar toward Athens. He couldn't let himself dwell on it, lest the sense of strangeness immobilize him.

They rounded the hill and the plain lay spread out before them. To the southeast the ground was choked with corpses, the detritus of the initial clash, where the inward-pivoting Greek flanks had crushed the Persian center a lesser trail of carnage extended northeast of that, following the path of the re-formed, grimly advancing phalanx that was now nearing the improvised Persian line defending the ships, almost directly to the east. Beyond that, the narrow beach was a scene out of hell, with the ships putting out to sea and the shallows choked with frantic men trying to find a ship, any ship, that would take them. On the Persian right, the Greek light troops were hunting scattered Persian stragglers into the great marsh.

The noise from the plain, compounded of the screams of the wounded, the panicked cries of the Persian fugitives, the shouted command, and the tramp of the phalanx's twenty thousand feet, was horrifying. But Jason knew it was about to rise to a truly hellish crescendo, for this was a lull in the battle, before the final clash.

Jason tried to imagine the exhaustion of the dust- and gore-encrusted hoplites of the phalanx, moving toward what by some accounts was to be the fiercest fighting of the day, where Callimachus and many others would fall. He

knew that their exhaustion would allow the Persians to hold
out long enough for all but seven of their ships to escape.
He also knew—although it almost defied belief—that these
same men would turn around later that same morning and
march twenty-six miles *in armor* to Phalerum, where the
Persian fleet would find them drawn up on the shore. Jason
had to wonder how much of a fight they would really have
been able to put up at that point, had it come to that. But
after what the Persians had just experienced, they would
have no appetite to put it to the test. They would sail away.

Then Jason turned the final corner of the goat-trail they
were following. There, on a ledge beyond a boulder, were
three Transhumanists—none of whom was Franco—and
Pan. He motioned his followers to a halt and crept forward
to peer over the boulder.

The Transhumanists, who had a good view of the
Persian line that Datis had somehow managed to
improvise, were aiming a subsonic projector of the kind he
had imagined they would use. It was a small model, with
barely enough range. But all that would be required of it
would be to induce emotional turmoil in just a few men,
here and there in a hastily organized formation of men
already badly shaken. That would be enough to dissolve
that formation. Off to the side was the Teloi aircar, an
open-topped model large enough to carry four passengers
besides the pilot, not quite as overdecorated as the
"chariots" Jason remembered.

Only three of them, Jason thought. No doubt there had
originally been a fourth, but that one—the murderer of
Bryan Landry and would-be murderer of Mondrago and
himself—now lay near the Greek camp with Mondrago's

sling-pellet in his brain. *And they're preoccupied. This ought to be easy.* He signaled the others to slide forward and join him behind the boulder. They noiselessly took up their positions and he prepared to give the signal.

At that instant, at the far end of the ledge beyond the Transhumanist group, an inhumanly tall figure appeared.

One of the Transhumanists cried out. They all whirled to face the new apparition. Pan cowered. Jason, his tactical calculations thrown off, motioned Mondrago and the others to lay quietly as he tried to evaluate the situation's new dynamics. Da Cunha and Logan stared over the top of the boulder wide-eyed, for this was their first sight of Teloi in the flesh.

Zeus stalked forward. Three other Teloi followed him: a male who somewhat resembled him, another male who seemed more powerfully built than the Teloi norm, and a female who, like Zeus, exhibited the Teloi indicia of aging. Jason didn't recognize any of the three, but certain hard-to-define qualities about them made him wonder if he was looking at Poseidon, Ares and Hera.

One thing was certain: none of them looked happy, Zeus least of all. And all wore, on the belts of their tunics, laser pistols of the kind that had killed Sidney Nagel on the island of Kalliste shortly before it had exploded, leaving the remnants that would one day be known as the Santorini group.

The Transhumanist who seemed to be the leader—he looked to be one of the varieties gengineered for intelligence and initiative, at the expense of some of the physical attributes—bowed and addressed Zeus in the tone of patently bogus servility Jason had heard Franco use.

"Why, greetings, Lord. This is most unexpected." He looked around in vain for an aircar. "How did you—?"

"The sky-chariot that brought us has departed," said Zeus, his voice thick with an emotion that made it even more disturbing than Teloi voices normally were. "Aphrodite took it away, for we will not be needing it. We mean to reclaim this one, which we unwisely let you use before we learned of your impious betrayal of us, your gods."

"Whatever do you mean, Lord?" The Transhumanist's reverential tone was getting a little frayed around the edges. As a member of one of the upper Transhumanist castes, he was struggling to suppress a heritage of arrogance. "As our leader Franco has repeatedly told you, we wish only to serve you."

"You lie, as Franco has lied to us from the beginning. He promised to enable the Persians to restore Hippias to power in Athens so he could complete his great work: the raising of a temple almost worthy of me. But now I see your true aim. You mean to give the victory to the Athenians!"

"A minor change in plans, Lord—a mere tactical adjustment." The Transhumanist's struggle to maintain his pose of obsequiousness was now comically obvious—or at least it would have been comical under any other circumstances. "Rest assured that our long-term goal is unchanged: leading Athens back into its proper reverence for you."

"More lies! It is all clear to me now! Your only concern is to establish a cult of this grotesque artificial being Pan which we enabled you to create but which is now under your control. And you intend to commit the ultimate blasphemy by establishing him as a god, for your own selfish purposes!"

Pan looked like he wanted to burrow into the stony soil of the hillside.

Zeus was raving now, his features working convulsively. "You are no better than all other humans—the original stock, and the Heroes we created in an effort to guide the others back to their proper role. You 'Transhumanists' claim to be a superior strain, but you are like all the rest: treacherous and disloyal and, above all, ungrateful to us, your creators and your gods! We should never have summoned your species up from apedom!"

A strong shudder convulsed the Transhumanist and his façade of worshipfulness seemed to fall from him and shatter, revealing what lay beneath. Not just his face but his entire body was one great sneer of loathing and contempt.

"Our gods? You senile, decayed, demented fool! You are inferior even to the lesser breeds of humans. You have long since outlived your time—and you have now outlived your usefulness to us, your supplanters—the new gods!" And with motion of almost insect-like quickness, possible only to genetically upgraded reflexes, the Transhumanist reached inside his chiton, pulled out an extremely compact laser pistol, and shot Zeus in the upper chest.

In the late twentieth century, after the invention of the laser but when weapon-grade applications of it had been only a theoretical possibility, people had had peculiar ideas about them. The vision of a blinding but silent beam of light was wrong in every particular; it was invisible in vacuum, and in atmosphere there was only a sparkling trail of ionized air, accompanied by a sharp but not very loud crack as air rushed in to fill the tube of vacuum that had been drilled through it. And a continuous laser beam swinging back and forth and reducing its target to sizzling salami slices was out of the question; even aside from the impossible energy demands, any attempt to do it in atmosphere would have come to grief on the hard facts of thermal bloom. Instead, a pulse of directed energy burned a hole in the victim, with a burst of superheated pinkish steam—the human or Teloi body is, after all, seventy percent water—whose knockback effect now sent Zeus' body toppling over backwards.

The other two Teloi drew their weapons, as did the two subordinate Transhumanists. There was an intense instant of crisscrossing, crackling beams. One of the Transhumanists went down, as did all the Teloi.

It all happened so quickly that the last Teloi was sinking to the ground before Jason could react.

"Get them!" he snapped, rising to his feet from behind the boulder and activating his "walking stick." He speared the Transhumanist leader with a series of rapid-fire laser pulses more powerful than those of the pistols. Mondrago and the others opened up at appreciably the same instant, and the Transhumanists died, practically incinerated by multiple laser burns.

Jason turned away toward Pan. But as he did he heard a low, croaking "Jason." Zeus was still barely alive.

Moved by some impulse, Jason walked over to the Teloi with whom he had once conspired the "imprisonment of the Titans," and looked down into the nonhuman face. It was contorted with pain, but the strange pale-blue-and-azure eyes held an odd clarity, as though the clouds of insanity had dissipated.

"Jason," Zeus repeated, though this time it was more a whisper than a croak. "Yes, I do remember you. It was so long ago, when Kalliste exploded and our older generation were trapped forever." He stated it matter-of-factly—nothing about imprisoning the Titans in Tartarus. All his delusions were gone, burned away by the fires of agony. "You made that possible."

"I and my two companions," Jason nodded. "Both of them died to do it. One was Oannes."

"Yes, I remember him too—one of the Nagommo." The Teloi's voice held none of the hate that would once have suffused it at the name of his race's mortal enemies. Even that was gone now. "And I remember Perseus, who afterwards established my worship at Mycenae as king of the gods. King of the gods!" The huge eyes closed, and Jason thought Zeus had spoken his last. But then they fluttered open, and were empty not just of lunacy but of everything, holding the ultimate horror of absolute nullity as he looked back over thousands of barren, pointless years with the pitiless clarity of impending death. His desolate whisper was barely audible.

"Lies. All lies. No, not even lies. Just . . . nothing." The Teloi's last breath whistled out in an oddly humanlike way.

Jason turned away and looked around him. In the usual way of laser firefights, it had been very quiet, without spectacular visual effects. None of the battling thousands on the plain below—none of whom were looking up the hill in any case—had noticed. Besides, even as the Transhumanists were dying, the Athenian war-cry of

Alleeee! had arisen again, and the grinding crash as the phalanx had rammed into the Persian holding force.

Jason couldn't pause to admire the view. He rushed over to where Pan crouched in a fetal position. Grabbing a shoulder, he rolled the being over. Large brown eyes went even wider.

"It's you!" squeaked Pan. "How—?"

"It's a long story, and we haven't got time. What I need to know is this: does the agreement we made a few minutes ago over there on Mount Agriliki still hold?"

"Yes. But now you're suddenly dressed differently, and you seem somehow changed. And who are these others?"

"Never mind. You said you knew how to pilot this Teloi aircar. I need for you to take us to Athens, as fast as it can possibly be managed while maximizing concealment."

"Yes . . . yes, that was always the plan. And there is a prearranged landing site—the precinct that's always been sacred to Zeus, and where his unfinished temple is located. Nobody ever goes there now."

"Good." The irony was not lost on Jason, as he glanced at the detritus of the erstwhile king of the gods. "Do you also know how to program the aircar's autopilot?"

"Yes, I do."

"Then let's go." Jason turned to his subordinates. "Put that sonic projector into the aircar's baggage compartment—it should fit, and we ought not to leave it here. Move!"

They piled into the aircar. Jason had intended to be the last one in, but Mondrago, standing on the rim of the ledge, called to him. "Sir, look down here."

Jason joined him. He had forgotten the roar of battle

from the plain below. But now he followed Mondrago's pointing finger to the east. The makeshift Persian line had given way, and the battle was dissolving into a chaotic melee on the narrow beach as the Greeks pursued the fleeing Persians through the sands and the shallows as they sought rescue, desperately scrambling aboard the ships that Datis' last stand had enabled to disembark before it had collapsed in—

"Panic," Mondrago stated. "The Persians panicked after all, even though the Transhumanists never got a chance to use that sonic projector! Ah . . . what's funny, sir?"

Jason brought his chuckling under control. "Of course the Persians panicked! I mean, after the hell they had been through in the first stage of the battle, the one we were involved in . . . and remember, this Persian battle-line was a pick-up force of stragglers Datis somehow put together to cover the embarkation. And now they saw that blood-spattered phalanx coming at them again. What could be more natural than panic? So you see . . . *it happened anyway!*"

Mondrago nodded his understanding. "And because of the 'prophecy' that Pan gave Pheidippedes on the road from Sparta a few days ago, the Athenians will attribute it to Pan and sacrifice to him in that grotto every year, just like history says."

"Exactly. As usual, reality protects itself. Come on, let's go."

They departed, leaving the bodies of the would-be gods to the carrion birds.

CHAPTER TWENTY-FOUR

THEY FLEW SOUTHWESTWARD, relying on the aircar's low altitude and high speed to avoid being observed—or, at least, to assure that anyone who *did* observe it would not be believed. As they curved around the lower northern slopes of Mount Pentelikon, Jason reflected that somewhere up there on the summit was at least one Transhumanist, ready to flash the "shield signal" that would so perplex contemporary Athenians and later historians. He would subsequently return to his own time and place, for they had no leisure to attempt a search for him. Then the mountain was behind them and they sped across the plain of Attica.

As they went, Jason spoke to Pan in haste, because they had little time. "Do you know anything about the beliefs of the Persians? The teachings of their prophet Zoroaster?"

"Some," said Pan, clearly puzzled by the question. "Franco and others have spoken of it."

"Good, because when you address the cultists, this is what I want you to say." Jason set it out in a few swift sentences, which was all he had time for. Pan frowned but claimed to understand. Jason could only accept that.

Pan brought them carefully around to approach Athens from the southwest, where no one's attention was fixed. There, tucked into an angle of this century's unimpressive city walls, was the dust-blown, weed-choked precinct sacred to Zeus. Here stood the forest of unfinished columns that had been intended to uphold the immense temple the tyrant Hippias had begun to erect, ostensibly to the glory of Zeus but in reality to his own and that of the Pisistratid dynasty of political bosses. It was what Napoleon might have built as a monument to his own ego if he had been a Classical Greek. Now it stood in its permanently unfinished state, left by the Athenian democracy as an object lesson in the futility of dictatorial megalomania.

Pan landed the aircar in the roofless space that was to have been the temple's vast central aisle. As they got out, alert to the possibility of stray bystanders—even more unlikely than ever, on this day—Jason spoke to Pan. "Now, I want you to set a course into the autopilot which will, when signaled to do so, send this aircar out over water—I don't care where, as long as it's a remote stretch of coast—and then into a crash dive. I don't really expect to use it," he added, seeing Pan's expression. "It's just in case of contingencies."

Pan obeyed, as he was conditioned to do, then handed Jason a remote-control unit, small and austerely functional by Teloi standards. "You need only press this stud to activate the command."

"Good." Jason put the unit in the pouch at his waist. "All right, everybody, let's go!"

It was only about a third of a mile to their destination-point on the Acropolis' north slope, as the crow flew. Of course, crows didn't have to negotiate the twisting narrow streets of Athens. But Jason's map display helped keep them from deviating from the most nearly direct route. And those streets were practically deserted, with the old men and women and children thronging the Agora on the far side of the Acropolis, waiting for news of the battle. The baggage compartment had held a hooded cloak in which the Transhumanists had customarily wrapped Pan when it was necessary to move him about where he might be observed. Swathed in it and hunched over, he might be mistaken for an elderly woman, as long as the cloak fell to the ground and concealed his hooves.

As they hastened through the streets, Jason briefly wondered if that slightly younger Jason Thanou was even now on the far side of Athens retrieving Chantal's TRD from Themistocles' house, or if he had already departed for Crete.

Moving along the narrow roadway that ran along the north side of the Acropolis, with the steep hillside immediately to their left, they reached a point directly below the grotto of Pan. The decaying Bronze Age wall did not extend here, for it only enclosed the area around the Acropolis' western end. The hillside here was regarded as unscalable. Jason understood why as they scrambled up it, not wishing to waste time and risk notice by proceeding around to the gate in the wall and backtracking along the pathway Jason and Mondrago had followed before.

There was no one outside the grotto. Pan had explained that the cultists would not arrive until later, although they were probably already on their way, following the pathway from the gate, which was another reason Jason hadn't wanted to take that route. The question was whether Franco was already inside. It was at this point that they were going to have to begin playing it by ear.

"Do you remember where you hit the rear wall?" Jason asked Mondrago.

"About here, I think." Still, Mondrago had to pound several times before finding the right spot. The door-sized segment they remembered swung open. He and Jason led the way in, down the crude, shallow steps and across the small cave and into the tunnel. They activated their laser weapons' "flashlight" feature as the light from the doorway dimmed. There was no light from up ahead, and no sound. Jason dared to breathe a sigh of relief.

They entered the large cavern holding the eerily archaic cult statue. But the idol was not on its dais. Rather, it was sunk into the floor, leaving the hatchway Jason remembered Pan emerging from in a glare of artificial light.

"Franco will be here any moment," said Pan nervously as he busied himself lighting oil lamps.

"With how many others?" demanded Mondrago.

"No more than one. Aside from the one on Mount Pentelikon, that's all he has left." Jason nodded; he'd always thought there had to be a limit to how many people the Transhumanists, however advanced their time-travel technology, could displace, especially when they were also displacing the mass of an aircar. "He'll be expecting the

four others from Marathon to be waiting here with me. Oh
. . . and he'll also probably bring the woman defector. He's
represented her to the cultists as a priestess."

Jason made no comment. He looked down into the
chamber into which the idol had sunk. "It looks like there
ought to be room for all of us to squeeze in down there.
Pan, you wait up here where Franco expects you."

The four of them descended a short ladder and crowded
together. It was at least as tight a fit as Jason had thought .
. . and though the cavern was cool, they had all been
sweating profusely in the outside August heat.

"It's just as well," whispered Mondrago, as though
reading Jason's thoughts, "that none of us have been eating
the local diet. All those beans—!"

"Shhh!" Jason shushed him, for there was a faint sound
of approaching footsteps above.

They hadn't long to wait before Franco's unmistakable
voice spoke, curtly and without preamble. "Where are my
men?"

"Dead, Lord," squeaked Pan. "Zeus and three other
Teloi arrived atop Mount Kotroni and accused you of
betraying them. A fight broke out and everyone, on both
sides, was killed. Afterwards, I took the aircar and came
here according to the plan, as I knew you would wish."

"You lie, you nauseating piece of filth! *All* of them, on
both sides killed? Do you take me for a fool?" There was a
meaty smack, followed by a high-pitched whimpering.

"Don't, Franco!" came a female voice—Chantal Frey's
voice. "After all, he came back as ordered."

"He had no choice." Franco's voice held a
dismissiveness that transcended contempt.

"They're coming!" said a male voice unknown to Jason.

Franco's voice muttered a non-verbal curse. "All right, we have no time. We'll get to the bottom of this later. You: get down there and be prepared to play your role." Franco didn't look down into the compartment below the dais, for he had no reason to. Pan scurried down the ladder and crammed himself in with Jason and the others. His body odor was oddly acrid, but none of them were particularly squeamish. Above, Franco must have activated a control, for the cult statue rose up to its position on the dais and the hatch closed. Darkness settled over them.

Sounds from above were now muffled, but Jason could discern shuffling feet as the cultists filed into the cavern. It didn't sound to him like as large a group as he had seen here before, but that made sense on this day; this would be mostly women and older men, with only those younger men who had managed to evade military service. Then he heard the droning, somehow sinister chant he had heard before. Soon the chanting began to be responsive, alternating with various ritual signals. Jason paid no attention to the sounds of the ceremony, which had probably been crafted to conform to the type of ritual that members of the various mystery religions would expect. Then it stopped abruptly, replaced by the stirring sound of Franco's voice.

"Rejoice! Civilization is saved! While other Athenians huddle in the Agora, quaking with fear, Pan now grants you, his elect, the news they await. Know, then, that at this very moment, the battle is already won. The barbarians, driven mad with fear by Pan, have fled shrieking to their ships. The only ones left on Attic soil now lie dead on the plain of Marathon or drowned in the marshes."

The rapturous collective sigh was audible.

Franco's voice dropped an octave. "But those barbarians who escaped still believe they can defy the will of the gods and vent their rage on Athens. They have now set their course for Cape Sunium, and Phalerum beyond it, where they mean to land and descend on this defenseless city."

There was a faint hissing sound of indrawn breath.

"But fear nothing!" Franco's remarkable voice again became a clarion. "Pan has granted to his priestess Cleothera a vision of the future. Hear the prophecy!"

There was a pause, either intentionally or unintentionally dramatic, before Chantal spoke. Jason thought he could discern a quavering hesitancy in her voice. To the cultists, the effect must have been one not of ambivalence but of eeriness. And her singsong tone of recitation by rote must have been exactly what they expected of an oracle through whom a god spoke to mortals.

"Rejoice," she intoned. "At this moment, the men of Athens have recognized the danger, and are girding themselves to march back. And they will arrive at Phalerum in time! The Persians, seeing the men who had just bested them drawn up on the shore, will wet their barbarian trousers in fear and sail away."

Another, even more relieved sigh arose.

"And now," Franco resumed, "your god has once again shown the favor in which he holds you. You have already received oracles that will enable your families to enrich themselves when the events they foretell—the second Persian invasion ten years from now, the wars between Athens and Sparta, and all the rest—come to pass. Thus you will be able to profit at the expense of this city that has never accorded Pan proper worship! And he will always hold you and your descendants in this same favor, as long as you unquestioningly obey his commands, as told to you by us, his messengers, while keeping your vow of secrecy."

There was a chorus of frantically affirmative noises.

"Finally, even though his previous appearance was spoiled by impious intruders, you will now receive the ultimate reward of your devotion . . . for now *the Great God Pan appears to you!*"

All at once, the hatch above Jason's head was outlined in light that shone through the cracks as the harsh electrical light he had seen before flooded the cavern. He heard the gasps of the cultists as they were temporarily blinded by the unnatural glare. Then the hatch, with the idol atop it, sank down, leaving the opening. Pan ascended the short ladder and the light above faded, allowing the cultists to see the apparition in the dimness.

Jason, crouched in the darkness below, heard the weird half-moan and half-sigh that arose above. It was a sound that no group of people in Jason's world could have produced, for it held the kind of skepticism-free terrified ecstasy that the human race had lost the capacity to feel when it had emerged from the shadows of superstition. Gradually it droned down into silence, leaving a breathless hush.

The silence seemed to last a long time.

Jason felt Mondrago's body, pressed up against his in the confines of the chamber, go rigid with tension.

Pan's not going to go through with it, thought Jason, with a sickening sense of defeat. *He can't. The habit of obedience is too strong, and now it's reasserting itself. He's going to do exactly as Franco told him to do. I was an idiot to think otherwise.*

All at once, the silence was shattered by a high-pitched sound. It took Jason a second to recognize the sound for what it was, for he had never heard it or even imagined it could be.

It was the sound of Pan laughing.

"You *fools!* Are you really such idiots that you still think I'm your god Pan? Now the time has come when I can enjoy telling you how you've been deceived."

Jason tried to imagine Franco's state of shock. It must, he thought, be as complete as that of the worshippers, though for different reasons. And there was nothing Franco could do. He could hardly shoot or otherwise silence the "god." He could only stand, paralyzed, and listen as his creation's jeering voice went on, tearing down his edifice of intrigue with every syllable.

"Know, then, simpletons, that I am come from the East, for I am of the *daiva*, the anti-gods who impersonate and thwart the gods just as black smoke rises along with the sacred fire. Even as the Ionians of Didyma worshipped one of my fellows thinking him to be their god Apollo, so you have worshiped me! Oh fools, fools, fools!"

As Zoroastrian theology it was, of course, perfect gibberish. But these people didn't know that. They had some vague knowledge of the religion's concepts and terminology, for their fellow Greeks in Ionia had long been in contact with the Persians. And they had heard of what Datis had told the Apollo-worshipers of Delos about the oracle at Didyma. So this all held a ring of horrible verisimilitude for them, and continued to do so as Pan raved on.

"You think what I have done at Marathon today was to save Athens, this stinking pig-wallow you call a city? Ha! I did it to punish the Persians for their failure to worship the one *true* God: Ahriman, lord of the darkness which must inevitably engulf the universe when the last light finally gutters out, no matter how many futile fires the priests of Ahura Mazda ignite. But the Persians have chosen to worship Ahura Mazda, following their stupid prophet Zoroaster, and now they have paid for their folly. *And so shall you, fools!* For my servants are here to destroy you!"

It took a fraction of a second for Jason to realize what Pan meant. Then he barked "Move!" at the others and forced his stiffened legs to propel him up the ladder, to stand beside Pan.

The light in the cavern was dim enough that his eyes required no real adaptation. He saw the cultists, still immobilized with shock, and, off to the side, Franco with Chantal beside him, staring wildly. Another figure, which he recognized as one of the middle-level Transhumanists, lunged at him, drawing a dagger as he moved. Jason brought up his "walking stick" and speared the man with a laser beam.

Behind him, Mondrago and the others were scrambling up the ladder and, as they emerged into the cavern, firing laser bolts into the mass of cultists. In this dimness, the trails of ionization were almost bright enough to resemble lightning. And the vicious crack was loud in this confined space.

The cultists went mad with terror. They pelted toward

the tunnel mouth, trampling and crushing each other in their hysterical haste to be gone from what had become a chamber of inexplicable horror.

The rapid-fire laser bolts stabbed again and again into that writhing, screaming mass of bodies, and the stench of burned flesh filled the cavern.

But Jason had eyes for none of that. He swung his weapon toward Franco.

With that unnatural quickness of his, Franco whipped out from under his tunic a small laser pistol of the same model his fellows had used earlier on Mount Kotroni. But he did not point it at Jason. Instead, he grasped Chantal by the upper arm, twisted it up in an obviously painful grip, and swung her in front of him, placing the pistol's focusing lens against her head.

Chantal gave a cry of pain and something worse than pain. "Franco . . . darling. . . ."

"Shut up, you pathetic Pug cunt!" Franco snarled, and yanked her arm further up, eliciting a fresh cry. "You're useless for my purposes without your TRD—except as a shield."

Jason forced himself to remain calm and do nothing reckless like trying for a head shot, for even if it succeeded it might well cause Franco's trigger finger to spasm in death. He looked around. The last of the surviving cultists had by now fled down the tunnel, and Mondrago, Da Cunha, and Logan were also covering Franco and his captive with their weapons. Pan groveled beside Jason's feet.

Franco looked them over for a moment, then smiled at Jason. "So . . . you've come back, while an earlier version of you is simultaneously here. The fuddy-duddies who run the Authority will never recover!"

Jason was in no mood to appreciate Franco's perspicacity, which would doubtless also enable him to recognize the falsity of any offer to let him live. "Let her go," he said evenly, "and you can have a quick, clean death. Your choice."

Franco gave another infuriating smile. "I believe I'll choose no death whatever. I'm taking her with me. If anyone tries to stop me, she dies. If I see anyone following me, she dies."

Jason put on a devil-may-care expression. "What makes you think a threat to the life of a defector is going to deter us?"

"It shouldn't. But if I know Pugs, it will." The false levity abruptly slid away, and Franco's face, for all its designer Classical handsomeness, grew very ugly. "No more childish bluffing! I'm going now, to the precinct of Zeus, where that repulsive little genetic monstrosity must have brought the Teloi aircar." He gave Pan a look of loathing. "I wish I were in a position to kill it now, for its betrayal. But no; that would be kinder than letting it live."

Beside his legs, Jason felt Pan stiffen, and a kind of convulsion go through the misshapen body. All at once a high-pitched scream of pent-up hate split the air of the cavern and Pan's goatish legs propelled him forward like a projectile.

Startled, Franco pulled Chantal with him as he tried to avoid that sudden attack. He almost succeeded. Pan careened against his and his prisoner's legs, knocking them both off balance. He tried to grapple Franco's legs.

Instinctively, Franco brought his laser pistol down hard. The butt struck Pan's right temple, under the horn, with a sickening crunching sound. Pan went limp.

Mondrago was the first to recover. With an inarticulate shout, he fired at the now partially exposed Transhumanist. But Franco was still staggering, and the aim was off. The laser beam brushed against his left arm, and also Chantal's, which Franco had never quite let go. Her scream immobilized them all just long enough for Franco to bring his laser pistol back up against her head.

"Now, where were we?" said Franco, although his face was too contorted with pain to manage a mocking smile. "Remember, nobody is to follow us, or she dies. After I reach the aircar, I'll let her go. After all, I think I've had the full use of her! You're welcome to her now, Thanou— not that I'd give her much of a recommendation." He gave Chantal's laser-burned left arm a particularly vicious jerk and pulled her along with him as he backed into the tunnel. The sound of their footsteps and Chantal's whimpering gradually receded.

Jason dropped to his knees beside Pan. As expected, the artificial being whose fragility Jason had thought he had sensed was dead.

"I'm sorry, sir," said Mondrago miserably. "I didn't mean to hurt her. I thought I could—"

"Forget it." Jason held up a hand for silence, and waited until he was sure Franco had had time to exit the tunnel. "All right. The three of you set up the explosive charge in the tunnel, as per the plan. And . . . leave Pan's body in here. After you've set the timer, come to the precinct of Zeus. I'm going there now."

"What?" Mondrago goggled. "But, sir—"

"Don't worry. Of course I'm not going to let Franco see me—at least not until he reaches the aircar. There . . . well, I think I have a way of dealing with him."

"Let me come too!"

"No. There's less chance of him spotting just one of us. Now just follow orders for once, damn it!" And Jason plunged into the tunnel.

Franco had closed the outer door, but like Houdini's safes it was easy to open from the *inside*. Jason scrambled down the steep, rocky slope of the Acropolis and slipped through the twisting alley-like streets. Once he caught a glimpse of Franco and Chantal far ahead, and instantly flattened himself against a wall before resuming his stealthy pursuit.

He emerged from the labyrinth of alleys and buildings into the open area where the unfinished temple stood, just in time to see Franco drag Chantal between two of the topless columns. He followed, circling around and passing through the colonnades at another point. Franco had mounted the open-topped aircar and was pulling Chantal up onto it.

"But you said you'd let me go!" she protested, struggling to resist.

"Don't be even stupider than you have to be. I lied, of course. No, I think I'll take you with me. I can amuse myself with you in various ways before my TRD activates. By then, you'll be begging me to kill you. But I probably won't. No, I believe I'll just leave you permanently stranded . . . an unattached woman with no family, in this society . . . maimed and disfigured, as you'll be by then after what I'll have done to you . . . yes." With a final heave of his good arm, Franco hauled her up onto the aircar.

Jason stepped out from behind his concealing column. "Hi!" he called out with a jaunty wave. In his hand was a small black object: the remote control unit Pan had given him.

Franco and Chantal, standing on the aircar's edge, both stared.

Jason pressed the stud.

The autopilot awoke, and under its control the aircar lurched aloft.

Chantal lost her balance and fell a few feet. The impact, landing on her burned left arm, brought a gasping shriek of pain.

But Jason's attention was fixed on the swiftly rising aircar. Franco was windmilling his arms, frantically trying to regain his balance. But he toppled over the side. He managed to catch the rim and hold on as the aircar rose still higher and began to swing into a southward course.

Jason took careful aim with his disguised laser carbine and burned Franco in his good right shoulder. With a cry of pain, the Transhumanist lost his grip and fell. He hit the stump of an unfinished column face-first with bone-cracking force, then fell the rest of the way to the ground and lay still. The aircar continued on its way, and would plunge into the sea, vanishing from an era in which it did not belong.

Jason walked over to Franco. The Transhumanist's ribcage was crushed, and when he tried to speak only a feeble, gurgling hiss of agony emerged from between his splintered teeth, along with a froth of blood.

Jason drew his dagger, but then stopped. *Why bother?* He sheathed the dagger, turned away and went to examine Chantal. Her breathing was shallow, and aside from her laser burn, she had broken her right leg. But she would live. Franco's noise had ceased by the time she regained consciousness.

"Lie still," he told her. "You're safe. Franco's dead."

"Jason," she whispered weakly, "I've been a fool. I wish I could make amends, but I know I can't, ever. I deserve to stay in this century and die."

"You're not going to. We're going to take you back."

"*What?* But how—?"

"Never mind. Just lie still," Jason repeated. He heard footsteps behind him. It was his team.

"All done, sir," Mondrago reported. "The charge is set. In fact, it ought to be—"

From the direction of the Acropolis, Jason thought he heard an extremely faint *crump*, but he knew it was probably his imagination. The explosive device they had used generated a momentary sound-deadening field at the instant of its detonation, rendering it effectively inaudible to Athens' preoccupied citizens. If he'd heard anything, it must have been the rumble as the subterranean tunnel collapsed.

"We left Pan in there as ordered, sir," Da Cunha added.

"Good. It's a fitting tomb for him." Jason smiled. "No one will ever know who's lying under the Acropolis."

"When the Athenians offer their annual sacrifices to Pan at the grotto," mused Logan in the thoughtfully deliberate way he always seemed to speak, on the rare occasions when he did it at all, "they'll never dream that the real thing is entombed inside it."

"Interesting point." Jason handed his "walking stick" to Mondrago and, with great care, put one arm under Chantal's knees and the other behind her back, and lifted her up. She gasped with pain but clung to his neck. He focused his mind, preparatory to giving a neural command. "All right. Is everybody ready? Let's go home."

CHAPTER TWENTY-FIVE

THE GREAT DOMED DISPLACER CHAMBER was almost exactly as they had left it a couple of hours earlier. Rutherford had to all appearances never moved. After his initial startlement at their appearance, he brusquely motioned forward the waiting medical team. Jason handed Chantal over to them.

"How is she?" he asked as soon as they had laid her on a stretcher and brought their medical sensors to bear.

"She's in a great deal of pain," a doctor replied as he gave her a hypospray injection against that same pain. "And she's in mild shock. But none of her injuries are life-threatening. She's going to be fine." He gestured, and his orderlies lifted the stretcher.

Chantal turned her head to meet Jason's eyes, and spoke weakly. "Jason . . . thank you. I'm—"

"Hush. Don't try to talk."

"No, let me finish. I already knew I was wrong. But

you've shown me just how very wrong I was, because what you've done has reminded me of what it is to be truly *human.* So now I know why—whatever humanity's imperfections—we must always *remain* human. That is too precious a thing to be gambled away against the chance of something 'superior'." The effort of speaking seemed to exhaust her. The doctor gave a more peremptory gesture, and she was borne away. Only when she was out of sight did Jason turn to face Rutherford.

"Mission accomplished," he reported wearily, "in all particulars. I'll tell you the details later, in private. But the Transhumanist operation has been scotched, and their leader was killed. And I don't think Dr. Frey's loyalties are going to be in any question after this."

"And the, uh, 'cleanup' aspects of the plan?" asked Rutherford anxiously.

"All done. The tunnel under the Acropolis behind the grotto was sealed, and no anachronistic hardware was left lying around."

"Good." Rutherford's relief was palpable.

"Also, the being 'Pan' was killed by his own Transhumanist master."

"Just as well," said Rutherford offhandedly.

Jason glared at him. So, he noticed to his surprise, did Mondrago. "I suppose it could be regarded that way, from the standpoint of 'cleanup.' But . . . well, he kept his bargain with me, and he died trying to aid us. I think he's entitled to just a little respect."

"I meant no offense." Rutherford seemed genuinely contrite, and Jason's annoyance ebbed.

"None taken. And before we head for your office,

there's one other thing you'll want to know, because it relates directly to one of the questions the original expedition sought to answer. As we learned then, the Olympian 'gods' were still alive and active in the flesh—at least the Teloi flesh—up to 490 B.C. But after that, for the most part, they became just what they've always been assumed to have been: myths."

Rutherford's eyes kept going to the sword that was his private office's prize exhibit. Jason wasn't sure why.

Finally Rutherford swung around to face Jason and Mondrago. "So not all of the Teloi were wiped out in this final confrontation with the Transhumanists?"

"No. Zeus, before he died, mentioned Aphrodite—or whatever names she was known by in the other Indo-European cultures—as being the pilot of the aircar that had dropped them off. So she and various others must have lived on afterwards; I can't account for Athena or Artemis or Apollo, for example. And they could have continued to play the god game with the help of the self-repairing Teloi techno-magic devices. But remember, they were all members of the youngest Earth-born generation, which Oannes assured me suffered from a drastic reduction in life expectancy. They must have died off, and even before they did, the literal belief in their pantheon began to dissipate, leaving a void that was filled by various Eastern mystery religions and, finally, by Christianity." Jason chuckled. "Knowing the Teloi, I have a feeling that the loss of human belief in them helped hasten their end."

"Quite likely." Rutherford turned brisk. "But, more to the point, about the Transhumanists. . . ."

"Yes. That's the real problem. At least one of them survived, as we knew from the first was going to happen, since we didn't have time to hunt down whoever sent the signal from Mount Pentelikon. So one or more of them were retrieved on schedule, as were the corpses of Franco and the others. The survivor or survivors didn't know the details of Franco's death, but they *did* know in general about our discovery of their presence. And they knew that Alexandre and I may have gotten back with that knowledge, even though we were earmarked for assassination down there on the battlefield.

"Incidentally, I've been using the past tense deliberately, because as you know, their expedition came from, and therefore returned to, a time somewhat prior to ours. So their linear present lies in our past—"

"I know," interjected Rutherford bleakly, for he understood the implications.

"—and therefore by now they know that their scheme for a Pan cult was foiled, although they don't know how. And they must regard it as at least a possibility that, as of a point slightly in their own future, we know about their underground and its extratemporal activities, so they'll be on their guard. One good thing: when we went back we killed all the ones who actually saw us, so just exactly what happened on Mount Kotroni and at the grotto in Athens must be a mystery to them."

"One other good thing," Mondrago spoke up. "They know that we got Dr. Frey's TRD back, so they'll assume she was left to die in the fifth century B.C."

"That's right," Jason agreed. "I suggest that we keep her presence here strictly under wraps, even to the extent of providing her with a new identity. I'm certain she'll cooperate. And a debriefing by intelligence specialists ought to be productive."

"Surely Franco didn't give her a great deal of detailed and specific data about the Transhumanist underground," said Rutherford dubiously.

"No, of course not, but he could hardly have avoided dropping some information in the course of her . . . association with him. He was an incorrigible braggart. She may turn out to be an ace in the hole for us." Jason paused. "I don't know what the final judicial determination of her case will be, or if it will even come to that. But if she ends up being sentenced to incarceration, I recommend that the time we keep her here be credited against her term."

"I will pass along your recommendation, with my endorsement. Coming from a man whose death she almost caused, it should carry some weight. And you may quite possibly be right about her usefulness to us. But it goes without saying that she can provide no information on what the Transhumanists have been doing since Franco's expedition. And as to what they may do in the future, the expeditions they may send back before we find this compact and energy-efficient temporal displacer of theirs, as we *must* find it . . . !" Rutherford shook his head slowly and looked at least his age.

"And," said Mondrago, "we don't know how riddled Earth is with these long-term secret organizations of theirs—we only aborted one of them, remember. We also don't know when 'The Day' is scheduled to be, when all their long-term schemes are scheduled to come to fruition.

Basically," he concluded with a kind of pessimistic relish, "we don't know much of anything at all."

"One thing we do know," said Jason grimly, and his eyes held Rutherford's. "We know that the Temporal Service is going to have to change. The days of us being a sort of glorified tour guides are over. Oh, of course we'll continue to send historical research expeditions back. But those expeditions are going to have to have more guards—very watchful guards. And above and beyond that, the Service is going to have to have a new unit whose full-time job is hunting down the Transhumanists across time the way we just did—a specialized combat section."

Rutherford winced. "Perhaps we could call it the 'Special Operations Section.'"

"Sounds good. Call it whatever you want. But for that section, at least, the old loose-jointed style isn't going to work anymore. It's going to have to be a military, or at least paramilitary, outfit—and outfits like that have the kind of organization they do, including a formalized rank structure, for a reason."

"And I think I know just the man to head it," Rutherford told him, with a very brief smile. Then his expression grew desolate again, as he contemplated the coming era of time wars. It was the look of an old man seeing his life's assumptions and verities slipping irretrievably away into the past and vanishing, leaving him face to face with a harsh, unfamiliar, and unfriendly future in which he did not belong.

But then his eyes strayed to the fifteenth-century sword in his display case, the sword that had been borne by she who had come to symbolize the capacity of human beings to fight bravely and die gallantly for something they knew in their souls was worth dying—and killing—for. He seemed to draw strength from it. He turned back to Jason and spoke matter-of-factly.

"You will, of course, need to commence recruiting without delay."

"Right. Da Cunha and Logan are, of course, obvious candidates. And we'll need as wide a range of ethnic types as possible."

"Sir," Modrago blurted. "I want to be the first to sign up for this Special Ops Section of yours."

"Satisfactory, Jason?" asked Rutherford with a lift of one eyebrow.

Jason pretended to consider. "Well, he's an insubordinate wise-ass—"

"I can see how there might be a certain affinity, however reluctantly acknowledged," Rutherford interjected drily.

"—but he's an insubordinate wise-ass who is very handy to have around in a fight." Jason turned to Mondrago. "I just might be able to use you. But I need to be sure you've got the right kind of motivation."

"Well, sir, let me put it this way. Of course I've always hated Transhumanists, but mostly just because *everybody* hates them, if you know what I mean. Now I understand why I *ought* to hate them." Mondrago seemed to seek for words to explain further, but then shook his head and spoke briefly. "It's just something that has to be done."

"Like what those men we fought beside at Marathon did," Jason nodded. "Yes, I think you may possibly do." He turned to Rutherford. "Will that be all for now?"

"Yes." Then, as Jason and Mondrago got to their feet,

Rutherford seemed to remember something. "Oh, yes, Jason, I almost forgot. A most remarkable coincidence occurred." He took out the little plastic case Jason had left in his care. It was empty. Then he held out his other hand. It held a tiny TRD.

"Do you recall our last exchange just before your departure? Afterwards, still thinking about it, I looked in the case and found it was empty. A subsequent search revealed this on the displacer stage. Would you like to keep it?"

"No. I don't think I need it anymore." Jason smiled. "Come on, Alexandre. We've got work to do."

HISTORICAL NOTE

THAT MARATHON was one of the most crucial battles of world history has been recognized by such diverse authorities as Sir Edward Creasy and the U.S. House of Representatives, in a resolution on its 2500th anniversary. I fail to see how any other view is possible.

The events of Xerxes' invasion of Greece ten years afterwards—the immensity of the Persian host, even when discounted for exaggeration; the heroic last stand of the three hundred Spartans (and their seven hundred forgotten Thespian allies) at Thermopylae; the stunning naval victory at Salamis; the titanic clash of massive armies at Plataea—have an epic quality which causes them to get most of the attention. But none of these things would ever have happened had the Athenians lost at Marathon, or submitted without fighting. No subsequent Persian invasion would have been necessary. It would have all been over in 490 B.C.—or perhaps the following year, if Sparta had not yielded and another campaigning season had been required to complete its obliteration.

A few historians—including Arnold Toynbee, in one of his less brilliant passages—have attempted to minimize the criticality of the Persian Wars. And in the 2006 collection *Unmaking the West*, Barry Strauss presented a counterfactual scenario suggesting that even if the Persians had conquered Greece and gone on to conquer the rest of the Mediterranean basin, it is not impossible that Western civilization—or at least *a* Western civilization, sharing many of the characteristics and values we associate with that term—still *could*, maybe, just possibly, have arisen. As an intellectual exercise, the essay is as original, ingenious and thought-provoking as one would expect from Professor Strauss . . . and it doesn't convince for an instant. Not even he can succeed in defending the indefensible.

No. When those ten thousand hoplites broke into a run and charged three times their number of a hitherto invincible enemy, our future went with them. We cannot calculate the debt we owe them.

The scholarly literature relevant to Marathon is intimidating in its voluminousness. For the interested reader with finite time, I recommend three books on which I have leaned heavily and to which I take this opportunity to acknowledge my debt.

The first is *The Western Way of War*, by Victor Davis Hanson, a brilliant study of Classical Greek warfare and its long-term historical repercussions, which latter theme is further developed in the author's subsequent *Carnage and Culture*. Hanson has been on the receiving end of a great deal of hysterical invective and politically correct name-calling. He must be doing something right.

The second is *Persian Fire*, by Tom Holland, a compulsively readable overview of the Persian Wars which achieves an almost unique degree of evenhandedness without ever seeming to lean over backwards to be evenhanded. Rather, the author simply accepts each side on its own terms while skewering both with his trademark sardonic wit. He is particularly good on the little-known and less-understood subject of what can only be called the ideology of the Persian Empire.

Third and most recent is *The First Clash*, by Jim Lacey, which focuses on the Marathon campaign and benefits from the fact that its author, aside from his academic credentials, is an experienced infantry officer and defense analyst. And unlike all too many historians, he does his math. On narrowly military questions I have tended to defer to his judgment, or at least to give it respectful weight when balancing it against Holland's. I have not always done so in less specialized areas such as the much-disputed chronology and sequence of events. For example, I agree with Holland and an ever-increasing number of other historians that the battle took place in August. Lacey, in his Prologue, does perfunctory obeisance to the traditional date of September 12, but he doesn't mention it again—which is understandable, inasmuch as his own reconstruction of the campaign (and, in particular, of the logistical constraints under which the Persians labored) makes nonsense of it. In fact, in a later chapter he himself refers to the "hot August sun" in the days immediately preceding the battle.

Finally, in addition to these books, I cannot forbear to mention *The Ancient City*, by Peter Connolly and Hazel Dodge. In the absence of actual time travel, it is the next best thing. After studying the segment on Classical Athens, I felt as though I had been there.

With the exception of Callicles, all the fifth century B.C. Greeks named in this novel are historical. Themistocles is the only one for whom we have what is self-evidently an individual portrait—the Ostia bust—free of artistic conventions and idealization. Otherwise, I have had to use my imagination about personal appearance, aided by hints from sculpture (the baldness of Aeschylus) and names ("Miltiades," derived from the word for red ochre clay, was often bestowed on reddish-haired children).

The dualistic theology of Zoroastrianism is complex and fascinating, but I have not gone into it as it deserves. The Persian kings of the period in question were far from consistent in their practice of it, for their imperial policy was based on scrupulous (if insincere) respect for the innumerable gods of their various conquered peoples. Even among the Iranians themselves, Ahura Mazda was by tradition merely the chief god of a pantheon almost as inchoate as that of the Greeks, rather than the one uncreated God proclaimed by Zoroaster. The Persian Empire was not in any sense a Zoroastrian theocracy. But Darius I, one of the greatest masters of spin who has ever lived, used Zoroastrian imagery and terminology to justify his usurpation of the Persian throne. It was in this spirit that Datis used a distorted version of it as a propaganda tool as I have described. I have followed in his footsteps, albeit with even more outrageous distortion.

In the matter of dialogue, I have permitted myself certain anachronisms in the interest of clarity.

The initial Persian conquerors of Ionia were Medes led by their General Harpagus, and since this was the Greeks' first contact with the Persian Empire they tended to refer to all the Persians as the "Medes," just as Near Easterners today call all Western Europeans "Feringhi," or Franks. In these pages the Persians are simply the Persians.

Conversely, the Greeks referred to themselves as "Hellenes," as in fact they still do. I have used the more familiar "Greeks," a name later applied to them by the Romans, who derived it from the Graeci, the inhabitants of the colony of Graeae in Italy. Interestingly, in light of the preceding paragraph, Near Eastern terms for the Greeks have always been some variation on "Ionians," the Greeks with whom the Near East was most directly in contact. (The Persian word was "Yauna"; in the Old Testament, one of the sons of Japheth, the son of Noah whose progeny peopled Europe, is "Javan.")

Likewise, I have used the well-known Latinized forms of Persian names rather than the originals. ("Cyrus," not "Kurush"; "Darius," not "Daryush.")

Whenever transliteration of Greek place-names is disputed, I cheerfully admit that I have simply picked whichever version struck my fancy, with a fine lack of that foolish consistency which as we all know is the bugbear of small minds. ("Mount Pentelikon," not "Mount Pentelicus"; "Phalerum," not "Phaleron.")

The Hero with Michael Z. Williamson
(pb) 1-4165-0914-3 • $7.99

■ ■ ■

Citizens ed. by John Ringo & Brian M. Thomsen
(trade pb) 978-1-4391-3347-7 • $16.00
(pb) 978-1-4391-3460-3 • $7.99

Master of Epic SF
The Council War Series
There Will Be Dragons
(pb) 0-7434-8859-8 • $7.99

Emerald Sea
(pb) 1-4165-0920-8 • $7.99

Against the Tide
(pb) 1-4165-2057-0 • $7.99

East of the Sun, West of the Moon
(pb) 1-4165-5518-87 • $7.99

Master of Real SF
The Troy Rising Series
Live Free or Die
(hc) 1-4391-3332-8 • $26.00
(pb) 978-1-4391-3397-2 • $7.99

Citadel
(hc) 978-1-4391-3400-9 • $26.00
(pb) 978-1-4516-3757-1 • $7.99

The Hot Gate
(hc) 978-1-4391-3432-0 • $26.00

■ ■ ■

Von Neumann's War with Travis S. Taylor
(pb) 1-4165-5530-8 • $7.99

"Murderous though they be, the Ellis Peters books set in twelfth-century Britain have the freshness of a new world at dawn. . . . Peters weaves a complex, colorful, and at times quite beautiful tapestry. Medieval, of course."   —*Houston Post*

"Some of the most elegant, unstilted prose being written in mystery novels. [Peters's] chronicles of twelfth-century abbey life in England, featuring Brother Cadfael as sleuth, have made her a best-selling phenomenon on both sides of the Atlantic."
                    —*Chicago Sun-Times*

"Peters continues to provide the type of superior medieval mystery that has spawned a host of unabashed imitations."   —*Booklist*

"Each book is an elegant little mystery, gracefully written, cleverly plotted and richly detailed, full of the sounds and the colors and the customs of twelfth-century England. . . . You can get so caught up in Cadfael's world that you might just look up from a long spell of reading and wonder for a moment where you are."
                    —*Cleveland Plain Dealer*

"Enchanting. . . . Medieval England comes marvelously alive."   —*Washington Post*

"An absorbing mystery . . . a colorfully sketched slice of medieval English history. . . . [Peters] has not lost her touch."   —*Indianapolis Star*

ELLIS PETERS

BROTHER · CADFAEL'S · PENANCE ·

THE MYSTERIOUS PRESS

Published by Warner Books

A Time Warner Company

MYSTERIOUS PRESS EDITION

Copyright © 1994 by Ellis Peters
All rights reserved.

Cover design and illustration by Bascove

The Mysterious Press name and logo are registered trademarks of Warner Books, Inc.

 Mysterious Press Books are published by
Warner Books, Inc.
1271 Avenue of the Americas
New York, NY 10020

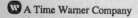 A Time Warner Company

Printed in the United States of America

Originally published in hardcover by The Mysterious Press
First US Printing: December, 1994
First Printed in Paperback: February, 1996

10 9 8 7 6 5 4 3 2 1

A SPECIAL NOTE TO READERS

Edith Pargeter, who, as Ellis Peters, was known to millions for her bestselling books about Brother Cadfael, died in her sleep on Saturday, October 14, 1995, at home in her beloved Shropshire. She was 82 years old.

Her first book was published in 1936 when she was 23; her last in 1994. Her more than 90 books include current affairs novels, historical novels such as the acclaimed Heaven Tree trilogy, and translations of Czech classics into English. The professionalism and scholarship that distinguished all her writing was self-taught; her formal education stopped at high school. She was especially proud of her contributions to Czech literature, the gold medal she received from the Czechoslovak Society for Foreign Relations, and the honorary MA degree she was awarded by Birmingham University.

Ellis Peters came into being in 1959 with the mystery *Death Mask*. (She created the pseudonym partly from the name of her brother, Ellis Pargeter, with whom she lived for many years.) She began the 20-volume Brother Cadfael series in 1977, setting the story in the place where she was born and would later die. As she wrote in *Shropshire: A Memoir of the English Countryside*, "I can travel joyfully to any of my favourite haunts abroad, but only to this place can I come home. . . . This is where I put my feet up and thank God."

Brother Cadfael's Penance, the last book written by Edith Pargeter, went to press before the initial biography on the inside back cover could be changed.

BROTHER · CADFAEL'S
· PENANCE ·

CHAPTER ONE

THE EARL of Leicester's courier came riding over the bridge that spanned the Severn, and into the town of Shrewsbury, somewhat past noon on a day at the beginning of November, with three months' news in his saddle-roll.

Much of it would already be known, at least in general outline, but Robert Beaumont's despatch service from London was better provided than anything the sheriff of Shropshire could command, and in a single meeting with that young officer the earl had marked him as one of the relatively sane in this mad world of civil war that had crippled England for so many years, and run both factions, king and empress alike, into exhaustion, without, unfortunately, bringing either sharply up against reality. Such able young men as Hugh Beringar, Earl Robert considered, were well worth supplying with information, against the day when reason would finally break through and put an end to such wasteful warfare. And in this year of the Lord, 1145, now drawing towards its close, chaotic events had seemed to be offering promise, however faint as yet, that even the two cousins battling wearily for the throne must despair of force and look round for another way of settling disputes.

The boy who carried the earl's despatches had made this journey once before, and knew his way across the bridge and up the curve of the Wyle, and round from the High Cross to

1

the castle gates. The earl's badge opened the way before him without hindrance. Hugh came out from the armoury in the inner ward, dusting his hands, his dark hair tangled by the funnelled wind through the archway, to draw the messenger within, and hear his news.

"There's a small breeze rising," said the boy, unloading the contents of his satchel upon the table in the anteroom of the gatehouse, "that has my lord snuffing the air. But warily, it's the first time he's detected any such stirring, and it could as easily blow itself out. And it has as much to do with what's happening in the East as with all this ceding of castles in the Thames valley. Ever since Edessa fell to the paynims of Mosul, last year at Christmas, all Christendom has been uneasy about the kingdom of Jerusalem. They're beginning to talk of a new Crusade, and there are lords on either side, here at home, who are none too happy about things done, and might welcome the Cross as sanctuary for their souls. I've brought you his official letters," he said briskly, mustering them neatly at Hugh's hand, "but I'll give you the gist of it before I go, and you can study them at leisure, for there's no date yet settled. I must return this same day, I have an errand to Coventry on my way back."

"Then you'd best take food and drink now, while we talk," said Hugh, and sent out for what was needed. They settled together confidentially to the tangled affairs of England, which had shifted in some disconcerting directions during the summer months, and now, with the shutter of the coming winter about to close down against further action, might at least be disentangled, and open a course that could be pursued with some hope of progress. "You'll not tell me Robert Beaumont is thinking of taking the Cross? There are some powerful sermons coming out of Clairvaux, I'm told, that will be hard to resist."

"No," said the young man, briefly grinning, "my lord's concerns are all here at home. But this same unease for Christendom is making the bishops turn their thoughts to enforcing some order here, before they make off to settle the affairs of Outremer. They're talking of one more attempt to bring king and empress together to talk sense, and find a means of breaking out of this deadlock. You'll have heard that the earl of Chester has sought and got a meeting with King Stephen, and pledged his allegiance? Late in the day, and no easy passage, but the king jumped at it. We knew about it before they ever met at Stamford, a week or so back, for Earl Ranulf has been preparing the ground for some time, making sweet approaches to some of Stephen's barons who hold grudges for old wrongs, trying to buy acceptance into the fold. There's land near his castle of Mountsorrel has been in dispute with my lord some years. Chester has made concessions now over that. A man must soften not only the king but all those who hold with the king if he's to change sides. So Stamford was no surprise, and Chester is reconciled and accepted. And you know all that business of Faringdon and Cricklade, and Philip FitzRobert coming over to Stephen, in despite of father and empress and all, and with a strong castle in either hand."

"That," said Hugh flatly, "I shall never understand. He, of all people! Gloucester's own son, and Gloucester has been the empress's prop and stay as good as singlehanded throughout, and now his son turns against him and joins the king! And no half-measures, either. By all accounts, he's fighting for Stephen as fiercely as he ever fought for Maud."

"And bear in mind, Philip's sister is wife to Ranulf of Chester," the courier pointed out, "and these two changes of heart chime together. Which of them swept the other away with him, or what else lies behind it, God he knows, not I. But there's the plain fact of it. The king is the fatter by two new allies and a very respectable handful of castles."

"And I'd have said, in no mood to make any concessions, even for the bishops," observed Hugh shrewdly. "Much more likely to be encouraged, all over again, to believe he can win absolute victory. I doubt if they'll ever get him to the council table."

"Never underestimate Roger de Clinton," said Leicester's squire, and grinned. "He has offered Coventry as the meeting-place, and Stephen has as good as agreed to come and listen. They're issuing safe conducts already, on both sides. Coventry is a good centre for all, Chester can make use of Mountsorrel to offer hospitality and worm his way into friendships, and the priory has housing enough for all. Oh, there'll be a meeting! Whether much will come of it is another matter. It won't please everyone, and there'll be those who'll do their worst to wreck it. Philip FitzRobert for one. Oh, he'll come, if only to confront his father and show that he regrets nothing, but he'll come to destroy, not to placate. Well, my lord wants your voice there, speaking for your shire. Shall he have it? He knows your mind," said the young man airily, "or thinks he does. You rank somewhere in the list of his hopes. What do you say?"

"Let him send me word of the day," said Hugh heartily, "and I'll be there."

"Good, I'll tell him so. And for the rest, you'll know already that it was only the handful of captains, with Brien de Soulis at their head, who sold out Faringdon to the king, and made prisoner all the knights of the garrison who refused to change sides. The king handed them out like prizes to some of his own followers, to profit by their ransom. My lord has got hold from somewhere of a list of those doled out, those among them who have been offered for ransom, and those already bought free. Here he sends you a copy, in case any names among them concern you closely, captors or captives. If anything comes of the meeting at Coventry their case will come up for consideration, and it's not certain who holds the last of them."

"I doubt there'll be any there known to me," said Hugh, taking up the sealed roll thoughtfully. "All those garrisons along the Thames might as well be a thousand miles from us. We do not even hear when they fall or change sides until a month after the event. But thank Earl Robert for his courtesy, and tell him I'll trust to see him in the priory of Coventry when the day comes."

He did not break the seal of Robert Beaumont's letter until the courier had departed, to make for Coventry and Bishop Roger de Clinton's presence on his way back to Leicester. In the last few years the bishop had made Coventry the main seat of his diocese, though Lichfield retained its cathedral status, and the see was referred to impartially by either name. The bishop was also titular abbot of the Benedictine monastery in the town, and the head of the household of monks bore the title of prior, but was mitred like an abbot. Only two years previously the peace of the priory had been sadly disturbed, and the monks temporarily turned out of their quarters, but they had been firmly reinstalled before the year ended, and were unlikely to be dispossessed again.

Never underestimate Roger de Clinton, Robert Beaumont's squire had said, no doubt echoing his formidable patron. Hugh already had a healthy respect for his bishop; and if a prelate of this stature, with the peril of Christendom on his mind, could draw to him a magnate like the Earl of Leicester, and others of similar quality and sense, from either faction or both, then surely in the end some good must come of it. Hugh unrolled the earl's despatches with a cautiously hopeful mind, and began to read the brief summary within, and the list of resounding names.

The sudden and violent breach between Robert, earl of Gloucester, the Empress Maud's half-brother and loyal champion, and his younger son Philip, in the heat of midsummer, had startled the whole of England, and still remained inadequately explained or understood. In the desultory but dangerous and explosive battlefield of the Thames valley Philip,

the empress's castellan of Cricklade, had been plagued by
damaging raids by the king's men garrisoned in Oxford and
Malmesbury, and to ease the load had begged his father to
come and choose a site for another castle, to try and disrupt
communications between the two royal strongholds, and put
them, in turn, on the defensive. And Earl Robert had duly
selected his site at Faringdon, built his castle and garrisoned
it. But as soon as the king heard of it he came with a strong
army and laid siege to the place. Philip in Cricklade had sent
plea after plea to his father to send reinforcements at all costs,
not to lose this asset barely yet enjoyed, and potentially so
valuable to the hard-pressed garrison of his son's command.
But Gloucester had paid no heed, and sent no aid. And suddenly it was the talk of the south that the castellan of Faringdon, Brien de Soulis, and his closest aides within the castle,
had made secret compact with the besiegers, unknown to the
rest of the garrison, let in the king's men by night, and delivered over Faringdon to them, with all its fighting men. Those
who accepted the fiat joined Stephen's forces, as most of the
ranks did, seeing their leaders had committed them; those
who held true to the empress's salt were disarmed and made
prisoner. The victims had been distributed among the king's
followers, to be held to ransom. And no sooner was this
completed than Philip FitzRobert, the great earl's son, in
despite of his allegiance and his blood, had handed over
Cricklade also to the king, and this time whole, with all its
armoury and all its manpower intact. As many considered, it
was his will, if not his hand, which had surrendered the keys
of Faringdon, for Brien de Soulis was known to be as close
to Philip as twin to twin, at all times in his councils. And
thereafter Philip had turned to, and fought as ferociously
against his father as once he had fought for him.

But as for why, that was hard to understand. He loved his
sister, who was married to Earl Ranulf of Chester, and Ranulf
was seeking to inveigle himself back into the king's favour,

and would be glad to take another powerful kinsman with him, to assure his welcome. But was that enough? And Philip had asked for Faringdon, and looked forward to the relief it would give his own forces, only to see it left to its fate in spite of his repeated appeals for help. But was even that enough? It takes an appalling load of bitterness, surely, to cause a man, after years of loyalty and devotion, to turn and rend his own flesh and blood.

But he had done it. And here in Hugh's hand was the tale of his first victims, some thirty young men of quality, knights and squires, parcelled out among the king's supporters, to pay dearly for their freedom at best, or to rot in captivity unredeemed if they had fallen into the wrong hands, and were sufficiently hated.

Robert Beaumont's clerk had noted, where it was known, the name of the captor against that of the captive, and marked off those who had already been bought free by their kin. No one else was likely to raise an exorbitant sum for the purchase of a young gentleman in arms, as yet of no particular distinction. One or two of the ambitious young partisans of the empress might be left languishing unfathered and without patron in obscure dungeons, unless this projected conference at Coventry produced some sensible agreement that must, among its details, spare a thought to insist on their liberation.

At the end of the scroll, after many names that were strange to him, Hugh came to one that he knew.

> "Known to have been among those overpowered and disarmed, not known who holds him, or where. Has not been offered for ransom. Laurence d'Angers has been enquiring for him without result: Olivier de Bretagne."

Hugh went down through the town with his news, to confer with Abbot Radulfus over this suddenly presented opportunity

to put an end to eight years of civil strife. Whether the bishops
would allow an equal voice to the monastic clergy only time
would tell; relations between the two arms of the Church
were not invariably cordial, though Roger de Clinton certainly
valued the abbot of Shrewsbury. But whether invited to the
conference or not, when the time came, Radulfus would need
to be prepared for either success or failure, and ready to act
accordingly. And there was also another person at the abbey
of Saint Peter and Saint Paul who had every right to be told
the content of Robert Beaumont's letter.

Brother Cadfael was standing in the middle of his walled
herb-garden, looking pensively about him at the autumnal
visage of his pleasance, where all things grew gaunt, wiry
and sombre. Most of the leaves were fallen, the stems dark
and clenched like fleshless fingers holding fast to the remnant
of the summer, all the fragrances gathered into one scent of age
and decline, still sweet, but with the damp, rotting sweetness of
harvest over and decay setting in. It was not yet very cold,
the mild melancholy of November still had lingering gold in
it, in falling leaves and slanting amber light. All the apples
were in the loft, all the corn milled, the hay long stacked, the
sheep turned into the stubble fields. A time to pause, to look
round, to make sure nothing had been neglected, no fence
unrepaired, against the winter.

He had never before been quite so acutely aware of the
particular quality and function of November, its ripeness and
its hushed sadness. The year proceeds not in a straight line
through the seasons, but in a circle that brings the world and
man back to the dimness and mystery in which both began,
and out of which a new seed-time and a new generation are
about to begin. Old men, thought Cadfael, believe in that new
beginning, but experience only the ending. It may be that God
is reminding me that I am approaching my November. Well,
why regret it? November has beauty, has seen the harvest into

the barns, even laid by next year's seed. No need to fret about not being allowed to stay and sow it, someone else will do that. So go contentedly into the earth with the moist, gentle, skeletal leaves, worn to cobweb fragility, like the skins of very old men, that bruise and stain at the mere brushing of the breeze, and flower into brown blotches as the leaves into rotting gold. The colours of late autumn are the colours of the sunset: the farewell of the year and the farewell of the day. And of the life of man? Well, if it ends in a flourish of gold, that is no bad ending.

Hugh, coming from the abbot's lodging, between haste to impart what he knew, and reluctance to deliver what could only be disturbing news, found his friend standing thus motionless in the middle of his small, beloved kingdom, staring rather within his own mind than at the straggling, autumnal growth about him. He started back to the outer world only when Hugh laid a hand on his shoulder, and visibly surfaced slowly from some secret place, fathoms deep in the centre of his being.

"God bless the work," said Hugh, and took him by the arms, "if any's been done here this afternoon. I thought you had taken root."

"I was pondering the circular nature of human life," said Cadfael, almost apologetically, "and the seasons of the year and the hours of the day. I never heard you come. I was not expecting to see you today."

"Nor would you have seen me, if Robert Bossu's intelligencers had been a little less busy. Come within," said Hugh, "and I'll tell you what's brewing. There's matter concerning all good churchmen, and I've just come from informing Radulfus. But there's also an item that will come close home to you. As indeed," he owned, thrusting the door of Cadfael's workshop open with a gusty sigh, "it does to me."

"You've heard from Leicester?" Cadfael eyed him thoughtfully from the threshold. "Earl Robert Bossu keeps in touch? He views you as one of his hopefuls, Hugh, if he's keeping that road open. What's he about now?"

"Not he, so much, though he'll be in it to the throat, whether he quite believes in it or not. No, it's certain of the bishops have made the first move, but there'll be some voices on either side, like Leicester's, to back their efforts."

Hugh sat down with him under the dangling bunches of drying herbs, stirring fragrantly along the beams in the draught from the open door, and told him of the proposed meeting at Coventry, of the safe conducts already being issued on either part, and of such prospects as existed of at any rate partial success.

"God he knows if either of them will so much as shift a foot. Stephen is exalted at having got Chester on his side, and Gloucester's own son into the bargain, but Maud knows her menfolk have made very sure of Normandy, and that will sway some of our barons who have lands over there to safeguard, as well as here. I can see more and more of the wiser sort paying mouth allegiance still, but making as little move in the martial kind as they can contrive. But by all means let's make the attempt. Roger de Clinton can be a powerful persuader when he's in good earnest, and he's in good earnest now, for his real quarry is the Atabeg Zenghi in Mosul, and his aim the recovery of Edessa. And Henry of Winchester will surely add his weight to the scale. Who knows? I've primed the abbot," said Hugh dubiously, "but I doubt if the bishops will call on the monastic arm, they'd rather keep the reins in their own hands."

"And how does this, however welcome and however dubious, concern me closely?" Cadfael wondered.

"Wait, there's more." He was carrying it carefully, for such news is brittle. He watched Cadfael's face anxiously as he asked: "You'll recall what happened in the summer at Robert of Gloucester's newly built castle of Faringdon? When

Gloucester's younger son turned his coat, and his castellan gave over the castle to the king?"

"I remember," said Cadfael. "The men-at-arms had no choice but to change sides with him, their captains having sealed the surrender. And Cricklade went over with Philip, intact to a man."

"But many of the knights in Faringdon," said Hugh with deliberation, "refused the treason, and were overpowered and disarmed. Stephen handed them out to various of his allies, new and old, but I suspect the new did best out of it, and got the fattest prizes, to fix them gratefully in their new loyalty. Well, Leicester has been employing his agents round Oxford and Malmesbury to good effect, to ferret out the list of those made prisoner, and discover to whom they were given. Some have been bought out already, briskly enough. Some are on offer, and for prices high enough to sell very profitably. But there's one name, known to have been there, listed with no word of who holds him, and has not been seen or heard of since Faringdon fell. I doubt if the name means anything to Robert Bossu, more than the rest. But it does to me, Cadfael." He had his friend's full and wary attention; the tone of his voice, carefully moderate, was a warning rather than a reassurance. "And will to you."

"Not offered for ransom," said Cadfael, reckoning the odds with careful moderation in return, "and held very privately. It argues a more than ordinary animosity. That will be a price that comes high. Even if he will take a price."

"And in order to pay what may be asked," said Hugh ruefully, "Laurence d'Angers, so Leicester's agent says, has been enquiring for him everywhere without result. That name would be known to the earl, though not the names of the young men of his following. I am sorry to bring such news. Olivier de Bretagne was in Faringdon. And now Olivier de Bretagne is prisoner, and God knows where."

*   *   *

After the silence, a shared pause for breath and thought, and
the mutual rearrangement of the immediate concerns that
troubled them both, Cadfael said simply: "He is a young man
like other young men. He knows the risks. He takes them
with open eyes. What is there to be said for one more than
the rest?"

"But this was a risk, I fancy, that he could not foresee. That
Gloucester's own son should turn against him! And a risk
Olivier was least armed to deal with, having so little concep-
tion of treachery. I don't know, Cadfael, how long he had
been among the garrison, or what the feeling was among the
young knights there. It seems many of them were with Olivier.
The castle was barely completed, Philip filled it and wanted
it defended well, and when it lay under siege Robert failed
to lift a finger to save it. There's bitterness there. But Leicester
will go on trying to find them all, to the last man. And if
we're all to meet soon at Coventry, at least there may be
agreement on a release of prisoners on both sides. We shall
all be pressing for it, men of goodwill from both factions."

"Olivier ploughs his own furrow, and cuts his own swathe,"
said Cadfael, staring eastward through the timber wall before
him, far eastward into drought and sand and sun, and the
glittering sea along the shores of the Frankish kingdom of
Jerusalem, now menaced and in arms. The fabled world of
Outremer, once familiar to him, where Olivier de Bretagne
had grown up to choose, in young manhood, the faith of his
unknown father. "I doubt," said Cadfael slowly, "any prison
can hold him long. I am glad you have told me, Hugh. Bring
me word if you get any further news."

But the voice, Hugh thought when he left his friend, was
not that of a man fully confident of a good ending, nor the
set of the face indicative of one absolute in faith and prepared
to sit back and leave all either to Olivier or to God.

When Hugh was gone, with his own cares to keep him fully

occupied, and his errand in friendship faithfully discharged, Cadfael damped down his brazier with turves, closed his workshop, and went away to the church. There was an hour yet to Vespers. Brother Winfrid was still methodically digging over a bed cleared of beans, to leave it to the frosts of the coming winter to crumble and refine. A thin veil of yellowed leaves still clung to the trees, and the roses were grown tall and leggy, small, cold buds forming at the tips, buds that would never open.

In the vast, dim quiet of the church Cadfael made amicable obeisance to the altar of Saint Winifred, as to an intimate but revered friend, but for once hesitated to burden her with a charge for another man, and one even she might find hard to understand. True, Olivier was half Welsh, but that, hand in hand with all that was passionately Syrian in his looks and thoughts and principles, might prove even more confusing to her. So the only prayer he made to her was made without words, in the heart, offering affection in a gush of tenderness like the smoke of incense. She had forgiven him so much, and never shut him out. And this same year she had suffered flood and peril and contention, and come back safely to a deserved rest. Why disturb its sweetness with a trouble which belonged all to himself?

So he took his problem rather to the high altar, directly to the source of all strength, all power, all faithfulness, and for once he was not content to kneel, but prostrated himself in a cross on the cold flags, like an offender presenting his propitiatory body at the end of penance, though the offence he contemplated was not yet committed, and with great mercy and understanding on his superior's part might not be necessary. Nevertheless, he professed his intent now, in stark honesty, and besought rather comprehension than forgiveness. With his forehead chill against the stone he discarded words to present his compulsion, and let thoughts express the need that found him lucid but inarticulate. This I must do, whether with a blessing or a ban. For whether I am blessed or banned is of no consequence, provided what I have to do is done well.

At the end of Vespers he asked audience of Abbot Radulfus, and was admitted. In the private parlour they sat down together.

"Father, I believe Hugh Beringar has acquainted you with all that he has learned in letters from the Earl of Leicester. Has he also told you of the fate of the knights of Faringdon who refused to desert the empress?"

"He has," said Radulfus. "I have seen the list of names, and I know how they were disposed of. I trust that at this proposed meeting in Coventry some agreement may be reached for a general release of prisoners, even if nothing better can be achieved."

"Father, I wish I shared your trust, but I fear they are neither of them in any mind to give way. Howbeit, you will have noted the name of Olivier de Bretagne, who has not been located, and of whom nothing is known since Faringdon fell. His lord is willing and anxious to ransom him, but he has not been offered the opportunity. Father, I must tell you certain things concerning this young man, things I know Hugh will not have told you."

"I have some knowledge of the man myself," Radulfus reminded him, smiling, "when he came here four years ago at the time of Saint Winifred's translation, in search of a certain squire missing from his place after the conference in Winchester. I have not forgotten him."

"But this one thing," said Cadfael, "is still unknown to you, though it may be that I should have told you long since, when first he touched my life. I had not thought that there was any need, for I did not expect that in any way my commitment to this place could be changed. Nor did I suppose that I should ever meet him again, nor he ever have need of me. But now it seems meet and right that all should be made plain. Father," said Cadfael simply, "Olivier de Bretagne is my son."

There was a silence that fell with surprising serenity and gentleness. Men within the pale as without are still men, vulnerable and fallible. Radulfus had the wise man's distant respect for perfection, but no great expectation of meeting it in the way.

"When first I came to Palestine," said Cadfael, looking back without regret, "an eighteen-year-old boy, I met with a young widow in Antioch, and loved her. Long years afterwards, when I returned to sail from Saint Symeon on my way home, I met with her again, and lingered with her in kindness until the ship was ready to sail. I left her a son, of whom I knew nothing, until he came looking for two lost children, after the sack of Worcester. And I was glad and proud of him, and with good reason. For a short while, when he came the second time, you knew him. Judge if I was glad of him, or no."

"You had good reason," said Radulfus readily. "However he was got, he did honour to his getting. I dare make no reproach. You had taken no vows, you were young and far from home, and humanity is frail. No doubt this was confessed and repented long since."

"Confessed," said Cadfael bluntly, "yes, when I knew I had left her with child and unfriended, but that is not long ago. And repented? No, I doubt if ever I repented of loving her, for she was well worth any man's love. And bear in mind, Father, that I am Welsh, and in Wales there are no bastards but those whose fathers deny their paternity. Judge if I would ever deny my right to that bright, brave creature. The best thing ever I did was to cause him to be brought forth into a world where very few can match him."

"However admirable the fruit may be," said the abbot drily, "it does not justify priding oneself on a sin, nor calling a sin by any other name. But neither is there any profit in passing today's judgement upon a sin some thirty years past. Since your avowal I have very seldom found any fault to chasten in you, beyond the small daily failings in patience or diligence, to which we are all prone. Let us deal, therefore, with what confronts us now. For I think you have somewhat to ask of me or to put to me concerning Olivier de Bretagne."

"Father," said Cadfael, choosing his words gravely and with deliberation, "if I presume in supposing that fatherhood imposes a duty upon me, wherever child of mine may be in trouble or misfortune, reprove me. But I do conceive of such a duty, and cannot heave it off my heart. I am bound to go and seek my son, and deliver him when found. I ask your countenance and your leave."

"And I," said Radulfus, frowning, but not wholly in displeasure, rather in profound concentration, "put to you the opposing view of what is now your duty. Your vows bind you here. Of your own will you chose to abandon the world and all your ties within it. That cannot be shed like a coat."

"I took my vows in good faith," said Cadfael, "not then knowing that there was in the world a being for whose very existence I was responsible. From all other ties my vows absolved me. All other personal relationships my vows severed. Not this one! Whether I would have resigned the world if I had known it contained my living seed, that I cannot answer, nor may you hazard at an answer. But he lives, and it was I engendered him. He suffers captivity and I am free. He may be in peril, and I am safe. Father, can the creator forsake the least of his creatures? Can a man turn away from his own imperilled blood? Is not procreation itself the undertaking of a sacred and inviolable vow? Knowing or unknowing, before I was a brother I was a father."

This time the silence was chiller and more detached, and lasted longer. Then the abbot said levelly: "Ask what you have come to ask. Let it be plainly said."

"I ask your leave and blessing," said Cadfael, "to go with Hugh Beringar and attend this conference at Coventry, there to ask before king and empress where my son is held, and by God's help and theirs see him delivered free."

"And then?" said Radulfus. "If there is no help there?"

"Then by whatever means to pursue that same quest, until I do find and set him free."

The abbot regarded him steadily, recognizing in the voice some echo from far back and far away, with the steel in it that had been blunted and sheathed as long as he had known this elderly brother. The weathered face, brown-browed and strongly boned, and deeply furrowed now by the wear and tear of sixty-five years, gazing back at him from wide-set and wide open eyes of a dark, autumnal brown, let him in honestly to the mind within. After years of willing submission to the claims of community, Cadfael stood suddenly erect and apart, again solitary. Radulfus recognized finality.

"And if I forbid," he said with certainty, "you will still go."

"Under God's eye, and with reverence to you, Father, yes."

"Then I do not forbid," said Radulfus. "It is my office to keep all my flock. If one stray, the ninety and nine left are also bereft. I give you leave to go with Hugh, and see this council meet, and I pray some good may come of it. But once they disperse, whether you have learned what you need or no, there your leave of absence ends. Return with Hugh, as you go with Hugh. If you go further and delay longer, then you go as your own man, none of mine. Without my leave or my blessing."

"Without your prayers?" said Cadfael.

"Have I said so?"

"Father," said Cadfael, "it is written in the Rule that the brother who by his own wrong choice has left the monastery may be received again, even to the third time, at a price. Even penance ends when you shall say: It is enough!"

CHAPTER TWO

THE DAY of the council at Coventry was fixed as the last day of November. Before that date there had been certain evidences that the prospect of agreement and peace was by no means universally welcome, and there were powerful interests ready and willing to wreck it. Philip FitzRobert had seized and held prisoner Reginald FitzRoy, another of the empress's half-brothers and Earl of Cornwall, though the earl was his kinsman, on the empress's business, and bearing the king's safe conduct. The fact that Stephen ordered the earl's release on hearing of it, and was promptly and correctly obeyed, did not lessen the omen.

"If that's his mind," said Cadfael to Hugh, the day they heard of it, "he'll never come to Coventry."

"Ah, but he will," said Hugh. "He'll come to drop all manner of caltrops under the feet of all those who talk peace. Better and more effective within than without. And he'll come, from all that I can make of him, to confront his father brow to brow, since he's taken so bitter a rage against him. Oh, Philip will be there." He regarded his friend with searching eyes; a face he could usually read clearly, but its grey gravity made him a little uneasy now. "And you? Do you really intend to go with me? At the risk of trespassing too far for return? You know I would do your errand for you gladly. If there's word to be had there of Olivier, I will uncover it. No need for you to stake what I know you value as your life itself."

"Olivier's life," said Cadfael, "has more than half its race to run, by God's grace, and is of higher value than my spent years. And you have a duty of your own, as I have mine. Yes, I will go. He knows it. He promises nothing and threatens nothing. He has said I go as my own man if I go beyond Coventry, but he has not said what he would do, were he in my shoes. And since I go without his bidding, I will go without any providing of his, if you will find me a mount, Hugh, and a cloak, and food in my scrip."

"And a sword and a pallet in the guardroom afterwards," said Hugh, shaking off his solemnity, "if the cloister discards you. After we have recovered Olivier, of course."

The very mention of the name always brought before Cadfael's eyes the first glimpse he had ever had of his unknown son, seen over a girl's shoulder through the open wicket of the gate of Bromfield Priory in the snow of a cruel winter. A long, thin but suave face, wide browed, with a scimitar of a nose and a supple bow of a mouth, proud and vivid, with the black and golden eyes of a hawk, and a close, burnished cap of blue-black hair. Olive-gold, cast in fine bronze, very beautiful. Mariam's son wore Mariam's face, and did honour to her memory. Fourteen years old when he left Antioch after her funeral rites, and went to Jerusalem to join the faith of his father, whom he had never seen but through Mariam's eyes. Thirty years old now, or close. Perhaps himself a father, by the girl Ermina Hugonin, whom he had guided through the snow to Bromfield. Her noble kin had seen his worth, and given her to him in marriage. Now she lacked him, she and that possible grandchild. And that was unthinkable, and could not be left to any other to set right.

"Well," said Hugh, "it will not be the first time you and I have ridden together. Make ready, then, you have three days yet to settle your differences with God and Radulfus. And at least I'll find you the best of the castle's stables instead of an abbey mule."

Within the enclave there were mixed feelings among the brothers concerning Cadfael's venture, undertaken thus with only partial and limited sanction, and with no promise of submission to the terms set. Prior Robert had made known in chapter the precise provisions laid down for Cadfael's absence, limited to the duration of the conference at Coventry, and had emphasized that strict injunction as if he had gathered that it was already threatened. Small blame to him, the implication had certainly been there in the abbot's incomplete instruction to him. As for the reason for this journey to be permitted at all, even grudgingly, there had been no explanation. Cadfael's confidence was between Cadfael and Radulfus.

Curiosity unsatisfied put the worst interpretation upon such facts as had been made public. There was a sense of shock, grieved eyes turning silently upon a brother already almost renegade. There was dread in the reactions of some who had been monastic from infancy, and jealousy among some come later, and uneasy at times in their confinement. Though Brother Edmund the infirmarer, himself an oblate at four years old, accepted loyally what puzzled him in his brother, and was anxious only at losing his apothecary for a time. And Brother Anselm the precentor, who acknowledged few disruptions other than a note off-key, or a sore throat among his best voices, accepted all other events with utter serenity, assumed the best, wished all men well, and gave over worrying.

Prior Robert disapproved of any departure from the strict Rule, and had for years disapproved of what he considered privileges granted to Brother Cadfael, in his freedom to move among the people of the Foregate and the town when there was illness to be confronted. And time had been when his chaplain, Brother Jerome, would have been assiduous in adding fuel to the prior's resentment; but Brother Jerome, earlier in the year, had suffered a shattering shock to his satisfaction with his own image, and emerged from a long penance deprived of his office as one of the confessors to the novices, and crushed into surprising humility. For the present, at least, he was much easier to live with, and less vociferous in denouncing the faults of others. In time, no doubt, he would recover his normal sanctimony, but Cadfael was spared any censure from him on this occasion.

So in the end Cadfael's most challenging contention was with himself. He had indeed taken vows, and he felt the bonds they wound about him tightening when he contemplated leaving this chosen field. He had told only truth in his presentation of his case to the abbot; everything was done and stated openly. But did that absolve him? Brother Edmund and Brother Winfrid between them would now have to supply his place, prepare medicines, provision the leper hospital at Saint Giles, tend the herb-garden, do not only their own work, but also his.

All this, if his defection lasted beyond the time allotted to him. By the very act of contemplating that possibility, he knew he was expecting it. So this decision, before ever he left the gates, had the gravity of life and death in it.

But all the while he knew that he would go.

Hugh came for him on the morning appointed, immediately after Prime, with three of his officers in attendance, all well mounted, and a led horse for Cadfael. Hugh remarked with satisfaction that his friend's sternly preoccupied eyes perceptibly brightened approvingly at the sight of a tall, handsome roan, almost as lofty as Hugh's raking grey, with a mettlesome gait and an arrogant eye, and a narrow white blaze down his aristocratic nose. Cloaked and booted and ready, Cadfael buckled his saddlebags before him, and mounted a little stiffly, but with plain pleasure. Considerately, Hugh refrained from offering help. Sixty-five is an age deserving of respect and reverence from the young, but those who have reached it do not always like to be reminded.

There was no one obviously watching as they rode out from the gate, though there may have been eyes on them from the shelter of cloister or infirmary, or even from the abbot's lodging. Better to pursue the regular routine of the day as though this was merely a day like any other, and nowhere in any mind a doubt that the departing brother would come back at the due time, and resume his duties as before. And if peace came home with him, so much the more welcome.

Once out past Saint Giles, with the town and Foregate behind them, and the hogback of the Wrekin looming ahead, Cadfael's heart lifted into eased resignation, open without grudging to whatever might come. There were consolations. With December on the doorstep the fields were still green, the weather mild and windless, he had a good horse under him, and riding beside Hugh was a pleasure full of shared memories. The highroad was open and safe, and the way they must take familiar to them both, at least as far as the forest of Chenet; and Hugh had set out three days before the council was due to meet formally.

"For we'll take it gently along the way," he said, "and be there early. I could do with a word with Robert Bossu before anything is said in session. We may even run into Ranulf of Chester when we halt overnight at Lichfield. I heard he had some last minute advice to pour into the ears of his half-brother of Lincoln. William is minding the winnings of both of them in the north while Ranulf comes demurely to council in Coventry."

"He'll be wise," said Cadfael thoughtfully, "not to flaunt his successes. There must be a good number of his enemies gathering."

"Oh, he'll still be courting. He's handed out several judicious concessions these last few weeks, to barons he was robbing of lands or privileges only last year. It costs," said Hugh cynically, "to change sides. The king is only the first he has to charm, and the king is apt to welcome allies with his eyes shut and his arms open, and be the giver rather than the getter. All those who have held by him throughout, and watched Ranulf flout him, won't come so cheaply. Some of them will take the sweets he offers, but forbear from delivering the goods he thinks he's buying. If I were Ranulf, I would walk very meekly and humbly for a year or so yet."

When they rode into the precinct of the diocesan guesthalls at Lichfield, early in the evening, there was certainly a lively bustle to be observed, and several noble devices to be seen among the grooms and servants in the common lodging where Hugh's men-at-arms rested. But none from Chester. Either Ranulf had taken another route, perhaps straight from his half-brother in Lincoln, or else he was ahead of them, already back in his castle of Mountsorrel, near Leicester, making his plans for the council. For him it was not so much an attempt at making peace as an opportunity to secure his acceptance on what he hoped and calculated would be the winning side in a total victory.

Cadfael went out before Compline into the chill of the dusk, and turned southward from the close to where the burnished surfaces of the minster pools shone with a sullen leaden light in the flat calm, and the newly cleared space where the Saxon church had stood showed as yet like a scar slow to heal. Roger de Clinton, continuing work on foundations begun years before, had approved the choice of a more removed and stable site for a projected weight far greater than Saint Chad, the first bishop, had ever contemplated. Cadfael turned at the edge of the holy ground blessed by the ministry of one of the gentlest and most beloved of prelates, and looked back to the massive bulk of the new stone cathedral, barely yet finished, if indeed there could ever be an end to adorning and enlarging it. The long roof of the nave and the strong, foursquare central

tower stood razor-edged against the paler sky. The choir was
short, and ended in an apse. The tall windows of the west
end caught a few glimpses of slanted light through walls
strong as a fortress. Invisible under those walls, the marks of
the masons' lodges and the scars of their stored stone and
timber still remained, and a pile of stacked ashlar where the
bankers had been cleared away. Now the man who had built
this castle to God had Christendom heavy on his mind, and
was already away in the spirit to the Holy Land.

Faint glints of lambent light pricked out the edge of the
pool as Cadfael turned back to Compline. As he entered the
close he was again among men, shadowy figures that passed
him on their various occasions and spoke to him courteously
in passing, but had no recognizable faces in the gathering
dark. Canons, acolytes, choristers, guests from the common
lodging and the hall, devout townspeople coming in to the
late office, wanting the day completed and crowned. He felt
himself compassed about with a great cloud of witnesses, and
it mattered not at all that the whole soul of every one of these
might be intent upon other anxieties, and utterly unaware of
him. So many passionate needs brought together must surely
shake the heavens.

Within the great barn of the nave a few spectral figures
moved silently in the dimness, about the Church's evening
business. It was early yet, only the constant lamps on the
altars glowing like small red eyes, though in the choir a deacon
was lighting the candles, flame after steady flame growing
tall in the still air.

There was an unmistakably secular young man standing
before a side altar where the candles had just been lighted.
He bore no weapon here, but the belt he wore showed the
fine leather harness for sword and dagger, and his coat, dark-
coloured and workmanlike, was none the less of fine cloth
and well cut. A square, sturdy young man who stood very
still and gazed unwaveringly at the cross, with a regard so

earnest and demanding that he was surely praying, and with grave intent. He stood half turned away, so that Cadfael could not see his face, and certainly did not recall that he had ever seen the man before; and yet there seemed something curiously familiar about the compact, neat build, and the thrust of the head upward and forward, as though he jutted his jaw at the God with whom he pleaded and argued, as at an equal of whom he had a right to demand help in a worthy cause.

Cadfael shifted his ground a little to see the fixed profile, and at the same moment one of the candles, the flame reaching some frayed thread, flared suddenly sidelong, and cast an abrupt light on the young man's face. It lasted only an instant, for he raised a hand and pinched away the fault briskly between finger and thumb, and the flame dimmed and steadied again at once. A strong, bright profile, straight-nosed and well chinned, a young man of birth, and well aware of his value. Cadfael must have made some small movement at the edge of the boy's vision when the candle flared, for suddenly he turned and showed his full face, still youthfully round of cheek and vulnerably honest of eye, wide-set brown eyes beneath a broad forehead and a thick thatch of brown hair.

The startled glance that took in Cadfael was quickly and courteously withdrawn. In the act of returning to his silent dialogue with his maker the young man as suddenly stiffened, and again turned, this time to stare as candidly and shamelessly as a child. He opened his mouth to speak, breaking into an eager smile, recoiled momentarily into doubt, and then made up his mind.

"Brother Cadfael? It *is* you?"

Cadfael blinked and peered, and was no wiser.

"You can't have forgotten," said the young man blithely, certain of his memorability. "You brought me to Bromfield. It's six years ago now. Olivier came to fetch me away, Ermina and me. I'm changed, of course I am, but not you—not changed at all!"

And the light of the candles was steady and bright between them, and six years melted away like mist, and Cadfael recognized in this square, sturdy young fellow the square, sturdy child he had first encountered in the forest between Stoke and Bromfield in a bitter December, and helped away with his sister to safety in Gloucester. Thirteen years old then, now almost nineteen, and as trim and assured and bold as he had promised from that first meeting.

"Yves? Yves Hugonin! Ah, now I do see . . . And you are not so changed after all. But what are you doing here? I thought you were away in the west somewhere, in Gloucester or Bristol."

"I've been on the empress's errand to Norfolk, to the earl. He'll be on his way to Coventry by now. She needs all her allies round her, and Hugh Bigod carries more weight than most with the baronage."

"And you're joining her party there?" Cadfael drew delighted breath. "We can ride together. You are here alone? Then alone no longer, for it's a joy to see you again, and in such good fettle. I am here with Hugh, he'll be as glad to see you as I am."

"But how," demanded Yves, glowing, "did you come to be here at all?" He had Cadfael by both hands, wringing them ardently. "I know you were sent out by right, that last time, to salve a damaged man, but what art did you use to be loosed out to a state conference like this one? Though if there were more of you, and all delegates," he added ruefully, "there might be more hope of accord. God knows I'm happy to see you, but how did you contrive it?"

"I have leave until the conference ends," said Cadfael.

"On what grounds? Abbots are not too easily persuaded."

"Mine," said Cadfael, "allows me limited time, but sets a period to it that I may not infringe. I am given leave to attend at Coventry for one reason, to seek for news of one of the prisoners from Faringdon. Where princes are gathered together I may surely get word of him."

He had not spoken a name, but the boy had stiffened into an intensity that tightened all the lines of his young, fresh face into a formidable maturity. He was not yet quite at the end of his growing, not fully formed, but the man was already there within, burning through like a stirred fire when some partisan passion probed deep into his heart.

"I think we are on the same quest," he said. "If you are looking for Olivier de Bretagne, so am I. I know he was in Faringdon, I know as all who know him must know that he would never change his allegiance, and I know he has been hidden away out of reach. He was my champion and saviour once, he is my brother now, my sister carries his child. Closer to me than my skin, and dear as my blood, how can I ever rest," said Yves, "until I know what they have done with him, and have haled him out of captivity?"

"I was with him," said Yves, "until they garrisoned Faringdon. I was with him from the time I first bore arms, I would not willingly be parted from him, and he of his kindness kept me close. Father and brother both he has been to me, since he and my sister married. Now Ermina is solitary in Gloucester, and with child."

They sat together on a bench beneath one of the torches in the guesthall, Hugh and Cadfael and the boy, in the last hush of the evening after Compline, with memories all about them in the dimness where the torchlight could not reach. Yves had pursued his quest alone since the fall of Faringdon had cast his friend into limbo, unransomed, unlisted, God knew where. It was relief now to open his heart and pour out everything he knew or guessed, to these two who valued Olivier de Bretagne as he did. Three together might surely do more than one alone.

"When Faringdon was finished, Robert of Gloucester took his own forces away and left the field to his son, and Philip made Brien de Soulis castellan of Faringdon, and gave him a strong garrison drawn from several bases. Olivier was among them. I was in Gloucester then, or I might have gone with him, but for that while I was on an errand for the empress, and she kept me about her. Most of her household were in Devizes still, she had only a few of us with her. Then we heard that King Stephen had brought a great host to lay siege to the new castle, and ease the pressure on Oxford and Malmesbury. And the next we knew was of Philip sending courier after courier to his father to come with reinforcements and save Faringdon. But he never came. Why?" demanded Yves helplessly. "Why did he not? God knows! Was he ill? Is he still a sick man? Very weary I well understand he may be, but to be inactive then, when most he was needed!"

"From all I heard," said Hugh, "Faringdon was strongly held. Newly armed, newly provisioned. Even without Robert, surely it could have held out. My king, with all the liking I have for him, is not known for constancy in sieges. He would have sickened of it and moved on elsewhere. It takes a long time to starve out a newly supplied fortress."

"It could have held," Yves said bleakly. "There was no need for that surrender, it was done of intent, of malice. Whether Philip was in it then or not, is something no man knows but Philip. For what happened certainly happened without his presence, but whether without his will is another matter. De Soulis is close in his counsels. However it was, there was some connivance between the leaders who had personal forces within, and the besiegers without, and suddenly the garrison was called to witness that all their six captains had come to an agreement to surrender the castle, and their men were shown the agreement inscribed and sealed by all six, and perforce they accepted what their lords decreed. And that left the knights and squires without following, to be

disarmed and made prisoner unless they also accepted the
fiat. The king's forces were already within the gates. Thirty
young men were doled out like pay to Stephen's allies, and
vanished. Some have reappeared, bought free by their kin and
friends. Not Olivier."

"This we do know," said Hugh. "The Earl of Leicester has
the full list. No one has offered Olivier for ransom. No one
has said, though someone must know, who holds him."

"My Uncle Laurence has been enquiring everywhere,"
agreed Yves, "but can learn nothing. And he grows older, and
is needed in Devizes, where she mainly keeps her court these
days. But in Coventry I intend to bring this matter into the
open, and have an answer. They cannot deny me."

Cadfael, listening in silence, shook his head a little, almost
fondly, at such innocent confiding. King and empress, with
absolute if imagined victory almost within sight, were less
likely to give priority to a matter of simple individual justice
than this boy supposed. He was young, candid, born noble,
and serenely aware of his rights to fair dealing and courteous
consideration. He had some rough awakenings coming to him
before he would be fully armoured against the world and the
devil.

"And then," said Yves bitterly, "Philip handed over
Cricklade whole and entire to King Stephen, himself, his
garrison, arms, armour and all. I can't for my life imagine
why, what drove him to it. I've worn my wits out trying to
fathom it. Was it a simple calculation that he was labouring
more and more on the losing side, and could better his fortunes
by the change? In cold blood? Or in very hot blood, bitter
against his father for leaving Faringdon to its fate? Or was it
he who betrayed Faringdon in the first place? Was it by his
orders it was sold? I cannot see into his mind."

"But you at least have seen him," said Hugh, "and served
with him. I have never set eyes on him. If you cannot account
for what he has done now, yet you have worked alongside

him, you must have some view of him, as one man of another in the same alliance. How old can he be? Surely barely ten years your elder."

Yves shook the baffled bewilderment impatiently from him, and took time to think, "Around thirty. Robert's heir, William, must be a few years past that. A quiet man, Philip—he had dark moods, but a good officer. I would have said I liked him, if ever I had considered to answer that at all. I never would have believed he would change his coat—certainly never for gain or for fear. . . ."

"Let it be," said Cadfael placatingly, seeing how the boy laboured at the thing he could not understand. "Here are three of us not prepared to let Olivier lie unransomed. Wait for Coventry, and we shall see what we can uncover there."

They rode into Coventry in mid-afternoon of the following day, a fine, brisk day with gleams of chilly sunshine. The pleasure of the ride had diverted Yves for a while from his obsession, brightened his eyes and stung high colour into his cheeks. Approaching the city from the north, they found Earl Leofric's old defences still in timber, but sturdy enough, and the tangle of streets within well paved and maintained since the bishops had made this city their main base within the see. Roger de Clinton had continued the practice, though Lichfield was dearer to his own heart, for in these disturbed times Coventry was nearer the seat of dissension, and in more danger from the sporadic raids of rival armies, and he was not a man to steer clear of perils himself while his flock endured them.

And certainly his redoubtable presence had afforded the city a measure of protection, but for all that there were some scars and dilapidations to be seen along the streets, and an occasional raw-edged gap where a house had been stripped down to its foundations and not yet replaced. In a country which for several years now had been disputed in arms between two very uncousinly cousins, it was no wonder if private enemies and equally acquisitive neighbours joined in the plundering for themselves, independently of either faction. Even the Earl of Chester's small timber castle within the town had its scars to show, and would hardly be suitable for his occupation with the kind of retinue he intended to bring to the conference table, much less for entertaining his newly appeased and reconciled king. He would prefer the discreet distance of Mountsorrel in which to continue his careful wooing.

The city was divided between two lordships, the prior's half and the earl's half, and from time to time there was some grumbling and discontent over privileges varying between the two, but there was a shared and acknowledged town moot for all, and by and large they rubbed shoulders with reasonable amity. There were few more prosperous towns in England, and none more resilient and alert to opportunity. It was to be seen in the bustle in the streets. Merchants and tradesmen were busy setting out their wares to the best advantage, to catch the eyes of the assembling nobility. Whether they expected that the gathering would last long or produce any advance towards peace might be doubtful, but trade is trade, and where earls and barons were massing there would be profits to be made.

There were illustrious pennants afloat against the leaning house fronts, and fine liveries passing on horseback towards the gates of the priory and the houses of rest for pilgrims. Coventry possessed the relics of its own Saint Osburg, as well as an arm of Saint Augustine and many minor relics, and had thrived on its pilgrims ever since its founding just over a hundred years previously. This present crop of the wealthy and powerful, thought Cadfael, eyeing the evidences of their presence all about him, could hardly, for reputation's sake, depart without giving profitable reward for their entertainment and the Church's hospitality.

They wove their way at an easy walk through the murmur

and bustle of the streets, and long before they reached the gateway of Saint Mary's Priory Yves had begun to flush into eagerness, warmed by the air of excitement and hope that made the town seem welcoming and the possibility of conciliation a little nearer. He named the unfamiliar badges and banneroles they encountered on the way, and exchanged greetings with some of his own faction and status, young men in the service of the empress's loyal following.

"Hugh Bigod has made haste from Norfolk, he's here before us. . . . Those are some of his men. And there, you see the man on the black horse yonder? That's Reginald FitzRoy, half-brother to the empress, the younger one, the one Philip seized not a month ago, and the king made him set him free. I wonder," said Yves, "how Philip dared touch him, with Robert's hand always over him, for they do show very brotherly to each other. But give him his due, Stephen does play fair. He'd granted safe conducts, he stood by them."

They had reached the broad gate of the priory enclave, and turned into a great court alive with colour and quivering with movement. The few habited Benedictine brothers who were doing their best to go about their duties and keep the horarium of the day were totally lost among this throng of visiting magnates and their servitors, some arriving, some riding out to see the town or visit acquaintances, grooms coming and going with horses nervous and edgy in such a crowd, squires unsaddling and unloading their lords' baggage. Hugh, entering, drew aside to give free passage to a tall horseman, splendid in his dress and well attended, who was just mounting to ride forth.

"Roger of Hereford," said Yves, glowing, "the new earl. He whose father was killed by mishap, out hunting, a couple of years ago. And the man just looking back from the steps yonder—that's the empress's steward, Humphrey de Bohun. She must be already arrived—"

He broke off abruptly, stiffening, his mouth open on the

unfinished sentence, his eyes fixed in an incredulous stare. Cadfael, following the direction of the boy's fixed gaze, beheld a man striding down the stone steps of the guesthall opposite, for once the sole figure on the wide staircase, and in clear sight above the moving throng below. A very personable man, trimly built and moving with an elegant arrogance, his fair head uncovered, a short cloak swinging on one shoulder. Thirty-five years old, perhaps, and well assured of his worth. He reached the cobbles of the court, and the crowd parted to give him passage, as if they accepted him at his own valuation. But nothing there, surely, to cause Yves to check and stare, gathering dark brows into a scowl of animosity.

"He?" said Yves through his teeth. "Dare *he* show his face here?" And suddenly his ice melted into fire, and with a leap he was out of the saddle and surging forward into the path of the advancing stranger, and his sword was out of the scabbard and held at challenge, spinning grooms and horses aside out of his way. His voice rose loud and hard.

"You, de Soulis! Betrayer of your cause and your comrades. Dare *you* come among honest men?"

For one shocked instant every other voice within the court was stunned into silence; the next, every voice rose in a clamour of alarm, protest and outrage. And as the first clash had sent people scurrying out of the vortex, so an immediate reaction drew many inward in recoil, to attempt to prevent the threatened conflict. But de Soulis had whirled to confront his challenger, and had his own sword naked in his hand, circling about him to clear ground for his defence. And then they were at it in earnest, steel shrieking against steel.

CHAPTER THREE

HUGH SPRANG down, flinging his bridle on his horse's neck for a groom to retrieve, and plunged into the ring of affrighted people surrounding the contestants, out of range of the flashing swords. Cadfael followed suit, with resigned patience but without haste, since he could hardly do more or better to quiet this disturbance than Hugh would be able to do. It could not go on long enough to be mortal, there were too many powers, both regal and clerical, in residence here to permit anything so unseemly, and by the noise now reverberating on all sides from wall to wall around the court, every one of those powers would be present and voluble within minutes.

Nevertheless, once on his feet he made his way hastily enough into the heaving throng, thrusting through to where he might at least be within reach, should any opportunity offer of catching at a whirling sleeve and hauling one of the combatants back out of danger. If this was indeed de Soulis, the renegade of Faringdon, he had a dozen years the advantage of Yves, and showed all too alert and practised with the sword. Experience tells. Cadfael burrowed sturdily, distantly aware of a great voice bellowing from behind him, somewhere in the gateway, and of a flashing of lustrous colours above him in the doorway of the guesthall, but so intent on breaking through the circle that he missed the most effective interven-

34

tion of all, until it was launched without warning over his left shoulder, sheering through clean into the circling sword play.

A long staff was thrust powerfully past him, prising bodies apart to shear a way through. A long arm followed it, and a long, lean, vigorous body, and silver flashed at the head of the stave, striking the locked swords strongly upward, bruising the hands that held them. Yves lost his grip, and the blade rang and re-echoed on the cobbles. De Soulis retrieved his hold with a lunge, but the hilt quivered in his hand, and he sprang back out of range of the heavy silver mount crowning the staff now upright between them. A breathless silence fell.

"Put up your weapons," said Bishop Roger de Clinton, without so much as raising his voice. "Think shame to bare your swords within this precinct. You put your souls in peril. Our intent here is peace."

The antagonists stood breathing hard, Yves flushed and half rebellious still, de Soulis eyeing his attacker with a chill smile and narrowed eyes.

"My lord," he said with smooth civility, "I had no thought of offending until this rash young man drew on me. For no sane reason that I know of, for I never set eyes on him before." He slid his blade coolly into the scabbard, with a deliberately ceremonious gesture of reverence towards the bishop. "He rides in here from the street, stranger to me, and begins to abuse me like a kennel brawler. I drew to keep my head."

"He well knows," flashed Yves, burning, "why I call him turncoat, renegade, betrayer of better men. Good knights lie in castle dungeons because of him."

"Silence!" said the bishop, and was instantly obeyed. "Whatever your quarrels, they have no place within these walls. We are here to dispose of all such divisions between honourable men. Pick up your word. Sheathe it! Do not draw it again on this sacred ground. Not upon any provocation! I so charge you, as for the Church. And here are also those who will lay the same charge on you, as your sovereigns and liege lords."

The great voice that had bellowed orders on entering the gate upon this unseemly spectacle had advanced upon the suddenly muted circle in the shape of a big, fair, commanding and very angry man. Cadfael knew him at once, from a meeting years past, in his siege camp in Shrewsbury, though the years between had sown some ashen threads in his yellow hair, and seams of anxiety and care in his handsome, open face. King Stephen, soon roused, soon placated, brave, impetuous but inconstant, a good-natured and generous man who had yet spent all the years of his reign in destructive warfare. And that flash of bright colours in the doorway of the guesthall, Cadfael realized at the same moment, was, must be, the other one, the woman who challenged Stephen's sovereignty. Tall and erect against the dimness within the hall, splendidly apparelled and in her proud prime, there stood old King Henry's sole surviving legitimate child, Empress Maud by her first marriage, countess of Anjou by her second, the uncrowned Lady of the English.

She did not condescend to come down to them, but stood quite still and viewed the scene with a disinterested and slightly disdainful stare, only inclining her head in acknowledgement of the king's reverence. She was regally handsome, her hair dark and rich under the gilded net of her coif, her eyes large and direct, as unnerving as the straight stare of a Byzantine saint in a mosaic, and as indifferent. She was past forty, but as durable as marble.

"Say no word, either of you," said the king, towering over the offenders, even over the bishop, who was tall by most men's standards, "for we'll hear none. Here you are in the Church's discipline, and had best come to terms with it. Keep your quarrels for another time and place, or better still, put them away for ever. They have no place here. My lord bishop, give your orders now as to this matter of bearing arms, and announce it formally when you preside in hall tomorrow. Banish all weapons if you will, or let us have some firm regulation as to their wear, and I will see to it that whoever offends against your rule shall pay his dues in full."

"I would not presume to deprive any man of the right to bear arms," said the bishop firmly. "I can, with full justification, take measures to regulate their use within these walls and during these grave discussions. In going about the town, certainly swords may be worn as customary, a man might well feel incomplete without his sword." His own vigorous form and aquiline face could as well have belonged to a warrior as a bishop. And was it not said of him that his heart was already set on playing more than a passive role in the defence of the Christian kingdom of Jerusalem? "Within these walls," he said with deliberation, "steel must not be drawn. Within the hall in session, not even worn, but laid by in the lodgings. And no weapon must ever be worn to the offices of the Church. Whatever the outcome, no man shall challenge another man in arms, for any reason soever, until we who are met here again separate. If your Grace is content so?"

"I am content," said Stephen. "This does well. You, gentlemen, bear it in mind, and see to it you keep faith." His blue, bright gaze swept over them both with the like broad, impersonal warning. Neither face meant anything to him, not even to which faction they belonged. Probably he had never seen either of them before, and would forget their faces as soon as he turned his back on them.

"Then I will put the case also to the lady," said Roger de Clinton, "and declare terms when we gather tomorrow morning."

"Do so, with my goodwill!" said the king heartily, and strode away towards the groom who was holding his horse within the gate.

The lady, Cadfael observed when he looked again towards the doorway of the guesthall, had already withdrawn her aloof

and disdainful presence from the scene, and retired to her
own apartments within.

Yves fumed his way in black silence to their lodging in one
of the pilgrim houses within the precinct, half in a boy's
chagrin at being chastened in public, half in a man's serious
rage at having to relinquish his quarrel.

"Why should you fret?" Hugh argued sensibly, humouring
the boy but warily considering the man. "De Soulis, if that
was de Soulis, has had his ears clipped, too. There's no denying
it was you began it, but he was nothing loth to spit you, if
he could have done it. Now you've brought about your own
deprivation. You might have known the Church would take
it badly having swords drawn here on their ground."

"I did know it," Yves admitted grudgingly, "if I'd ever
stopped to think. But the sight of him, striding around as if
in his own castle wards . . . I never thought he would show
here. Good God, what must she feel, seeing him so brazen,
and the wrong he has done her! She favoured him, she gave
him office!"

"She gave office to Philip no less," said Hugh hardly. "Will
you fly at his throat when he comes into the conference hall?"

"Philip is another matter," said Yves, flaring. "He gave over
Cricklade, yes, that we know, but that whole garrison went
willingly. Do you think I do not know there could be good
reasons for a man to change his allegiance? Honest reasons?
Do you think she is easy to serve? I have seen her turn cold
and insolent even to Earl Robert, seen her treat him like a
peasant serf when the mood was on her. And he her sole
strength, and enduring all for her sake!"

He wrung momentarily at a grief Cadfael had already
divined. The Lady of the English was gallant, beautiful, contending for the rights of her young son rather than for her
own. All these innocent young men of hers were a little in
love with her, wanted her to be perfect, turned indignant backs

on all manifestations that she was no such saint, but knew very well in their sore hearts all her arrogance and vindictiveness, and could not escape the pain. This one, at least, had got as far as blurting out the truth of his knowledge of her.

"But this de Soulis," said Yves, recovering his theme and his animosity, "conspired furtively to let the enemy into Faringdon, and sold into captivity all those honest knights and squires who would not go with him. And among them Olivier! If he had been honest in his own choice he would have allowed them theirs, he would have opened the gates for them, and let them go forth honourably in arms, to fight him again from another base. No, he sold them. He sold Olivier. That I do not forgive."

"Possess your soul in patience," said Brother Cadfael, "until we know what we most need to know, where to look for him. Fall out with no one, for who knows which of them here may be able to give us an answer?" And by the time we get that answer, he thought, eyeing Yves' lowering brows and set jaw tolerantly, revenges may well have gone by the board, no longer of any significance.

"I have no choice now but to keep the peace," said Yves, resentfully but resignedly. None the less, he was still brooding when a novice of the priory came looking for him, to bid him to the empress's presence. In all innocence the young brother called her the Countess of Anjou. She would not have liked that. After the death of her first elderly husband she had retained and insisted on her title of empress still; the descent to mere countess by her second husband's rank had displeased her mightily.

Yves departed in obedience to the summons torn between pleasure and trepidation, half expecting to be taken to task for the unbecoming scene in the great court. She had never yet turned her sharp displeasure on him, but once at least he had witnessed its blistering effect on others. And yet she could charm the bird from the tree when she chose, and he had been thrown the occasional blissful moment during his brief sojourn in her household.

This time one of her ladies was waiting for him on the threshold of the empress's apartments in the prior's own guest-house, a young girl Yves did not know, dark-haired and bright-eyed, a very pretty girl who had picked up traces of her mistress's self-confidence and boldness. She looked Yves up and down with a rapid, comprehensive glance, and took her time about smiling, as though he had to pass a test before being accepted. But the smile, when it did come, indicated that she found him something a little better than merely acceptable. It was a pity he hardly noticed.

"She is waiting for you. The earl of Norfolk commended you, it seems. Come within." And crossing the threshold into the presence she lowered her eyes discreetly, and made her deep reverence with practised grace. "Madame, Messire Hugonin!"

The empress was seated in a stall-like chair piled with cushions, her dark hair loosed from its coif and hanging over her shoulder in a heavy, lustrous braid. She wore a loose gown of deep blue velvet, against which her ivory white skin glowed with a live sheen. The light of candles was kind to her, and her carriage was always that of a queen, if an uncrowned queen. Yves bent the knee to her with unaffected fervour, and stood to wait her pleasure.

"Leave us!" said Maud, without so much as a glance at the lingering girl, or the older lady who stood at her shoulder. And when they were gone from the room: "Come closer! Here are all too many stretched ears at too many doors. Closer still! Let me look at you."

He stood, a little nervously, to be studied long and thoughtfully, and the huge, Byzantine eyes passed over him at leisure, like the first stroking caress of the flaying knife.

"Norfolk says you did your errand well," she said then.

"Like a natural diplomat. It's true I was in some doubt of him, but he is here. I marked little of the diplomat about you this afternoon in the great court."

Yves felt himself flushing to the hair, but she hushed any protest or excuse he might have been about to utter with a raised hand and a cool smile. "No, say nothing! I admired your loyalty and your spirit, if I could not quite compliment you on your discretion."

"I was foolish," he said. "I am sensible of it."

"Then that is quickly disposed of," said the empress, "for at this moment I am, officially, reproving you for the folly, and repeating the bishop's orders to you, as the aggressor, to curb your resentment hereafter. For the sake of appearances, as no doubt Stephen is chastising the other fool. Well, now you have understood me, and you know you may not offer any open affront or injury to any man within these walls. With that in agreement between us, you may leave me."

He made his obeisance, somewhat confused in mind, and turned again to the closed door. Behind him the incisive voice, softened and still, said clearly: "All the same, I must confess I should not be greatly grieved to see Brien de Soulis dead at my feet."

Yves went out in a daze, the soft, feline voice pursuing him until he had closed the door between. And there, standing patiently a few yards away, waiting with folded hands to be summoned back to her mistress, the elder lady turned her thin oval face and dark, incurious eyes upon him, asking nothing, confiding nothing. No doubt she had seen many young men emerge from that imperial presence, in many states of mortification, elation, devotion and despair, and refrained, as she did now, from making them aware how well she could read the signs. He drew his disrupted wits together, and made the best he could of his withdrawal, passing by her with a somewhat stiff reverence. Not until he was out in the darkened court, with the chill of the November twilight about him, did he pause to draw breath, and recall, with frightening clarity, every word that had been said in that brief encounter.

Had the empress's gentlewoman overheard the valedictory words? Could she have heard them, or any part of them, as the door opened to let him out? And would she, even for an instant, have interpreted them as he had? No, surely impossible! He remembered now who she was, closer than any other to her liege lady: the widow of a knight in the earl of Surrey's following, and herself born a de Redvers, from a minor branch of the family of Baldwin de Redvers, the empress's earl of Devon. Impeccably noble, fit to serve an empress. And old enough and wise enough to be a safe repository for an empress's secrets. Perhaps too wise to hear even what she heard! But if she had caught the last words, how did she read them?

He crossed the court slowly, hearing again the soft, insistent voice. No, it was he who was mangling the sense of her words. Surely she had been doing no more than giving bitter expression to a perfectly natural hatred of a man who had betrayed her. What else could be expected of her? No, she had not been even suggesting a course of action, much less ordering. We say these things in passion, into empty air, not with intent.

And yet she had quite deliberately instructed him: You may not offer any *open* affront or injury . . . And then: But all the same, I should not be greatly grieved . . . And with that you may leave me. Yves Hugonin! You have wit enough to get my meaning.

Impossible! He was doing her great wrong, it was he who had the devious mind, seeing her words twisted and askew. And he must and would put this unworthiness clean out of his mind and his memory.

He said no word to Hugh or to Cadfael, he would have been ashamed to probe the wound openly. He shrugged off

Hugh's teasing: "Well, at any rate she did not eat you!" with an arduous smile, and declined to be drawn. But not even Compline, in solemn state among bishops and magnates in preparation for the next day's conference, could quite cleanse the disquiet from his mind.

In the chapter-house of Saint Mary's Priory, after solemn Mass, the sovereignty and nobility of England met in full session. Three bishops presided, Winchester, Ely, and Roger de Clinton of Coventry and Lichfield. All three, inevitably, had partisan inclination towards one or other of the contending parties, but it appeared that they made a genuine effort to put all such interest aside, and concentrate with profound prayer on the attempt to secure agreement. Brother Cadfael, angling for a place outside the open door, where observers might at least glimpse and overhear the exchanges within, took it as a warning against any great optimism that those attending tended to group defensively together with their own kind, the empress and her allies on one side in solid phalanx, King Stephen and his magnates and sheriffs on the other. So marked a tendency to mass as for battle boded no good, however freely friends might come together across the divide once out of the chapter-house. There was Hugh, shoulder to shoulder with the Earl of Leicester and only four or five places from the king's own seat, and Yves upon the other side, in attendance on Hugh Bigod, earl of Norfolk, who had commended him to the empress for an errand well done. Once loosed from this grave meeting they would come together as naturally as right hand and left on a job to be done; within, they were committed to left and right in opposition.

Cadfael viewed the ranks of the great with intent curiosity, for most of them he had never seen before. Leicester he already knew: Robert Beaumont, secure in his earldom since the age of fourteen, intelligent, witty and wise, one of the few, perhaps, who were truly working behind the scenes towards a

just and sensible compromise. Robert Bossu they called him,
Robert the Hunchback, by reason of his one misshapen shoulder, though in action the flaw impeded him not at all, and
scarcely affected the compact symmetry of his body. Beside
him was William Martel, the king's steward, who had covered
Stephen's retreat a few years back at Wilton, and himself been
made prisoner, and bought free by Stephen at the cost of a
valuable castle. William of Ypres was beside him, the chief
of the king's Flemings, and beyond him Cadfael, craning and
peering in the doorway between the heads of others equally
intent, could just see Nigel, Bishop of Ely, newly reconciled
to the king after some years of disfavour, and no doubt wishful
to keep his recovered place among the approved.

On the other side Cadfael had in full view the man who
was the heart and spirit of the empress's cause, Robert, earl
of Gloucester, constant at his half-sister's side here as he
fought her battles in the field. A man of fifty, broad built,
plain in his clothing and accoutrements, a lacing of grey in
his brown hair, lines of weariness in his comely face. Grey
in his short beard, too, accentuating the strong lines of his
jaw in two silver streaks. His son and heir, William, stood at
his shoulder. The younger son, Philip, if he was present here,
would be among those on the opposing side. This one was
built sturdily, like his father, and resembled him in the face.
Humphrey de Bohun was there beside them, and Roger of
Hereford. Beyond that Cadfael could not see.

But he could hear the voices, even identify some whose
tones he had heard on rare occasions before. Bishop de Clinton
opened the session by welcoming all comers in goodwill to
the house of which he was titular abbot as well as bishop,
and asserting, as he had promised, the ban on the carrying of
weapons either here in hall, or, under any circumstances, when
attending the office of the Church, then he handed over the
opening argument to Henry of Blois, King Stephen's younger
brother and bishop of Winchester. This high, imperious voice

Cadfael had never heard before, though the effects of its utterances had influenced the lives of Englishmen for years, both secular and monastic.

It was not the first time that Henry of Blois had attempted to bring his brother and his cousin to sit down together and work out some compromise that would at least put a stop to active warfare, even if it meant maintaining a divided and guarded realm, for ever in danger of local eruptions. Never yet had he had any success. But he approached this latest endeavour with the same vigour and force, whatever his actual expectations. He drew for his audience the deplorable picture of a country wracked and wasted in senseless contention, through years of struggle without positive gain to either party, and a total loss to the common people. He painted a battle which could neither be won by either party nor lost by either, but would be solved only by some compounding that bound them both. He was eloquent, trenchant, and brief. And they listened; but they had always listened, and either never really heard, never understood, or never believed him. He had sometimes wavered and shifted in his own allegiance, and everyone knew it. Now he challenged both combatants with equal asperity. When he ended, by his rising cadence inviting response, there was a brief silence, but with a curious suggestion in its hush that two jealous presences were manoeuvring for the advantage. No good omen there!

It was the empress who took up the challenge, her voice high and steely, raised to carry. Stephen, thought Cadfael, had left her the opening of the field not out of policy, as might have been supposed, since the first to speak is the first to be forgotten, but out of his incorrigible chivalry towards all women, even this woman. She was declaring, as yet with cautious mildness, her right to be heard in this or any other gathering purporting to speak for England. She was chary of revealing all her keenest weapons at the first assay, and went, for her, very circumspectly, harking back to old King Henry's lamentable loss of his only remaining legitimate son in the wreck of the White Ship off Barfleur, years previously, leaving her as unchallenged heiress to his kingdom. A status which he had taken care to ensure while he lived, by summoning all his magnates to hear his will and swear fealty to their future queen. As they had done, and afterwards thought better of acknowledging a woman as sovereign, and accepted Stephen without noticeable reluctance, when for once he moved fast and decisively, installed himself, and assumed the crown. The small seed which had proliferated into all this chaos.

They talked, and Cadfael listened. Stephen asserted with his usual vulnerable candour his own right by crowning and coronation, but also refrained as yet from inviting anger. A few voices, forcefully quiet, argued the case of those lower in the hierarchies, who were left to bear the heaviest burden. Robert Bossu, forbearing from this seldom regarded plea, bluntly declared the economic idiocy of further wasting the country's resources, and a number of his young men, Hugh among them, echoed and reinforced his argument by reference to their own shires. Enough words were launched back and forth to supply a Bible, but not too often mentioning "agreement," "compromise," "reason" or "peace." The session was ending before an unexpected minor matter was raised.

Yves had chosen his time. He waited until Roger de Clinton, scanning the ranks which had fallen silent, rose to declare an end to this first hearing, relieved, perhaps even encouraged, that it had passed without apparent rancour. Yves' voice rose suddenly but quietly, with deferential mildness; he had himself well in hand this time. Cadfael shifted his position vainly to try and get a glimpse of him, and clasped his hands in a fervent prayer that this calm should survive.

"My lords, your Grace . . ."

The bishop gave way courteously and let him speak.

"My lords, if I may raise a point, in all humility . . ."

The last quality the young and impetuous should lay claim to, but at least he was trying.

"There are some outstanding minor matters which might tend to reconciliation, if they could be cleared up now. Even agreement on a detail must surely tend to agreement on greater things. There are prisoners held on both sides. While we are at truce for this good purpose would it not be just and right to declare a general release?"

A murmur arose from partisans of both factions, and grew into a growl. No, neither of them would concede that, to put back into the opposing ranks good fighting men at present disarmed and out of the reckoning. The empress swept the idea aside with a gesture of her hand. "These are matters to be dealt with in the terms of peace," she said, "not priorities."

The king, for once in agreement upon not agreeing, said firmly: "We are here first to come to terms upon the main issue. This is a matter to be discussed and negotiated afterwards."

"My lord bishop," said Yves, fixing sensibly upon the one ally upon whom he could rely in considering the plight of captives, "if such an exchange must be deferred, at least may I ask for information concerning certain knights and squires made prisoner at Faringdon this past summer. There are some among them held by unnamed captors. Should not their friends and kin, who wish to ransom them, at least be provided that opportunity?"

"If they are held for gain," said the bishop, with a slight edge of distaste in his voice, "surely the holder will be the first to offer them for his profit. Do you say this has not been done?"

"Not in all cases, my lord. I think," said Yves clearly, "that some are held not for gain but for hate, in personal revenge for some real or imagined offence. There are many private feuds bred out of faction."

The king shifted in his chair impatiently, and repeated

loudly: "With private feuds we are not concerned. This is irrelevant here. What is one man's fate beside the fate of the realm?"

"Every man's fate *is* the fate of the realm," cried Yves boldly. "If injustice is done to one, it is one too many. The injury is to all, and the whole realm suffers."

Over the growing hubbub of many voices busily crying one another down, the bishop raised authoritative hands. "Silence! Whether this is the time and place or no, this young man speaks truth. A fair law should apply to all." And to Yves, standing his ground apprehensive but determined: "You have, I think, a particular case in mind. One of those made prisoner after Faringdon fell."

"Yes, my lord. And held in secret. No ransom has been asked, nor do his friends, or my uncle, his lord, know where to enquire for his price. If his Grace would but tell me who holds him . . ."

"I did not parcel out my prisoners under my own seal," blared the king, growing louder and more restive, but as much because he wanted his dinner, Cadfael judged, as because he had any real interest in what was delaying him. It was characteristic of him that, having gained a large number of valuable prizes, he should throw the lot of them to his acquisitive supporters and walk away from the bargaining, leaving them to bicker over the distribution of the booty. "I knew few of them, and remember no names. I left them to my castellan to hand out fairly."

Yves took that up eagerly, before the point could be lost. "Your Grace, your castellan of Faringdon is here present. Be so generous as to let him give me an answer." And he launched the question before it could be forbidden. "Where is Olivier de Bretagne, and in whose keeping?"

He had kept his voice deliberate and cool, but he hurled the name like a lance for all that, and not at the king, but clean across the open space that divided the factions, into the face of de Soulis. Stephen's tolerance he needed if he was to get an answer. Stephen could command where no one else could do more than request. And Stephen's patience was wearing thin, not so much with the persistent squire as with the whole process of this overlong session.

"It is a reasonable request," said the bishop, with the sharp edge still on his voice.

"In the name of God," agreed the king explosively, "tell the fellow what he wants to know, and let us be done with the matter."

The voice of de Soulis rose in smooth and prompt obedience, from among the king's unseen minor ranks, well out of Cadfael's sight, and so modestly retired from prominence that it sounded distant. "Your Grace, I would willingly, if I knew the answer. At Faringdon I made no claim for myself, but withdrew from the council and left it to the knights of the garrison. Those of them who returned to your Grace's allegiance, of course," he said with acid sweetness. "I never enquired as to their decisions, and apart from such as have already been offered for ransom and duly redeemed, I have no knowledge of the whereabouts of any. The clerks may have drawn up a list. If so, I have never asked to see it."

Long before he ended, the deliberate sting against those of the Faringdon garrison who had remained true to their salt had already raised an ominous growl of rage among the empress's followers, and a ripple of movement along the ranks, that suggested swords might have been half out of scabbards if they had not been forbidden within the hall. Yves' raised voice striking back in controlled but passionate anger roused a counter roar from the king's adherents. "He lies, your Grace! He was there every moment, he ordered all. He lies in his teeth!"

Another moment, and there would have been battle, even without weapons, barring the common man's weapons of fists, feet and teeth. But the Bishop of Winchester had risen in indignant majesty to second Roger de Clinton's thunderous demand for order and silence, king and empress were both on their feet and flashing menacing lightnings, and the mounting hubbub subsided gradually, though the acrid smell of anger and hatred lingered in the quivering air.

"Let us adjourn this session," said Bishop de Clinton grimly, when the silence and stillness had held good for uneasy and shaming minutes, "without further hot words that have no place here. We will meet again after noon, and I charge you all that you come in better and more Christian condition, and further, that after that meeting, whatever it brings, you who truly mean in the heart what your mouths have uttered, that you seek peace here, shall attend at Vespers, unarmed, in goodwill to all, in enmity towards none, to pray for that peace."

CHAPTER FOUR

HE IS lying," repeated Yves, still flushed and scowling over the priory's frugal board, but eating like a hungry boy nevertheless. "He never left that council for a moment. Can you conceive of him forgoing any prize for himself, or being content with less than the best? He knows very well who has Olivier in hold. But if Stephen cannot force him to speak out—or will not!—how can any other man get at him?"

"Even a liar," reflected Hugh judicially, "for I grant you he probably is that!—may tell truth now and again. For I tell you this, there seem to be very few, if any, who do know what happened to Olivier. I've been probing where I could, but with no success, and I daresay Cadfael has been keeping his ears open among the brothers. Better, I do believe the bishop will be making his own enquiries, having heard what he heard from you this morning."

"If I were you," said Cadfael, profoundly pondering, "I would keep the matter out of the chapter-house. It's certain king and empress will have to declare themselves, and neither will relish being pestered to go straying after the fate of one squire, when their own fortunes are in the balance. Go round about, if there are any others here who were in Faringdon. And I will speak to the prior. Even monastic ears can pick up whatever rumours are passed around, as fast as any, and all the better for being silent themselves."

But Yves remained blackly brooding, and would not be deflected. "De Soulis knows, and I will have it out with him, if I must carve it out of his treacherous heart. Oh, say no word!" he said, waving away whatever Cadfael might have had on the tip of his tongue. "I know I am hobbled within here, I cannot touch him."

Now why, thought Cadfael, should he state the obvious with so much lingering emphasis, yet so quietly, as if to remind himself rather than reassure anyone else. And why should his normally wide-eyed, candid gaze turn dubiously inward, looking back, very wearily, on something imperfectly understood and infinitely disquieting?

"But both he and I will have to leave the pale of the Church soon," said Yves, shaking himself abruptly out of his brooding, "and then nothing hinders but I should meet him in arms, and have the truth out of his flesh."

Brother Cadfael went out through the crowds in the great court, and made his way into the priory church. The grandees would not yet have left their high table to resume discussions so little likely to produce profitable results; he had time to retire into some quiet corner and put the world away from him for a while. But quiet corners were few, even in the church. Numbers of the lesser partisans had also found it convenient to gather where they could confer without being overheard, and had their heads together in the shelter of altars and in the carrels of the cloister. Visiting clergy were parading nave and choir and studying the dressing of the altars, and a few of the brothers, returning to their duties after the half-hour of rest, threaded their way silently among the strangers.

There was a girl standing before the high altar, with modestly folded hands and lowered eyes. In prayer? Cadfael doubted it. The altar lamp shed a clear, rosy light over her slight, confident smile, and the man who stood close at her shoulder was speaking very discreetly and respectfully into her ear, but with something of the same private smile in the curve of his lips. Ah, well! A young girl here among so many personable young men, and herself virtually the only one of her sex and years in this male assemblage, might well revel in her privileges while they lasted, and exploit her opportunities. Cadfael had seen her before, blithely following the empress to Mass that morning, bearing the imperial prayer-book and a fine wool shawl in case the lady felt the cold in this vast stony cavern before service ended. The niece of the older gentlewoman, he had been told. And those three, one royal, two from the ranks of the baronage, the only women in this precinct among the entire nobility of the land. Enough to turn any girl's head. Though by her pose and her carriage, and the assurance with which she listened and made no response, Cadfael judged that this one would not lightly make any concessions, or ever lose sight of her real advantages. She would listen and she would smile, and she might even suggest the possibility of going further, but her balance was secure. With a hundred or more young men here to see and admire, and flatter her with enjoyable attentions, the first and boldest was not likely to advance very far until others had shown their paces. She was young enough to take delight in the game, and shrewd enough to survive it untouched.

Now she had recalled the approaching hour and the exigence of her service, and turned to depart, to attend her mistress again to the door of the chapter-house. She moved decisively, walking briskly enough to indicate that she did not care whether her courtier followed her or not, but not so rapidly as to leave him behind. Until that moment Cadfael had not recognized the man. The first and boldest—yes, so he would be. The fair head, the elegant, self-assured stride, the subtle, half-condescending smile of Brien de Soulis followed the girl out of the church with arrogant composure, to all appearances as certain that there was no haste, that she would come his way whenever he chose, as she was certain she could play him and discard him. And which of two such overweening creatures would prevail was a matter for serious speculation.

Cadfael felt curious enough to follow them out into the court. The older gentlewoman had come out from the guesthall looking for her niece. She contemplated the pair of them without any perceptible emotion, her face impassive, and turned to re-enter the hall, looking back for the girl to follow her. De Soulis halted to favour them both with a courtly reverence, and withdrew at leisure towards the chapter-house. And Cadfael turned back into the cloister garth, and paced the bleached wintry sward very thoughtfully.

The empress's gentlewoman could hardly approve her niece's dalliance, however restrained, with the empress's traitor and renegade. She would be concerned to warn the girl against any such foolishness. Or perhaps she knew her own kin better, and saw no reason for concern, being well aware that this was a shrewd young woman who would certainly do nothing to compromise her own promising future in the empress's household.

Well, he had better be turning his mind to graver matters than the fortunes of young women he had never seen before. It was almost time for the feuding factions to meet yet again in session. And how many of them on either side were genuinely in search of peace? How many in pursuit of total victory with the sword?

When Cadfael manoeuvred his way as close as he could to the doorway of the chapter-house, it seemed that Bishop de Clinton had ceded the presidium on this occasion to the Bishop of Winchester, perhaps hopeful that so powerful a prelate would exert more influence upon obdurate minds, by virtue of his royal blood, and his prestige as recently filling the office of papal legate to the realm of England. Bishop Henry was just rising to call the assembly to order, when hasty footsteps and a brusque but civil demand for passage started the crowding watchers apart, and let through into the centre of the chapter-house a tall newcomer, still cloaked and booted for riding. Behind him in the court a groom led away the horse from which he had just dismounted, the hoofbeats receding slowly towards the stables. Eased to a walk now after a long ride, and the horseman dusty from the wind-dried roads.

The latecomer crossed the open space between the partisans with a long, silent stride, made a deferential obeisance to the presiding bishop, who received it with a questioning frown and the merest severe inclination of his head, and bent to kiss the king's hand, all without compromising for an instant his own black dignity. The king smiled on him with open favour.

"Your Grace, I ask pardon for coming late. I had work to do before I could leave Malmesbury." His voice was pitched low, and yet had a clear, keen edge to it. "My lords, forgive my travel-stained appearance, I hoped to come before this assembly with better grace, but am come too late to delay the proceedings longer."

His manner towards the bishops was meticulously courteous. To the empress he said no word, but made her a bow of such ceremonious civility and with such an aloof countenance that its arrogance was plainly apparent. And his father he had passed by without a glance, and now, turning, confronted with a steady, distant stare, as though he had never seen him before.

For this was certainly Philip FitzRobert, the earl of Gloucester's younger son. There was even a resemblance, though they were built differently. This man was not compact and foursquare, but long and sinewy, abrupt but graceful of movement and dark of colouring. Above the twin level strokes of his black brows the cliff of forehead rose loftily into thick, waving hair, and below them his eyes were like damped-down fires, muted but alive. Yet the likeness was there, stressed most strongly by the set of long, passionate lips and formidable jaw. It was the image carried one generation further into extremes. What would be called constant in the father would be more truly stubborn in the son.

His coming, it seemed, had cast a curious constraint upon the company, which could not be eased without his initiative. He took pains to release them from the momentary tension, with an apologetic gesture of hand and head in deference to the bishops. "My lords, I beg you'll proceed, and I'll withdraw." And he drew back into the ranks of King Stephen's men, and melted smoothly through them to the rear. Even so, his presence was almost palpable in the air, stiffening spines, causing ears to prick and hackles to rise in the nape of the neck, all about him. Many there had held that he would not dare to come where his affronted father and his betrayed liege lady were. It appeared, after all, that there was very little this man would not dare, nor much that he could not carry off with steely composure, too commanding to be written off lightly as effrontery.

He had somewhat discomposed even the bishop of Winchester, but the hesitation was only a moment long and the impressive voice rose with authority, calling them peremptorily to prayer, and to the consideration of the grave matters for which they were gathered together.

As yet the principals had done no more than state, with caution, the bases of their claims to sovereignty. It was high time to elicit from them some further consideration of how far they were willing to go, by way of acknowledging each the other's claim. Bishop Henry approached the empress very circumspectly; he had long experience of trying to manipulate her, and breaking his forehead against the impregnable wall of her obstinacy. Above all, avoid ever referring to her as the countess of Anjou. Accurate enough, that was yet a title she regarded as derogatory to her status as a king's daughter and an emperor's consort.

"Madam," said the bishop weightily, "you know the need and the urgency. This realm has suffered dissension all too long, and without reconciliation there can be no healing. Royal cousins should be able to come together in harmony. I entreat you, search your heart and speak, give a lead to your people as to the way we should take from this day and this place, to put an end to the wastage of life and land."

"I have given years of consideration already," said the empress crisply, "to these same matters, and it seems to me that the truth is plain, and no amount of gazing can change it, and no amount of argument make it untrue. It is exactly as it was when my father died. He was king unquestioned, undisputed, and by the loss of a brother, I was left the sole living child of my father by his lawful wife, Matilda, his queen, herself daughter to the king of Scots. There is no man here present who does not know these things. There is no man in England who dare deny them. How then could there be any other heir to this kingdom when the king my father died?"

Not a word, of course, reflected Cadfael, stretching his ears outside the doorway, of the dozen or so children the old king had left behind, scattered about his realm, by other mothers. They did not count, not even the best of them, who stood patient and steadfast at her shoulder, and could have out-royalled both these royal rivals had his pedigree accorded with Norman law and custom. In Wales he would have had his rights, the eldest son of his father, and the most royal.

"Yet to make all sure," pursued the dominant voice proudly, "my father the king himself broached the matter of succession, at his Christmas court, nine years before his death, and called on all the magnates of his realm to take a solemn oath to receive me, descendant of fourteen kings, as his heiress, and their queen after him. And so they did, every man. My lords bishops, it was William of Corbeil, then Archbishop of Canterbury, who first took the oath. My uncle, the king of Scots, was the second, and the third who swore his allegiance to me," she said, raising her voice and honing it like a dagger, "was Stephen, my cousin, who now comes here with argument of royalty against me."

A dozen voices were murmuring by then, deprecatory and anxious on one side, in rumbling anger on the other. The bishop said loudly and firmly: "It is no place here to bring forward all the deeds of the past. There have been enough, not all upon one part. We stand now where these faults and betrayals, from whatever source, have left us, and from where we stand we must proceed, we have no other choice. What is to be done *now*, to undo such ills as may be undone, is what we have to fathom. Let all be said with that in mind, and not revenges for things long past."

"I ask only that truth be recognized as truth," she said inflexibly. "I am lawful queen of England by hereditary right, by my father's royal decree and by the solemn oaths of all his magnates to accept and acknowledge me. If I wished, I cannot change my status, and as God sees me, I will not. That I am denied my right alters nothing. I have not surrendered it."

"You cannot surrender what you do not possess," taunted a voice from the rear ranks of Stephen's supporters. And instantly there were a dozen on either side crying out provocation, insult and mockery, until Stephen crashed his fist down on the arms of his chair and bellowed for order even above the bishop's indignant plea.

"My imperial cousin is entitled to her say," he proclaimed firmly, "and has spoken her mind boldly. Now for my part I have somewhat to say of those symbols which not so much decree or predict sovereignty, but confer it and confirm it. For the countess of Anjou to inherit that crown to which she lays claim by inheritance, it would be needful to deprive me of what I already hold. I hold by coronation, by consecration, by anointing. That acceptance she was promised, I came, I asked for, I won fairly. The oil that consecrated me cannot be washed away. That is the right by which I claim what I hold. And what I hold I will not give up. No part of anything I have won, in any way soever, will I give up. I make no concession, none."

And with that said, upon either part, the one pleading by blood-right, the other by both secular and clerical acknowledgement and investiture, what point was there in saying anything further? Yet they tried. It was the turn of the moderate voices for a while, and not urging brotherly or cousinly forgiveness and love, but laying down bluntly the brutal facts; for if this stalemate, wrangling and waste continued, said Robert Bossu with cold, clear emphasis, there would eventually be nothing worth annexing or retaining, only a desolation where the victor, if the survivor so considered himself, might sit down in the ashes and moulder. But that, too, was ignored. The empress, confident in her knowledge that her husband and son held all Normandy in their grasp, and most of these English magnates had lands over there to protect, and must cling to what favour they had with the house of Anjou to accomplish that feat, felt certain of eventual victory in England no less. And Stephen, well aware that his star was in the ascendant here in England, what with this year's glittering gains, was equally sure the rest must fall into his hands, and was willing to risk what might be happening overseas, and leave it to be dealt with later.

The voices of cold reason were talking, as usual, to deaf ears. The bulk of the talk now was little more than an exchange of accusations and counter accusations. Henry of Winchester held the balance gallantly enough, and fended off actual conflict, but could do no better than that. And there were many, Cadfael noted, who listened dourly and said nothing at all. Never a word from Robert of Gloucester, never a word from his son and enemy, Philip FitzRobert. Mutually sceptical, they refrained from waste of breath and effort, in whatever direction.

"Nothing will come of it," said Robert Bossu resignedly

in Hugh Beringar's ear, when the two monodies had declined
at last into one bitter threnody. "Not here. Not yet. This is
how it must end at last, and in an even bleaker desolation.
But no, there'll be no end to it yet."

They were adjured, when the fruitless session finally closed,
at least to keep this last evening together in mutual tolerance,
and to observe the offices of the Church together at Vespers
and Compline before parting the next morning to go their
separate ways. A few, not far from home, left the priory this
same evening, despairing of further waste of time, and perhaps
even well satisfied that nothing had resulted from the hours
already wasted. Where most men are still dreaming of total
victory, the few who would be content with an economical
compromise carry no weight. And yet at the last, as Robert
Bossu had said, this was the way it must go, there could be
no other ending. Neither side could ever win, neither side
lose. And they would sicken at last of wasting their time, their
lives and their country.

But not here. Not yet.

Cadfael went out into the stillness of early dusk, and
watched the empress sweep across the court towards her lodging, with the slender, elderly figure of Jovetta de Montors at
her elbow, and the girl Isabeau demurely following, a pace
or two behind them. There was an hour left before Vespers
for rest and thought. The lady would probably content herself
with the services of her own chaplain instead of attending the
offices in the priory church, unless, of course, she saw fit to
make a final splendid state appearance in vindication of her
legitimate right, before shaking off the very dust of compromise and returning to the battlefield.

For that, Cadfael thought sadly, is where they are all bound,
after this regrouping of minds and grudges. There will be
more of siege and raid and plunder, they will even have stored
up reserves of breath and energy and hatred during this pause.

For a while the fires will be refuelled, though the weariness will come back again with the turn of another year. And I am no nearer knowing where my son lies captive, let alone how to conduct the long journey to his deliverance.

He did not look for Yves or for Hugh, but went alone into the church. There were now quiet corners enough within there for every soul who desired a holy solitude and the peopled silence of the presence of God. In entering any other church but his own he missed, for one moment, the small stone altar and the chased reliquary where Saint Winifred was not, and yet was. Just to set eyes on it was to kindle a little living fire within his heart. Here he must forgo that particular consolation, and submit to an unfamiliar benediction. Nevertheless, there was an answer here for every need.

He found himself a dim place in a transept corner, on a narrow stone ridge that just provided room to sit, and there composed himself into patient stillness and closed his eyes, the better to conjure up the suave olive face and startling eyes, black within gold, of Mariam's son. Other men engendered sons, and had the delight of their infancy and childhood, and then the joy of watching them grow into manhood. He had had only the man full grown and marvellous, launched into his ageing life like the descent of an angelic vision, as sudden and as blinding; and that only in two brief glimpses, bestowed and as arbitrarily withdrawn. And he had been glad and grateful for that, as more than his deserving. While Olivier went free and fearless and blessed about the world, his father needed nothing more. But Olivier in captivity, stolen out of the world, hidden from the light, that was not to be borne. The darkened void where he had been was an offence against truth.

He did not know how long he had sat silent and apart, contemplating that aching emptiness, unaware of the few people who came and went in the nave at this hour. It had grown darker in the transept, and his stillness made him invisible to

the man who entered from the mild twilight of the cloister
into his chosen and shadowy solitude. He had not heard footsteps. It startled him out of his deep withdrawal when a body
brushed against him, colliding with arm and knee, and a hand
was hurriedly reached to his shoulder to steady them both.
There was no exclamation. A moment's silence while the
stranger's eyes took time to adjust to the dimness within, then
a quiet voice said: "I ask pardon, brother, I did not see you."

"I was willing," said Cadfael, "not to be seen."

"There have been times," agreed the voice, unsurprised,
"when I would have welcomed it myself."

The hand on Cadfael's shoulder spread long, sinewy fingers
strongly into his flesh, and withdrew. He opened his eyes
upon a lean, dark figure looming beside him, and a shadowed
oval face, high-boned and aquiline, looking down at him
impersonally, with a grave and slightly unnerving intelligence.
Eyes intent and bright studied him unhurriedly, without reticence, without mercy. Confronted with a mere man, neither
ally nor enemy to him, Philip FitzRobert contemplated humanity with a kind of curious but profound perception, hard to
evade.

"Are there griefs, brother, even here within the pale?"

"There are griefs everywhere," said Cadfael, "within as
without. There are few hiding-places. It is the nature of this
world."

"I have experienced it," said Philip, and drew a little aside,
but did not go, and did not release him from the illusionless
penetration of the black, aloof stare. In his own stark way a
handsome man, and young, too young to be quite in control
of the formidable mind within. Not yet quite thirty, Olivier's
own age, and thus seen in semidarkness the clouded mirror
image of Olivier.

"May your grief be erased from memory, brother," said
Philip, "when we aliens depart from this place, and leave you

at least in peace. As we shall be erased when the last hoofbeat dies."

"If God wills," said Cadfael, knowing by then that it would not be so.

Philip turned and went away from him then, into the comparative light of the nave, a lithe, light-stepping youth as soon as the candles shone upon him; round into the choir, up to the high altar. And Cadfael was left wondering why, in this moment of strange fellowship, mistaken, no doubt, for a brother of this house, he had not asked Gloucester's son, face to face, who held Olivier de Bretagne; wondering also whether he had held his tongue because this was not the time or the place, or because he was afraid of the answer.

Compline, the last office of the day, which should have signified the completion of a cycle of worship, and the acknowledgement of a day's effort, however flawed, and a day's achievement, however humble, signified on this night only a final flaunting of pride and display, rival against rival. If they could not triumph on the battlefield, not yet, they would at least try to outdo each other in brilliance and piety. The Church might benefit by the exuberance of their alms. The realm would certainly gain nothing.

The empress, after all, was not content to leave even this final field to her rival. She came in sombre splendour, attended not by her gentlewomen, but by the youngest and handsomest of her household squires, and with all her most powerful barons at her back, leaving the commonalty to crowd in and fill the last obscure corners of the nave. Her dark blue and gold had the sombre, steely sheen of armour, and perhaps that was deliberate, and she had left the women out of her entourage as irrelevant to a battlefield on which she was the equal of any man, and no other woman was fit to match her. She preferred to forget Stephen's able and heroic queen, dominant without rival in the south-east, holding inviolable the heart and source of her husband's sovereignty.

And Stephen came, massively striding, carelessly splendid, his lofty fair head bared, to the eye every inch a king. Ranulf of Chester, all complacent smiles, kept his right flank possessively, as if empowered by some newly designed royal appointment specially created for a new and valuable ally. On his left William Martel, his steward, and Robert de Vere, his constable, followed more staidly. Long and proven loyalty needs no sleeve-brushing and hand-kissing. It was some minutes, Cadfael observed from his remote dark corner of the choir, before Philip FitzRobert came forward unhurriedly from wherever he had been waiting and brooding, and took his place among the king's adherents; nor did he press close, to be certain of royal notice as in correct attendance, but remained among the rearguard. Reticence and withdrawal did not diminish him.

Cadfael looked for Hugh, and found him among the liegemen of the earl of Leicester, who had collected about him a number of the more stable and reliable young. But Yves he did not find. There were so many crowding into the church by the time the office began that latecomers would be hard put to it to find a corner in nave or porch. Faces receded into a dappled dimness. The windows were darkening, banishing the outer world from the dealings within. And it seemed that the bishops had accepted, with sadness, the failure of their efforts to secure any hope of peace, for there was a valedictory solemnity about the terms in which Roger de Clinton dismissed his congregation.

"And I adjure you, abide this last night before you disperse and turn your faces again to warfare and contention. You were called here to consider on the sickness of the land, and though you have despaired of any present cure, you cannot therefore shake off from your souls the burden of England's sorrows. Use this night to continue in prayer and thought, and if your hearts are changed, know that it is not too late to speak out and change the hearts of others. You who lead—we also to whom God has committed the wellbeing of souls—not one of us can evade the blame if we despoil and forsake our duties to the people given into our care. Go now and consider these things."

The final blessing sounded like a warning, and the vault cast back echoes of the bishop's raised and vehement voice like distant minor thunders of the wrath of God. But neither king nor empress would be greatly impressed. Certainly the reverberations held them motionless in their places until the clergy had almost reached the door of their vestry, but they would forget all warnings once they were out of the church and into the world, with all their men of war about them.

Some of the latecomers had withdrawn quietly to clear the way for the brothers' orderly recession, and the departure of the princes. They spilled out from the south porch into the deep dusk of the cloister and the chill of nightfall. And somewhere among the first of them, a few yards beyond into the north walk, a sudden sharp cry arose, and the sound of a stumble, recovered just short of the fall. It was not loud enough to carry into the church, merely a startled exclamation, but the shout of alarm and consternation that followed it next moment was heard even in the sanctity of the choir. And then the same voice was raised urgently, calling: "Help here! Bring torches! Someone's hurt . . . A man lying here . . ."

The bishops heard it, and recoiled from their robing-room threshold to stand stockstill for a moment, ears stretched, before bearing down in haste upon the south door. All those nearest to it were already jamming the doorway in their rush to get out, and bursting forth like seeds from a dehiscent pod in all directions as the pressure behind expelled them into the night. But the congestion was miraculously stricken apart like the Red Sea when Stephen came striding through, not even yielding the precedence to the empress, though she was not far behind him, swept along in the momentum of his passage. She emerged charged and indignant, but silent, Stephen loud and peremptory.

"Lights, some of you! Quickly! Are you deaf?" And he was off along the north walk of the cloister, towards the alarm that had now subsided into silence. The dimness under the vault halted him long enough for someone to run with a guttering torch, until a gust of wind, come with the evening chill, cast a sudden lick of flame down to the holder's fingers, and he dropped it with a yell, to sputter out against the flags.

Brother Cadfael had discarded the idea of candles, aware of the sharp evening wind, but recalled that he had seen a horn lantern in the porch, and carried one of the candlesticks with him to retrieve and light it. One of the brothers was beside him with a torch plucked from its sconce, and one of Leicester's young men had possessed himself of one of the iron fire-baskets from the outer court, on its long pole. Together they bore down on the congestion in the north walk of the cloister, and thrust a way through to shed light upon the cause of the outcry.

On the bare flags outside the third carrel of the walk a man lay sprawled on his right side, knees slightly drawn up, a thick fell of light brown hair hiding his face, his arms spilled helplessly along the stones. Rich dark clothing marked his status, and a sheathed sword slanted from his left hip, its tip just within the doorway of the carrel, as his toes just brushed the threshold. And stooped over him, just rising from his knees, Yves Hugonin stared up at them with shocked, bewildered eyes and white face.

"I stumbled over him in the dark. He's wounded . . ."

He stared at his own hand, and there was blood on his fingers. The man at his feet lay more indifferently still than any living thing should be, with king and empress and half the nobility of the land peering down at him in frozen fascination. Then Stephen stooped and laid a hand on the hunched shoulder, and rolled the body over onto its back, turning up to the light of the torches a face now fixed in blank astonishment, with half-open eyes glaring, and a broad breast marred by a blot of blood that spread and darkened slowly before their eyes.

From behind Stephen's shoulder issued a muted cry, not loud, but low, tightly controlled and harsh, as brief as it was chilling; and Philip FitzRobert came cleaving through the impeding crowd to kneel over the motionless body, stooping to lay a hand on the still warm flesh at brow and throat, lift one upper eyelid and glare into an eye that showed no reaction to light or darkness, and then as brusquely, almost violently, sweep both lids closed. Over dead Brien de Soulis he looked up to confront Yves with a bleak, glittering stare.

"Through the heart, and he had not even drawn! We all know the hate that you had for him, do we not? You were at his throat the moment you entered here, as I have heard from others who witnessed it. Your rage against him after, that I have seen with my own eyes. Your Grace, you see here murder! Murder, my lords bishops, in a holy place, during the worship of God! Either lay hold on this man for the law to deal with him, or let me take him hence and have his life fairly for this life he has taken!"

CHAPTER FIVE

YVES HAD recoiled a stumbling pace backward from the whiplash voice and ferocious glare, gaping in blank shock and disbelief. In the confident armour of his status and privilege it had not even dawned on him that he had put himself in obvious peril of such suspicions. He stared open-mouthed, fool innocent that he was, he was even tempted into a grin of incredulity, almost into laughter, before the truth hit home, and he blanched whiter than his shirt, and flashed a wild glance round to recognize the same wary conviction in a dozen pairs of eyes, circling him every way. He heaved in breath gustily, and found a voice.

"I? You think that *I* . . .? I came from the church this moment. I stumbled over him. He lay here as you see him . . ."

"There's blood on your hand," said Philip through set teeth. "And on your hands by right! Who else? Here you stand over his body, and no man else abroad in the night but you. You, who bore a blood grudge against him, as every soul here knows."

"I found him so," protested Yves wildly. "I kneeled to handle him, yes, it was dark, I did not know if he was dead or alive. I cried out when I stumbled over him. You heard me! I called you to come, to bring lights, to help him if help was possible . . ."

"What better way," Philip demanded bitterly, "to show as innocent, and bring witnesses running? We were on your heels, you had no time to vanish utterly and leave your dead man lying. This was my man, my officer, I valued him! And I will have his price out of you if there is any justice."

"I tell you I had but just left the church, and fell over him lying here. I came late, I was just within the door." He had grasped his dire situation by now, his voice had settled into a strenuous level, reasoning and resolute. "There must be some here who were beside me in the church, latecomers like me. They can bear out that I have but just come forth into the cloister. De Soulis wears a sword. Am I in arms? Use your eyes! No sword, no dagger, no steel on me! Arms are forbidden to all who attend the offices of the Church. I came to Compline, and I left my sword in my lodging. How can I have killed him?"

"You are lying," said Philip, on his feet now over the body of his friend. "I do not believe you ever were in the church. Who speaks up for you? I hear none. While we were within you had time enough, more than enough, to clean your blade and bestow it in your quarters, while you waited for the office to end, to cry out to us and bring us running to discover him in his blood, and you unarmed and crying murder on some unknown enemy. You, the known enemy! Nothing hinders but this can be, must be, *is* your work."

Cadfael, hemmed in among many bodies pressing close, could not thrust a way through towards king and empress, or make himself heard above the clamour of a dozen voices already disputing across the width of the cloister. He could see between the craning heads Philip's implacable face, sharply lit by the torchlight. Somewhere among the hubbub of partisan excitement and consternation, no doubt, the voices of the bishops were raised imploring reason and silence, but without effect, without even being heard. It took Stephen's imperious bellow to shear through the noise and cut off all other sound.

"Silence! Hush your noise!"

And the silence fell like a stone, crushingly; for one instant all movement froze, and every breath was held. A moment only, then almost stealthily feet shuffled, sleeves brushed, breath was drawn in gustily, and even comment resumed in hushed undertones and hissing whispers, but Stephen had his field, and bestrode it commandingly.

"Now let us have some room for thought before we accuse or exonerate any man. And before all, let someone who knows his business make good sure that the man is out of reach of help, or we are *all* guilty of his death. One lad falling over him in the dark, whether he himself struck the blow or not, can hardly give a physician's verdict. William, do you make sure."

William Martel, long in experience of death by steel through many campaigns, knelt beside the body, and turned it by the shoulder to lie flat, exposing to the torchlight the bloody breast, the slit coat, and the narrow, welling wound. He drew wide an eyelid and marked the unmoving stare.

"Dead. Through the heart, surely. Nothing to be done for him."

"How long?" asked the king shortly.

"No telling. But very recently."

"During Compline?" The office was not a long one, though on this fateful evening it had been drawn out somewhat beyond its usual time.

"I saw him living," said Martel, "only minutes before we went in. I thought he had followed us in. I never marked that he wore steel."

"So if this young man is shown to have been within throughout the office," said the king practically, "he cannot be guilty of this murder. Not fair fight, for de Soulis never had time to draw. Murder."

A hand reached softly for Cadfael's sleeve. Hugh had been

worming his way inconspicuously through the press to reach him. In Cadfael's ear his voice whispered urgently: "Can you speak for him? *Was* he within? Did you see him?"

"I wish to God I had! He says he came later. I was well forward in the choir. The place was full, the last would be pinned just within the doors." In corners unlit, and possibly with none or few of their own acquaintance nearby to recognize or speak to them. All too easy not to be noticed, and a convincing reason why Yves should be one of the first to move out into the cloister and clear the way, to stumble over a dead man. The fact that his first cry had been a wordless one of simple alarm when he fell should speak for him. Only a minute later had he cried out the cause.

"No matter, let be!" said Hugh softly. "Stephen has his finger on the right question. Someone surely will know. And if all else fails, the empress will never let Philip FitzRobert lay a finger on any man of hers. Not for the death of a man she loathes! Look at her!"

Cadfael had to crane and shift to do so, for tall though she was, for a woman, she was surrounded by men far taller. But once found, she shone fiercely clear under the torchlight, her handsome face composed and severe, but her large eyes glittering with a suggestion of controlled elation, and the corners of her lips drawn into the austere shadow of an exultant smile. No, she had no reason at all to grieve at the death of the man who had betrayed Faringdon, or to sympathize with the grief and anger of his lord and patron, who had handed over her castle of Cricklade to the enemy. And as Cadfael watched, she turned her head a little, and looked with sharp attention at Yves Hugonin, and the subtle shadows that touched the corners of her lips deepened, and for one instant the smile became apparent. She did not move again, not yet. Let other witnesses do all for her, if that was possible. No need to spend her own efforts until or unless they were needed. She had her half-brother beside her, Roger of Hereford at one shoulder, Hugh Bigod at the other, force enough to prevent any action that might be ventured against any protégé of hers.

"Speak up!" said Stephen, looking round the array of watchful faces, guarded and still now, side-glancing at near neighbours, eyeing the king's roused countenance. "If any here can say he saw this man within the church throughout Compline, then speak up and declare it, and do him right. He says he came unarmed, in all duty, to the worship of God, and was with us to the end of the office. Who bears him out?"

No one moved, beyond turning to look for reaction from others. No one spoke. There was a silence.

"Your Grace sees," said Philip at length, breaking the prolonged hush, "there is no one willing to confirm what he says. And there is no one who believes him."

"That is no proof that he lies," said Roger de Clinton. "Too often truth can bring no witness with it, and find no belief. I do not say he is proven true, but neither is he proven a liar. We have not here the testimony of every man who came to Compline this night. Even if we had, it would not be proof positive that he is lying. But if one man only can come forward and say: I stood by him close to the door until the last prayer was said, and we went out to leave the doorway clear: then truth would be made manifest. Your Grace, we should pursue this further."

"There is no time," said the king, frowning. "Tomorrow we leave Coventry. Why linger? Everything has been said."

Back to the battlefield, thought Cadfael, despairing for a moment of his own kind, and with their fires refuelled by this pause.

"Within these walls," said Roger de Clinton, roused, "I forbid violence even in return for violence, and even outside these walls I charge you forswear all revenges. If there cannot be proper enquiry after justice, then even the guilty among us must go free."

"They need not," said Philip grimly. "I require a blood price for my man. If his Grace wills justice, then let this man be left in fetters here, and let the constables of the city examine him, and hold him for trial. There is the means of justice in the laws of this land, is there not? Then use them! Give him to the law, as surely as death he has broken the law, and owes a death for a death. How can you doubt it? Who else was abroad? Who else had picked so fierce a quarrel with Brien de Soulis, or held so bitter a grudge against him? And we find him standing over the dead man, and barely another soul loose in the night, and you still doubt?"

And indeed it seemed to Cadfael that Philip's bitter conviction was carrying even the king with him. Stephen had no great cause to believe in an unknown youth's protestations of innocence against the odds, a youth devoted to the opposing cause, and suspect of robbing him of a useful fighting man who had recently done such signal service. He hesitated, visibly only too willing to shift the burden to other shoulders, and be off about his martial business again. The very suggestion that he was failing to maintain strict law in his own domain prompted him to commit Yves to the secular authorities, and wash his hands of him.

"I have a thing to say to that," said the empress deliberately, her voice raised to carry clearly. "This conference was convened upon the issue of safe conducts on both sides, that we might come together without fear. Whatever may have happened here, it cannot break that compact. I came here with a certain number of people in my following, and I shall go hence tomorrow with that same number, for all were covered by safe conduct, and against none of them has any wrong been proved, neither this young squire nor any other. Touch him, and you touch him unlawfully. Detain him, and you are forsworn and disgraced. We leave tomorrow as many as we came."

She moved decisively then, brushing aside those who stood

between, and held out her hand imperiously to Yves. Her sleeve brushed disdainfully past Philip's braced arm as the white-faced boy obeyed her gesture and turned to go with her wherever she directed. The ranks gave back and opened before her. Cadfael saw her turn to smile upon her escort, and marvelled that the boy's face should gaze back at her so blanched and empty of gratitude, worship or joy.

He came back to their lodging half an hour later. She did not even allow him to walk the short distance between without a guard, for fear Philip or some other aggrieved enemy would attempt revenge while he was here within reach. Though her interest in him, Yves reflected wretchedly, probably would not last long. She would keep him jealously from harm until her whole entourage was safely away on the road back to Gloucester, and then forget him. It was to herself she owed it to demonstrate her power to hold him immune. The debt she owed, or believed she owed to him was thereby amply repaid. He was not of any permanent importance.

And yet the vital touch of her hand on his, leading him contemptuously out of the circle of his enemies, could not but fire his blood. Even though he felt it freeze again as he reminded himself what she believed of him, what she was valuing in him. Of all those who truly believed he had murdered Brien de Soulis, the Empress Maud was the most convinced. The soft voice he recalled, giving subtle orders by roundabout means, haunted him still. A loyal young man, clay in her hands, blindly devoted like all the rest, and nothing she could not ask of him, however circuitously, and he understood and obeyed. And of course he would deny it, even to her. He knew his duty. The death of de Soulis must not be spoken of, must never be acknowledged in any way.

He was short to question, that night, even by his friends; by his friends most of all. They were none too sure of his safety, either, and stayed close beside him, not letting him out of their sight until he should be embarked in the protective company of all the empress's escort next morning, and bound away for Gloucester.

He put together his few belongings before sleeping. "I must go," he said, and added nothing to explain the note of reluctance in his voice. "And we are no nearer to finding out what they have done with Olivier."

"With that matter," said Cadfael, "I have not finished yet. But for you, best get away from here, and let it lie."

"And that cloud still over my name?" said Yves bitterly.

"I have not finished with that, either. The truth will be known in the end. Hard to bury truth for ever. Since you certainly did not kill Brien de Soulis, there's somewhere among us a man who did, and whoever uncovers his name removes the shadow from yours. If, indeed, there is anyone who truly believes you guilty."

"Oh, yes," said Yves, with a wry and painful smile. "Yes, there is. One at least!"

But it was the nearest he got to giving that person a name; and Cadfael pressed him no more.

In the morning, group by group, they all departed. Philip FitzRobert was gone, alone as he had come, before ever the bell rang for Prime, making no farewells. King Stephen waited to attend High Mass before gathering all his baronage about him and setting forth briskly for Oxford. Some northern lords left for their own lands to make all secure before returning their attention to either king or empress. The empress herself mustered for Gloucester in mid-morning, having lingered to be sure her rival was out of the city before her, and not delaying to use even this opportunity for recruiting support behind her back.

Yves had gone alone into the church when the party began to gather, and Cadfael, following at a discreet distance, found him on his knees by a transept altar, shunning notice in his

private devotions before departure. It was the stiff unhappiness
of the boy's face that caused Cadfael to discard discretion
and draw closer. Yves heard him come, and turned on him a
brief, pale smile, and hurriedly raised himself. "I'm ready."

The hand he leaned upon the prie-dieu wore a ring Cadfael
had never seen before. A narrow, twisted gold band, no way
spectacular, and so small that it had to be worn on the boy's
little finger. The sort of thing a woman might give to a page
as reward for some special service. Yves saw how Cadfael's
eyes rested upon it, and began an instinctive movement to
withdraw it from sight, but then thought better of it, and let
it lie. He veiled his eyes, himself staring down at the thin
band with a motionless face.

"She gave you this?" Cadfael asked, perceiving that he was
permitted, even expected, to question.

Half resigned, half grateful, Yves said simply: "Yes." And
then added: "I tried to refuse it."

"You were not wearing it last night," said Cadfael.

"No. But now she will expect . . . I am not brave enough,"
said Yves ruefully, "to face her and discard it. Halfway to
Gloucester she'll forget all about me, and then I can give it
to some shrine—or a beggar along the way."

"Why so?" said Cadfael, deliberately probing this manifest
wound. "If it was for services rendered?"

Yves turned his head with a sharp motion of pain, and started
towards the door. Aside he said, choking on the utterance: "It
was unearned." And again, more gently: "I had not earned
it."

They were gone, the last of the glittering courtiers and the
steel captains, the kings and the kingmakers, and the two
visiting bishops, Nigel of Ely to his own diocese, Henry of
Blois with his royal brother to Oxford, before going beyond,
to his see of Winchester. Gone with nothing settled, nothing

solved, peace as far away as ever. And one dead man lying in a mortuary chapel here until he could be coffined and disposed of wherever his family, if he had family, desired to bury him. In the great court it was even quieter than normally, since the common traffic between town and priory had not yet resumed after the departure of the double court of a still divided land.

"Stay yet a day or two," Cadfael begged of Hugh. "Give me so much grace, for if I then return with you I am keeping to terms. God knows I would observe the limits laid on me if I can. Even a day might tell me what I want to know."

"After king and empress and all their following have denied any knowledge of where Olivier may be?" Hugh pointed out gently.

"Even then. There were some here who did know," said Cadfael with certainty. "But, Hugh, there is also this matter of Yves. True, the empress has spread her cloak over him and taken him hence in safety, but is that enough? He'll have no peace until it's known who did the thing he surely did not do. Give me a few more days, and let me at least give some thought to this death. I have asked the brothers here to let me know of anything they may have heard concerning the surrender of Faringdon, give me time at least to be sure the word has gone round, and to get an answer if any man here has an answer to give me."

"I can stretch my leave by a day or two," Hugh allowed doubtfully. "And indeed I'd be loth to go back without you. Let us by all means put the boy's mind at rest if we can, and lay the blame where it belongs. If," he added with a grimace, "there should be any great measure of blame for removing de Soulis from the world. No, say nothing! I know! Murder is murder, as much a curse to the slayer as to the slain, and cannot be a matter of indifference, whoever the dead may be. Do you want to look at him again? An accurate stab wound, frontal, no ambush from behind. But it was dark there. A knowledgeable swordsman, if he had been waiting and had his night eyes, would have no difficulty."

Cadfael considered. "Yes, let's take another look at the man. And his belongings? Are they still here in the prior's charge? Could we ask, do you think?"

"The bishop might allow it. He's no better pleased at having a murderer active within the pale than you are."

Brien de Soulis lay on the stone slab in the chapel, covered with a linen sheet, but not yet shrouded, and his coffin still in the hands of the carpenters. It seemed money had been left to provide a noble funeral. Was that Philip's doing?

Cadfael drew down the sheet to uncover the body as far as the wound, a mere thin blue-black slit now, with slightly ribbed edges, a stroke no more than a thumbnail long. The body, otherwise unmarked, was well muscled and comely, the face retained its disdainful good looks, but cold and hard as alabaster.

"It was no sword did that," said Cadfael positively. "The flow of blood hid all when he was found. But that was made by a dagger, not even a long one, but long enough. It's not so far into the heart. And fine, very fine. The hilt has not bruised him. It was plunged in and withdrawn quickly, quickly enough for the slayer to draw off clean before ever the bleeding came. No use looking for stained clothing, so fine a slit does not open and gush like a fountain. By the time it was flowing fast the assailant was gone."

"And never stayed to be sure of his work?" wondered Hugh.

"He was sure of it. Very cool, very resolute, very competent." Cadfael drew up the sheet again over the stone-still face. "Nothing more here. Shall we consider once again the place where this happened?"

They passed through the south door, and emerged into the north walk of the cloister. Outside the third carrel the body had lain, its toes just trailing across the threshold. There was a faint pink stain, a hand's length, still visible, where his blood had seeped down under his right side and fouled the flags. Someone had been diligent in cleaning it away, but the shape still showed. "Yes, here," said Hugh. "The stones will show no marks, even if there was a struggle, but I fancy there was none. He was taken utterly by surprise."

They sat down together there in the carrel to consider the alignment of this scene.

"He was struck from before," said Cadfael, "and as the dagger was dragged out he fell forward with it, out of the carrel into the walk. Surely he was the one waiting here within. For someone. He wore sword and dagger himself, so he was not bound for Compline. If he designed to meet someone here in private, it was surely someone he trusted, someone never questioned, or how did he approach so close? Had it been Yves—as we know it was not—de Soulis would have had the sword out of the scabbard before ever the boy got within reach. The open hostility between those two was not the whole story. There must have been fifty souls within these walls who hated the man for what he did at Faringdon. Some who were there, and escaped in time, many others of the empress's following who were not there, but hold the treason bitterly against him no less. He would be wary of any man fronting him whom he did not know well, and trust, men of his own faction and his own mind."

"And this one he mistook fatally," said Hugh.

"How should treason be prepared for counter-treason? He turned in the empress's hand, now one of his own has turned in his. And he as wholly deceived as she was in him. So it goes."

"I take it," said Hugh, eyeing his friend very gravely, "that we can and do accept all that Yves says as truth? I do so willingly only from knowledge of him. But should we not consider how the thing must have looked to others who do not know him?"

"So we may," said Cadfael sturdily, "and still be certain. True, no one has owned to seeing him among the last who came into the church, but that is well possible. He says he came late and spoke to no one, because the office had already begun. He was in a dark corner just within the door, and hence among the first out, to clear the way at the end. We heard him cry out, the first simply a gasp of surprise as he stumbled, then the alarm. Now if he had indeed avoided Compline, and had time to act at leisure while almost all were within, why cry out at all? Out of cunning, as Philip charged, to win the appearance of innocence? Yves is clever, but certainly has no cunning at all. And if he had the whole cloister at his back, he had time enough to slip away and leave others to find his dead man. He bore no arms, his sword was found, as he said, clean and sheathed in his quarters, and showed no sign of having been blooded. He had had, said Philip, the whole time of Compline to blood it, clean it and restore it to his lodging. But I saw the blade, and I could find no sign of blood. No, if he had had all the time of Compline at his disposal, he would never have sounded the alarm himself, but taken good care to be elsewhere when the dead man was found, and among witnesses, well away from the first outcry."

"And if he had come forth from the church as he says, then he had no time to encounter and kill, and no sword or dagger on him."

"Manifestly. And I think you know, as I know, that the death came earlier, though how much earlier it's hard to tell. He had had time to bleed, you still see there the extent of the pool that gathered under him. No, you need not have any doubts. What you know of our lad you know rightly."

"And of the rest of this great household," said Hugh reflectively, "most were in the church. It need not be all, however. And as you say, he had enemies here, one at least more discreet than Yves, and more deadly."

"And one," Cadfael elaborated sombrely, "of whom he was no way wary. One who could approach him closely and rouse no suspicion, one he was waiting for, for surely he was standing here, in this carrel, and stepped forth willingly when the other came, and was spitted on the very threshold."

Hugh retraced in silence the angle of that fall, the way the body had lain, the ominous rim of the bloodstain, and could find no flaw in this account of that encounter. In their well-meant efforts to bring together in reconciliation all the power and force and passion of both sides in the contention, the bishops had succeeded also in bringing within these walls a great cauldron of hatred and malice, and infinite possibilities of further treachery.

"More intrigue, more plotting for advantage," said Hugh resignedly. "If two were meeting here in secret while the baronage was at worship, then it was surely for mischief. What more can we do here? Did you say you wanted to see what belongings de Soulis left behind him? Come, we'll have a word with the bishop."

"The man's possessions," said the bishop, "such as he had here with him, are here in my charge, and I await word from his brother in Worcester as to future arrangements for his burial. I have no doubt the brother will be responsible for that. But if you think that examination of his effects can give us any indication as to how he died, yes, certainly we should at least put it to the test. We may not neglect any means of finding out the truth. You are fully convinced," he added anxiously, "that the young man who called us to the body bears no guilt for the death?"

"My lord," said Hugh, "from all I know of him, he is as poor a hand at deceit or stealth as ever breathed. You saw him yourself on the day we entered here, how he sprang out of the saddle and made straight for his foe, brow to brow.

That is more his way of going about it. Nor had he any weapon about him. You cannot know him as we do, but for my part and Brother Cadfael's, we are sure of him."

"In any case," agreed the bishop heavily, "it can do no harm to see if there is anything, letter or sign of any kind, in the dead man's baggage that may shed light, on his movements intended on leaving here, or any undertaking he had in hand. Very well! The saddle-bags are here in the vestment room."

There was a horse in the stables, too, a good horse waiting to be delivered, like all the rest, to the younger de Soulis in Worcester. The bishop unbuckled the straps of the first bag with his own hands, and hoisted it to a bench. "One of the brothers packed them and brought them here from the guesthall where he lodged. You may view them." He stayed to observe, in duty bound, being now responsible for all that was done with these relics.

Spread out upon the bench before their eyes, handled scrupulously as another man's property, Brien de Soulis's equipment showed Spartan and orderly. Changes of shirt and hose, the compact means of a gentleman's toilet, a well-furnished purse. Plainly he travelled light, and was a man of neat habit. A leather pouch in the second saddle-bag yielded a compartmented box with flint and tinder, wax and a seal. A man of property, travelling far, would certainly not be without his personal seal. Hugh held it on his palm for the bishop's inspection. The device, sharply cut, was a swan with arched neck, facing left, and framed between two wands of willow.

"That is his," Hugh confirmed. "We saw it on the buckle of his sword-belt when we carried in the body. But embossed and facing the other way, of course. And that is all."

"No," said Cadfael, his hand groping along the seams of the empty bag. "Some other small thing is here at the bottom." He drew it out and held it up to the light. "Also a seal! Now what would a man want with carrying two on a journey?"

What indeed? For to risk carrying both, if two had actually

been made, was to risk theft or loss of one, with all the dire possibilities of having it fall into the hands of an enemy or a sharper, and being misused in many and profitable ways, to its owner's loss.

"It is not the same," said Hugh sharply, and carried it to the window to examine it more carefully. "A lizard—like a little dragon—no, a salamander, for he's in a nest of little pointed flames. No border but a single line at the rim. Engraved deep—little used. I have never seen this. Do you know it, my lord?"

The bishop studied it, and shook his head. "No, strange to me. For what purpose could one man be carrying another man's personal seal? Unless it had been confided to him as the owner's proxy, for attachment to some document in absence?"

"Certainly not here," said Hugh wryly, "for here there have been no documents to seal, no agreement on any matter, the worse for us all. Cadfael, do you see any significance in this?"

"Of all his possessions," said Cadfael, "a man would be least likely to be parted from his seal. The thing carries his sanction, his honour, his reputation with it. If he did trust it to a known friend, it would be kept very securely, not dropped into the corner of a saddle-bag, thus disregarded. Yes, Hugh, I should very much like to know whose device this is, and how it came into de Soulis's possession. His recent history has not shown him as a man to be greatly trusted by his acquaintances, or lightly made proxy for another man's honour."

He hesitated, turning the small artifact in his fingers. A circlet measuring as far across as the length of his first thumb joint, its handle of a dark wood polished high, fitting smoothly in the palm. The engraving was skilled and precise, the little conventional flames sharply incised. The head with its open mouth and darting tongue faced left. The positive would face right. Mirror images, the secret faces of real beings, hold terrifying significances. It seemed to Cadfael that the sharp ascending flames of the salamander's cradling fire were searing the fingers that touched them, and crying out for recognition and understanding.

"My lord bishop," he said slowly, "may I, on my oath to return it to you unless I find its true owner, borrow this seal? In my deepest conscience I feel the need of it. Or, if that is not permitted, may I make a drawing of it, in every detail, for credentials in its place?"

The bishop gave him a long, penetrating look, and then said with deliberation: "At least in taking the copy there can be no harm. But you will have small opportunity of enquiring further into either this death, or the whereabouts of the prisoner you are seeking if, as I suppose, you are going home to Shrewsbury now the conference is over."

"I am not sure, my lord," said Cadfael, "that I shall be going home."

CHAPTER SIX

"YOU KNOW, do you not," said Hugh very gravely, as they came from one more Compline together in the dusk, "that if you go further, I cannot go with you. I have work of my own to do. If I turn my back upon Madog ap Meredudd many more days he'll be casting covetous eyes at Oswestry again. He's never stopped hankering after it. God knows I'd be loth to go back without you. And you know, none better, you'll be tearing your own life up by the roots if you fail to keep your time."

"And if I fail to find my son," said Cadfael, gently and reasonably, "my life is nothing worth. No, never fret for me, Hugh, one alone on this labour can do as much as a company of armed men, and perhaps more. I have failed already to find any trace here, what remains but to go where he served, where he was betrayed and made prisoner? There someone must know what became of him. In Faringdon there will be echoes, footprints, threads to follow, and I will find them."

He made his drawings with care, on a leaf of vellum from the scriptorium, one to size, with careful precision, one enlarged to show every detail of the salamander seal. There was no motto nor legend, only the slender lizard in its fiery nest. Surely that, too, harked back in some way to the surrender of Faringdon, and had somewhat to say concerning the death of Brien de Soulis, if only its language could be interpreted.

Hugh cast about, without overmuch comfort, for something to contribute to these vexed puzzles that drove his friend into unwilling exile, but there was little of help to be found. He did venture, for want of better: "Have you thought, Cadfael, that of all those who may well have hated de Soulis, there's none with better reason than the empress? How if she prompted some besotted young man to do away with him? She has a string of raw admirers at her disposal. It could be so."

"To the best of my supposing," said Cadfael soberly, "it was so. Do you remember she sent for Yves that first evening, after she had seen the lad show his paces against de Soulis? I fancy she had accepted the omen, and found him a work he could do for her, a trace more privately, perhaps, than at his first attempt."

"No!" gasped Hugh, stricken, and halted in mid-stride. "Are you telling me that *Yves* . . ."

"No, no such matter!" Cadfael assured him chidingly. "Oh, he took her meaning, or I fear he did, though he surely damned himself for ever believing it was meant so. He did not *do* it, of course not! Even she might have had the wit to refrain, with such an innocent. But stupid he is not! He understood her!"

"Then may she not have singled out a second choice for the work?" suggested Hugh, brightening.

"No, you may forget that possibility. For she is convinced that Yves took the nudge, and rid her of her enemy. No, there's no solution there."

"How so?" demanded Hugh, pricked. "How can you know so much?"

"Because she rewarded him with a gold ring. No great prize, but an acknowledgement. He tried to refuse it, but he was not brave enough, small blame to the poor lad. Oh, nothing was ever openly said, and of course he would deny it, she would avoid even having to make him say as much. The child is out of his depth with such women. He's bent on getting rid of her gift as soon as he safely may. Her gratitude is short, that he knows. But no, she never hired another murderer, she is certain she needed none."

"That can hardly have added to his happiness," said Hugh with a sour grimace. "And no help to us in lifting the weight from him, either."

They had reached the door of their lodging. Overhead the sky was clear and cold, the stars legion but infinitesimal in the early dark. The last night here, for Hugh had duties at home that could not be shelved.

"Cadfael, think well what you are doing. I know what you stake, as well as you know it. This is not simple going and returning. Where you will be meddling a man can vanish, and no return ever. Come back with me, and I will ask Robert Bossu to follow this quest to its ending."

"There's no time," said Cadfael. "I have it in my mind, Hugh, that there are more souls than one, and more lives than my son's, to be salvaged here, and the time is very short, and the danger very close. And if I turn back now there will be no one to be the pivot at the centre, on whom the wheel of all those fortunes turns, the demon or the angel. But yes, I'll think well before you leave me. We shall see what the morning will bring."

What the morning brought, just as the household emerged from Mass, was a dust-stained rider on a lathered horse, cantering wearily in from the street and sliding stiffly and untidily to a clattering stop on the cobbles of the court. The horse stood with drooping head and heaving sides, steaming into the air sharpened with frost, and dripping foam between rolled-back lips into the stones. The rider doubled cramped fists on the pommel, and half clambered, half fell out of the saddle to stiffen collapsing knees and hold himself upright by his mount.

"My lord bishop, pardon . . ." He could not release his hold to make due reverence, but clung to his prop, bending his head as deep and respectfully as he might. "My mistress sends me to bring you word—the empress—she is safe in Gloucester with all her company, all but one. My lord, there was foul work along the road . . ."

"Take breath, even evil news can wait," said Roger de Clinton, and waved an order at whoever chose to obey it. "Bring drink—have wine mulled for him, but bring a draught now. And some of you, help him within, and see to his poor beast, before he founders."

There was a hand at the dangling bridle in an instant. Someone ran for wine. The bishop himself lent a solid shoulder under the messenger's right arm, and braced him erect. "Come, let's have you within, and at rest."

In the nearest carrel of the cloister the courier leaned back against the wall and drew in breath long and gratefully. Hugh, lissome and young, and mindful of some long, hard rides of his own after Lincoln, dropped to his knees and braced experienced hands to ease off the heavy riding boots.

"My lord, we had remounts at Evesham, and made good time until fairly close to Gloucester, riding well into the dusk to be there by nightfall. Near Deerhurst, in woodland, with the length of our company past—for I was with the rearguard—an armed band rode out at our tail, and cut out one man from among us before ever we were aware, and off with him at speed into the dark."

"What man was that?" demanded Cadfael, stiffening. "Name him!"

"One of her squires, Yves Hugonin. He that had hard words with de Soulis, who is dead. My lord, there's nothing surer than some of FitzRobert's men have seized him, for suspicion of killing de Soulis. They hold him guilty, for all the empress would have him away untouched."

"And you did not pursue?" asked the bishop, frowning.

"Some little way we did, but they were fresh, and in forest they knew well. We saw no more of them. And when we sent ahead to let our lady know, she would have one of us ride back to bring you word. We were under safe conduct, this was foul work, after such a meeting."

"We'll send to the king," said the bishop firmly. "He will order this man's release as he did before when FitzRobert seized the Earl of Cornwall. He obeyed then, he will obey again, whatever his own grudge."

But would he, Cadfael wondered? Would Stephen lift a finger in this case, for a man as to whose guilt he had said neither yea nor nay, but only allowed him to leave under safe conduct at the empress's insistence. No valuable ally, but an untried boy of the opposing side. No, Yves would be left for the empress to retrieve. He had left here under her wing, it was for her to protect him. And how far would she go on Yves' behalf? Not so far as to inconvenience herself by the loss of time or advantage. His supposed infamous service to her had been acknowledged and rewarded, she owed him nothing. And he had withdrawn deliberately to the tail end of her cortège, to be out of sight and out of mind.

"I think they had a rider alongside us for some way, in cover," said the courier, "making sure of their man, before they struck. It was all over in a moment, at a bend in the path where the trees grow close."

"And close to Deerhurst?" said Cadfael. "Is that already in FitzRobert's own country? How close are his castles? He left here early, in time to have his ambush ready. He had this in mind from the first, if he was thwarted here."

"It might be twenty miles or so to Cricklade, more to Faringdon. But closer still there's his new castle at Green-hamsted, the one he took from Robert Musard a few weeks back. Not ten miles from Gloucester."

"You are sure," said Hugh, a little hesitantly and with an anxious eye on Cadfael, "that they did carry him off prisoner?"

"No question," said the messenger with weary bluntness, "they wanted him whole, it was done very briskly. No, they're more wary what blood they spill, these days. Men on one side have kin on the other who could still take offence and make trouble. No, be easy for that, there was no killing."

The courier was gone into the prior's lodging to eat and rest, the bishop to his own palace to prepare letters to carry the news, notably to Oxford and Malmesbury, in the region where this raid had taken place. Whether Stephen would bestir himself to intervene in this case was doubtful, but someone would surely pass the news on to the boy's uncle in Devizes, who carried some weight with the empress. At least everything must be tried.

"Now," said Cadfael, left contemplating Hugh's bleak and frustrated face through a long silence, "I have two hostages to buy back. If I asked for a sign, I have it. And now there is no doubt in my mind what I must do."

"And I cannot come with you," said Hugh.

"You have a shire to keep. Enough for one of us to break faith. But may I keep your good horse, Hugh?"

"If you'll pledge me to bring him safely back, and yourself in the saddle," said Hugh.

They said their farewells just within the priory gate, Hugh to return north-west along the same roads by which they had come, with his three men-at-arms at his back, Cadfael bearing south. They embraced briefly before mounting, but when they issued from the gate into the street, and separated, they went briskly, and did not look back. With every yard the fine thread that held them together stretched and thinned, attenuated to breaking point, became a fibre, a hair, a cobweb filament, but did not break.

For the first stages of that journey Cadfael rode steadily, hardly aware of his surroundings, fully absorbed in the effort to come to terms with the breaking of another cord, which had parted as soon as he turned south instead of towards home. It was like the breaking of a tight constriction which had bound his life safely within him, though at the cost of pain; and the abrupt removal of the restriction was mingled relief and terror, both intense. The ease of being loose in the world came first, and only gradually did the horror of the release enter and overwhelm him. For he was recreant, he had exiled himself, knowing well what he was doing. And now his only justification must be the redemption of both Yves and Olivier. If he failed in that he had squandered even his apostasy. *Your own man*, Radulfus had said, *no longer any man of mine. Vows abandoned, brothers forsaken, heaven discarded.*

The first need was to recognize that it had happened, the second to accept it. After that he could ride on composedly, and be his own man, as for the former half of his life he had been, and only rarely felt a need beyond, until he found community and completion in surrendering himself. Life could and must be lived on those same terms for this while, perhaps for all the while remaining.

So by that time he could look about him again, pay attention to the way, and turn his mind to the task that lay before him.

Close to Deerhurst they had closed in and cut out Yves from his fellows. And strictly speaking, there was no proof as to who had so abducted him; but Philip FitzRobert, who alone was known to bear a great grudge against the boy, and who was patently a man bent on revenge, had three castles and a strong following in those parts, and could venture such a raid with impunity, secure of his power. Then they would not risk being abroad with their captive, even by night, longer than they must, but have him away into hold in one of the castles, out of sight and out of mind, as quickly and privately as possible. Greenhamsted, said the empress's courier, was the nearest. Cadfael did not know the region well, but he had questioned the messenger concerning the lie of the land. Deerhurst, a few miles north of Gloucester, Greenhamsted about as far to the south-east. La Musarderie, the courier had called the castle, after the family that had held it since Domesday. At Deerhurst there was an alien priory belonging to St. Denis in Paris, and if he lodged there overnight he might be able to elicit some local information. Country people keep a sharp eye on the devious doings of their local lords, especially in time of civil war. For their own preservation they must.

By all accounts there had been a castle there at La Musarderie ever since King William gave the village to Hascoit Musard some time before the Domesday survey was taken. That argued enough time to have built in stone, after the first hurried timber erection to secure a foothold. Faringdon had been thrown up in a few weeks of the summer, and laid under siege almost before it was finished. Earthwork and wood, no other possibility in the time, though evidently care had been taken to make it as strong as possible. And Cricklade, whatever its defensive state might be, was not as close as Greenhamsted to the spot where Yves had been abducted. Well, he could see if anyone at Deerhurst could enlighten him on any of these matters.

He rode steadily, intending to ride late and be well on his way before night. He took no food, and said the office at tierce and sext in the saddle. Once he fell in with a mounted merchant and his packman on the way, and they rode together some miles, to a flow of talk that went in at Cadfael's left ear and out at the right, punctuated by his amicable but random murmurs of acknowledgement, while all the while his mind was on those as yet unknown fields of enterprise that awaited him in the valley of the Thames, where the lines of battle were drawn. At the approach to Stratford the merchant and his man turned off to make for the town, and Cadfael rode on alone once again, exchanging preoccupied greetings here and there with other travellers on a well-used and relatively safe highway.

In the dusk he came to Evesham, and it fell upon him suddenly with chilling shock that he had been taking for granted his welcome as a brother of the Order, he who now had no right to any privilege here, he who had with deliberation broken his vow of obedience, knowing well what he did. Recreant and self-exiled, he had no right even to the habit he wore, except of charity to cover his nakedness.

He bespoke for himself a pallet in the common hall, on the plea that his journey was penitential, and he was not deserving of entering among the choir monks until it was fully accomplished, which was as near to the truth as he cared to come. The hospitaller, gravely courteous, would not press him beyond what he cared to confide, but let him have his way, offered a confessor should he be in need, and left him to lead his horse to the stables and tend him before taking his own rest. At Vespers and at Compline Cadfael chose for himself an obscure corner of the nave, but one from which he could see the high altar. He was not excommunicate, except by his own judgement. Not yet.

But all through the office he felt within himself an impossible paradox, a void that weighed heavier than stone.

He came through the woodlands flanking the vale of Gloucester during the next afternoon. All these midland shires of England seemed to him richly treed and full of game, one great, lavish hunting chase. And in these particular glades Philip FitzRobert had hunted a man. One more desperate loss to that gallant girl now solitary in Gloucester, and with child.

He had left Tewkesbury aside on his right hand, following the most direct road for Gloucester, as the empress and her train would have done. The forest stretches were on good, broad rides that narrowed only in a few short stretches, making use of level ground. At a bend in the path where the trees grew close, the messenger had said. Nearing her journey's end, the empress would have quickened her pace to be in before dark, and they had taken fresh horses at Evesham. The rearguard had straggled somewhat; easy enough to close in from both sides and cut out a single man. Somewhere here, and two nights past now, and even the traces left by several riders in haste would be fading.

The thicker woodland opened out on the southern side of the track, letting light through the trees to enrich the grasses and wild ground plants below, and someone had chosen this favourable spot to cut out an assart for himself. The hut lay some yards aside, among the trees, with a low wooden fence round it, and a byre beyond. Cadfael heard a cow lowing, very contentedly, and marked how a small space to one side had been cleared of what larger timber it had carried, to allow of modest coppicing. The man of the house was digging within his enclosure, and straightened his back to stare alertly when he heard the soft thudding of hooves along the ride. Beholding a Benedictine brother, he perceptibly relaxed his braced shoulders, slackened his grip on the spade, and called a greeting across the dozen yards or so between.

"Good day to you, brother!"

"God bless the work!" said Cadfael, and checked his horse, turning in between the trees to draw nearer. The man put down his spade and dusted his hands, willing to interrupt his labours for a gossip with a harmless passerby. A square, compact fellow with a creased brown face like a walnut, and sharp blue eyes, well established in his woodland holding, and apparently solitary, for there was no sound or sign of any other creature about the garden or within the hut. "A right hermitage you have here," said Cadfael. "Do you not want for company sometimes?"

"Oh, I've a mind for quietness. And if I tire of it, I have a son married and settled in Hardwicke, barely a mile off, that way, and the children come round on holy days. I get my times for company, but I like the forest life. Whither bound, brother? You'll be in the dusk soon."

"I'll bide the night over at Deerhurst," said Cadfael placidly. "So you never have troubles yourself, friend, with wild men also liking the forest life, but for no good reasons like yours?"

"I'm a man of my hands," said the cottar confidently. "And it's not modest prey like me the outlaws are after. Richer pickings ride along here often enough. Not that we see much trouble of that kind. Cover here is good, but narrow. There are better hunting-grounds."

"That depends on the quarry," said Cadfael, and studied him consideringly. "Two nights back, I think you had a great company through here, on their way to Gloucester. About this time of day, perhaps an hour further into the dark. Did you hear them pass?"

The man had stiffened, and stood regarding Cadfael with narrowed thoughtful eyes, already wary but not, Cadfael thought, of either this enquiry or the enquirer.

"I saw them pass," he said evenly. "Such a stir a wise man does not miss. I did not know then who came. I know now. The empress, she that was all but queen, she came with her men from the bishops' court at Coventry, back into Gloucester. Nothing good ever comes to men like me from her skirts brushing by, nor from the edge of King Stephen's mantle, either. We watch them go by, and thank God when they're gone."

"And did they go by in peace?" asked Cadfael. "Or were there others abroad, lying in ambush for them? Was there fighting? Or any manner of alarm that night?"

"Brother," said the man slowly, "what's your interest in these matters? I stay within doors when armed men pass by, and let alone all who let me alone. Yes, there was some sort of outcry—not here, a piece back along the way, heard, not seen. Shouting, and sudden crashing about among the trees, but all was over in minutes. And then one man came riding at a gallop after the company, crying news, and later another set off back along the route in haste. Brother, if you know more of all this than I do who heard it, why question me?"

"And next morning, by daylight," said Cadfael, "did you go to view that place where the attack was made? And what signs did you find there? How many men, would you judge? And which way did they go, afterwards?"

"They had been waiting in hiding," said the man, "very patiently, most on the southern side of the track, but a few to the north. Their horses had trampled the sward among the trees. I would say at least a dozen in all. And when it was done, whatever was done, they massed and rode at speed, southward. There is a path there. Bushes broken and torn as they crashed through."

"Due south?" said Cadfael.

"And in a hurry. Men who knew their way well enough to hurry, even in the dark. And now that I've told you what I heard and saw—and but for your cloth I would have kept my mouth shut—do you tell me what business you have with such night surprises."

"To the best of my understanding," said Cadfael, consenting to a curiosity as practical and urgent as his own, "those who struck at the empress's rearguard and rode away in haste southward have seized and taken with them into captivity a young man of my close acquaintance, who has done nothing wrong but for incurring the hatred of Philip FitzRobert. And my business is to find where they have taken him, and win him free."

"Gloucester's son, is it? In these parts it's he calls the tune, true enough, and has boltholes everywhere. But, brother," urged the cottar, appalled, "you'd as well beard the devil himself as walk into La Musarderie and confront Philip Fitz-Robert."

"La Musarderie? Is that where he is?" echoed Cadfael.

"So they're saying. And has a hostage or two in there

already, and if there's one more since that tussle here, you have as much chance of winning him free as of being taken up to heaven living. Think twice and again before you venture."

"Friend, I will. And do you live safe here from all armed men, and say a prayer now and then for all prisoners and captives, and you'll be doing your share."

Here among the trees the light was perceptibly fading. He had best be moving on to Deerhurst. At least he had gleaned a crumb of evidence to help him on his way. A hostage or two in there already. And Philip himself installed there. And where he was, surely he would bring with him his perverse treasure of bitterness and hatred, and hoard up his revenges.

Cadfael was about to turn his horse to the track once more, when he thought of one more thing he most needed to know, and brought out the rolled leaf of vellum from the breast of his habit, and spread it open on his thigh to show the drawings of the salamander seal.

"Have you ever seen this badge, on pennant, or harness, or seal? I am trying to find its owner."

The man viewed it attentively, but shook his head. "I know nothing of these badges and devices of the gentles, barring the few close hereabouts. No, I never saw it. But if you're bound for Deerhurst, there's a brother of the house studies such things, and prides himself on knowing the devices of every earl and baron in the land. He can surely give this one a name."

He emerged from the dusk of the woodland into the full daylight of the wide water-meadows flanking that same Severn he had left behind at Shrewsbury, but here twice the width and flowing with a heavy dark power. And there gleaming through trees no great way inland from the water was the creamy silver stone of the church tower, solid Saxon work, squat and strong as a castle keep. As he approached, the long line of the nave roof came into view, and an apse at the east end, with a semicircular base and a faceted upper part. An old, old house, centuries old, and refounded and endowed by the Confessor, and bestowed by him upon Saint Denis. The Confessor was always more Norman in his sympathies than English.

Once again Cadfael found himself approaching almost with reluctance the Benedictine ambience that had been home to him for so many years, and feeling that he came unworthily and without rights. But here his conscience must endure its own deception if he was to enquire freely after the knowledge he needed. When all was done, if he survived the doing, he would make amends.

The porter who admitted him into the court was a round and amiable soul in his healthy middle years, proud of his house, and happy to show off the beauties of his church. There was work going on south of the choir, a masons' lodge shelved out against the wall of the apse, and ashlar stacked for building. Two masons and their labourers were just covering the banker and laying by their tools as the light faded. The porter indicated fondly the foundations of walls outlining the additions to be made to the fabric.

"Here we are building another south-east chapel, and the like to balance it on the northern side. Our master mason is a local man, and the works of the Church are his pride. A good man! He gives work to some unfortunates other masters might find unprofitable. You see the labourer who goes lame of one leg there, from an injury. A man-at-arms until recently, but useless to his lord now, and Master Bernard took him on, and has had no cause to regret it, for the man works hard and well."

The labourer who went heavily on the left leg, surely after some very ill-knit fracture, was otherwise a fine, sturdy fellow, and very agile for all his disability. Probably about thirty years old, with large, able hands, and a long reach. He stood back civilly to give them passage, and then completed the covering of the stacked timber under the wall, and followed the master-mason towards the outer gate.

As yet there had been nothing harder than mild ground frosts, or building would have ceased already for the winter, and the growing walls been bedded down in turf and heather and straw to sleep until spring.

"There'll be work within for them when the winter closes in," said the porter. "Come and see."

Within Deerhurst's priory church there was as yet no mark of the Norman style, all was Saxon, and the first walls of the nave centuries old. Not until the porter had shown forth all the curiosities and beauties of his church to the visitor did he hand Cadfael over to the hospitaller, to be furnished with a bed, and welcomed into the community at supper in the frater.

Before Compline he asked after the learned brother who was knowledgeable about the devices and liveries of the noble houses of England, and showed the drawings he had made in Coventry. Brother Eadwin studied them and shook his head. "No, this I have not seen. There are among the baronage some families who use several personal variations among their many members and branches. This is certainly none of the most prominent. I have never seen it before."

Neither, it seemed, had the prior, or any of the brethren. They studied the drawings, but could not give the badge a family name or a location.

"If it belongs in these parts," said Brother Eadwin, willing to be helpful, "you may find an answer in the village rather than within here. There are some good but minor families holding manors in this shire, besides those of high rank. How did it come into your hands, brother?"

"It was in the baggage of a dead man," said Cadfael, "but not his. And the original is in the hands of the bishop of Coventry now, until we can discover its owner and restore it." He rolled up the leaf of vellum, and retied the cord that bound it. "No matter. The lord bishop will pursue it."

He went to Compline with the brothers, preoccupied rather with the pain and guilt of his own self-exile from this monastic world than with the responsibility he had voluntarily taken upon himself in the secular world. The office comforted him, and the silence afterwards came gratefully. He put away all thought until the morrow, and rested in the quietness until he fell asleep.

Nevertheless, after Mass next morning, when the builders had again uncovered their stores to make use of one more working day, he remembered the porter's description of Master Bernard as a local man, and thought it worth the trial to unroll his drawings upon the stacked ashlar and call the mason to study them and give judgement. Masons may be called upon to work upon manors and barns and farmsteads as well as churches, and use brands and signs in their own mysteries, and so may well respect and take note of them elsewhere.

The mason came, gazed briefly, and said at once: "No, I do not know it." He studied it with detached interest, but shook his head decidedly. "No, this I've never seen."

Two of his workmen, bearing a laden hand-barrow, had checked for a moment in passing to peer in natural curiosity at the leaf which was engaging their master's interest. The lame man, braced on his good right leg, looked up from the vellum to Cadfael's face for a long moment, before they moved on, and smiled and shrugged when Cadfael returned the glance directly.

"No local house, then," said Cadfael resignedly.

"None that's known to me, and I've done work for most manors round here." The mason shook his head again, as Cadfael re-rolled the leaf and put it back securely within his habit. "Is it of importance?"

"It may be. Somewhere it will be known."

It seemed he had done all that could be done here. What his next move should be he had not considered yet, let alone decided. By all the signs Philip must be in La Musarderie, where most probably his men had taken Yves into captivity, and where, according to the woodsman, he already had another hostage, or more than one, in hold. Even more convincing it seemed to Cadfael, was the argument that a man of such powerful passions would be where his hatreds anchored him. Beyond doubt Philip believed Yves guilty. Therefore if he could be convinced he was wronging the boy, his intent could and would be changed. He was an intelligent man, not beyond reason.

Cadfael took his problem with him into the church at the hour of tierce, and said the office privately in a quiet corner. He was just opening his eyes and turning to withdraw when a hand was laid softly on his sleeve from behind.

"Brother . . ."

The lame man, for all his ungainliness, could move silently in his scuffed felt shoes on the floor tiles. His weathered face, under a thatch of thick brown hair, was intent and sombre. "Brother, you are seeking the man who uses a certain seal to his dealings. I saw your picture." He had a low, constrained voice, well suited to confidences.

"I was so seeking," agreed Cadfael ruefully, "but it seems no one here can help me. Your master does not recognize it as belonging to any man he knows."

"No," said the lame man simply. *"But I do."*

CHAPTER SEVEN

CADFAEL HAD opened his mouth to question eagerly, seizing upon this unforeseen chance, but he recalled that the man was at work, and already dependent on his master's goodwill, and lucky to have found such a patron. "You'll be missed," he said quickly. "I can't bring you into reproof. When are you free?"

"At sext we rest and eat our bit of dinner. Long enough," said the lame man, and briefly smiled. "I feared you might be for leaving before I could tell you what I know."

"I would not stir," said Cadfael fervently. "Where? Here? You name the place, I'll be waiting."

"The last carrel of the walk, next to where we're building." With the stacked ashlar and all the timber at their backs, Cadfael reflected, and a clear view of anyone who should appear in the cloister. This one, whatever the reason, natural suspicion or well-grounded caution, kept a close watch on his back, and a lock on his tongue.

"No word to any other?" said Cadfael, holding the level grey eyes that met him fairly.

"In these parts too much has happened to make a man loose-mouthed. A word in the wrong ear may be a knife in the wrong back. No offence to your habit, brother. Praise God, there are still good men." And he turned, and went limping back to the outer world and his labours on God's work.

* * *

In the comparative warmth of noon they sat together in the end carrel of the north walk of the cloister, where they could see down the full length of the walk across the garth. The grass was dry and bleached after an almost rainless autumn, but the sky was overcast and heavy with the foreshowing of change.

"My name," said the lame man, "is Forthred. I come from Todenham, which is an outlier of this manor of Deerhurst. I took service for the empress under Brien de Soulis, and I was in Faringdon with his force, the few weeks the castle stood for the cause. It's there I've seen the seal you have there in the drawings. Twice I've seen it set to documents he witnessed. No mistaking it. The third time I saw it was on the agreement they drew up and sealed when they handed over Faringdon to the king."

"It was done so solemnly?" said Cadfael, surprised. "I thought they simply let in the besiegers by night."

"So they did, but they had their agreement ready to show to us, the men of the garrison, proving that all six captains with followings among us had accepted the change, and committed us with them. I doubt they would have carried the day but for that. A nay word from one or two of the best, and their men would have fought, and King Stephen would have paid a stiff price for Faringdon. No, it was planned and connived at beforehand."

"Six captains with their own companies," said Cadfael, brooding, "and all under de Soulis's command?"

"So it was. And some thirty or so new knights or squires without personal following, only their own arms."

"Of those we know. Most refused to turn their coats, and are prisoners now among the king's men. But all these six who had companies of their own men were agreed, and set their seals to the surrender?"

"Every one. It would not have been done so easily else.

Fealty among the common soldiery is to their own leaders. They go where their captains go. One seal missing from that vellum, and there would have been trouble. One in particular, and there would have been a battle. One who carried the most weight with us, and was the best liked and trusted."

There was something in his voice as he spoke of this man, elect and valued, that conveyed much more than had been said. Cadfael touched the rolled leaf of vellum.

"This one?"

"The same," said Forthred, and for a moment volunteered nothing more, but sat mute, gazing along the grass of the garth with eyes that looked inward rather than outward.

"And he, like the rest, set his seal to the surrender?"

"His seal—this seal—was certainly there to be seen. With my own eyes I saw it. I would not have believed it else."

"And his name?"

"His name is Geoffrey FitzClare, and the Clare whose son he is is Richard de Clare, who was earl of Hertford, and the present earl, Gilbert, is his half-brother. A by-blow of the house of Clare. Sometimes these sons come by astray are better than the true coin. Though Gilbert, for all I know, is a good man, too. At least he and his half-brother have always respected and liked each other, seemingly, although all the Clares are absolute for Stephen, and this chance brother chose the empress. They were raised together, for Earl Richard brought his bastard home almost newborn, and the grandam took him up in care, and they did well by him, and set him up in life when he was grown. That is the man whose seal you're carrying with you, or the picture of it, at least." He had not asked how Cadfael had come by it, to make the copy.

"And where," wondered Cadfael, "is this Geoffrey to be found now? If he pledged himself and his men to Stephen along with the rest, is he still with the garrison at Faringdon?"

"At Faringdon he surely is," said the lame man, his low voice edged like steel, "but not with the garrison. The day after the surrender they brought him into the castle in a litter, after a fall from his horse. He died before night. He is buried in the churchyard at Faringdon. He has no more need now of his seal."

The silence that fell between them hung suspended, like a held breath, upon Cadfael's senses, before the echoes began, echoes not of the words which had been spoken, but of those which had not been spoken, and never need be. There was an understanding between them that needed no ritual form. A man certainly had need to keep a lock on his tongue, a man who had perilous things to tell, was already crippled, and had to live all too close, still, to men of power who had things to hide. Forthred had gone far in trusting even the Benedictine habit, and must not be made to utter openly what he had already conveyed clearly enough by implication.

And as yet he did not even know how Cadfael had come by the salamander seal.

"Tell me," said Cadfael carefully, "about those few days, how events fell out. The timing is all."

"Why, we were pressed, that was true, and hot summer, and none too well provided with water, seeing we had a strong garrison. And Philip from Cricklade had been sending to his father for relief, time and time again, and no reply. And come that one morning, there were the king's officers let in by night, and Brien de Soulis calls on us not to resist, and brings before us this sealed agreement, to be seen by all of us, his own seal and all five of the others, the command of the entire garrison but for the young men who brought only their own proficiency in arms to the defence. And those who would not countenance the change of allegiance were made prisoner, as all men know. And the men-at-arms—small choice, seeing our masters had committed us."

"And Geoffrey's seal was there with the rest?"

"*It* was there," said Forthred simply. "*He* was not."

No, that had begun to be apparent. But no doubt it had been adequately accounted for.

"They told us he had ridden to Cricklade in the night, to report to Philip FitzRobert what had been done. But before leaving he had set his seal to the agreement. First among equals he had set it there, with his own hand."

And without it there would have been no such easy passage from empress to king. Lacking his consent, his own men and others would have taken station at his back, and there would have been a battle.

"And the next day?" said Cadfael.

"The next day he did not come back. And they began to seem anxious—as were we all," said Forthred with level and expressionless voice, "and de Soulis and two who were nearest to him rode out to follow the way he would have ridden. And in the dusk they brought him back in a litter, wrapped in a cloak. Found in the woodland, they said, thrown from his horse and badly hurt, and the beast led back riderless. And in the night he died."

In the night he died. But which night, thought Cadfael, and felt the same conviction burning and bitter in the man who sat beside him. A dead man can easily be removed to some private place in one night, the night of the betrayal in which he refused to take part, and brought back publicly the next night, lost by tragic accident.

"And he is buried," said Forthred, "there in Faringdon. They did not show us the body."

"Had he wife or child?" asked Cadfael.

"No, none. De Soulis sent a courier to tell the Clares of his death, Faringdon being now of their party. They have had masses said for him in all good faith." With the house of Clare he had no quarrel.

"I have an uneasy thought," said Cadfael tentatively, "that there is more to tell. So soon thereafter—how did you come by your injuries?"

A dark smile crossed the composed face of the lame man. "A fall. I had a perilous fall. From the keep into the ditch. I did not like my new service as well as the old, but it was not wisdom to show it. How did they know? How do they always know? There was always someone between me and the gate. I was letting myself down from the wall when someone cut the rope."

"And left you there broken and unaided?"

"Why not? Another accident, they come in twos and threes. But I could crawl as far as cover, and there decent poor men found me. It has knit awry, but I am alive."

There were monstrous debts here to be repaid some day, the worth of a life, the price of a body deliberately and coldly maimed. Cadfael suddenly felt burdened by a debt of his own, since this man had so resolutely trusted and confided in him for no return. One piece of knowledge he had, that after its perverse and inadequate fashion might at least provide proof that justice, however indirect or delayed, is certain in the end.

"I have a thing to tell you, Forthred, that you have not asked me. This seal, that was so used to confirm a betrayal, is now in the hands of my bishop in Coventry. And as to how it came there, it was among the baggage of a man who attended the conference there, and there was killed, no one knows by whose hand. His own seal he had on him, that was nothing strange. But he also had this other, from which I made these drawings. The seal of Geoffrey FitzRichard of Clare travelled from Faringdon to Coventry in the saddlebags of Brien de Soulis, and Brien de Soulis is dead in Coventry with a dagger through his heart."

At the end of the cloister walk the master-mason passed by returning to his work. Forthred rose slowly to follow, and his smile, bleak but assuaged, shone exultantly for an instant, and then was suppressed and veiled in his normal stony indifference. "God is neither blind nor deaf," he said, low-voiced, "no, nor forgetful. Praise be!" And he stepped out into the empty walk and crossed the turf of the garth, limping heavily, and Cadfael was left gazing after him.

And now there was no cause to remain here another hour, and no doubt whither he must go. He sought out the hospitaller, and made his farewells, and went to saddle up in the stable yard. As yet he had not given a thought to how he should proceed when he came to Greenhamsted. But there are more ways than one of breaking into a castle, and sometimes the simplest is the best. Especially for a man who has forsworn arms, and taken vows that bar him from both violence and duplicity. Truth is a hard master, and costly to serve, but it simplifies all problems. And even an apostate may find it honourable to keep such vows as are not already broken.

Hugh's handsome young chestnut roan was glad to be on the move again, and came forth from his stall dancing, the light silvering into lustre the white bloom tempering the brightness of his coat. They set forth from Deerhurst southward. They had some fifteen miles to go, Cadfael judged, and would do well to give Gloucester a wide berth, leaving it on the right hand. There was heavy cloud closing in on the afternoon; it would be a pleasure to ride briskly.

They came up from the broad valley meadows into the edges of the hill country, among the high sheep villages where the wool merchants found some of their finest fleeces. They were already in the fringes of the most active battleground, and local farming had not gone quite unscathed, but most of the fighting was a matter of sporadic raiding by the garrisons of the castles, each faction plaguing the other, in a series of damaging exchanges in which Faringdon had been designed to play the central part for the empress, and now balanced King Stephen's line and held open communications between Malmesbury and Oxford. Somewhat tired warfare now, Cadfael realized, though still venomous. Earl Robert Bossu was right, in the end they must come to terms, because neither side was capable of inflicting defeat upon the other.

Could that, he wondered, once grasped, be a sound reason for changing sides, and transferring all one's powers and weapons to the other faction? On the consideration, for instance: I have fought for the empress nine years now, and I know we are not one step nearer winning a victory that can bring back order and government to this land. I wonder if the other party, should I transfer to them and take others with me, could do what we have failed to do, settle the whole score, and put the weapons away. Anything to put an end to this endless waste. Yes, it might even seem worth the trial. But partisanship must have ebbed wholly and horribly away into exhaustion in order to reach the despairing knowledge that any end to the anarchy would be better than none.

Then what could there be beyond that stage, when the new alliance proved as wasteful, incompetent and infuriating as the old? Only total disgust with both factions, and withdrawal to spend the last remaining energies on something better worth.

The road Cadfael was travelling had levelled on the uplands, and stretched before him arrow-straight into distance. Villages here were prosperous from the wool trade, but far between, and tended to lie aside from the highway. He was forced to turn off in order to find a house at which to ask guidance, and the cottar who came out to greet him eyed him with sharp attention when he asked for La Musarderie.

"You're not from these parts, brother? Likely you don't know the place has fallen into fresh hands. If your business is with the Musards, you'll not find them. Robert Musard was taken in an ambush weeks, months back now, and had to give up his castle to the Earl of Gloucester's son, he that's declared for King Stephen recently."

"So I had heard," said Cadfael. "But I have an errand there

I have undertaken and must fulfill. I take it the change is not well thought of hereabouts."

The man shrugged. "Church and village he lets alone, provided neither priest nor reeve gets in his way. But Musards have been there ever since the first King William gave the manor to this one's great-grandsire, and no man now expects change to be for the better. So go softly, brother, if you must go. He'll be ware of any stranger before ever you get close to his walls."

"He'll hardly fear any feats of arms from me," said Cadfael. "And what I have to fear from him I'll be prepared for. And thanks, friend, for the warning. Now, how must I go?"

"Go back to the road," he was advised, with a shrug for his probably ill-fated persistence, "and ride on for a mile or more, and there's a track on the right will bring you to Winstone. Cross the river beyond by the ford, and up through the woodland the other side, and when you come clear of the trees you'll see the castle ahead of you, it stands high. The village stands higher still, up on the crest beyond," he said. "Go gently, and come again safely."

"By God's favour I hope for it," said Cadfael, and thanked him, and turned his horse to return to the highroad.

There are more ways than one of getting into a castle, he reasoned as he rode through the village of Winstone. The simplest of all, for a lone man without an army or any means of compulsion, is to ride up to the gate and ask to be let in. I am manifestly not in arms, the day is drawing towards an early and chilly evening, and hospitality is a sacred duty. Especially is it incumbent on the nobility to open roof and board to clerics and monastics in need. Let us see, then, how far Philip FitzRobert's nobility extends.

And following the same sequence of thought: if you want to have speech with the castellan, the most obvious means is to ask; and the most unshakable story to get you into his presence is the truth. He holds two men—surely by now that is as good as certain!—two men to whom he means no good. You want them released unharmed, and have good reasons to advance why he should reconsider his intent towards them. Nothing could be simpler. Why complicate matters by going roundabout?

Beyond Winstone the road proceeded virtually due west, and gradually dwindled into a track, though a well-made and well-used one. From open, scattered woodland and heath it plunged almost suddenly into thick forest, and began to descend steeply by winding traverses among trees into a deep valley. He heard water flowing below, no great flood but the purling sound of a little river with a stony bed; and presently he came out on a narrow slope of grass on its banks, and a narrower tongue of gravel led out into the water, marking the passage of the ford. On the further side the track rose again almost as steeply as on the side where he had descended, and old, long-established trees hid all that awaited him beyond.

He crossed, and began to climb out of the valley. Light and air showed suddenly between the trees, and he emerged from forest into cleared land, bare even of bushes; and there before and above him, at perhaps a half-mile distance, on a level promontory, stood the castle of La Musarderie.

He had been right, four generations of the same family in unchallenged possession had afforded time to build in local stone, to enlarge and to strengthen. The first hasty palisades thrown up in timber seventy-five years ago, to establish and assure ownership, had vanished long since. This was a massive bulk, a battlemented curtain wall, twin gate-towers, squat and strong, fronting this eastward approach, and the serrated crests of other flanking towers circling a tall keep within. Beyond, the ground continued to rise steeply in complex folds and levels to a long crest above, where Cadfael could just distinguish above the trees the top of a church tower, and the occasional slope of a roof, marking the village of Greenhamsted. A rising causeway, stripped of all cover and dead straight, led up to the castle gates. No one was allowed to approach La Musarderie unseen. All round it the ground had been cleared of cover.

Cadfael embarked on that climb with deliberation, willing to be seen, waiting to be challenged. Philip FitzRobert would not tolerate any inefficient service. They were already alerted, long before he came within hailing distance. He heard a horn call briefly within. The great double doors were closed. It was sufficiently late in the day to have everything secured, but there was a wicket left open, lofty enough and wide enough to let in a mounted man, even a galloping man if he came pursued, and easy and light enough to slam shut after him and bar once he was within. In the twin short towers that flanked the gate there were arrow-slits that could bring to bear a dual field of fire on any pursuers. Cadfael approved, his instincts harking back to encounters long past but not forgotten.

Such a gateway, however innocently open, a man approaches with discretion, keeping both hands in clear view, and neither hastening nor hesitating. Cadfael ambled the last few yards and halted outside, though no one had appeared either to welcome or obstruct. He called through the open wicket: "Peace on all within!" and moved on gently through the opening and into the bailey, without waiting for an answer.

In the dark, vaulted archway of the gate there were men on either side of him, and when he emerged into the ward two more were ready for him, prompt to bridle and stirrup, unhurried and unthreatening, but watchful.

"And on whoever comes in peace," said the officer of the guard, coming out from the guardroom smiling, if a little narrowly. "As doubtless you do, brother. Your habit speaks for you."

"It speaks truly," said Cadfael.

"And what's your will in these parts?" asked the sergeant. "And where are you bound?"

"Here, to La Musarderie," said Cadfael directly, "if you'll afford me houseroom a while, till I speak with your lord. My business is nothing beyond that. I come to beg audience with Philip FitzRobert, and they tell me he's here within. At your disposal and his, whenever he sees fit. I'll wait his pleasure as long as need be."

"You're messenger for another?" the sergeant questioned, no more than mildly curious. "He's come back from a clutch of bishops, are you here to speak for yours?"

"After a fashion, yes," Cadfael conceded. "But for myself also. If you'll be so good as to carry him my request, no doubt he'll also speak his mind."

They surrounded him, but at a tolerant distance, curious and alert, faintly grinning, while their sergeant considered at leisure what to think of him and what to do with him. The bailey was not very large, but the wide clearance of cover all round the castle walls compensated for that. From the guardwalk along the wall the view would be broad enough to give ample warning of any force coming in arms, and provide a murderous field for archers, who almost certainly figured large in the garrison. The encrustation of sheds, stores, armouries and cramped living quarters all round the wall within consisted mainly of timber. Fire, Cadfael considered, might be a threat, but even so a limited one. Hall and keep and towers and curtain wall were all of stone. He wondered why he was studying the place as an objective in battle, a stronghold to be taken. So it might prove to him, but not that way.

"Light down and be welcome, brother," said the sergeant amiably. "We never turn away men of your cloth. As for our lord, you'll need to wait a while, for he's out riding this moment, but he shall hear your asking, never fear. Let Peter

here take your horse, and he'll bring your saddle bags into
the lodging for you."

"I tend my own horse," said Cadfael placidly, mindful of
the precaution of knowing where to find him at need; though
the sergeant was so assured of having only a simple monastic
courier on his hands that there was no need to suspect him
of any deception. "I was a man-at-arms myself, long years
ago. Once learned, you never lose the habit."

"True enough," said the sergeant indulgently, humouring
this old ex-warrior. "Then Peter will show you, and when
you're done, you'll find someone in hall to see to your needs.
If you've borne arms yourself you'll be used to a soldier's
keep."

"And content with it," agreed Cadfael heartily, and led his
horse away after the groom, well satisfied to be within the
wards. Nor did he miss any of the evidences that Philip kept
an alert and well-run household here. Recalling the dark and
courteous presence encountered so briefly and privately in
the priory church at Coventry, he would have expected nothing
less. Every castle ward has a multifarious life of its own, that
goes on without fuss, in well-house, bakery, armoury, store
and workshops, in two parallel disciplines, one military, one
domestic. Here in a region of warfare, however desultory
the dangers might be, the domestic side of castle life in La
Musarderie seemed to have been scaled down to a minimum,
and almost womanless. Possibly Philip's steward had a wife
somewhere, in charge of such women servants as might be
kept here, but the economy within was starkly military and
austerely male, and functioned with a ruthless efficiency that
surely stemmed from its lord. Philip was unmarried and without children, wholly absorbed into the demonic conflict that
no one seemed able to end. His castle reflected his obsession.

There was human activity enough about the ward and in
the stables, men came and went about their proper businesses,
without haste but briskly, and the babel of voices was as

constant as the buzzing about a beehive. The groom Peter was easy and talkative about helping Cadfael to unsaddle and unload, groom and water the horse and settle him in a stall, and pointed him amiably to the hall when that was done. The steward's clerk who received him there with no more than momentary surprise and an acquiescent shrug, as though accepting a visitor of an unexpected but harmless kind, offered him a bed as of right, and told him where to find the chapel, for the proper hour of Vespers was past, and he had need of a pause to give thanks for present blessings and invoke help in future contentions. An elderly Benedictine wanting shelter for the night, what was there in that to enlist any man's interest for more than a moment, even where voluntary guests were few and far between?

The chapel was in the heart of the keep, and he wondered a little that they should let him into it unwatched and solitary. Philip's garrison had no hesitation in allowing a monastic access to the central defences of the castle, they had even housed him within the keep, and there could be no other reason for such confidence than simple trust in his integrity and reverence for his habit. That caused him to look more closely into his own motives and methods, and confirmed him in the directness of his approach. There was no other way but straight forward, whether to success or ruin.

He paid his belated devotions very gravely, in the chill, stony chapel, on his knees before an altar austerely draped and lit only by one small, steady lamp. The vault above withdrew into darkness, and the cold honed his mind as it stiffened his flesh. Lord God, how must I approach, how can I match, such a man? One who in casting off one coat has stripped himself naked to reproach and condemnation, and in donning another has merely covered his wounds, not healed them. I do not know what to make of this Philip.

He was rising from his knees when he heard, distantly from the outer ward, the brisk clatter of hooves on the cobbles, a small, sharp sound. One horse only; one man only, like himself, not afraid to ride out from a castle or into a castle alone, in a region where castles were prizes to be seized at the least opportunity, and prisons to be avoided at all costs. After a moment Cadfael heard the horse being led away to the stable yard, treading out sober walking paces across the stones, ebbing into silence. He turned to leave the chapel, and went out between the guardrooms and gates of the keep, where the twilight hung pale against the black pillars of the portal. He emerged into what seemed by contrast almost daylight, and found himself crossing the path of Philip FitzRobert, just dismounted after his ride and striding across the ward to his hall, shrugging off his cloak onto one arm as he went. They met and halted, two or three yards between them, mutually at gaze.

The rising wind of evening had ruffled Philip's black hair, for he had ridden with head uncovered. The short, blown strands laced his high forehead, and caused him to frown as he stared. He went in the plainest of dark gear, independent of any manner of ornament or finery. His own bearing was his distinction. Physically, in motion or in stillness, he had an elongated elegance, and a tension like a strung bow.

"They told me I had a guest," he said, and narrowed his full, dark brown eyes. "Brother, I think I have seen you before."

"I was in Coventry," said Cadfael, "among many others. Though whether you ever noticed me is more than I can say."

There was a brief silence, and neither of them moved. "You were present," Philip said then, "close by, but you did not speak. I do remember, you were by when we found de Soulis dead."

"I was," said Cadfael.

"And now you come to me. To have speech with me. So they have said. On whose behalf?"

"On behalf of justice and truth," said Cadfael, "at least in my view. On behalf of myself, and of some for whom I am advocate. And ultimately, perhaps, my lord, even on yours."

The eyes narrowed to sharpen vision through the fading light studied him in silence for a moment, without, apparently, finding any fault with the boldness of this address.

"I shall have time to listen," said Philip then, the courteous level of his voice unshaken even by curiosity, "after supper. Come to me after I leave the hall. Any man of the household will show you where to find me. And if you wish, you may assist my chaplain at Compline. I respect your habit."

"That I cannot," said Cadfael bluntly. "I am not a priest. Even the full right of this habit I cannot now claim. I am absent without leave from my abbot. I have broken the cord. I am apostate."

"For cause!" said Philip, and stared upon him steadily for a long moment, his interest both caught and contained within measure. Then he said abruptly: "Nevertheless, come!" and turned and walked away into his hall.

CHAPTER EIGHT

IN PHILIP FitzRobert's hall the service was Spartan, and the company exclusively male. He presided at the high table among his knights, and the young men of his following used him with confident candour, not in awe, but to all appearances in willing duty. He ate sparingly and drank little, talked freely with his equals and courteously with his servants. And Cadfael, from his place beside the chaplain at a lower table, watched him and wondered what went on behind the lofty forehead and the deep brown eyes like slow-burning fires, and all that was mysterious in him, if not ominous.

He rose from the table early, leaving the men of his garrison to continue at their leisure, and after his going there was an easing of manners and further circling of ale and wine, and some who could make music fetched their instruments to enliven the evening. Small doubt there was a strong guard set, and all gates closed and barred. Musard, so the chaplain had reported, had foolishly gone forth hunting, and ridden straight into Philip's ambush, and been forced to surrender his castle in order to regain his freedom, and possibly also to keep himself man alive; though threats against life in order to gain possession of a fortress were more likely to remain threats than to be put into action, and often met with obstinate defiance even with necks noosed and hangmen ready, in the assurance that they dared not be carried out. Family loyalties and complex intermarriages had baulked a great many such attempts. But Musard, not having a powerful relative on Stephen's side, of greater importance to the king than Philip himself, had been less confident of his safety, and given in. That was hardly likely ever to happen to Philip. He showed no fear of any man, but neither would he leave gates unbarred, or fail to set good sentries on the walls.

"I am bidden to your lord's presence," said Cadfael, "after he withdraws from the hall. Will you point me the way? I think he is not a man to be kept waiting when he has named the time."

The chaplain was old and experienced, beyond surprise. In any case nothing that their castellan did, nothing he denied, nothing he granted, no princeling he rejected, no humble travelling monastic he welcomed, seemed to occasion surprise here. There would be sufficient reason for all, and whether that reason proved comprehensible or not, it would not be questioned.

The old priest shrugged, and rose obligingly from table to lead the way out from the hall. "He keeps early hours as a rule. So he set you a time, did he? You're favoured. But he's hospitable to any who wear your habit, or come in the Church's name."

Cadfael forbore from following that lead. It was known here that he came from the conference at Coventry, and probably assumed that he bore some further exhortation from his bishop to insinuate into Philip's ear. Let them by all means think so; it accounted for him very satisfactorily. As between himself and Philip there could be no pretences.

"In here. He lives almost priestly," commented the chaplain, "here in the cold of the keep, close to his chapel, none of your cushioned solars." They were in a narrow stone passage, lit only by a small, smoky torch in a bracket on the wall. The door they approached was narrow, and stood ajar. At the chaplain's knock a voice from within called: "Come!"

Cadfael entered a small, austere room, high-windowed on a single lancet of naked sky, in which a faint dusting of starlight showed. They were one lofty floor raised, high enough to clear the curtain wall on this sheltered side. Below the window a large, shaded candle burned on a heavy table, and behind the table Philip sat on a broad stool buttressed with massive carved arms, his back against the dark hangings on the wall. He looked up from the book that lay open before him. It was no surprise that he was lettered. Every faculty he had he would push to the limit.

"Come in, brother, and close the door."

His voice was quiet, and his face, lit sidelong by the candle at his left elbow, showed sharply defined in planes of light and ravines of shadow, deep hollows beneath the high cheekbones and in the ivory settings of dark, thoughtful eyes. Cadfael marvelled again how young he was, Olivier's own age. Something of Olivier, even, in his clear, fastidious face, fixed at this moment in a searching gravity, that hung upon Cadfael in continued speculation.

"You had something to say to me. Sit, brother, and say it freely. I am listening."

A motion of his hand indicated the wooden bench against the wall at his right hand, draped with sheepskin. Cadfael would rather have remained standing, facing him directly, but he obeyed the gesture, and the contact of eyes was not broken; Philip had turned with him, maintaining his unwavering regard.

"Now, what is it you want of me?"

"I want," said Cadfael, "the freedom of two men, two whom, as I believe, you have in close hold."

"Name them," said Philip, "and I will tell you if you believe rightly."

"The name of the first is Olivier de Bretagne. And the name of the second is Yves Hugonin."

"Yes," said Philip without hesitation, and without any change in the quiet level of his voice. "I hold them both."

"Here, in La Musarderie?"

"Yes. They are here. Now tell me why I should release them."

"There are reasons," said Cadfael, "why a fairminded man should take my request seriously. Olivier de Bretagne, I judge from all I know of him, would not consider turning his coat with you when you handed over Faringdon to the king. There were several who held with him, and would not go with you. All were overpowered and made prisoner, to be held for ransom by whoever should be given them as largesse by the king. That is known openly. Why, then, has Olivier de Bretagne not been offered for ransom? Why has it not been made known who holds him?"

"I have made it known now to you," said Philip, with a small, dry smile. "Proceed from there."

"Very well! It is true I had not asked you until now, and now you have not denied. But it was never published where he was, as it was for the others. Is it fair that his case should be different? There are those who would be glad to buy him free."

"However high the price asked?" said Philip.

"Name it, and I will see it raised and paid to you."

There was a long pause, while Philip looked at him with eyes wide and clear, and yet unreadable, so still that not a single hair on his head quivered. "A life, perhaps," he said then, very softly. "Another life in place of his to rot here solitary as he will rot."

"Take mine," said Cadfael.

In the arched lancet of the high window clouds had blotted out the faint starlight, the stones of the wall were now paler than the night without.

"Yours," said Philip with soft deliberation, not questioning, not exclaiming, only saying over the single word to himself as if to incise it on the steely metal of his mind. "What satisfaction would your life be to me? What grudge have I against you, to give me any pleasure in destroying you?"

"What grudge had you against him? What bitter pleasure will you experience in destroying him? What did he ever do to you, except hold fast to his cause when you deserted yours? Or when he so thought of what you did," Cadfael corrected himself stoutly, "for I tell you, I do not know how to interpret all that you have done, and he, as I well know, would be less ready to look not once, but twice, thrice and again, before judging."

No, the protest was pointless. Olivier's fiery scorn would be enough offence. A match for Philip in his towering pride, blazing forth in unrestrained reproach, as if Philip's own mirror image cried out against him. Perhaps the only way to put that mortal wound out of mind had been to bury the accuser out of sight and out of memory.

"You valued him!" said Cadfael, enlightened and unwary.

"I valued him," Philip repeated, and found no fault with the statement. "It is not the first time I have been denied, rejected, misprized, left out of the reckoning, by some I most valued. There is nothing new in that. It takes time to reach the point of cutting off the last of them, and proceeding alone. But now, since you have made me an offer, why should you, why do you, offer me your old bones to moulder in his place? What is Olivier de Bretagne to you?"

"He is my son," said Cadfael.

In the long, profound silence that followed, Philip released held breath at last in a prolonged soft sigh. The chord that had been sounded between them was complex and painful, and echoed eerily in the mind. For Philip also had a father, severed from him now in mutual rejection, irreconcilable.

There was, of course, the elder brother, William, Robert's heir. Was that where the breakage began? Always close, always loved, always sufficient, and this one passed over, his needs and wants as casually attended to as his pleas for Faringdon had been? That might be a part of Philip's passion of anger, but surely not the whole. It was not so simple.

"Do fathers owe such regard to their sons?" he said dryly. "Would mine, do you suppose, lift a hand to release me from a prison?"

"For ought that I know or you know," said Cadfael sturdily, "so he would. You are not in need. Olivier is, and deserves better from you."

"You are in the common error," said Philip indifferently. "I did not first abandon him. He abandoned me, and I have accepted the judgement. If that was the measure of resolution on one side, to bring this abominable waste to an end, what is left for a man but to turn and throw his whole weight into the other scale? And if that prove as ineffective, and fail us as bitterly? How much more can this poor land endure?"

He was speaking almost in the same terms as the Earl of Leicester, and yet his remedy was very different. Robert Bossu was trying to bring together all the wisest and most moderate minds from both factions, to force a compromise which would stop the fighting by agreement. Philip saw no possibility but to end the contention with a total victory, and after eight wasteful years cared very little which faction triumphed, provided the triumph brought back some semblance of law and normality to England. And as Philip was branded traitor and turncoat, so, some day, when he withheld his powers from battle to force his king's hand, would Robert Bossu be branded. But he and his kind might be the saviours of a tormented land, none the less.

"You are speaking now of king and empress," said Cadfael, "and what you say I understand, better than I did until this moment. But I am speaking of my son Olivier. I am offering you a price for him, the price you named. If you meant it, accept it. I do not think, whatever else I might think of you, that you go back on your bargains, bad or good."

"Wait!" said Philip, and raised a hand, but very tolerantly. "I said: perhaps a life. I am not committed by so qualified a declaration. And—forgive me, brother!—would you consider yourself fair exchange, old as you are, against his youth and strength? You appealed to me as a fairminded man, so do I turn to you."

"I see the imbalance," said Cadfael. Not in age and beauty and vigour, however glaring that discrepancy might be, but in the passion of confident trust and affection that could never be adequately paid by the mild passing liking this man felt now for his challenger. When it came to the extreme of testing, surely those two friends had failed to match minds, and that was a disintegration that could never be forgiven, so absolute had been the expectation of understanding. "Nevertheless, I have offered you what you asked, and it is all that is mine to offer you. I cannot raise my stake. There is no more to give. Now be as honest, and admit to me, it is more than you expected."

"It is more," said Philip. "I think, brother, you must allow me time. You come as a surprise to me. How could I know that Olivier had such a father? And if I asked you concerning this so strangely fathered son of yours, I doubt you would not tell me."

"I think," said Cadfael, "that I would."

The dark eyes flared into amused interest. "Do you confide so easily?"

"Not to every man," said Cadfael, and saw the sparks burn down into a steady glow. And again there was a silence, that lay more lightly on the senses than the previous silences.

"Let us leave this," said Philip abruptly. "Unresolved, not abandoned. You came on behalf of two men. Speak of the second. You have things to argue for Yves Hugonin."

"What I have to argue for Yves Hugonin," said Cadfael, "is that he had no part in the death of Brien de Soulis. Him you have altogether mistaken. First, for I know him, have known him from a child, as arrow-straight for his aim as any living man. I saw him, as you did not, not that time, I saw him when first he rode into the priory gate at Coventry, and saw de Soulis in his boldness, armed, and cried out on him for a turncoat and traitor, and laid hand to hilt against him, yes, but face to face before many witnesses. If he had killed, that would have been his way, not lurking in dark places, in ambush with a bared blade. Now consider the night of the man's death. Yves Hugonin says that he came late to Compline, when the office had begun, and remained crowded into the last dark corner within the door, and so was first out to clear the way for the princes. He says that he stumbled in the dark over de Soulis's body, and knelt to see how bad was the man's case, and called out to us to bring lights. And so was taken in all men's sight with bloody hands. All which is patently true, whatever else you attribute to him. For you say he never was in the church, but had killed de Soulis, cleaned his sword and bestowed it safely and innocently in his lodging, where it should be, and returned in good time to cry the alarm in person over a dead man. But if that were true, why call to us at all? Why be there by the body? Why not elsewhere, in full communion with his fellows, surrounded by witnesses to his innocence and ignorance of evil?"

"Yet it could be so," said Philip relentlessly. "Men with limited time to cover their traces do not always choose the most infallible way. What do you object to my most bitter belief?"

"A number of things. First, that same evening I examined Yves' sword, which was sheathed and laid by as he had said. It is not easy to cleanse the last traces of blood from a grooved blade, and of such quests I have had experience. I found no blemish there. Second, after you were gone, with the bishop's leave I examined de Soulis's body. It was no sword that made that wound, no sword ever was made so lean and fine. A thin, sharp dagger, long enough to reach the heart. And a firm stroke, in deep and out clean before he could bleed. The flow of blood came later as he lay, he left the mark outlined on the flagstones under him. And now, third, tell me how his open enemy can have approached him so close, and de Soulis with sword and poniard ready to hand. He would have had his blade out as soon as he saw his adversary nearing, long before ever he came within dagger range. Is that good sense, or no?"

"Good sense enough," Philip allowed, "so far as it goes."

"It goes to the heart of the matter. Brien de Soulis bore arms, he had no mind to be present at Compline, he had another assignation that night. He waited in a carrel of the cloister, and came forth into the walk when he heard and saw his man approaching. A quiet time, with everyone else in the church, a time for private conference with no witnesses. Not with an avowed enemy, but with a friend, someone trusted, someone who could walk up to him confidently, never suspected of any evil intent, and stab him to the heart. And walked away and left him lying, for a foolish young man to stumble over, and yell his discovery to the night, and put his neck in a noose."

"His neck," said Philip dryly, "is still unwrung. I have not yet determined what to do with him."

"And I am making your decision no easier, I trust. For what I tell you is truth, and you cannot but recognize it, whether you will or no. And there is more yet to tell, and though it does not remove from Yves Hugonin all cause for hating Brien de Soulis, it does open the door to many another who may have better cause to hate him even more. Even among some he may formerly have counted his friends."

"Go on," said Philip equably. "I am still listening."

"After you were gone, under the bishop's supervision we

put together all that belonged to de Soulis, to deliver to his brother. He had with him his personal seal, as was to be expected. You know the badge?"

"I know it. The swan and willow wands."

"But we found also another seal, and another device. Do you also know this badge?" He had drawn the rolled leaf out of the breast of his habit, and leaned to flatten it upon the table, between Philip's long muscular hands. "The original is with the bishop. Do you know it?"

"Yes, I have seen it," said Philip with careful detachment. "One of de Soulis's captains in the Faringdon garrison used it. I knew the man, though not well. His own raising, a good company he had. Geoffrey FitzClare, a half-brother to Gilbert de Clare of Hertford, the wrong side the sheets."

"And you must have heard, I think, that Geoffrey FitzClare was thrown from his horse, and died of it, the day Faringdon was surrendered. He was said to have ridden for Cricklade during the night, after he had affixed his seal, like all the other captains who had their own followings within, to the surrender. He did not return. De Soulis and a few with him went out next day to look for him, and brought him home in a litter. Before night they told the garrison he was dead."

"I do know of this," said Philip, his voice for the first time tight and wary. "A very ill chance. He never reached me. I heard of it only afterwards."

"And you were not expecting him? You had not sent for him?"

Philip was frowning now, his level black brows knotted tightly above the deep eyes. "No. There was no need. De Soulis had full powers. There is more to this. What is it you are saying?"

"I am saying that it was convenient he should die by accident so aptly, the day after his seal was added to the agreement that handed over Faringdon to King Stephen. If, indeed, he did not die in the night, before some other hand impressed his seal there. For there are those, and I have spoken with one of them, who will swear that Geoffrey FitzClare never would have consented to that surrender, had he still had voice to cry out or hand to lift and prevent. And if voice and hand had been raised against it, his men within, and maybe more than his would have fought on his side, and Faringdon would never have been taken."

"You are saying," said Philip, brooding, "that his death was no accident. And that it was another, not he, who affixed that seal to the surrender with all the rest. After the man was dead."

"That is what I am saying. Since he would never have set it there himself, nor let it go into other hands while he lived. And his consent was essential, to convince the garrison. I think he died as soon as the thing was broached to him, and he condemned it. There was no time to lose."

"Yet they rode out next day to look for him, and brought him back to Faringdon openly, before the garrison."

"Wrapped in cloaks, in a litter. No doubt his men saw him pass, saw the recognizable face plainly. But they never saw him close. They were never shown the body after they were told that he had died. A dead man in the night can very easily be carried out to lie somewhere in hiding, against his open return next day. The postern that was opened to let the king's negotiators in could as well let FitzClare's dead body out, to some hiding-place in the woods. And how else, for what purpose," said Cadfael heavily, "should FitzClare's seal go with Brien de Soulis to Coventry, and be found in his saddle-bag there."

Philip rose abruptly from his seat, and rounded the table sharply to pace across the room. He moved in silence, with a kind of contained violence, as if his mind was forcing his body into motion as the only means of relief from the smouldering turmoil within. He quartered the room like a prowling cat, and came to rest at length with clenched fists braced on the heavy chest in the darkest corner, his back turned to Cadfael and the source of light. His stillness was as tense as his pacing, and he was silent for long moments. When he turned, it was clear from the bright composure of his face that he had come to a reconciliation with everything he had heard.

"I knew nothing of all this. If it is truth, as my blood in me says it is truth, I had no hand in it, nor never would have allowed it."

"I never thought it," said Cadfael. "Whether the surrender was at your wish—no, at your decree!—I neither know nor ask, but no, you were not there, whatever was done was done at de Soulis's orders. Perhaps by de Soulis's hand. It would not be easy to get four other captains, with followings to be risked, to connive at murder. Better to draw him aside, man to man, and give out that he had been sent to confer with you at Cricklade, while one or two who had no objection to murder secretly conveyed away a dead man and the horse he was said to be riding on his midnight mission. And his seal was first on the vellum. No, you I never thought of as conniving at murder, whatever else I may have found within your scope. But FitzClare is dead, and de Soulis is dead, and you have not, I think, the reason you believed you had to mourn or avenge him. Nor any remaining cause to lay his death at the charge of a young man openly and honestly his enemy. There were many men in Faringdon who would be glad enough to avenge the murder of FitzClare. Who knows if some of them were also present at Coventry? He was well liked, and well served. And not every man of his following believed what he was told of that death."

"De Soulis would have been as ready for such as for Hugonin," said Philip.

"You think they would betray themselves as enemies? No, whoever set out to get close to him would take good care not to give any warning. But Yves had already cried out loud

before the world his anger and enmity. No, yourself you know
it, he would never have got within a sword's reach, let alone
a slender little knife. Set Yves Hugonin free," said Cadfael
"and take me in my son's stead."

Philip came back slowly to his place at the table, and sa
down, and finding his book left open and unregarded, quietly
closed it. He leaned his head between long hands, and fixed
his unnerving eyes again on Cadfael's face. "Yes," he said
rather to himself than to Cadfael, "yes, there is the matter o
your son Olivier. Let us not forget Olivier." But his voice
was not reassuring. "Let us see if the man I have known,
thought well, is the same as the son you have known. Never
has he spoken of a father to me."

"He knows no more than his mother told him, when he
was a child. I have told him nothing. Of his father he know
only a too kindly legend, coloured too brightly by affection.

"If I question too close, refuse me answers. But I feel a
need to know. A son of the cloister?"

"No," said Cadfael, "a son of the Crusade. His mother live
and died in Antioch. I never knew I had left her a son unti
I met with him here in England, and he named her, mentione
times, left me in no doubt at all. The cloister came later."

"The Crusade!" Philip echoed. His eyes burned up int
gold. He narrowed their brightness curiously upon Cadfael'
grizzled tonsure and lined and weathered face. "The Crusad
that made a Christian kingdom in Jerusalem? You were there
Of all battles, surely the worthiest."

"The easiest to justify, perhaps," Cadfael agreed ruefully
"I would not say more than that."

The bright, piercing gaze continued to weigh and measur
and wonder, with a sudden personal passion, staring throug
Cadfael into far distances, beyond the fabled Midland Sea
into the legendary Frankish kingdoms of Outremer. Ever sinc
the fall of Edessa Christendom had been uneasy in its hope

and fears for Jerusalem, and popes and abbots were stirring in their sleep to consider their beleaguered capital, and raise their voices like clarions calling to the defence of the Church. Philip was not yet so old but he could quicken to the sound of the trumpet.

"How did it come that you encountered him here, all unknown? And once only?"

"Twice, and by God's grace there will be a third time," said Cadfael stoutly. He told, very briefly, of the circumstances of both those meetings.

"And still he does not know you for his sire? You never told him?"

"There is no need for him to know. No shame there, but no pride, either. His course is nobly set, why cause any tremor to deflect or shake it?"

"You ask nothing, want nothing of him?" The perilous bitterness was back in Philip's voice, husky with the pain of all he had hoped for from his own father, and failed to receive. Too fierce a love, perverted into too fierce a hate, corroded all his reflections on the anguished relationship between fathers and sons, too close and too separate, and never in balance.

"He owes me nothing," said Cadfael. "Nothing but such friendship and liking as we have deserved of each other by free will and earned trust, not by blood."

"And yet it is by blood," said Philip softly, "that you conceive you owe him so much, even to a life. Brother, I think you are telling me something I have learned to know all too well, though it took me years to master it. We are born of the fathers we deserve, and they engender the sons they deserve. We are our own penance and theirs. The first murderous warfare in the world, we are told, was between two brothers, but the longest and the bitterest is between fathers and sons. Now you offer me the father for the son, and you are offering me nothing that I want or need, in a currency I cannot spend.

How could I ease my anger on you? I respect you, I like you,
there are even things you might ask of me that I would give
you with goodwill. But I will not give you Olivier."

It was a dismissal. There was no more speech between them
that night. From the chapel, hollowly echoing along the corridors of stone, the bell chimed for Compline.

CHAPTER NINE

CADFAEL ROSE at midnight, waking by long habit even without the matins bell, and being awake, recalled that he was lodged in a tiny cell close to the chapel. That gave him further matter for thought, though he had not considered earlier that it might have profound implications. He had declared himself honestly enough in his apostasy to Philip, and Philip, none the less, had lodged him here, where a visiting cleric might have expected such a courtesy. And being so close, and having been so considerately housed there, why should he not at least say Matins and Lauds before the altar? He had not surrendered or compromised his faith, however he had forfeited his rights and privileges.

The very act of kneeling in solitude, in the chill and austerity of stone, and saying the familiar words almost silently, brought him more of comfort and reassurance than he had dared to expect. If grace was not close to him, why should he rise from his knees so cleansed of the doubts and anxieties of the day, and clouded by no least shadow of the morrow's uncertainties?

He was in the act of withdrawing, and a pace or two from the open door, which he had refrained from closing in case it should creak loudly enough to wake others, when one who was awake, and as silent as he, looked in upon him. The faint light showed them to each other clearly enough.

"For an apostate," said Philip softly, "you keep the hours very strictly, brother." He wore a heavy furred gown over his nakedness, and walked barefooted on the stone. "Oh, no, you did not disturb me. I sat late tonight. For that you may take the blame if you wish."

"Even a recusant," said Cadfael, "may cling by the hems of grace. But I am sorry if I have kept you from sleep."

"There may be better than sorrow in it for you," said Philip. "We will speak again tomorrow. I trust you have all you need here, and lie at least as softly as in the dortoir at home? There is no great difference between the soldier's bed and the monk's, or so they tell me. I have tried only the one, since I came to manhood."

Truth, indeed, since he had taken up arms in this endless contention in support of his father before he reached twenty.

"I have known both," said Cadfael, "and complain of neither."

"So they told me, I recall, at Coventry. Some who knew of you. As I did not—not then," said Philip, and drew his gown closer about him. "I, too, had a word to say to God," he said, and passed Cadfael and entered his chapel. "Come to me after Mass."

"Not behind a closed door this time," said Philip, taking Cadfael by the arm as they came out from Mass, "but publicly in hall. No, you need not speak at all, your part is done. I have considered all that has emerged concerning Brien de Soulis and Yves Hugonin, and if the one matter is still unproven, guilty or no, the other cries out too loud to be passed over. Let Brien de Soulis rest as well as he may, it is too late to accuse him, at least here. But Hugonin—no, there is too great a doubt. I no longer accuse him, I dare not. Come, see him released to ride and rejoin his own faction, wherever he pleases."

In the hall of La Musarderie trestle tables and benches were all cleared away, leaving the great space stark and bare, the central fire roused and well tended, for winter was beginning to bite with night frosts, and for all the shelter of the deep river valley the winds found their bitter way in by every shutter and every arrow-slit. Philip's officers gathered there turned impartial faces as he entered, and a cluster of men-at-arms held off and watched, awaiting his will.

"Master of arms," said Philip, "go and bring up Yves Hugonin from his cell. Take the smith with you, and strike off his chains. It has been shown me that in all probability I have done him wrong in thinking him guilty of de Soulis's death. At least I have doubt enough in me to turn him loose and clear him of all offence against me. Go and fetch him here."

They went without hesitation, with a kind of indifferent briskness that came naturally to these men who served him. Fear had no part in their unquestioning promptness. Any who feared him would have fallen off from him and taken themselves elsewhere.

"You have given me no chance to be grateful," said Cadfael in Philip's ear.

"There is no occasion for gratitude here. If you have told me truth, this is due. I make too much haste, sometimes, but I do not of intent spit in the face of truth." And to some of the men who hovered in the doorway: "See his horse saddled, and his saddle-roll well provided. No, wait a while for that. His own grooming may take a while, and we must send our guests forth fed and presentable."

They went to do his bidding, to heat water and carry it to an empty apartment, and install there the saddle-roll that had been hoisted from the horse when Yves had been brought in prisoner. So it was more than half an hour later when the boy was brought into the hall before his captor, and baulked and stared at the sight of Brother Cadfael standing at Philip's side.

"Here is one says I have grossly mistaken you," said Philip

directly, "and I have begun to be of his opinion. I make known now that you are free to go, no enemy henceforth of mine, and not to be meddled with where my writ runs."

Yves looked from one to the other, and was at a loss, so suddenly hailed out of his prison and brought forth into the light. He had been captive for so short a time that the signs hardly showed on him at all. His wrists were bruised from the irons, but there was no more than a thin blue line to be seen, and either he had been housed somewhere clean and dry, or he had changed into fresh clothes. His hair, still damp, curled about his head, drying fluffy as a child's. But there were the dark shadows of anger and suspicion in the stiffness of his face when he looked at Philip.

"You won him fairly," said Philip indifferently, smiling a little at the boy's black stare. "Embrace him!"

Bewildered and wary, Yves tensed at the very touch of Cadfael's hands on his shoulders, but as suddenly melted, and inclined a flushed and still half-reluctant cheek for the kiss, quivering. In a stumbling breath he demanded helplessly: "What have you done? What brings you here? You should never have followed."

"Question nothing!" said Cadfael, putting him off firmly to the length of his arms. "No need! Take what is offered you, and be glad. There is no deceit."

"He said you had won me." Yves turned upòn Philip, frowning, ready to blaze. "What has he done? How did he get you to let go of me? I do not believe you do it for nothing. What has he pledged for me?"

"It is true," said Philip coolly, "that Brother Cadfael came offering a life. Not, however, for you. He has reasoned me out of you, my friend, no price has been paid. Nor asked."

"That is truth," said Cadfael.

Yves looked from one to the other, swayed between belief in the one and disbelief in the other. "Not for me," he said slowly. "It's true, then, it must be true. Olivier is here! Who else?"

"Olivier is here," agreed Philip equably, and added with finality: "And stays here."

"You have no right." Yves was too intent and solemn now to have room for anger. "What you held against me was at least credible. Against him you have no justification. Let him go now. Keep me if you will, but let Olivier go free."

"I will be the judge," said Philip, his brows drawn formidably, but his voice as level as before, "whether I have ground of bitter complaint against Olivier de Bretagne. As for you, your horse is saddled and provided, and you may ride where you will, back to your empress without hindrance from any man of mine. The gate will open for you. Be on your way."

The curtness of the dismissal raised a flush in Yves' smooth, scrubbed cheeks, and for a moment Cadfael feared for the young man's newly achieved maturity. Where would be the sense in protesting further when the situation put all but dignified compliance out of his reach? A few months back, and he might have blazed in ineffective rage, in the perilous confusion of the transition from boy to man. But somewhere beneath one of the curtain towers of La Musarderie Yves had completed his growing up. He confronted his antagonist with mastered face and civil bearing.

"Let me at least ask," he said, "what is your intent with Brother Cadfael. Is he also prisoner?"

"Brother Cadfael is safe enough with me. You need not fear for him. But for the present I desire to retain his company, and I think he will not deny me. He is free to go when he will, or stay as long as he will. He can keep the hours as faithfully in my chapel as in Shrewsbury. And so he does," said Philip with a brief smile, remembering the night encounter, "even the midnight matin. Leave Brother Cadfael to his own choice."

"I have still business here," said Cadfael, meeting the boy's earnest eyes, that widened to take in more meanings than the mere words conveyed.

"I go, then," he said. "But I give you to know, Philip FitzRobert, that I shall come back for Olivier de Bretagne in arms."

"Do so," said Philip, "but do not complain then of your welcome."

He was gone, without looking back. A hand to the bridle, a foot in the stirrup, and a light spring into the saddle, and the reins were gathered in one hand, and his spurless heels drove into the horse's dappled flanks. The ranks of curious soldiers, servants and retainers parted to let him through, and he was out at the gate and on the descending causeway, towards the rim of the trees in the river valley below. There he would cross, and climb out again through the thick belt of woodland that everywhere surrounded Greenhamsted. By the same way that Cadfael had come, Yves departed, out to the great, straight road the Romans had made long ago, arrow-straight across the plateau of the Cotswolds, and when he reached it he would turn left, towards Gloucester and back to his duty.

Cadfael did not go towards the gate to watch him depart. The last he saw of him that day was clear against a sullen sky in the gateway, his back as straight as a lance, before the gates were closed and barred behind him.

"He means it," said Cadfael by way of warning. For there are young men who say things they do not really mean, and those who fail to understand how to distinguish between the two may live to regret it. "He will come back."

"I know it," said Philip. "I would not grudge him his flourish even if it was no more than a flourish."

"It is more. Do not disdain him."

"God forbid! He will come, and we shall see. It depends how great a force she has now in Gloucester, and whether my father is with her." He spoke of his father quite coldly, simply estimating in his competent mind the possible forces arrayed against him.

The men of the garrison had dispersed to their various duties. A wind from the courtyard brought in the scent of fresh, warm bread carried in trays from the bakery, sweet as clover, and the sharp, metallic chirping of hammers from the armoury.

"Why," asked Cadfael, "should you wish to retain my company? It is I who had business unfinished with you, not you with me."

Philip stirred out of his pondering to consider question and questioner with sharp attention. "Why did you choose to remain? I told you you might go whenever you wished."

"The answer to that you know," said Cadfael patiently. "The answer to my question I do not know. What is it you want of me?"

"I am not sure myself," Philip owned with a wry smile. "Some signpost into your mind, perhaps. You interest me more than most people."

That, if it was a compliment, was one which Cadfael could have returned with fervent truth. Some signpost into this man's mind, indeed, might be a revelation. To get some grasp of the son might even illuminate the father. If Yves found Robert of Gloucester with the empress in the city, would he urge her to the attack against Philip with a bitterness the match of Philip's own, or try to temper her animosity and spare his son?

"I trust," said Philip, "you will use my house as your own, brother, while you are here. If there is anything lacking to you, ask."

"There is a thing lacking." He stepped directly into Philip's path, to be clearly seen and heard, and if need be, denied, eye to eye. "My son is withheld from me. Give me leave to see him."

Philip said simply: "No." Without emphasis or need of emphasis.

"Use your house as my own, you said. Do you now place any restriction on where I may go within these walls?"

"No, none. Go where you will, open any unlocked door, wherever you please. You may find him, but you will not be able to get in to him," said Philip dispassionately, "and he will not be able to get out."

In the early twilight before Vespers, Philip made the rounds of his fortress, saw every guard set, and all defences secured. On the western side, where the ground rose steeply towards the village on the ridge, the wall was bratticed with a broad timber gallery braced out from its crest, since this was the side which could more easily be approached closely to attack the walls with rams or mining. Philip paced the length of the gallery to satisfy himself that all the traps built into its floor to allow attack from above on any besiegers who reached the wall, without exposing the defenders to archery, were clear of all obstacles and looked down stark stone to the ground, uncluttered by outside growth of bush or sapling. True, the brattice itself could be fired. He would have preferred to replace the timber with stone, but was grateful that Musard had at least provided this temporary asset. The great vine that climbed the wall on the eastern side had been permitted to remain, clothing a corner where a tower projected, but approach from that direction, climbing steeply over ground cleared of cover, was no great threat.

On this loftier side, too, he had stripped a great swathe of the hillside bare, so that siege engines deployed along the ridge must stay at a distance to remain in cover, and unless heavy engines were brought up for the attack, the walls of La Musarderie would be safely out of range.

His watchmen on the towers were easy with him, sure of his competence and their own, respected and respecting. Many of his garrison had served him for years, and come here with him from Cricklade. Faringdon had been a different matter, a new garrison patched together from several bases, so that he had had less cause to expect absolute trust and understanding from them. Yet it was the man deepest in his affection and confidence, the one on whom he had most relied for understanding, who had turned upon him with uncomprehending contempt, and led the recusants against him. A failure of language? A failure somewhere in the contact of minds? Of vision? Of reading of the stages in the descent to despair? A failure of love. That, certainly.

Philip looked down from the wall into his own castle wards, where torches began to flare, resinous fires in the deepening dusk. Overhanging the towers on this western side the clouds were heavy, perhaps with snow, and the watchmen on the wall swathed themselves in their cloaks and gathered themselves stolidly against a biting wind. That gallant, silly boy must have reached Gloucester by now, if indeed Gloucester was where he was bound.

Philip recalled Yves' stiff-necked simplicity with a faint, appreciative smile. No, the Benedictine was almost certainly right about him. Folly to suppose such a creature could kill by stealth. He showed as a minor copy of that other, all valour and fealty; no room there for the troubled mind that might look for a way through the labyrinth of destruction by less glorious ways than the sword. White on white on the one hand, black on black on the other, and nowhere room for those unspectacular shades of grey that colour most mortals. Well, if some of us mottled and maimed souls can somehow force a way to a future for the valiant and disdainful innocents, why grudge it to them? But why, having achieved that effort of the mind, is it so hard to come by the tough resignation that should go with it? Burning is never easy to bear.

The activity in the ward below, customary and efficient, sealed in La Musarderie for the night, small, foreshortened

figures going about from the buildings under the wall to hall
and keep, a tiny hearth of reflected light from the smith'
furnace red on the cobbles outside the forge. Two gowned
figures swept their dark skirts in at the door of the keep
Chaplain and Benedictine monk together, heading for Vespers
An interesting man, this Benedictine from Shrewsbury,
brother but deprecating his own brotherhood, no priest and
yet a father, and having experienced a son's confrontation
with a father of his own in youth, since doubtless he was
engendered like the rest of humankind. And now himself a
father for more than twenty years without knowing it, until
he was suddenly presented with the revelation of his offspring
in the fullness of manhood, with none of the labours, frustra-
tions and anxieties that go to the making of a mature man
And such a man, perfect and entire, but for the saving leaven
of self-doubt which keeps a man humble. And I have not
shown much of that myself, thought Philip wryly.

Well, it was time. He descended the narrow stone staircase
that led down from the guardwalk, and went to join them at
Vespers.

They were a reduced company at the office that night, the
guard having been strengthened, and the smiths still at work
in forge and armoury. Philip listened with an open mind as
the Benedictine brother from Shrewsbury read the psalm. I
was the feast day of Saint Nicholas, the sixth day of December

"I am numbered among such as go down into the pit; I am
made as one having no more strength:

"Thou hast committed me to the lowest pit, in darkness,
in the depths . . ."

Even here he reminds me, thought Philip, accepting the
omen. Yet the psalm was set for this day, and not by Cadfael

"Thou hast put away my acquaintance, far distant from me
thou hast made me an abomination to them. I am shut up
and I cannot come forth."

How easy it is to be persuaded into believing that God puts words into the office of the day of intent, for the appropriate mouth to utter them. The *sortes* by another way. But I, thought Philip, between regret and defiance, do not believe it. All this chaotic world fumbles along by chance.

"Wilt thou show forth thy marvels to men entombed? Shall the dead arise and praise thee?"

Well? Philip challenged in silence: Shall they?

After the evening meal in hall Philip withdrew alone to his own quarters, took the most private of his keys, and went out from the keep to the tower at the north-western corner of the curtain wall. A thin sleet was falling, not yet snow, though it made a faint and fleeting white powdering upon the cobbles. By morning it would be gone. The watchman on the tower marked the passage of the tall figure across the ward, and was motionless, knowing the man and his errand. It had not happened now for a matter of weeks. There was a name which had been banished from mention, but not from mind. What could have recalled it on this particular night the guard speculated, but without overmuch curiosity.

The door at the foot of the tower, which opened to the first key, was narrow and tall. One swordsman, with an archer three steps up the stair at his back and aiming above his head, could hold it against an army. There was a short brand burning in a sconce on the wall within, shedding light down the well of the continuing stair that spiralled downwards. Even the airshafts that slanted up to the light on the two levels below, through the thick stone of the walls, gave only onto the enclosed and populous ward, not the outer world. Even could a man slough off his chains and compress himself painfully into the narrowing shaft, he would emerge only to be thrust back into his prison. There was no escape there.

On the lower level Philip thrust his second key into the lock of another door, narrow and low. It functioned as smoothly and quietly as everything else that served him. Nor did he trouble to lock it behind him when he entered.

This lower cell was carved out from the rock for more than half the height of the walls, clenched together with stone above, and spacious enough for a wary captor, if he visited at all, to stay well out of reach of a prisoner in irons. The cold within was sharp but dry. The shaft that slanted up to a grid in the tower wall within the ward sent a chill draught across the cell. On a bracket in the solid rock a massive candle burned steadily, well aside from the current of air, and within reach from the levelled rock ledge on which the prisoner's bed was laid. At the edge of the bracket there was a new candle standing ready, for the present one was burning down to its ending.

And on the bed, rigidly erect at the first grate of key in lock, and eyes levelled like javelins upon the doorway, was Olivier de Bretagne.

"No greeting for me?" said Philip. The candle guttered for the first time in the counter-draught he had let in with him. He observed it, and meticulously closed the door at his back. "And after so long? I have neglected you."

"Oh, you are welcome," said Olivier, coldly gracious. The tones of the two voices, a little complicated by an immediate and yet distant echo, matched and clashed. The echo made an unnerving third in the room, listener and commentator. "I regret I have no refreshment to offer you, my lord, but no doubt you have dined already."

"And you?" said Philip, and briefly smiled. "I see the empty trays returning. It has been a reassurance to me that you have not lost your appetite. It would be a disappointment if ever you weakened in your will to keep all your powers intact against the day when you kill me. No, say nothing, there is no need, I acknowledge your right, but I am not ready yet. Be still, let me look at you."

He looked, with grave attention, for some time, and all the

while the levelled eyes, wide, round, golden-irised and fierce
as a hawk's, stared back unwaveringly into his. Olivier was
thin, but with the restless leanness of energy confined, not
with any bodily deprivation, and bright with the intolerable
brightness of frustration, anger and hatred. It was, it had been
from the first, a mutual loss, their rage and anguish equal,
either of them bereaved and embittered. Even in this they
were matched, a perfect pairing. And Olivier was neat,
decently clothed, his bed well furnished, his dignity discreetly
preserved by the stone vessel and leather bucket for his physical needs, and the candle that gave him light or darkness at
will.

For he had even the means of relighting it to hand beside
his pallet, flint and steel and tinder in a wooden box. Fire is
a dangerous gift, but why not? It cannot set light to stone,
and no sane man cased in stone is going to set light to his
own bed, or what else within will burn, and himself with it.
And Olivier was almost excessively sane, so much so that he
could see only by his own narrow, stainless standards, and
never so far as the hopes and despairs and lame and sorry
contrivances by which more vulnerable people cope with a
harsh world.

Confinement, resentment and enforced patience had only
burnished and perfected his beauty, the eager bones accentu-
ated, the suave flesh polished into ivory. The black, glossy
hair clasped his temples and hollow cheeks like hands loving
but alien, blue-black, live with tension. Daily he had plunged
into the water brought to him, like a swimmer into the sea,
urgent to be immaculate whenever his enemy viewed him,
never to decline, never to submit, never to plead. That above
all.

There in the east, Philip thought, studying him, from that
Syrian mother, he must have brought this quality in him that
will not rust or rot or any way submit to desecration. Or was
it, after all, from that Welsh monk I have left outside this

meeting? What a mating that must have been, to bring forth such a son.

"Am I so changed?" Olivier challenged the fixed stare. When he moved, his chains chimed lightly. His hands were untrammelled, but thin steel bands encircled his ankles, and tethered him by a generous length of chain to a ring in the stone wall beside his pallet. Knowing his ingenuity and his mettle, Philip was taking no chances. Even if helpers could penetrate here, they would have much ado to hammer him loose from his prison. There was no will to mar or defile him, but an absolute will to keep him immured from the world, a solitary possession on which no price could ever be set.

"Not changed," said Philip, and moved nearer, within arm's length of his captive. Fine hands Olivier had, elegant and large and sinewy; once they had established a first well-judged grip on a throat it would not be easy to break free. Perhaps the temptation and the provocation would have been even more irresistible if those hands had been chained. A fine chain round a throat would have choked out life even more efficiently.

But Olivier did not move. Philip had tempted him thus more than once since the irredeemable breakage of Faringdon; and failed to rouse him. His own death, of course, would probably have followed. But whether that in itself was what restrained him there was no guessing.

"Not changed, no." And yet Philip watched him with a new, intense interest, searching for the subtle elements of those two disparate creatures who had brought this arrogant excellence into being. "I have a guest in my hall, Olivier, who has come on your behalf. I am learning things about you that I think you do not know. It may be high time that you did."

Olivier looked back at him with a fixed and hostile face, and said never a word. It was no surprise that he should be sought, he knew he had his value, and there would be those anxious to retrieve him. That any of those well disposed to him should by reason or luck have tracked him down to this place was more surprising. If Laurence d'Angers had indeed sent here to ask after his lost squire, it was a bow drawn at a venture. And the arrow would not hit the mark.

"In truth," said Philip, "I had here two equally concerned for your fate. One of them I have sent away empty-handed, but he says he will be back for you in arms. I have no cause to doubt he'll keep his word. A young kinsman of yours, Yves Hugonin."

"Yves?" Olivier stiffened, bristling. "Yves has been here? How could that be? What brought him here?"

"He was invited. Somewhat roughly, I fear. But never fret, he's away again as whole as he came, and in Gloucester by this time, raising an army to come and drag you out of hold. I thought for a time," said Philip consideringly, "that I had a quarrel with him, but I find I was in error. And even if I had not been, it turned out the cause was valueless."

"You swear it? He's unharmed, and back to his own people? No, I take that back," said Olivier fiercely. "I know you do not lie."

"Never, at any rate, to you. He is safe and well, and heartily hating me for your sake. And the other—I told you there were two—the other is a monk of the Benedictines of Shrewsbury, and he is still here in La Musarderie, of his own will. His name is Cadfael."

Olivier stood utterly confounded. His lips moved, repeating the familiar but most unexpected name. When he found a voice at last, he was less than coherent.

"How can he be here? A cloistered brother—no, they go nowhere, unless ordered—his vows would not allow—And why here? For *me* . . .? No, impossible!"

"So you do know of him? His vows—yes, he declares himself recusant, he is absent and unblessed. For cause. For you. Do me justice, it was you said I do not lie. I saw this brother at Coventry. He was there seeking news of you, like the young one. By what arts he traced you here I am not wholly sure, but so he did, and came to redeem you. I thought that you should know."

"He is a man I revere," said Olivier. "Twice I have met with him and been thankful. But he owes me nothing, nothing at all."

"So I thought and said," agreed Philip. "But he knows better. He came to me openly, asking for what he wanted. You. He said there were those who would be glad to buy you free; and when I asked, at whatever price? . . . he said, name it, and he would see it paid."

"This is out of my grasp," said Olivier, lost. "I do not understand."

"And I said to him: 'A life, perhaps.' And he said: 'Take mine!'"

Olivier sat down slowly on the rugs of the bed, astray between the present wintry reality and memories that crowded back upon him fresh as Spring. A brother of the Benedictines, habited and cowled, who had used him like a son. They were together waiting for midnight and Matins in the priory of Bromfield, drawing plans upon the floor to show the way by which Olivier could best be sure of getting his charges safely away out of Stephen's territory and back to Gloucester. They were under the rustling, fragrant bunches of herbs hanging from the rafters of Cadfael's workshop, that last time, when, without even giving it a thought, Olivier before departing had stooped his cheek for the kiss proper between close kin, and blithely returned it.

"And then I asked him: 'Why should you offer me your old bones to moulder in his place? What is Olivier de Bretagne to you?' And he said: 'He is my son.'"

After long silence, the dying candle suddenly sputtered and flowed into molten wax, and the wick lolled sidewise into the pool and subsided into a last spreading, bluish flame. Philip tilted the new one to pick up the fading spark out of the enclosing darkness, and blew out the last remnant, anchoring the renewed light upon the congealing remains of the old. Olivier's face, briefly withdrawn into twilight, burned slowly bright again as the flame drew constant and tall. He was quite still, the focus of his wide, astonished eyes lengthened into infinite distance.

"Is it true?" he asked almost soundlessly, but not of Philip, who did not lie. "He never told me. Why did he never tell me?"

"He found you already mounted and launched and riding high. A sudden father clutching at your arm might have thrust you off your course. He let well alone. As long as you remained in ignorance, you owed him nothing." Philip had drawn back a pace or two towards the door, the key ready in his hand, but he checked a moment to correct his last utterance. "Nothing, he says, but what is fairly earned between man and man. For until you knew, that was all you were. It will not be so easy between father and son, that I know. Debts proliferate, and the prices set come all too high."

"Yet he comes offering all for me," said Olivier, wrestling with this paradox almost in anger. "Without sanction, exiled, leaving his vocation, his quietude, his peace of mind, offering his life. He has cheated me!" he said in a grievous cry.

"I leave it with you," said Philip from the open doorway. "You have the night for thinking, if you find it hard to sleep."

He went out quietly, and closed and relocked the door.

CHAPTER TEN

YVES MAINTAINED his disdainful withdrawal down the open causeway only as far as he was in full view from the gateway and the guardwalk above. Once secure in cover he found himself a place where he could look back between the trees at the stony outline of the castle. From here, so far below, it looked formidably lofty and solid, yet it was not so great a stronghold. It was well garrisoned and well held, yet with force enough it could be taken. Philip had got it cheaply, by ambushing its lord well out of his own ground, and forcing him to surrender it under threats. Siege was of little use here, it takes far too long to starve out a well-provided garrison. The best hope was a total assault with all the force available, and a quick resolution.

Meantime, the surrounding forests circled the open site on all sides, and even the cleared ground did not remove the walls too far for Yves' excellent distant sight to record details, gradients, even weaknesses if Philip had left any. If he could bring any helpful observations with him to Gloucester, so much the better, and well worth losing a couple of hours in the inspection.

He took a long look at this frontal approach, for hitherto he had seen only the interior of a cell under one of the towers, being hustled within there with a cloak swathed round his head, and his arms bound. The flanking towers of the gatehouse afforded clear ground for archers across the gate and both left and right to the next towers along the wall. Across all this face the brattice had not been continued, approach up this slope being the most difficult to sustain. Yves turned his horse in the thick cover of the trees, to circle the castle widdershins. That would bring him out at the end on the high ground near the village, with the way clear to make for the fastest route to Gloucester.

Through the edges of the woodland he had a clear view of the most northerly of the towers, and the stretch of wall beyond. In the corner between them, a great coiling growth, blackened now in its winter hibernation, stripped of leaves, clambered as high as the battlements where the brattice began. A vine, very old, stout as a tree. When it had its foliage, he thought, it might partially obscure at least one arrow-slit. No great risk to leave it there. It might admit one man, with care and by night, but it could hardly let in more than one, and even the first would be risking his life. There was a guard on the wall there, pacing between towers. He caught the gleam of light on steel. Still, bear it in mind. He wondered which of four generations of Musards had planted the vine. The Romans had had vineyards in these border shires, centuries ago.

There were four towers in all, in the circuit of the walls, besides the twin towers of the gatehouse, and a watchman on every guardwalk between. Sometimes, in that circuit, Yves had to withdraw further into the trees, but he pursued his inspection doggedly, looking for possible weak spots, but finding none. By the time he was viewing the last tower he was already on ground much higher than the castle itself, and nearing the first cottages of the village. After this last rise the ground levelled into the Cotswold plateau, wide and flat on top of its elevated world, with great, straight roads, big open fields and rich villages fat with sheep. Here, just short of the crest, would be the place to deploy mangonels. And from here would be the best place to launch a mining party or a ram, in a rapid downhill rush to reach the wall by night. At the foot of this last tower there was masonry of a differing colour, as if repairs had been done there. If it could be breached there by a ram, firing might bring down part of the weight of the tower.

At least note even the possibility. There was no more he could do here. He knew the lie of the land now, and could report it accurately. He left the houses of the village behind him and made due east by the first promising track, to reach the highroad that went striding out north-west for Gloucester, and south-east for Cirencester.

He entered the city by the Eastgate late in the afternoon. The streets seemed to him busier and more crowded than he had ever seen them, and before he reached the Cross he had picked out among the throng the badges or the livery of several of the empress's most powerful adherents, among them her younger half-brother Reginald FitzRoy, Baldwin de Redvers, earl of Devon, Patrick of Salisbury, Humphrey de Bohun, and John FitzGilbert the marshall. Her court officers he had expected to see in close attendance, but the more distant partisans he had supposed to be by now dispersed to their own lands. His heart rose to the omen. All those bound south and west must have halted and foregathered again here to take counsel after the failure of the bishops' endeavours for peace, and see how best to take advantage of the time, before their enemies forestalled them. She had an army here assembled, force enough to threaten greater strongholds than La Musarderie. And in the castle here she had assault engines, light enough to be moved quickly, heavy enough in load to breach a wall if used effectively; and most formidable weapon of all, she had the unswerving loyalty of Robert of Gloucester, his person to confront and disarm his renegade son, his blood to lay claim to Philip's blood and render him helpless.

Certainly Philip had fought for King Stephen as relentlessly as ever he had for the empress, but never yet face to face with the father he had deserted. The one enormity, the only one, that had been ruled out in this civil war, was the killing of close kinsmen, and who could be closer kin than father and son. Fratricidal war, they called it, the very thing it was not. When Robert declared himself at the gates of La Musarderie and demanded surrender, his own life in the balance, Philip must give way. Or even if he fought, for very pride's sake, it must be with no more than half his heart, always turning away from confrontation with his own progenitor. Loved or hated, that was the most sacred and indissoluble tie that bound humankind. Nothing could break it.

He must take his story straight to the earl of Gloucester, and trust to him to know how to set about the errand. At the Cross, therefore, he turned away from the abbey, and towards the castle, down a busy and populous Southgate towards the river, and the water-meadows that still grew green in the teeth of winter. The great grey bulk of the castle loomed above the streets on this townward side, above the jetties and the shore and the wide steely waters on the other. The empress preferred somewhat more comfort when she could get it, and would certainly have installed herself and her women in the guest apartments of the abbey. Earl Robert was content in the sterner quarters of the castle with his men. By the bustle and the abundance of armed men and noble liveries about the town a considerable number of other billets must have been commandeered temporarily to accommodate the assembled forces. So much the better, there was more than enough power here to make short work of storming La Musarderie.

Yves dreamed ardently of climbing up by the great vine and remaining within, in concealment, long enough to find a postern that could be opened, or a guard who could be overpowered and robbed of his keys. The less fighting the better, the less time wasted, the less destruction to be made good, and the less bitter ill-will afterwards to smooth away into forgetfulness. Between faction and faction, between father and son. There might even be a reconciliation.

Before he reached the gates, Yves began to be hailed by some of his own kind, squires of this nobleman or that, astonished to see Philip FitzRobert's victim come riding in merrily, as if he had never fallen foul of that formidable enemy. He called greetings back to them gladly, but waved them off from delaying him now. Only when he entered the outer ward of the castle did he rein in beside the guardhouse, and stop to question, and to answer questions. Even then he did not dismount, but leaned from the saddle to demand, a little breathlessly from the excitement of the message he bore and the pleasure of being welcomed back among friends:

"The earl of Gloucester? Where shall I find him? I have news he should hear quickly."

The officer of the guard had come out to view the arrival, and stared up at him in amazement. A squire in the earl of Devon's following shouted aloud from among the multifarious activities in the ward beyond, and came running in delight to catch at his bridle.

"Yves! You're free? How did you break out? We heard how you were seized, we never thought to see you back so soon."

"Or ever?" said Yves, and laughed, able to be light-hearted about that possibility now the danger was past. "No, I'm loosed to plague you yet a while. I'll tell you all later. Now I need to find Earl Robert quickly."

"You'll not find him here," said the guard. "He's in Hereford with Earl Roger. No word yet when we can expect him back. What's so urgent?"

"Not here?" echoed Yves, dismayed.

"If it's that vital," said the officer briskly, "you'd better take it to her Grace the empress herself, at the abbey. She doesn't care to be passed over, even for her brother, as you should know if you've been in her service long. She won't thank you if she has to hear it from another, when you come riding in hot with it."

That was exactly what Yves was very reluctant to do. Her favour and her disfavour were equally scarifying, and equally to be avoided. No doubt she was still under the misapprehension that he had done her, at her clear suggestion, an appalling service, but also he had been the unfortunate cause of some disruption in her passage home to Gloucester, and put her to some trouble in consequence, for which she certainly would not thank him. And if she looked for her ring on his little finger, and failed to find it, that was hardly likely to count in his favour. Yves admitted to himself that he was afraid to confront her, and shook himself indignantly at the thought.

"She's at the abbey with her women. In your shoes I'd make for there as fast as may be," said the guard shrewdly. "She was roused enough when you were taken, go and show your face, and set her mind at rest on one count, at least."

"I'd advise it," agreed the squire with a good-humoured grin, and clapped Yves heartily on the back. "Get that over, and come and take your ease. You come as a welcome sight, we've been in a taking over you."

"Is FitzGilbert with her?" demanded Yves. If Robert of Gloucester was not available, at least he would rather deal with the marshall than with the lady alone, and it was the marshall who would have to talk good sense into the lady as to how to deal with this opportunity.

"And Bohun, and her royal uncle of Scotland. Her close council, nobody else."

Yves waved away the brief, inevitable delay, and turned his horse to return to the Southgate and the Cross, and so to the abbey enclave where the empress kept her court. A pity to have missed Gloucester himself. It meant delay, surely. She would not act on her own, without her brother's counsel and support, and Olivier had been in durance long enough. But make the best of it. She had the means to act, the town was bursting with troops. She could well afford to allow the raising of a voluntary force to try what could be done by stealth, if she would not move in strength. Yves had no doubts of her courage and valour, but all too many of her competence and generalship.

He rode into the great court of the abbey, and crossed to the guest apartments, through the preoccupied bustle of the court. The carrying of arms and presence of armed men was discreetly limited here, but for all that there were as many fighting men as brothers within the precinct, out of armour and not carrying steel, but unmistakably martial. The presence of a guard on the stairway to the great door of the hall indicated that the whole building had been taken over for Maud's use, and lesser mortals approached her presence only after proving the validity of their business. Yves submitted to being crisply halted and questioned.

"Yves Hugonin. I serve in the empress's household. My lord and uncle is Laurence d'Angers, his force is now in Devizes. I must see her Grace. I have a report to make to her. I went first to the castle, but they told me to come to her here."

"You, is it?" said his questioner, narrowing sharp eyes to view him more attentively. "I remember, you're the one they cut out from her retinue, on the way from Coventry. And we'd heard never a word of you since. Seemingly it's turned out better than we feared. Well, she should be glad to see you alive and well, at any rate. Not every man is getting a welcome these days. Come in to the hall, and I'll send a page in to let her know."

There were others waiting in the hall to be summoned to the presence, more than one minor magnate among them, besides some of the merchants of the town who had favours to ask or merchandise to offer for sale. While she kept her court here, with a substantial household about her, she was a source of profit and prosperity to Gloucester, and her resident armies a sure protection.

She kept them all waiting for some time. Half an hour had passed before the door to her apartments opened, and a girl came through it to call two names, and usher two minor lords, if not yet into the empress's presence, at least into her anteroom. Yves recognized the bold, self-assured young woman who had submitted him to such a close scrutiny at Coventry before she decided that he would do. Dark hair, with russet lights in its coils, and bright eyes, greenish hazel, that summed up men in sweeping glances and pigeon-holed them ruthlessly, discarding, it seemed, all who were past thirty. Her own age might have been nineteen, which was also Yves'. While she summoned, surveyed and dismissed the two lordlings she had been sent to bring in, she did not fail to devote one long glance to Yves, not altogether dismissively, but his mind was on other matters, and he did not observe it. She was gone with her charges almost before he had recalled where he had first encountered her. A favourite among the royal gentlewomen, probably; certainly she had adopted some of her mistress's characteristics.

Another half-hour had passed, and one or two of the townsmen had given up and departed the hall, before she returned for Yves.

"Her Grace is still in council, but come within and be seated, and she will send for you shortly."

He followed her along a short corridor and into a large, light room where three girls were gathered in one corner with embroideries in their laps, and their chatter subdued to low tones because there was only a curtained door between them and the imperial council. Occasionally they put in a dutiful stitch or two, but very desultorily. Their attendance was required, but it need not be made laborious. They were instantly more interested in Yves, when he entered, all the

more because he showed a grave, preoccupied face, and no
particular interest in them. Brief silence saluted his coming,
and then they resumed their soft and private conversation,
with a confidential circumspection that suggested he figured
in it. His guide abandoned him there, and went on alone into
the inner room.

There was an older woman seated on a cushioned bench
against the wall, withdrawn from the gaggle of girls. She had
a book in her lap, but the light was dimming towards evening,
and she had ceased to read. The empress would need a few
literate ladies about her, and this one seemed to be an essential
member of her retinue. Her, too, he remembered from Coventry. Aunt and niece, they had told him, the only gentlewoman
Maud had brought with her into that stark male assembly.
She looked up at him now, and knew him. She smiled, and
made a slight gesture of her hand that was clearly an invitation
to join her.

"Yves Hugonin? It *is* you? Oh, how good to see you here,
alive and well. And free! I had heard you were lost to us.
Most of us knew nothing of that outrage until after we reached
Gloucester."

She was perfectly composed, indeed he could not imagine
her calm ever being broken; and yet he was dazzled for an
instant by the widening and warming of her eyes when she
had recognized him. She had the illusionless eyes of middle
age, experienced, lined, proof against most surprises, and yet
in that one flash of glad astonishment they had a lustre and
depth that shook him to the heart. It had mattered to her
deeply, that even after the empress's protection extended to
him at Coventry, he should again be put in peril of his life.
It mattered to her now that he came thus unexpectedly back
to Gloucester, free and unharmed.

"Come, sit! You may as well, waiting for audience here is
a weary business. I am so glad," she said, "to see you alive
and well. When you left Coventry with us, and no one tried

to prevent, I thought that trouble was safely over, and no one would dare accuse you of any wrong deed again. It was very ill fortune that ever you fell under such suspicion. But her Grace stood firm for your right, and I thought that would be the end of it. And then that assault . . . We never heard until next day. How did you escape him? And he so bitter against you, we feared for you."

"I did not escape him," said Yves honestly, and felt boyishly diminished by having to admit it. It would have been very satisfying to have broken out of La Musarderie by his own ingenuity and daring. But then he would not even have known that Brother Cadfael was there within, nor could he have been certain that Olivier was held there, and he would not have stated his resolve and laid down his challenge to return for him in arms. That was of more importance than his own self-esteem. "I was set free by Philip FitzRobert. Dismissed, indeed! He acquits me of any part in de Soulis's death, and so has no more use for me."

"The more credit to him," said Jovetta de Montors. "He has cooled and come to reason."

Yves did not say that Philip had had some encouragement along the road to reason. Even so, it was credit to him indeed, that he had acknowledged his change of heart, and acted upon it.

"He did believe I had done murder," said Yves, doing his enemy justice, though still with some resentment and reluctance. "And he valued de Soulis. But I have other quarrels with him that will not be so easily settled." He looked earnestly at the pale profile beside him, tall brow under braided silver hair, straight, fine nose and elegantly strong line of the jaw, and above all the firm, full, sensitive way her lips folded together over her silences, containing in dignified reticence whatever she had learned in her more than fifty years of life. "You never believed me a murderer?" he asked, and himself was startled to find how he ached for the right answer.

She turned to him fully, wide-eyed and grave. "No," she said, "never!"

The door to the audience chamber opened, and the girl Isabeau came out with a swirl of brocaded skirts and held it open. "Her Grace will receive you now." And she mouthed at him silently: "I am dismissed. They are talking high strategy. Go in to her, and tread softly."

There were four people in the room he entered, besides two clerks who were just gathering up the tools of their trade, and the scattering of leaves of vellum spread across the large table. Wherever the empress moved her dwelling there would be charters to draw up and witness, sweets of property and title to dole out to buy favour, minor rewards to be presented to the deserving, and minor bribes to those who might be most useful in future, the inevitable fruits of faction and contention. King Stephen's clerks were occupied with much the same labour. But these had finished their work for this day, and having cleared the table of all signs of their profession, went out by a further door, and quietly closed it behind them.

The empress had pushed back her large, armed stool to allow the clerks to circle the table freely. She sat silent, with her hands on the broad, carved arms of her seat, not gripping, simply laid along the brocaded tissue, for once at rest. Her rich and lustrous dark hair was plaited into two long braids over her shoulders, intertwined with cords of gold thread, and lay upon the breast of her purple bliaut stirring and quivering to her long, relaxed breathing as though it had a life of its own. She looked a little tired, and a little as though she had recently been out of temper, but was beginning to put by the vexations of business and emerge from her darker mood. Behind her sombre magnificence the wall was draped with hangings, and the benches adorned with cushions and rich coverings. She had brought her own furnishings with her to create this audience room, the largest and lightest the abbey could provide.

The three who at the moment composed her closest council had risen from the table when the last charter was ready for copying and witnessing, and moved some paces apart after a long session. Beside one darkening window King David of Scotland stood, drawing in the chilling air, half turned away from his imperial niece. He had been at her side through most of the years of this long warfare, with staunch family loyalty, but also with a shrewd eye on his own and his nation's fortunes. Contention in England was no bad news to a monarch whose chief aim was to gain a stranglehold on Northumbria, and push his own frontier as far south as the Tees. Able, elderly and taciturn, a big man and still handsome for all the grey in his hair and beard, he stood stretching his wide shoulders after too long of sitting forward over tedious parchments and challenging maps, and did not turn his head to see what further petitioner had been admitted so late in the day.

The other two hovered, one on either side of the empress; Humphrey de Bohun, her steward, and John FitzGilbert, her marshall. Younger men both, the props of her personal household, while her more spectacular paladins paraded their feats of arms in the brighter light of celebrity. Yves had seen something of these two during his few weeks in the empress's entourage, and respected them both as practical men with whom their fellowmen could deal with confidence. They turned on him preoccupied but welcoming faces now. Maud, for her part, took a long moment to recall the circumstances in which he had come to absent himself, and did so with a sudden sharp frown, as though he had been to blame for causing her considerable trouble.

Yves advanced a few paces, and made her a deep reverence.

"Madam, I am returned to my duty, and not without news. May I speak freely?"

"I do remember," she said slowly, and shook off her abstraction. "We have known nothing of you since we lost you, late in the evening, on the road through the forest near Deerhurst. I am glad to see you alive and safe. We wrote that capture down to FitzRobert's account. Was it so? And where have you been in his hold, and how did you break free?" She grew animated, but not, he thought, greatly concerned. The misuse of one squire, even his death, would not have added very much to the score she already held against Philip FitzRobert. Her eyes had begun to burn up in small, erect flames at the mention of his name.

"Madam, I was taken to La Musarderie, in Greenhamsted, the castle he took from the Musards a few months back. I cannot claim to have broken free by any effort of mine, he has loosed me of his own will. He truly believed I had murdered his man de Soulis." His face flamed at the recollection of what she had believed of him, and still believed, and he shrank from trying to imagine with what amused approval she was listening to this discreet reference to that death. Probably she had not expected such subtlety from him. She might even have had some uneasy moments at his reappearance, and have scored up even that embarrassment against Philip, for not making an end of his captive. "But he has abandoned that belief," Yves rushed on, making short work of what, after all, was of no importance now. "He set me at liberty. For myself I have no complaint, I have not been misused, considering what he held against me."

"You have been in chains," said de Bohun, eyeing the boy's wrists.

"So I have. Nothing strange in that, as things were. But madam, my lords, I have discovered that he has Olivier de Bretagne, my sister's husband, in his dungeons in that same castle, and has so held him ever since Faringdon, and will listen to no plea to let him go freely, or offer him for ransom. There are many would be glad to buy him out of prison, but he will take no price for Olivier. And, madam, strong as La Musarderie is, I do believe we have the force here to take it by storm, so quickly they shall not have time to send to any of his other fortresses for reinforcements."

"For a single prisoner?" said the empress. "That might cost a very high price indeed, and yet fail of buying him. We have larger plans in mind than the well-being of one man."

"Olivier has been a very profitable man to our cause," urged Yves strenuously, evading provoking her with "*your* cause" just in time. It would have sounded like censure, and that was something not even those nearest to her and most regarded would have dared. "My lords," he appealed, "you know his mettle, you have seen his valour. It is an injustice that he should be held in secret when all the others from Faringdon have been honourably offered for ransom, as the custom is. And there is more than one man to win, there is a good castle, and if we move quickly enough we may have it intact, almost undamaged, and a mass of arms and armour with it."

"A fair enough prize," agreed the marshall thoughtfully, "if it could be done by surprise. But failing that, not worth a heavy loss to us. I do not know the ground well. Do you? You cannot have seen much of their dispositions from a cell underground."

"My lord," said Yves eagerly, "I went about the whole place before I rode here. I could draw out plans for you. There's ground cleared all about it, but not beyond arrow range, and if we could move engines to the ridge above . . ."

"No!" said the empress sharply. "I will not stir for one captive, the risk is too great, and too little to gain. It was presumptuous to ask it of me. Your sister's husband must abide his time, we have greater matters in hand, and cannot afford to turn aside for a luckless knight who happens to have made himself well hated. No, I will not move."

"Then, madam, will you give me leave to try and raise a lesser force, and make the attempt by other means? For I have told Philip FitzRobert to his face, and sworn it, that I will return for Olivier in arms. I said it, and I must and will make it good. There are some who would be glad to join me," said Yves, flushed and vehement, "if you permit."

He did not know what he had said to rouse her, but she was leaning forward over the table now, gripping the curved arms of the stool, her ivory face suddenly burningly bright. "Wait! What was that you said? To his face! You told him to his face? He was there this very morning, in person? I had not understood that. He gave his orders—that could be done from any of his castles. We heard that he was back in Cricklade, days ago."

"No, it's not so. He is there in La Musarderie. He has no thought of moving." Of that, for some reason, Yves was certain. Philip had chosen to keep Brother Cadfael, and Brother Cadfael, no doubt for Olivier's sake, had elected to stay. No, there was no immediate plan to leave Greenhamsted. Philip was waiting there for Yves to return in arms. And now Yves understood the working of her mind, or thought he did. She had believed her hated enemy to be in Cricklade, and to get at him there she would have had to take her armies well to the south-east, into the very ring of Stephen's fortresses, surrounded by Bampton, Faringdon, Purton, Malmesbury, all ready to detach companies to repel her, or, worse still, surround her and turn the besiegers into the besieged. But Greenhamsted was less than half the distance, and if tackled with determination could be taken and regarrisoned before Stephen's relief forces could arrive. A very different proposition, one that caused the fires in her eyes to burn up brilliantly, and the stray tresses escaping from her braids to quiver and curl with the intensity of her resolution and passion.

"He is within reach, then," she said, vengefully glowing. "He is within reach, and I will have him! If we must turn out every man and every siege engine we have, it is worth it."

Worth it to take a man she hated, not worth it to redeem

a man who had served her all too faithfully, and lost his liberty for her. Yves felt his blood chill in apprehension. But what could she do with Philip when she had him, but hand him over to his father, who might curb and confine him, but surely would not harm him. She would grow tired of her own hatred once she had suppressed and had the better of her traitor. Nothing worse could happen. There might even be a reconciliation, once father and son were forced to meet, and either come to terms or destroy each other.

"I will have him," said the empress with slow and burning resolve, "and he shall kneel to me before his own captive garrison. And then," she said with ferocious deliberation, "he shall hang."

The breath went out of Yves in a muted howl of consternation and disbelief. He gulped in air to find a voice to protest, and could not utter a word. For she could not mean it seriously. Her brother's son, a revolted son perhaps, but still his own flesh and blood, her own close kin, and a king's grandson. It would be to shatter the one scruple that had kept this war from being a total bloodbath, a sanction that must not be broken. Kinsman may bully, cheat, deceive, outmanoeuvre kinsman, but not kill him. And yet her face was set in iron resolution, smouldering and gleeful, and she did mean it, and she would do it, without a qualm, without pause for relenting.

King David had turned sharply from his detached contemplation of the darkening world outside the window, to stare first at his niece, and then at the marshall and the steward, who met his eyes with flashing glances, acknowledging and confirming his alarm. Even the king hesitated to say outright what was in his mind; he had long experience of the empress's reaction to any hint of censure, and if he had no actual fear of her rages, he knew their persistency and obstinacy, and the hopelessness of curbing them, once roused. It was in the most reasonable and mild of voices that he said:

"Is that wise? Granted his offence and your undoubted right, it would be well worth it to hold your hand at this moment. It might rid you of one enemy, it would certainly raise a dozen more against you. After talk of peace this would be one way to ensure the continuance of war, with more bitterness than ever."

"And the earl," added the steward with emphasis, "is not here to be consulted."

No, thought Yves, abruptly enlightened, for that very reason she will move this same night, set forward preparations to shift such of her siege engines as can be transported quickly, take every man she can raise, leave all other plans derelict, all to smash her way into La Musarderie before the earl of Gloucester hears what is in the wind. And she will do it, she has the hardihood and the black ingratitude. She will hang Philip and present Earl Robert with a fait accompli and a dead son. She dare do it! And then what awful disintegration must follow, destroying first her own cause, for that she does not care, provided she can get a rope round the neck of this one enemy.

"Madam," he cried, tearing King David's careful moderation to shreds, "you cannot do it! I offered you a good castle, and the release of an honourable soldier to add to your ranks, I did not offer you a death, one Earl Robert will grieve for to his life's end. Take him, yes, give him to the earl, prisoner, let them settle what lies between them. That is fair dealing. But this—this you must not and cannot do!"

She was on her feet by then, raging but contained, for Yves was only a minor insolence to be brushed aside rather than crushed, and at this moment she still had a use for him. He had seen her blaze up like this to flay other unfortunates, now the fire scorched him, and even in his devouring anger he shrank from it.

"Do you tell me what I can and cannot do, boy? Your part is to obey, and obey you shall, or be slung back into a worse dungeon and heavier irons than you've suffered yet. Marshall, call Salisbury and Reginald and Redvers into council at once, and have the engineers muster the mangonels, all that can be moved quickly. They shall set forth before us, and by noon tomorrow I want the vanguard on the road, and the main army mustering. I want my traitor dead within days, I will not rest until I see him dangling. Find me men who know the roads and this Greenhamsted well, we shall need them. And you," she turned her flashing eyes again upon Yves, "wait in the anteroom until you are called. You say you can draw us plans of La Musarderie, now you shall prove it. Make it good! If you know of any weak spots, name them. Be thankful I leave you your liberty and a whole skin, and take note, if you fall short of delivering what you have promised me, you shall lose both. Now go, get out of my sight!"

CHAPTER ELEVEN

SO NOW there was nothing to be done but to go along with what had already been done and could not be undone, make the best of it, and try by whatever means offered to prevent the worst. Nothing was changed in his determination to return to La Musarderie, and do his part to the limit in the battle to release Olivier. He would do all he could to press the assault. He had spent some hours of the night drawing out plans of the castle, and the ground from the ridge to the river below, and done his best to estimate the extent of the cleared land all round the fortress, and the range the siege engines would have to tackle. He had even indicated the curtain tower where there had been damage and repair, according to his observations, and where possibly a breach might be effected. The empress was welcome to the castle, once Olivier was safely out of captivity, but she was not, if he could prevent it, entitled to kill the castellan. Challenged by others more daring and more established than himself, she had argued vehemently that Earl Robert was as mortally affronted by Philip's treason as she herself was, and would not hesitate to approve the death. But she was in ruthless haste to be about the business before any word of her intention could get to her brother's ears, all the same. Not that she was afraid of Robert, or willing to acknowledge that she could do nothing effective without him. She had been known to humiliate him in public, on occasion, as arrogantly and ruthlessly as any other. No, what she aimed at was to present him with a death already accomplished, past argument, past redemption, her own unmistakable and absolute act, the statement of her supremacy. For surely all these years, while she had used and relied on him, she had also been jealous of him, and grudged him his preeminence.

Yves slept the few hours left to him after the council ended rolled in his cloak on a bench in the darkened hall, without a notion in his troubled head as to how to circumvent the empress's revenge. It was not simply that such an act would disrupt and alienate half her following, and fetch out of their scabbards every sword that was not bared and blooded already, to prolong and poison this even now envenomed warfare. It was also, though he had not the penetration to probe into motives after such a day, that he did not want Philip's death. A daunting, inward man, hard to know, but one he could have liked in other circumstances. One whom Olivier had liked, but equally did not understand.

Yves slept fitfully until an hour before dawn. And in the bleak morning hours he made ready, and rode with the main body of the empress's army, under John FitzGilbert, to the assault of La Musarderie.

The deployment of the siege force around the castle was left to the marshall, and the marshall knew his business, and could get his engineers and their mangonels into position along the ridge without noise or commotion enough to reach the ears of the watchmen on the walls, and his companies strategically placed within cover all about the site, from the bank of the river round to the fringes of the village above, where the empress and her women had taken possession of the priest's house, rather than face the ardours of a camp. The operation might have been much more difficult, and the secret out before the end of the day, had not the villagers of Greenhamsted

fared rather well under the Musards, and felt no inclination
at all to send warning to the present castellan of La Musarderie.
Their complacency with the present total occupation would
stand them in good stead with one faction, the one that had
appeared among them with convincing strength. They held
their peace, sat circumspectly among their invading soldiery,
and awaited events.

The dispersal went on into the darkness, and the first fire
in the camp above, insufficiently covered and damped, alerted
the guards on the wall. A round of the guardwalks discovered
a number of similar sparks dispersed among the trees, all
round the perimeter of the cleared ground.

"He has brought down the whole mass of her army on us,"
said Philip dispassionately to Cadfael, up on the south tower
watching the minute glints that showed the ring of besiegers.
"A lad of his word! Pure chance that she seems to have
mustered a council of earls about her in Gloucester, with all
their companies, when I could well have done without them.
Well, I invited him to the feast. I am as ready as I can be
with such odds against me. Tomorrow we shall see. At least
now we're warned." And he said to his monastic guest, very
civilly: "If you wish to withdraw, do so freely, now, while
there's time. They will respect and welcome you."

"I take that offer very kindly," said Cadfael with equally
placid formality, "but I do not go from here without my son."

Yves left his station among the trees to northward when it
was fully dark, and with a sky muffled by low-hanging clouds
that hid moon and stars. Nothing would happen this night.
With such a show of force there would certainly be a demand
for surrender, rather than set out from the beginning to batter
a valuable asset to pieces. At dawn, then. He had this one
night to make contact if he could.

Yves' memory was excellent. He could still repeat word
for word what Philip had said of his unexpected guest: "He

can keep the hours as faithfully in my chapel as in Shrewsbury. And so he does, even the midnight matin." Moreover, Yves knew where that chapel must be, for when they had plucked him out of his cell and brought him forth from the keep to the hall he had seen the chaplain emerge from a dim stone corridor with his missal in his hand. Somewhere along that passage Cadfael might, if God willed, keep his solitary office this night also, before the clash of battle. This night of all nights he would not neglect his prayers.

The darkness was great blessing. Even so, black-cloaked and silent, movement may be perceptible by a quiver in the depth of the blackness, or the mere displacement of air. And the stripped slope he had to cross seemed to him at this moment a matter of tedious miles. But even a shaven hillside can undulate, providing shallow gullies which nevertheless would be deep enough to offer a consistent path from trees to curtain wall, and the shadowy corner under the north tower where the great vine grew. Even a dip in the ground can provide some kind of shelter in the gradations of shadow. He wished he could see the head of the guard who paced the length of wall between those two towers, but the distance was too great for that. Beyond the halfway mark there might be enough variation between solid bulk and sky to show the outline of towers and crenellations, if without detail; perhaps even the movement of the head against space as the watchman patrolled his length of guardwalk. Pointless to hope for a greater degree of visibility, it would mean only that he, too, could be seen.

He wrapped the heavy black frieze about him, and moved forward clear of the trees. From within the wards a faint reflection of light from torches below made a just perceptible halo under the thick cloud cover. He fixed his eyes on that, and walked forward towards it, his feet testing the invisible ground, doing the function of eyes as they do for the blind. He went at a steady pace, and there was no wind to flap at his cloak and hair, and make itself palpable, even over distance.

The black bulk against the sky loomed nearer. His ears began to catch small sounds that emanated from within, or from the watchmen on the walls when they changed guard. And once there was a sudden torch-flare and a voice calling, as someone mounted from the ward, and Yves dropped flat to the ground, burying head and all under the cloak, and lay silent where everything round him was silent, and motionless where nothing moved, in case those two above should look over from the embrasure, and by some infinitesimal sign detect the approach of a living creature. But the man with the torch lit himself briskly down the stair again, and the moment passed.

Yves gathered himself up cautiously, and stood a moment still, to breathe freely and stare ahead, before he resumed his silent passage. And now he was close enough to be able to distinguish, as movement makes the invisible perceptible even in the dark, the passage of the guard's head, as he paced the length of wall between the towers. Here in the corner of tower and wall the brattice began; he had taken careful note of it again before darkness fell, and he had seen how the thick, overgrown branches of the vine reached crabbed arms to fasten on the timber gallery that jutted from the stone. It should be possible to climb over into the gallery while the watchman's beat took him in the other direction. And after that?

Yves came unarmed. Sword and scabbard are of little use in climbing either vines or castle walls, and he had no intention of attacking Philip's guard. All he wanted was to get in and out undetected, and leave the word of warning he had to deliver, for the sake of whatever fragile chance of reconciliation and peace remained alive after the débacle of Coventry. And how he accomplished it, well or ill, must depend on chance and his own ingenuity.

The guard on the wall was moving away towards the further tower. Yves seized the moment and ran for it, risking the rough ground, to drop thankfully under the wall, and edge his way along it until he reached the corner, and drew himself in under the maze of branches. Here the brattice above was a protection to him instead of a threat. Midnight must still be almost an hour away, he could afford to breathe evenly for some minutes, and listen for the footsteps above, very faint even when they neared this point, fading out altogether as soon as the guard turned away.

The cloak he must leave behind, to climb in it would be awkward and possibly dangerous, but he had seen to it that the clothing he wore beneath it was equally black. He let the footsteps return over him twice, to measure the interval, for at each return he would have to freeze into stillness. The third time, as the sound faded, he felt his way to a firm grip among the branches, and began to climb.

Almost leafless, the vine made no great stir or rustle, and the branches were twisted and gnarled but very strong. Several times on the way he had to suspend all movement and hang motionless while the watchman above halted briefly at the turn to stare out over the cleared ground, as he must have been staring at intervals all the time Yves was making his way here to the precarious shelter of the curtain wall. And once, feeling for a hold against the rounded masonry of the tower, he put his hand deep into an arrow-slit, and caught a glimmer of light within, reflected through a half-open door, and shrank back into the corner of the stonework in dread that someone might have seen him. But all continued quiet, and when he peered cautiously within there was nothing to be seen but the edge of that inner door and the sharp rim of light. Now if there should also be an unlocked door into the tower from the guardwalk. . . . They would have been moving weapons during the day, as soon as they knew the danger, and the place for light mangons and espringales was on the

wall and the towers. And stones and iron for the mangons,
surely by now piled here in store, and the darts and javelins
for the espringales. . . .

Yves waited to move again, and hoped.

The towers of La Musarderie jutted only a shallow height
beyond the crenellated wall, and the vine had pushed its
highest growth beyond the level of the brattice, still clinging
to the stone. He reached the stout timber barrier before he
realized it, and hung still to peer over it along the gallery. He
was within three paces of the guard this time when the man
reached the limit of his patrol, and turned again. Yves let him
withdraw half the length of his charge before daring to reach
out for the solid rail where the brattice began, and swing
himself over into the gallery. One more interval now before
he could climb over to the guardwalk. He lay down close
under one of the merlons, and let the pacing feet pass by
him and again return. Then he crept cautiously through the
embrasure onto the solid level of stone, and turned to the
tower. Here beside it the garrison had indeed been piling
missiles for the defence engines, but the door was now fast
closed, and would not give to his thrust. They had not needed
to use the tower to bring up their loads, there was a hoist
standing by over the drop into the bailey, and just astride from
it the head of one of the stairways from bailey to wall. There
was but one way to go, before the watchman turned at the
end of his beat. Yves went down the first steps of the flight
in desperate haste, and then lowered himself by his hands
over the edge, and worked his way down step by step, dangling
precariously over the drop.

He hung still as the guard passed and repassed, and then
continued his aching descent, into this blessedly remote and
dark corner of the ward. There was still light and sound in the
distant armoury, and shadowy figures crossing in purposeful
silence from hall to stores, and smithy to armoury. La Musarderie went about its siege business calmly and efficiently, not

yet fully aware of the numbers ranged against them. Yves
dropped the last steps of the stairway, and flattened himself
back against the wall to take stock of his ground.

It was not far to the keep, but too far to risk taking at a
suspect run. He schooled himself to come out of his hiding-
place and cross at a rapid, preoccupied walk, as the few other
figures out thus late in the night were doing. They were sparing
of torches where everything was familiar, all he had to do
was keep his face averted from any source of light, and seem
to be headed somewhere on garrison business of sharp importance. Had he encountered someone closely he would have
had to pass by with a muttered word, so intent on his errand
that he had no attention to spare for anything else. And that
would have been no lie. But he reached the open door and
went in without challenge, and heaved a great sigh to have
got so far in safety.

He was creeping warily along the narrow, stone-flagged
passage when the chaplain emerged suddenly from a door
ahead, and came towards him, with a small oil flask in his
hand, fresh from feeding and trimming the altar lamp. There
was no time to evade, and to have attempted it would have
penetrated even the tired old man's preoccupation. Yves drew
to the wall respectfully to let him pass, and made him a deep
reverence as he went by. Short-sighted eyes went over him
gently, and a resigned but tranquil voice blessed him. He was
left trembling, almost shamed, but he took it for a good omen.
The old man had even shown him where the chapel was to
be found, and pointed him to the altar. He went there humbly
and gratefully, and kneeled to give thanks for a dozen unde-
served mercies that had brought him thus far. He forgot even
to be careful, to be ready to take alarm at a sound, to regard
his own life or take thought for how he should ever find his
way out again. He was where he had set out to be. And Cadfael
would not fail him.

The chapel was lofty, cramped and stonily cold, but its

austerity had been tempered a little by draping the walls with thick woollen hangings, and curtaining the inner side of the door. In the dim light of the corner behind the door, where the folds of curtain and wall hanging met amply, a man could stand concealed. Only if someone entering closed the door fully behind him would the alien presence risk detection. Yves took his stand there, shook the folds into order to cover him, and settled down to wait.

In the several days that he had been a guest in La Musarderie Cadfael had awakened and risen at midnight largely from habit, but also from the need to cling at least to the memory of his vocation, and of the place where his heart belonged. If he did not live to see it again, it mattered all the more that while he lived that link should not be broken. It was also a solemn part of his consolation in keeping the monastic observances that he could do it in solitude. The chaplain observed every part of the daily worship due from a secular priest, but did not keep the Benedictine hours. Only once, on that one occasion when Philip had also had a word to say to God, had Cadfael had to share the chapel at Matins with anyone.

On this night he came a little early, without the necessity of waking from sleep. There would be little sleep for most of the garrison of La Musarderie. He said the office, and continued on his knees in sombre thought rather than private prayer. All the prayers he could make for Olivier had already been uttered and heard, and repeated in the mind over and over, reminders to God. And all that he might have pleaded for himself was seen to be irrelevant in this hour, when the day is put away, with all its unresolved anxieties, and the morrow's troubles are not yet, and need not be anticipated.

When he rose from his knees and turned towards the door, he saw the folds of the curtain behind it quiver. A hand emerged at the edge, putting the heavy cloth aside. Cadfael made no sound and no movement, as Yves stepped forth before his eyes, soiled and dishevelled from his climb, with urgent gesture and dilated eyes enjoining caution and silence. For a moment they both hung still, staring at each other. Then Cadfael flattened a hand against Yves' breast, pressing him back gently into hiding, and himself leaned out from the doorway to look both ways along the stone corridor. Philip's own chamber was close, but it was questionable whether he would be in it this night. Here nothing stirred, and Cadfael's narrow cell was not ten yards distant. He reached back to grip Yves' wrist, and pluck him hastily along the passage into sanctuary there, and close the door against the world. For a moment they embraced and stood tense, listening, but all was still.

"Keep your voice low," said Cadfael then, "and we are safe enough. The chaplain sleeps nearby." The walls, even these interior walls, were very thick. "Now, what are you doing here? And how did you get in?" He was still gripping the boy's wrist, so tightly as to bruise. He eased his grip, and sat his unexpected visitor down on the bed, holding him by both shoulders, as if to touch was to hold inviolable. "This was madness! What can you do here? And I was glad to know that you were out of it, whatever comes."

"I climbed up by the vine," said Yves, whispering. "And I must go back the same way, unless you know of a better." He was shivering a little in reaction; Cadfael felt him vibrating between his hands like a bowstring gradually stilling after the shot. "No great feat—if the guard can be distracted while I reach the gallery. But let that wait. Cadfael, I had to get word in here to you somehow. He must be told what she intends . . ."

"He?" said Cadfael sharply. "Philip?"

"Philip, who else? He has to know what he may have to deal with. She—the empress—she has half a dozen of her barons with her, they were all gathered in Gloucester, and all their levies with them. Salisbury, Redvers of Devon, FitzRoy, Bohun, the king of Scots and all, the greatest army she has had to hand for a year or more. And she means to use everything against this place. It may cost her high, but she will have it, and quickly, before Gloucester can get word what's in the wind."

"Gloucester?" said Cadfael incredulously. "But she needs him, she can do nothing without him. All the more as this is his son, revolted or not."

"No!" said Yves vehemently. "For that very reason she wants him left ignorant in Hereford until all's over. Cadfael, she means to hang Philip and be done with him. She has sworn it, and she'll do it. By the time Robert knows of it, there'll be nothing for him but a body to bury."

"She would not dare!" said Cadfael on a hissing breath.

"She will dare. I saw her, I heard her! She is hellbent on killing, and this is her chance. Her teeth are in his throat already, I doubt if Robert himself could break her death-grip, but she has no mind to give him the opportunity. It will all be over before ever he knows of it."

"She is mad!" said Cadfael. He dropped his hands from the boy's shoulders, and sat staring down the long procession of excesses and atrocities that would follow that death: every remaining loyalty torn apart, every kinship disrupted, the last shreds of hope for conciliation and sanity ripped loose to the winds. "He would abandon her. He might even turn his hand against her." And that, indeed, might have ended it, and brought about by force the settlement they could not achieve by agreement. But no, he would not be able to bring himself to touch her, he would only withdraw from the field with his bereavement and grief, and let others bring her down. A longer business, and a longer and more profound agony for the country fought over, back and forth to the last despair.

"I know it," said Yves. "She is destroying her own cause,

and damning to this continued chaos every man of us, on either side, and God knows, all the poor souls who want nothing but to sow and reap their fields and go about their buying and selling, and raising their children in peace. I tried to tell her so, to her face, and she flayed me for it. She listens to no one. So I had to come."

And not only to try and avert a disastrous policy, Cadfael thought, but also because that imminent death was an offence to him, and must be prevented solely as the barbaric act it was. Yves did not want Philip FitzRobert dead. He had come back in arms for Olivier, certainly, and he would stand by that to his last breath, but he would not connive at his liege lady's ferocious revenge.

"To me," said Cadfael. "You come to me. So what is it you want of me, now you are here?"

"Warn him," said Yves simply. "Tell him what she has in mind for him, make him believe it, for she'll never relent. At least let him know the whole truth, before he has to deal with her demands. She would rather keep the castle and occupy it intact than raze it, but she'll raze it if she must. It may be he can make a deal that will keep him man alive, if he gives up La Musarderie." But even the boy did not really believe in that ever happening, and Cadfael knew it never would. "At least tell him the truth. Then it is his decision."

"I will see to it," said Cadfael very gravely, "that he is in no doubt what is at stake."

"He will believe you," said Yves, sounding curiously content. And he stretched and sighed, leaning his head back against the wall. "Now I had better be thinking how best to get out of here."

They were quite used to Cadfael by that time, he was accepted in La Musarderie as harmless, tolerated by the castellan, and respectably what his habit represented him as being. He mixed

freely, went about the castle as he pleased, and talked with
whom he pleased. It stood Yves in good stead in the matter
of getting out by the same route by which he had entered.

The best way to escape notice, said Cadfael, was to go
about as one having every right and a legitimate reason for
going wherever he was seen to be going, with nothing furtive
about him. Risky by daylight, of course, even among a large
garrison of reasonably similar young men, but perfectly valid
now in darkness, crossing wards even less illuminated than
normally, to avoid affording even estimates of provision for
defence to the assembled enemy.

Yves crossed the ward to the foot of the staircase up to
the guardwalk by Cadfael's side, quite casually and slowly,
obeying orders trustfully, and melted into the dark corner to
flatten himself against the wall, while Cadfael climbed the
steps to lean into an embrasure between the merlons of the
wall and peer out towards the scattered sparkle of fires, out
there among the trees. The watchman, reaching this end of
his patrol, lingered to lean beside him and share his specula-
tions for a moment, and when he resumed his march back to
the distant tower, Cadfael went with him. Yves, listening
below, heard their two low voices recede gradually. As soon
as he felt they should be sufficiently distant, he crept hastily
up the steps and flung himself through the embrasure, to
flatten himself on the floor of the brattice under a merlon. He
was at the end of the gallery, the gnarled black branches and
twisted tendrils of the vine leaned inward over him, but he
did not dare to rise and haul himself in among them until the
guard had made one more turn, and again departed, leaving
Cadfael to descend to the ward and seek his bed for what
remained of the night.

Above Yves' head the familiar voice said very softly: "He's
away. Go now!"

Yves rose and heaved himself over the parapet and into
the sinewy coils of the vine, and began to let himself down

cautiously towards the ground far below. And Cadfael, when the boy had vanished, and the first shaking and rustling of the branches had subsided, descended the steps to the ward, and went to look for Philip.

Philip had made the rounds of his defences alone, and found them as complete as he had the means to make them. This assault came early, young Hugonin must have been uncommonly persuasive, and the empress unusually well provided with men and arms, or he would have had more time to prepare. No matter, it would be decided the sooner.

He was on the walk above the gate when Cadfael found him, looking down upon the open causeway by which, in the early morning, the first challenger would approach under flag of truce.

"You, brother?" he said, turning a mildly surprised face. "I thought you would have been sleeping hours ago."

"This is no night for sleeping," said Cadfael, "until all's done that needs to be done. And there is yet something needed, and I am here to see it done. My lord Philip, I have to tell you, and take it in earnest, for so it is, that the empress's mind against you is deadly. Yves Hugonin has brought all this host down upon you to deliver his friend and kinsman. But not she! She is here, not even to take a castle, though she must do that first. She is here to take a man. And when she has you, she means to hang you."

There was a silence. Philip stood gazing eastward, where the first grey blanching of the day would come, before dawn. At length he said quietly: "Her mind I never doubted. Tell me, if you know so much, brother, is that also my father's mind towards me?"

"Your father," said Cadfael, "is not here in arms. He does not know her army has moved, and she will take good care he does not find out, not until all is over. Your father is in Hereford with Earl Roger. For once she has moved without him. For good reason. She sees her chief enemy within her grasp. She is here to destroy you. And since she goes to such pains to keep this from him," said Cadfael, his voice detached and mild, "it would seem that she, at any rate, is by no means certain of his mind towards you."

A second silence fell between them. Then Philip said, without turning his head: "I knew her well enough to be out of reach now of surprise. I looked for nothing better, should it ever come to this. I made her of none account when I turned to the king, that is true, though less true, or only partial truth, that I turned against her. She was of none effect, that was the heart of it. And here, if not in Normandy, Stephen was and is in the ascendant. If he can win, as she could not, and put an end to this chaos and waste, let as many coats turn as may be needed to bring it about. Any end that will let men live, and till their fields, and ride the roads and ply their trades in safety, is to be desired above any monarch's right and triumph. My father," he said, "determined the way I went. As lief Stephen as Maud, to me, if he can enforce order. But I understand her rage. I grant her every fibre of her grudge against me. She has a right to hate me, and I'll abide her hate."

It was the first time he had spoken thus freely, temperately, without regret or penitence.

"If you have believed me," said Cadfael, "that she means your shameful death, that is my mission done. If you know the whole truth, you can dispose yourself to meet it. She has an eye to gain, as well as to revenge. If you choose, you could bargain."

"There are things I will not trade," said Philip, and turned his head, and smiled.

"Then hear me yet a moment," said Cadfael. "You have spoken of the empress. Now speak to me of Olivier."

The dark head turned sharply away again. Philip stood mute, staring eastward, where there was nothing to see, unless his own mind peopled the darkness.

"Then I will speak of him," said Cadfael. "I know my son. He is of a simpler mode than you, you asked too much of him. I think you had shared many dangerous moments with him, that you had come to rely on each other and value each other. And when you changed course, and he could not go with you, the severance was doubly bitter, for each of you felt that the other had failed him. All he saw was treason, and what you saw was a failure of understanding that was equally a betrayal."

"It is your story, brother," said Philip with recovered serenity, "not mine."

"There is as sharp a point to it as to a dagger," said Cadfael. "You do not grudge the empress her resentment. Why can you not extend the same justice to my son?"

He got no answer from Philip, but he needed none; he already knew. Olivier had been dearly loved. The empress never had.

CHAPTER TWELVE

THE EXPECTED embassage came with the dawn, and it was the marshall who brought it. The party appeared out of the woods, taking to the open causeway to be seen as soon as they left cover: a knight with a white pennant before, then FitzGilbert with three attendant officers at his back, not in mail or showing weapons, to indicate clearly that at this moment they intended no threat and expected none. Philip, roused from his brief sleep as soon as they were sighted, came out to the guardwalk over the gate, between the two towers, to receive them.

Cadfael, below in the ward, listened to the exchange from the doorway of the hall. The stillness within the walls was like the hush before storm, as every man halted and froze to hear the more clearly; not from fear, rather with a piercing tremor of excitement, many times experienced and by now customary and almost welcome.

"FitzRobert," called the marshall, halted some yards from the closed gates, the better to look up at the man he challenged, "open your gates to her Grace the empress, and receive her envoy."

"Do your errand from there," said Philip. "I hear you very well."

"Then I give you to know," said FitzGilbert forcefully, "that this castle of yours is surrounded, and strongly. No relief can get in to your aid, and no man of you can get out unless by agreement with her Grace. Make no mistake, you are in no case to withstand the assault we can make upon you, can and will, if you are obdurate."

"Make your offer," said Philip, unmoved. "I have work to do, if you have none."

FitzGilbert was too old a hand at the manoeuvrings of civil war to be shaken or diverted by whatever tone was used to him. "Very well," he said. "Your liege lady the empress summons you to surrender this castle forthwith, or she will take it by storm. Give it up intact, or fall with it."

"And on what conditions?" said Philip shortly. "Name the terms."

"Unconditional surrender! You must submit yourself and all you hold here to her Grace's will."

"I would not hand over a dog that had once barked at her to her Grace's will," said Philip. "On reasonable terms I might consider. But even then, John, I should require your warranty to back hers."

"There'll be no bargaining," said the marshall flatly. "Surrender or pay the price."

"Tell the empress," said Philip, "that her own costs may come high. We are not to be bought cheaply."

The marshall shrugged largely, and wheeled his horse to descend the slope. "Never say you were not warned!" he called back over his shoulder, and cantered towards the trees with his herald before him and his officers at his back.

After that they had not long to wait. The assault began with a volley of arrows from all the fringes of cover round the castle. For a good bowman the walls were within range, and whoever showed himself unwisely in an embrasure was a fair mark; but it seemed to Cadfael, himself up on the south-western tower, which came nearest to the village on the crest,

that the attackers were being lavish of shafts partly to intimi-
date, having no fear of being left short of arrows. The defenders were more chary of waste, and shot only when they
detected a possible target unwarily breaking cover. If they
ran down their stock of shafts there was no way of replenishing
it. They were reserving the espringales, and the darts and
javelins they shot, to repel a massed attack. Against a company
they could scarcely fail to find targets, but against one man
on the move their bolts would be wasted, and waste was
something they could not afford. The squat engines, like large
crossbows, were braced in the embrasures, four of them on
this south-westerly side, from which attack in numbers was
most likely, two more disposed east and west.

Of mangonels they had only two, and no target for them,
unless the marshall should be unwise enough to despatch a
massed assault. They were the ones who had to fear the
battering of siege engines, but at need heavy stones flung into
a body of men making a dash to reach the walls could cut
disastrous swathes in the ranks, and render the method too
expensive to be persisted in.

The activity was almost desultory for the first hours, but
one or two of the attacking archers had found a mark. Only
minor grazes as yet, where some unwary youngster had shown
himself for a moment between the merlons. No doubt some
of these practised bowmen on the walls had also drawn blood
among the fringes of the trees on the ridge. They were no
more than feeling their way as yet.

Then the first stone crashed short against the curtain wall
below the brattice, and rebounded without more damage than
a few flying chips of masonry, and the siege engines were
rolled out to the edge of cover, and began to batter insistently
at the defences. They had found their range, stone after heavy
stone howled through the air and thudded against the wall,
low down, concentrating on this one tower, where Yves had
detected signs of previous damage and repair. This, thought

Cadfael, would continue through the day, and by night they might try to get a ram to the walls, and complete the work of battering a way through. In the meantime they had lost at any rate one of their engineers, who had ventured into view too clearly in his enthusiasm. Cadfael had seen him dragged back into the trees.

He looked out over the high ground that hid the village of Greenhamsted, probing for movement among the trees, or glimpses of the hidden machines. This was a battleground in which he should have had no part. Nothing bound him to either the besiegers or the besieged, except that both were humankind like himself, and could bleed. And he had better by far be making himself useful in the one way he could justify here. But even as he made his way along the guardwalk, sensibly from merlon to merlon like an experienced soldier with a proper regard for his own skin, he found himself approving Philip's deployment of his bowmen and his espringales, and the practical way his garrison went about their defence.

Below in the hall the chaplain and an elderly steward were attending to such minor injuries as had so far been suffered, bruises and cuts from flying splinters of stone spattered high by the battering of the wall, and one or two gashes from arrows, where an arm or a shoulder had been exposed at the edge of the protecting merlons. No graver harm; not yet. Cadfael was all too well aware that before long there would be. He added himself to the relieving force here, and took comfort in the discovery that for some hours he had little enough to do. But before noon had passed it became clear that FitzGilbert had his orders to bring to bear upon La Musarderie every means of assault he had at his disposal, to assure a quick ending.

One frontal attack upon the gatehouse had been made early, under cover of the continued impact of stone upon stone under the tower to westward, but the espringales mounted above

the gate cut a swathe with their javelins through the ranks of
the attackers, and they were forced to draw off again and drag
their wounded with them. But the alarm had distracted some
degree of attention from the main onslaught, and diverted a
number of the defenders to strengthen the gate-towers. The
besiegers on the ridge took the opportunity to run their heaviest
mangonel forward clear of the trees, and let loose all the
heaviest stones and cases of iron rubble at the defences, raising
their aim to pound incessantly at the timber brattice, more
vulnerable by far than the solid masonry of the wall. From
within, Cadfael felt the hall shaken at every impact, and the
air vibrating like impending thunder. If the attackers raised
their range yet again, and began lobbing missiles over among
the buildings within the ward, they might soon have to transfer
their activities and their few wounded into the rocklike solidity
of the keep.

A young archer came down dangling a torn arm in a bloody
sleeve, and sat sweating and heaving at breath while the cloth
was cut away from his wound, and the gash cleaned and
dressed.

"My drawing arm," he said, and grimaced. "I can still loose
the espringale, though, if another man winds it down. A great
length of the brattice is in splinters, we nearly lost a mangonel
over the edge when the parapet went, but we managed to haul
it in over the embrasure. I leaned out too far, and got this.
There's nothing amiss with Bohun's bowmen."

The next thing, Cadfael thought, smoothing his bandage
about the gashed arm, will be fire arrows into the splintered
timbers of the gallery. The range, as this lad has proved to
his cost, is well within their capabilities, there is hardly any
deflecting wind, indeed by this stillness and the feel of the
air there will be heavy frost, and all that wood will be dry as
tinder.

"They have not tried to reach the wall under there?" he
asked.

"Not yet." The young man flexed his bandaged arm gingerly, winced, and shrugged off the twinge, rising to return to his duty. "They're in haste, surely, but not such haste as all that. By night they may try it."

In the dusk, under a moonless sky with heavy low cloud, Cadfael went out into the ward and climbed to the guardwalk on the wall, and peered out from cover at the splintered length of gallery that sagged outward drunkenly in the angle between tower and curtain wall. Within the encircling woodland above there were glimmerings of fires, and now and then as they flared they showed the outlines of monstrous black shapes that were the engines of assault. Distance diminished them into elusive toys, but did not diminish their menace. But for the moment there was a lull, almost a silence. Along the wall the defenders emerged cautiously from the shelter of the merlons to stare towards the ridge and the village beyond. The light was too far gone for archery, unless someone offered an irresistible target by stepping full into the light of a torch.

They had their first dead by then, laid in the stony cold of the chapel and the corridors of the keep. There could be no burying.

Cadfael walked the length of the wall between the towers, among the men braced and still in the twilight, and saw Philip there at the end of the walk, where the wreckage of the brattice swung loose from the angle of the tower. Dark against the dark, still in mail, he stood sweeping the rim of the trees for the gleams of fire and the location of the mangonels the empress had brought against him.

"You have not forgotten," said Cadfael, close beside him, "what I told you? For I told you absolute truth."

"No," said Philip, without turning his head, "I have not forgotten."

"Nor disbelieved it?"

"No," he said, and smiled. "I never doubted it. I am bearing it in mind now. Should God forestall the empress, there will

be provision to make for those who will be left." And then
he did turn his head, and looked full at Cadfael, still smiling.
"You do not want me dead?"

"No," said Cadfael, "I do not want you dead."

One of the tiny fires in the distance, no bigger than a first
spark from the flint, burned up suddenly into a bright red
glow, and flung up around it shadows of violent movement,
a little swirl of just perceptible chaos in the night and the
woodland, where the branches flared in a tracery like fine
lace, and again vanished. Something soared into the darkness
hissing and blazing, a fearful comet trailing a tail of flames.
One of the young archers, ten yards from where Cadfael stood,
was staring up in helpless fascination, a mere boy, unused to
siegecraft. Philip uttered a bellow of alarm and warning, and
launched himself like a flung lance, to grasp the boy round
the body and haul him back with him into the shelter of the
tower. The three of them dropped together, as men were
dropping under every merlon along the wall, pressed into the
angle of wall and flagged walk. The comet, spitting sparks
and flashes of flaming liquid, struck the centre of the length
of damaged gallery, and burst, hurling burning tar from end
to end of the sagging timbers, and splashing the guardwalk
through every embrasure. And instantly the battered wood
caught and blazed, the flames leaping from broken planks and
splintered parapet all along the wall.

Philip was on his feet, hauling the winded boy up with
him.

"Are you fit? Can you go? Down with you, never mind
fighting it. Go get axes!"

There would be burns and worse to deal with afterwards,
but this was more urgent now. The young man went scrambling down into the ward in frantic haste, and Philip, stooping
under the shelter of the wall, went running the length of the
blaze, hoisting his men up, despatching those worst damaged
down to take refuge below and find help. Here the brattice

would have to be hacked free, before it spread the fire within, flashed into the woodwork of the towers, spat molten tar over the ward. Cadfael went down the steps with a moaning youth in his arms, nursing him down stair by stair, his own scapular swathed round the boy's body to quench the lingering smouldering of cloth and the smell of scorched flesh. There were others below waiting to receive him, and more like him, and hoist them away into cover. Cadfael hesitated, almost wishing to go back. On the guardwalk Philip was hacking away the blazing timbers among his remaining guards, wading through lingering puddles of flaming tar to reach the beams that still clung to their shattered hold upon the wall.

No, he was not of the garrison, he had no right to take a hand in this quarrel upon either side. Better go and see what could be done for the burned.

Perhaps half an hour later, from among the pallets in the hall, with the stench of burned woollens and flesh in his nostrils, he heard the timbers of the gallery break free and fall, creaking as the last fibres parted, flaring with a windy roar as they fell, fanned by their flight, to crash under the tower and settle, in a series of spitting collapses, against the stones.

Philip came down some time later, blackened to the brow and parched from breathing smoke, and stayed only to see how his wounded fared. He had burns of his own, but paid them little attention.

"They will try and breach the wall there before morning," he said.

"It will still be too hot," objected Cadfael, without pausing in anointing a badly burned arm.

"They'll venture. Nothing but wood, a few hours of the night's cold. And they want a quick ending. They'll venture."

"Without a sow?" They could hardly have hauled a whole stout wooden shelter, long enough to house and cover a team

of men and a heavy ram, all the way from Gloucester, Cadfael
surmised.

"They'll have spent most of the day building one. They
have plenty of wood. And with half the brattice on that side
down, we'll be vulnerable." Philip settled his mail over a
bruised and scorched shoulder, and went back to his guardwall
to watch out the night. And Cadfael, drawing breath at length
among the injured, guessed at the approach of midnight, and
made a brief but fervent office of Matins.

Before first light the assault came, without the precaution
of the shelter a sow would have afforded, but with the added
impetus of speed to balance that disadvantage. A large party
issued from the woods and made a dash downhill for the wall,
and though the mounted espringales cut some furrows in their
ranks, they reached the foot of the tower, just aside from the
glowing remnants of the fire. Cadfael heard from the hall the
thudding of their ram against the stone, and felt the ground
shake to the blows. And now, for the want of that length of
gallery, the defenders were forced to expose themselves in
order to hoist stones over the embrasures, and toss down oil
and flares to renew the blaze. Cadfael had no knowledge of
how that battle must be going; he had more than enough to
do where he was. Towards morning Philip's second in command, a border knight from near Berkeley named Guy Camville, touched him on the shoulder, rousing him out of a half-
doze of exhaustion, and told him to get away into comparative
quiet in the keep, and snatch a couple of hours of honest
sleep, while it was possible.

"You've done enough, brother," he said heartily, "in a quarrel that's been none of your making."

"None of us," said Cadfael ruefully, clambering dazedly
to his feet, "has ever done enough—or never in the right
direction."

*   *   *

The ram was withdrawn, and the assault party with it, before full light, but by then they had made a breach, not through the curtain wall, but into the base of the tower. A fresh approach by full daylight was too costly to contemplate without cover, but the besiegers were certainly hard at work by now building a sow to shelter the next onslaught, and if they contrived to get branches and brushwood inside they might be able to burn their way through into the ward. Not, however, without delaying their own entry in any numbers until the passage was cool enough to risk. Time was the only thing of which they lacked enough. Philip massed his own mangonels along the threatened south-western wall, and set them to a steady battering of the edge of the woodland, to hamper the building of the sow, and reduce the number of his enemies, or confine them strictly to cover until nightfall.

Cadfael observed all, tended the injured along with every other man who could be spared for the duty, and foresaw an ending very soon. The odds were too great. Weapons spent here within, every javelin, every stone, could not be replaced. The empress had open roads and plenteous wagons to keep her supplied. No one knew it better than Philip. In the common run of this desultory war she would not have concentrated all this fury, costly in men and means, upon one solitary castle like La Musarderie. In just one particular she justified the expenditure, without regard to those she expended: her most hated enemy was here within. No cost was too great to provide her his death. That also he knew, none better. It had hardly needed telling; yet Cadfael was glad that Yves had risked his liberty, and possibly his own life, to bring the warning, and that it had been faithfully delivered.

While the attackers waited for night to complete the breach, and the defenders laboured to seal it, all the siege engines on the ridge resumed their monotonous assault, this time dividing their missiles between the foot of the tower and a new diver-

sion, raising their trajectory to send stones and butts of iron
fragments and tar casks over the wall into the ward. Twice
roofs were fired within, but the fires were put out without
great damage. The archers on the walls had begun selecting
their quarries with care, to avoid profitless expense in shafts
from a dwindling store. The engineers managing the siege
machines were their main target, and now and again a good
shot procured a moment's respite, but there were so many
practised men up there that every loss was soon supplied.

They set to work damping down all the roofs within the
curtain wall, and moved their wounded into the greater safety
of the keep. There were the horses to be thought of, as well
as the men. If the stables caught they would have to house
the beasts in the hall. The ward was full of purposeful activity
unavoidably in the open, though the missiles kept flying over
the wall, and to be in the open there was one way of dying.

It was in the dark that Philip emerged from the breached
tower, with all done there that could be done against the
inevitable night assault; the breach again barricaded, the tower
itself sealed, locked and barred. If the enemy broke in there
for hours at least they would be in possession of nothing
beyond. Philip came forth last, with the armourer's boy beside
him, fetcher and carrier for the work of bolting iron across
the gap in the wall. The armourer and one of his smiths had
climbed to the guardwalk, to ensure there should be no easy
way through at that level. The boy came out on Philip's arm,
and was restrained from bolting at once for the door of the
keep. They waited close under the wall a moment, and then
crossed at a brisk walk.

They were halfway across when Philip heard, as every man
heard, the howling, whistling flight as perhaps the last missile
of the day hurtled over the wall, black, clumsy and murderous,
and crashed on the cobbles a few feet before them. Even
before it had struck he had caught the boy in his arms, whirled

about with no time to run, and flung them both down on the ground, the boy face-down beneath him.

The great, ramshackle wooden crate crashed at the same moment, and burst, flinging bolts and twisted lumps of iron, furnace cinder, torn lengths of chain-mail, for thirty yards around in all directions. The weary men of the garrison shrank into the walls on every side, hugging their cowering flesh until the last impact had passed in shuddering vibration round the shell of the ward, and died into silence.

Philip FitzRobert lay unmoving, spread along the cobbles, head and body distorted by two misshapen lumps of iron of the empress's gift. Under him the terrified boy panted and hugged the ground, heaving at breath, undamaged.

They took him up, the trembling boy hovering in tears, and carried him into the keep and into his own austere chamber, and there laid him on his bed, and with difficulty eased him of his mail and stripped him naked to examine his injuries. Cadfael, who came late to the assembly, was let in to the bedside without question. They were accustomed to him now, and to the freedom with which their lord had accepted him, and they knew something of his skills, and had been glad of his willingness to use them on any of the household who came by injury. He stood with the garrison physician, looking down at the lean, muscular body, defaced now by a torn wound in the left side, and the incisive dark face just washed clean of blood. A lump of waste iron from a furnace had struck him in the side and surely broken at least two ribs, and a twisted, discarded lance-head had sliced deep through his dark hair and stuck fast in the left side of his head, its point at the temple. Easing it free without doing worse damage took them a grim while, and even when it was out, there was no knowing whether his skull was broken or not. They swathed his body closely but not too tightly, wincing at the short-

drawn breaths that signalled the damage within. Throughout
he was deep beneath the pain. The head wound they cleansed
carefully, and dressed. His closed eyelids never quivered, and
not a muscle of his face twitched.

"Can he live?" whispered the boy, shivering in the doorway.

"If God wills," said the chaplain, and shooed the boy away,
not unkindly, going with him the first paces with a hand on
his shoulder, and dropping hopeful words into his ear. But in
such circumstances, thought Cadfael grievously, remembering
the fate that awaited this erect and stubborn man if God did
please to have him survive this injury, which of us would
care to be in God's shoes, and how could any man of us bear
to dispose his will to either course, life or death?

Guy Camville came, the burden of leadership heavy on
him, made brief enquiry, stared down at Philip's imper-
vious repose, shook his head, and went away to do his best
with the task left to him. For this night might well be the
crisis.

"Send me word if he comes to his senses," said Camville,
and departed to defend the damaged tower and fend off the
inevitable assault. With a number of men out of the battle
now, it was left to the elders and those with only minor grazes
to care for the worst wounded. Cadfael sat by Philip's bed,
listening to the short, stabbing breaths he drew, painful and
hard, that yet could not break his swoon and recall him to
the world. They had wrapped him well against the cold, for
fear fever should follow. Cadfael moistened the closed lips
and the bruised forehead under the bandages. Even thus in
helplessness the thin, fastidious face looked severe and composed, as the dead sometimes look.

Close to midnight, Philip's eyelids fluttered, and his brows
knotted in a tightly drawn line. He drew in deeper breaths,
and suddenly hissed with pain returning. Cadfael moistened
the parted lips with wine, and they stirred and accepted the

service thirstily. In a little while Philip opened his eyes, and looked up vaguely, taking in the shapes of his own chamber, and the man sitting beside him. He had his senses and his wits again, and by the steady intelligence of his eyes as they cleared, memory also.

He opened his lips and asked first, low but clearly:

"The boy—was he hurt?"

"Safe and well," said Cadfael, stooping close to hear and be heard.

He acknowledged that with the faintest motion of his head, and lay silent for a moment. Then: "Bring Camville. I have affairs to settle."

He was using speech sparingly, to say much in few words; and while he waited he closed lips and eyes, and hoarded the clarity of his mind and the strength left to his body. Cadfael felt the force with which he contained and nursed his powers, and feared the fall that might follow. But not yet, not until everything had been set in order.

Guy Camville came in haste, to find his lord awake and aware, and made rapid report of what he might most want to hear. "The tower is holding. No breakthrough yet, but they're under the wall, and have rigged cover for the ram."

Philip perceptibly gathered his forces, and drew his deputy down by the wrist beside his bed. "Guy, I give you charge here. There'll be no relief. It is not La Musarderie she wants. She wants me. Let her have me, and she'll come to terms. At first light—flag FitzGilbert and call him to parley. Get what terms you best can, and surrender to her. If she has me, she'll let the garrison march out with honour. Get them safe to Cricklade. She'll not pursue. She'll have what she wants."

Camville cried in strong protest: "No!"

"But I say yes, and my writ still runs here. Do it, Guy! Get my men out of her hands, before she kills them all to get her hands on me."

"But it means your life—" Camville began, shaken and dismayed.

"Talk sense, man! My life is not worth one death of those within here, let alone all. I am within a hair's breadth of my death already, I have no complaint. I have been the cause of deaths here among men I valued, spare me any more blood on my head in departing. Call truce, and get what you can for me! At first light, Guy! As soon as a white banner can be seen."

And now there was no denying him. He spoke as he meant, sanely and forcefully, and Camville was silenced. Only after he had departed, shocked but convinced, did Philip seem suddenly to shrink in his bed, as if air and sinew had gone out of him with the urgency. He broke into a heavy sweat, and Cadfael wiped it away from forehead and lip, and trickled drops of wine into his mouth. For a while there was silence, but for the husky breaths that seemed to have grown both easier and shallower. Then a mere thread of a voice said, with eerie clarity: "Brother Cadfael?"

"Yes, I am here."

"One more thing, and I have done. The press yonder . . . open it."

Cadfael obeyed without question, though without understanding. What was urgent was already done. Philip had delivered his garrison free from any association with his own fate. But whatever still lay heavy on his mind must be lifted away.

"Three keys . . . hanging under the lock within. Take them."

Three on one ring, dwindling in size from large and ornate to small, crude and plain. Cadfael took them, and closed the press.

"And now?" He brought them to the bedside, and waited. "Tell me what it is you want, and I will get it."

"The north-west tower," said the spectral voice clearly. "Two flights below ground, the second key. The third unlocks his irons." Philip's black, burningly intelligent eyes hung nwaveringly upon Cadfael's face. "It might be well to leave im where he is until she makes her entry. I would not have im charged with any part of what she holds against me. But o to him now, as soon as you will. Go and find your son."

CHAPTER THIRTEEN

CADFAEL DID not stir until the chaplain came to take [his] place by the bedside. Twice the sick man had opened his ey[es] that now lay sunken in bluish pits in the gaunt face, a[nd] watched him sitting there unmoving with the keys in his ha[nd] but given no sign of wonder or disapproval, and uttered [no] more words. His part was done. Cadfael's part could be l[eft] to Cadfael. And gradually Philip sank again beneath the s[ur]face of consciousness, having no more affairs to set in ord[er.] None, at least, that it was in his power to better. What remain[ed] awry must be left to God.

Cadfael watched him anxiously, marking the sunken h[ol]lows beneath the cheekbones, the blanching of the brow, [the] tension of drawn lips, and later the heavy sweat. A stro[ng] tenacious life, not easy to quench. These wounds he had mi[ght] well put an end to it, but it would not be yet. And surely [by] noon tomorrow FitzGilbert would be in La Musarderie, a[nd] Philip his prisoner. Even if the empress delayed her entry [a] day or two more, to have proper apartments prepared for [her] reception, the respite could last no longer. She would [be] implacable. He had made her of none account, and she wou[ld] requite the injury in full. Even a man who cannot stand a[nd] is barely alive can be hoisted the extra yard or two in a noo[se] for an example to all others.

So there were still vital affairs to be set in order, as [

roper before an imminent death. And under the prompting
f God, who was to make provision?

When the chaplain came to relieve his watch, Cadfael took
is keys, and went out from the comparative quiet of the keep
nto the din of battle in the ward. Inevitably the besiegers had
ursued their assault upon the same spot they had already
weakened, and this time with a hastily constructed sow to
hield the ram and the men who wielded it. The hollow,
urposeful rhythm of the ram shook the ground underfoot,
nd was perforated constantly by the irregular thudding of
tones and iron flung down on the sow's wooden roof from
he damaged brattice above, and the embrasures along the
uardwalk. The soft, sudden vibration of bowstrings and hiss
f arrows came only very rarely from the air above. Archers
were of less use now.

From wall to wall the clash and roar of steel and voices
washed in echoing waves from the foot of the damaged
ower, round the bulk of the keep, to die in the almost-
ilence under the other tower, that north-western tower
nder which Olivier lay in chains. But here where the hand-
o-hand battle was joined the mass of men-at-arms, lancers,
wordsmen, pikemen, heaved round and within the base
f the breached tower. Above their heads, framed in the
rotesque shapes left standing in the shattered outer wall,
Cadfael could see fractured spaces of sky, paler than the
paque black of masonry, and tinted with the surviving
low of fire. The inner wall was pierced, the door and the
tonework that surrounded it battered into the ward, lying
ere and there among the massed defenders. Not a great
gap, and it seemed that the onslaught had been repelled,
nd the breach successfully filled up with men and steel;
ut a gap nonetheless. Not worth repairing, if tomorrow the
astle was to be surrendered, but still worth holding to
revent further dying. Philip had dealt in accordance with
is office; from the situation he had created he was extricat-

ing as many lives as he could, at the expense merely of h
own.

It was still good policy to hug the walls when moving abc
the ward, though in the night the rain of missiles had cease
and only the occasional fire-arrow was launched over the w
to attempt the diversion of a roof in flames. Cadfael circl
the mass of the keep and came to the almost deserted nort
western corner of the ward, where only the wall and t
brattice were manned, and even much of the noise from t
turmoil at the breach was strangely withdrawn into distanc
The keys had grown warm in his hand, and the air this nig
was not frosty. Tomorrow, after the surrender, they might
able to bury their dead, and rest their many wounded.

The narrow door at the foot of the tower opened to the fi
key without so much as a creak. Two flights down, Philip h
said. Cadfael descended. There was a flare in a sconce halfw
down the winding staircase; nothing had been forgotten her
even in the stresses of siege. At the cell door he hesitate
breathing deeply and long. There was no sound from withi
the walls were too thick; and here no sound from witho
only the dim light pulsating silently as the flare flickered.

With the key in the lock, his hand trembled, and sudden
he was afraid. Not of finding some emaciated wreck with
the cell; any such fear had long since left his mind. He w
afraid of having achieved the goal of his journey, and bei
left with only the sickening fall after achievement, and t
way home an endless, laborious descent into a long darknes
ending in nothing better than loss.

It was the nearest he had ever come to despair, but it last
only a moment. At the metal kiss of key in lock it was gon
and his heart rose in him to fill his throat like a breakin
wave. He thrust open the door, and came face to face wi
Olivier across the bare cell.

The captive had sprung erect at the first inward moveme
of his prison door, and stood braced, expecting to be co

fronted by the only visitor he ever had now, apart from the
gaoler who attended him, and confounded by this unexpected
apparition. He must have heard, funnelled downwards through
the slanting shaft from the ward to his cell, the clamour of
battle, and fretted at his own helplessness, wondering what
was happening above. The glare he had fixed upon the doorway was suddenly softened and shaken by bewilderment; then
his face was still, intent and wary. He believed what he saw;
he had his warning. But he did not understand. His wide,
wild, golden stare neither welcomed nor repelled; not yet.
The chains at his ankles had clashed one sharp peal, and lay
still.

He was harder, leaner, unnervingly bright, bright to incan-
descence with energy frustrated and restrained. The candle
on its shelf of rock cast its light sidelong over him, honing
every sharp line of his face into a quivering razor-edge, and
flaming in the dazzling irises of his eyes, dilated with doubt
and wonder. Neat, shaven clean, no way defaced, only the
fetters marking him as a prisoner. He had been lying on his
bed when the key turned in the lock; his burnished black
hair clasped his olive cheeks with ruffled wings, casting blue
shadows into the hollows there beneath the smooth, salient
bones. Cadfael had never seen him more beautiful, not even
on that first day when he had glimpsed this face through the
open gate at the priory of Bromfield, stooping suave cheek
to cheek with the girl who was now his wife. Philip had not
failed to respect, value and preserve this elegance of body
and mind, even though it had turned irrevocably against him.

Cadfael took a long step forward towards the light, uncertain whether he was clearly seen. The cell was spacious beyond
what he had expected, with a low chest in a dark corner, and
items of clothing or harness folded upon it. "Olivier?" he said
hesitantly. "You know me?"

"I know you," said Olivier, low-voiced. "I have been taught
to know you. You are my father." He looked from Cadfael's

face to the open door, and then to the keys in Cadfael's hand
"There's been fighting," he said, struggling to make sense of
all these chaotic factors that crowded in on him together.
"What has happened? Is he dead?"

He. Philip. Who else could have told him? And now he
asked instantly after his sometime friend, supposing, Cadfael
divined, that only after that death could these keys have come
into other hands. But there was no eagerness, no satisfaction
in the voice that questioned, only a flat finality, as one
accepting what could not be changed. How strange it was,
thought Cadfael, watching his son with aching intensity, that
this complex creature should from the first have been crystal
to the sire who engendered him.

"No," he said gently, "he is not dead. He gave them to
me."

He advanced, almost cautiously, as though afraid to startle
a bird into flight, and as warily opened his arms to embrace
his son, and at the first touch the braced body warmed and
melted, and embraced him ardently in return.

"It is true!" said Olivier, amazed. "But of course, true! He
never lies. And you knew? Why did you never tell me?"

"Why break into another man's life, midway, when he is
already in noble transit and on his way to glory? One breath
of a contrary wind might have driven you off course." Cadfael
stood him off between his hands to look closely, and kissed
the hollow oval cheek that leaned to him dutifully. "All the
father you needed you had from your mother's telling, better
than truth. But now it's out, and I am glad. Come, sit down
here and let me get you out of these fetters."

He knelt beside the bed to fit the last key into the anklet,
and the chains rang again their sharp, discordant peal as he
opened the gyves and hoisted the irons aside, dropping the
coil against the rock wall. And all the time the golden eyes
hung upon his face, with passionate concentration, searching
for glimpses that would confirm the continuity of the blood

that bound them together. And after a moment Olivier began to question, not the truth of this bewildering discovery, but the circumstances that surrounded it, and the dazzling range of possibilities it presented.

"How did you know? What can I ever have said or done to make you know me?"

"You named your mother," said Cadfael, "and time and place were all as they should be. And then you turned your head, and I saw her in you."

"And never said word! I said once, to Hugh Beringar I said it, that you had used me like a son. And never trembled when I said it, so blind I was. When he told me you were here, I said it could not be true, for you would not leave your abbey unless ordered. Recusant, apostate, unblessed, he said, he is here to redeem you. I was *angry*!" said Olivier, wrenching at memory and acknowledging its illogical pain. "I said you had cheated me! You should not so have thrown away all you valued, for me, made yourself exile and sinner, offered your life. Was it fair to load me with such a terrible burden of debt? Lifelong I could not repay it. All I felt was the sting of my own injury. I am sorry! Truly I am sorry! I know better now."

"There is no debt," said Cadfael, rising from his knees. "All manner of reckoning or bargaining is for ever impossible between us two."

"I know it! I do know it! I felt so far outdone, it scalded my pride. But that's gone." Olivier rose, stretched his long legs, and stalked his cell back and forth. "There is nothing I will not take from you, and be grateful, even if there never comes the day when I can do whatever needs to be done in your worship and for your sake. But I trust it may come, and soon."

"Who knows?" said Cadfael. "There is a thing I want now, if I could see how to come by it."

"Yes?" Olivier shook off his own preoccupations in penitent

haste. "Tell me!" He came back to his bed, and drew Cadfael down beside him. "Tell me what is happening here. You say he is not dead—Philip. He *gave* you the keys?" It seemed to him a thing only possible from a deathbed. "And who is it laying siege to this place? He made enemies enough, that I know, but this must be an army battering the walls."

"The army of your liege lady the empress," said Cadfael ruefully. "And stronger than commonly, since she was accompanied home into Gloucester by several of her earls and barons. Yves, when he was loosed, rode for Gloucester to rouse her to come and rescue you, and come she most surely has, but not for your sake. The lad told her Philip was here in person. She has vowed, too publicly to withdraw even if she wished, and I doubt she does, to take his castle and his body and hang him from his own towers, and before his own men. No, she won't withdraw. She is determined to take, humiliate and hang him. And I am equally resolute," said Cadfael roundly, "that she shall not, though how it's to be prevented is more than I yet know."

"She cannot do it," said Olivier, aghast. "It would be wicked folly. Surely she knows it? Such an act would have every able man in the land, if he had laid down his weapons, rushing to pick them up again and get into the field. The worst of us, on either side, would hesitate to kill a man he had bested and captured. How do you know this is truth, that she has so sworn?"

"I know it from Yves, who was there to hear it, and is in no doubt at all. She is in earnest. Of all men she hates Philip for what she holds to be his treason—"

"It was treason," said Olivier, but more temperately than Cadfael had expected.

"By all the rules, so it was. But also it was more than simply treason, however extreme the act. Before long," said Cadfael heavily, "some of the greatest among us, on both sides of the argument, and yes, the best, will be accused of treason on the same grounds. They may not turn to fight upon the other side, but to leave their swords in the sheath and decline to continue killing will just as surely be denounced as treachery. Whatever his crime may be called, she wants him in her grasp, and means to be his death. And I am determined she shall not have him."

Olivier thought for a moment, gnawing his knuckles and frowning. Then he said: "It would be well, for her more than any, that someone should prevent." He turned the intensity of his troubled stare upon Cadfael. "You have not told me all. There is something more. How far has this attack gone? They have not broken through?" The use of "they" might simply have been because he was enforcedly out of this battle, instead of fighting for his chosen cause with the rest, but it seemed to set him at an even greater distance from the besiegers. Cadfael had almost heard the partisan "we" springing to mind to confront the "they."

"Not yet. They have breached one tower, but have not got in, or had not when I came down to you," he amended scrupulously. "Philip refused surrender, but he knows what she intends to do with him . . ."

"How does he know?" demanded Olivier alertly.

"He knows because I told him. Yves brought the message at his own risk. At no risk to me I delivered it. But I think he knew. He said then that if God, by chance, should choose to forestall the empress, he must take thought for the men of his garrison. He has done so. He has handed over the charge of La Musarderie to his deputy Camville, and given him leave—no, orders!—to get the best terms he can for the garrison, and surrender the castle. And tomorrow that will be done."

"But he would not . . ." began Olivier, and cried out abruptly: "You said he is not dead!"

"No, he is not dead. But he is badly hurt. I don't say he will die of his wounds, though he may. I do say he will not die of his wounds in time to escape being dragged aloft, whatever his condition, in the empress's noose, once she gets into La Musarderie. He has consented in his own shameful death to procure the release of his men. She cares nothing for any of them, if she has Philip. She'll keep the castle and the arms, and let the men depart alive."

"He has consented to this?" asked Olivier, low-voiced.

"He has ordered it."

"And his condition? His injuries?"

"He has badly broken ribs, and I fear some lacerations inside from the broken bones. And head injuries. They tossed in a crate of lumps of iron, broken lance-heads, cinder from the furnaces. He was close when it struck and burst. A bad head wound from a piece of a lance, and maybe foul at that. He came to his senses long enough to make his dispositions, and that he did clearly, and will be obeyed. When they enter, tomorrow, he will be her prisoner. Her only prisoner, for if FitzGilbert agrees to terms he'll keep his word."

"And it is bad? He cannot ride? He cannot even stand and walk? But what use," said Olivier helplessly, "even if he could? Having bought their freedom he would not make off and leave the price unpaid. Never of his own will. I know him! But a man so sick, and at her mercy. . . . She would not!" said Olivier strenuously, and looked along his shoulder at Cadfael's face, and ended dubiously: "Would she?"

"He struck her to the heart, where her pride is. Yes, I fear she would. But when I left him to come to you, Philip was again out of his senses, and I think may well remain so for many hours, even days. The head wound is his danger."

"You think we might move him, and he not know? But they are all round us, no easy way out. I do not know this castle well. Is there a postern that might serve? And then, it would need a cart. There are those in the village that I do know," said Olivier, "but they may be no friends to Philip.

But at the mill by Winstone I'm known, and they have carts. Now, while the night is black, is there anywhere a man could get out? For if they get their truce, by morning they'll cease their close watch. Something might yet be done."

"There's a clear way out where they've breached the tower," said Cadfael, "I saw sky through it. But they're still outside there with the ram, and only held outside by force of arms. If a man of the garrison tried to slip out there, it would be one way of dying quickly. Even if they draw off, he could hardly go along with them."

"But I can!" Olivier was on his feet, glowing. "Why not? I'm one of them. I'm known to have kept my fealty. I have her badge on my sword-belt, and her colours on my surcoat and my cloak. There may be some there who know me." He crossed to the chest, and swept the covering cloak from sword and scabbard and light chain-mail coat, the links ringing.

"You see? All my harness, everything that came with me when I was dragged out of Faringdon, and the lions of Anjou, that the old king gave to Geoffrey when he married his daughter to him, clear to be seen, marking me for hers. He would not so much as displace the least of another man's possessions, though he might kill the man. In chain-mail and armed, and in the dark, who's to pick me out from any of the other besiegers outside the walls? If I'm challenged I can openly answer that I've broken out in the turmoil. If not, I can keep my own counsel, and make for the mill. Reinold will help me to the loan of a cart. But it would be daylight before I could get it here," he checked, frowning. "How can we account for it then?"

"If you are in earnest," said Cadfael, carried away in this gale, "something might be attempted. Once there's truce, there can be movement in and out, and traffic with the village. For all I know, there may be local men within here, and some wounded or even among the dead, and their kin will be wanting to get news of them, once the way's open."

Olivier paced, hugged his body in embracing arms, and considered. "Where is the empress now?"

"She set up her court in the village, so they say. I doubt if she'll make her appearance here for a day or so, she'll need a degree of state, and a grand entrance. But even so," said Cadfael, "all the time we have is the rest of this night, and the first few hours of truce, while there's still confusion, and no such close watch."

"Then we must make it enough," said Olivier. "And say we do begin well . . . Where would you have him taken? To have the care he needs?"

Cadfael had given thought to that, though then without much hope of ever being able to pursue it. "There is a house of the Augustinians in Cirencester. I remember the prior at Haughmond has regular correspondence with one of the canons there, and they have a good name as physicians. And with them sanctuary would be inviolable. But it is a matter of ten miles or more."

"But the best and fastest road," said Olivier, gleaming brightly in this fury of planning, "and would not take us near the village. Once through Winstone we should be on the straight run to Cirencester. Now, how are we to get him out of the castle and keep him man alive?"

"Perhaps," said Cadfael slowly, "as a man already dead. The first task, when the gates are open, will be to carry out the dead and lay them ready for burial. We know how many there should be, but FitzGilbert does not. And should there be a man from Winstone shrouded among them, his kin might very well come with a cart, to fetch him home."

With his eyes burning steadily upon Cadfael's face, Olivier voiced the final question and the final fear: "And if he is in his senses then, and forbids—as he might—what then?"

"Then," said Cadfael, "I will remove him at least into the chapel, and we'll put her and any other under the ban of the Church if they dare break his sanctuary. But there is no more

I can do. I have no medicines here that could put a man to sleep for hours. And even if I had—you said that I had cheated you by laying you in my debt without your knowledge. He might accuse me of forcing him to default on a debt, to his dishonour. I have not the hardihood to do that to Philip."

"No," agreed Olivier, and suddenly smiled. "So we had better make a success of it while he is still senseless. Even that may be straining our rights, but we'll argue that afterwards. And if I am going, as well go quickly. This once, my father, will you be my squire and help me to arm?"

He put on the mail hauberk, to make one more among the besiegers who were massed outside the walls, drawn off for a few minutes to regroup and attack yet again, and over it the surcoat of linen that bore the lions of Anjou plain to be seen. Cadfael buckled the sword-belt round his son's loins, and for a moment had the world in his arms.

The cloak was necessary cover here within the walls, to hide Geoffrey's blazon, for no one but Cadfael yet knew that Philip had set his prisoner free, and some zealous man-at-arms might strike first and question afterwards. True, it bore on the shoulder the imperial eagle which the empress had never consented to relinquish after her first husband's death, but the badge was dark and unobtrusive on the dark cloth, and would not be noticed. If Olivier could inveigle himself successfully in among the defenders in the obscurity and confusion within the tower, he must discard the cloak before attempting to break out and venture among the attackers, so that the lions might show clear on the pallor of the linen, even by night, and be recognized.

"Though I would rather pass unrecognized," admitted Olivier, stretching his broad shoulders under the weight of the mail, and settling the belt about his hips. "Every moment of this night I need, without wasting any in questioning and accounting. Well, my father, shall we go and make the assay?"

Cadfael locked the door after them, and they climbed the spiral stair. At the outer door Cadfael laid a hand on Olivier's arm, and peered out cautiously into the ward, but in the shelter of the keep all was still, only the movements of the guards on the wall came down to them almost eerily.

"Stay by me. We'll make our way close along the wall until we're among them. Then take your moment when you see it. Best when the next thrust comes, and they crowd into the tower to fend it off. And no goodbyes! Go, and God go with you!"

"It will not be goodbye," said Olivier. Cadfael felt him tensed and quivering at his back, confident, almost joyous. After long confinement his frustrated energy ached for release. "You will see me tomorrow, whether in my own or another shape. I have kept his back many a time, and he mine. This one more time, with God's help and yours, I'll do him that same service, whether he will or no."

The door of the tower Cadfael also locked, leaving all here as it should be. They crossed the open ward to the keep, and circled in its shadow to reach the threatened tower on the other side. Even here the clamour of battle had subsided into the shifting murmur of recoil between onsets, and even that subdued, to keep the hearing sharp and ready for the next alarm. They stirred restlessly, like the sea in motion, spoke to one another briefly and in lowered voices, and kept their eyes fixed upon the foremost ranks, filling the jagged gap in the base of the tower. Fragments of masonry and rubble littered the ground, but the torn hole was not yet so big as to threaten the tower's collapse. The fitful light of torches, such as still burned, and the dull glow in the sky outside the wall, where fire had burned out half the roof of the sow, left the ward almost in darkness.

A sudden warning outcry from within the tower, taken up and echoed back over the ranks within the ward, foretold the next assault. The mass drove in, tightening in support, to seal the breach with their bodies. Cadfael, on the fringe of the throng, felt the instant when Olivier slipped away from him like the tearing of his own flesh. He was gone, in among the men of the garrison, lithe and rapid and silent, lost to view in a moment.

Nevertheless, Cadfael drew back only far enough to be out of the way of the fighting men, and waited patiently for this assault, like the last, to be driven back. It never reached the ward. Certainly there was bitter fighting within the shell of the tower, but never a man of the attackers got beyond. It took more than half an hour to expel them completely, and drive them to a safe distance away from the walls, but after that the strange, tense quietness came back and with it a number of those who had fought the foremost came back to draw breath in safety until the next bout. But not Olivier. Either he was lurking somewhere in the broken shell, or else he was out into the turmoil of the night with the repelled invaders, and on his way, God grant, to cover in the woodland, and thence to some place where he could cross the river, and emerge on the road to the mill at Winstone.

Cadfael went back to the chamber where Philip lay, the chaplain nodding gently beside him. Philip's breathing scarcely lifted the sheet over his breast, and then in a short, rapid rhythm. His face was livid as clay, but impenetrably calm, no lines of pain tightening his forehead or lips. He was deep beyond awareness of any such trivial matters as peril, anger or fear. God keep him so a while yet, and prevent impending evil.

There would be need of help in carrying this body towards its peace along with the rest, but it must be in innocence. For a moment Cadfael considered asking the priest, but discarded the idea almost as soon as it was conceived. There could be no embroiling this tired old man in an enterprise which could incur the empress's deadly disfavour, and place him in reach of her immediate and implacable rage. What was to be done

must be done in such a way that no one else could be blamed,
or feel any betraying uneasiness.

But now there was nothing to be done but be still and pray,
and wait for the summons to action. Cadfael sat in a corner
of the room, and watched the old man drowse, and the
wounded man's withdrawal into something far more profound
than sleep. He was still sitting there motionless when he heard
the sound of the blown trumpets, calling the attention of the
investing forces to the white banners fluttering from the towers
of La Musarderie in the first dim light of predawn.

FitzGilbert rode down from the village, ceremoniously
attended, and talked with Guy Camville before the gate.
Brother Cadfael had come out into the ward to hear the terms
of the exchange, and was not surprised when the first words
the marshall uttered were: "Where is Philip FitzRobert?" Blunt
and urgent: patently he had his orders.

"My lord," said Camville from the walk above the gate,
"is wounded, and has authorized me to make terms with you
to surrender the castle. I ask that you will treat the garrison
fairly and with honour. Upon reasonable conditions La
Musarderie shall be yielded to the empress, but we are not
so pressed as to accept shameful or ungenerous usage. We
have wounded, we have dead. I ask that we may have truce
from this hour, and will open the gates to you now, that you
may see we are prepared to observe that truce and lay by all
arms. If you are satisfied we are in good faith, give us the
morning hours until noon to restore some order here within,
and marshal our wounded, and carry out our dead for burial."

"Fair asking so far," said the marshall shortly. "What then?"

"We were not the attackers here," said Camville equally
briskly, "and have fought according to our sworn allegiance,
as men owing fealty must. I ask that the garrison may be
allowed to march out at noon and depart without hindrance,
and that we take with us all our wounded who are fit to go.

Those with worse injuries I ask that you will see tended as well as may be, and our dead we will bury."

"And if I do not like your terms?" asked FitzGilbert. But it was plain from the complacency of his voice that he was well satisfied to be gaining, without further effort or waste of time, what all the empress's host had come to win. The common soldiery here within would have been only so many more mouths to feed, and a continuing risk if things went wrong. To have them depart was a satisfaction.

"Then you may go back empty-handed," said Camville boldly, "and we will fight you to the last man and the last arrow, and make you pay dear for a ruin you may have intact if you choose well."

"You abandon here all your arms," said the marshall, "even personal arms. And leave all engines undamaged."

Camville, encouraged by this indication of consent, made a token objection, hardly meant to be taken seriously, and withdrew it when it was rejected. "Very well, we go disarmed."

"So far, good! We allow your withdrawal. All but one! Philip FitzRobert stays here!"

"I believe you have agreed, my lord," said Camville, "that the wounded who cannot go with us shall be properly tended. I trust you make no exceptions to that? I have told you my lord is wounded."

"In the case of FitzRobert I gave no assurances," said the marshall, goaded. "You surrender him into the empress's hands unconditionally or there will be no agreement."

"On that head," said Camville, "I am already instructed by my lord Philip, and it is at his orders, not at yours, FitzGilbert, that I leave him here at your mercy."

There was a perilous silence for a long moment. But the marshall was long experienced in accommodating himself to these embarrassments endemic in civil warfare.

"Very well! I will confirm truce, as I have already called a halt to action. Be ready to march out by noon, and you may

go unhindered. But hark, I shall leave a party here outsi
the gates until noon, when we enter formally, to view ever
thing and every man you take away with you. You will hav
to satisfy them that you are keeping to terms."

"The terms I make I keep," said Camville sharply.

"Then we shall not renew the quarrel. Now open the ga
to me, let me see in what state you leave all within."

By which he meant, Cadfael judged, let him see that Phil
lay wounded and helpless within, and could not slip throug
the empress's fingers. Cadfael took the hint, and went bac
hastily to the bedchamber, to be there in attendance whe
FitzGilbert reached it, which he did very promptly. Priest an
monastic flanked the bed when Camville and the marsha
entered. Philip's shallow breathing had begun to rasp hollow
in throat and breast. His eyes were still closed, the full, arche
lids had an alabaster pallor.

FitzGilbert came close, and stood looking down at th
drawn face for a long time, whether with satisfaction or com
punction Cadfael could not determine. Then he said indiffe
ently: "Well ..." and shrugged, and turned away abruptl
They heard his footsteps echoing along the stony corrido
of the keep, and out into the ward. He departed assured tha
the empress's arch-enemy could not so much as lift a han
to ward off the noose, much less rise from his bed and rid
away out of reach of her vengeance.

When the marshall was gone, and the trumpets exchangin
their peremptory signals across the bleached grass of the ope
ground between the armies, Cadfael drew breath deep, an
turned to Philip's chaplain.

"There'll be no worse now. It's over. You have watche
the night through. Go and get your proper rest. I'll stay wit
him now."

CHAPTER FOURTEEN

ALONE WITH Philip, Cadfael searched the chest and the press for woollen rugs to swathe his patient against cold and the buffeting of the roads, and wound him in a sheet, with only a single thickness of linen over his face, so that air might still reach him. One more dead man prepared for burial; and now all that remained was to get him either into the chapel with the rest, or out among the first to the turf of the meadow, where several of his men-at-arms were digging a communal grave. And which was the more hazardous course was a moot question. Cadfael had locked the door of the room while he went about his preparations, and hesitated to open it too soon, but from within he could not determine what was going on. It must be midmorning by this time, and the garrison mustering for their withdrawal. And FitzGilbert in his rapid tour of the damage within must have taken note of the perilous state of one tower, and would be bringing masons in haste to make the stonework safe, even if proper repairs must wait.

Cadfael turned the key in the lock, and opened the door just wide enough to peer out along the passage. Two young men of the garrison passed by towards the outer door of the keep, bearing between them one of the long shutters from the inward-facing windows, with a shrouded body stretched upon it. It had begun already, as well move quickly. The bearers had no weapons now, with all arms already piled in the arm-

oury, but at least their lives were secured. They handled the
less fortunate souls they carried with rueful respect. And aft
this present pair came one of the officers of the marshall
guard, in conversation with a workman clearly from the vi
lage, leather-jerkined, authoritative and voluble.

"You'll need timber props under that wall as fast as I ca
bring them in," he was saying as they passed. "Stone ca
wait. Keep your men well away from there when you ente
and I'll have my lads here with props by the afternoon."

The wind of his passing smelled of wood; and of wood the
was plenty around Greenhamsted. The dangling stonework
the breached tower, inner wall and outer wall alike, wou
soon be braced into stability again, waiting for the mason
And by the sound of it, thought Cadfael, I at least had bett
venture in there before they come, for somewhere in the rubb
there may well be a discarded cloak with the imperial eag
on the shoulder, and what I need least, at this moment, is th
empress's officers asking too many questions. True, such
thing might have belonged to one of the besiegers who ha
managed to penetrate within, but he would hardly be mannir
the ram hampered by his cloak. The less any man wonder
the better.

For the moment, however, his problem was here, and h
needed another pair of hands, and needed them now, befor
more witnesses came on the scene. The officer had accompa
nied the master-builder only as far as the door of the keej
Cadfael heard him returning, and emerged into the passag
full in his path, thrusting the door wide open at his back. H
habit gave him a kind of right, at any rate, to be dealing wit
the dead, and possibly a slight claim on any handy help i
the work.

"Sir, of your kindness," he said civilly, "will you lend m
a hand with this one more here? We never got him as far a
the chapel."

The officer was a man of fifty or so, old enough to be tolerar of officious Benedictine brothers, good-natured enough to comply with casual demands on some minutes of his time, where he had little work to do but watch others at work, and already gratified at being spared any further fighting over La Musarderie. He looked at Cadfael, looked in without curiosity at the open door, and shrugged amiably. The room was bare enough and chill enough not to be taken at sight for the castellan's own apartment. In his circuit of the hall and living quarters he had seen others richer and more comfortable.

"Say a word in your prayers for a decent soldier," he said, "and I'm your man, brother. May someone do as much for me if ever I come to need it."

"Amen to that!" said Cadfael. "And I won't forget it to you at the next office." And that was fervent truth, considering what he was asking.

So it was one of the empress's own men who advanced to the head of the bed, and stooped to take up the swathed body by the shoulders. And all the while Philip lay like one truly dead, and it was in Cadfael's mind, resist it as he would, that so he might be before ever he left these walls. The stillness when the senses are out of the body, and only a thread of breath marks the border not yet crossed, greatly resembles the stillness after the soul is out. The thought aroused in him a strangely personal grief, as if he and not Robert of Gloucester had lost a son; but he put it from him, and refused belief.

"Take up pallet and all," he said. "We'll reclaim it afterwards if it's fit for use, but he bled, and there's no want of straw."

The man shifted his grip compliantly, and lifted his end of the bier as lightly as if it had been a child they carried. Cadfael took the foot, and as they emerged into the passage sustained his hold one-handed for a moment while he drew the door closed. God prevent the accidental discovery too soon! But to linger and turn the key on an empty room would have been cause for immediate suspicion.

They passed through all the activity in the ward, and ou
at the gatehouse into the dull grey December light, and th
guard on the paved apron without passed them through indi
ferently. They had no interest in the dead; they were ther
only to ensure that no arms and accoutrements of value wer
taken away when the garrison departed, and perhaps to chec
that Philip FitzRobert should not pass as one of the woundec
A short space to the left from the causeway there was a leve
place where the common grave was being opened, and besid
the plot the dead were laid decently side by side.

Between this mournful activity and the rim of the woodlan
several people from the village, and perhaps from furthe
afield, had gathered to watch, curious but aloof. There wa
no great love among the commonalty for either of these fac
tions, but the present threat was over. A Musard might ye
come back to Greenhamsted. Four generations had left th
family still acceptable to their neighbours.

A cart, drawn by two horses, came up the slope from th
river valley, and ground steadily up the causeway towards th
gatehouse. The driver was a thickset, bearded, well-fleshe
man of about fifty, in dark homespun and a shoulder cap
and capuchon of green, but all their colours faintly veiled an
dusted over from long professional days spent in an air mist
with the milling of grain. The lad at his back had sackclo
draped over his shoulders and the opened end of a sack ove
his head, a long young fellow in the common dun-coloure
cotte and hose of the countryside. Cadfael watched their
approach and gave thanks to God.

Beholding the work in progress in the meadow, the row o
shrouded bodies, the last of them just brought forth and la
beside the rest, and the chaplain, drooping and disconsolat
stumbling after, the driver of the cart, blithely ignoring th
guards at the gate, turned his team aside, and made straig
for the place of burial. There he climbed down briskly, leavir
his lad to descend after him and wait with the horses. It w

to Cadfael the miller addressed himself, loudly enough to reach the chaplain's ears also.

"Brother, there was a nephew of mine serving here under Camville, and I'd be glad to know how he's fared, for his mother's sake. We heard you had dead, and a deal more wounded. Can I get news of him?"

He had lowered his voice by then as he drew close. For all it gave away his face might have been oak.

"Rid your mind of the worst before you need go further," said Cadfael, meeting shrewd eyes of no particular colour, but bright with sharp intelligence. The chaplain was halted a little apart, talking to the officer of FitzGilbert's guard. "Walk along the line with me, and satisfy yourself that none of these here is your man. And take it slowly," said Cadfael quietly. Any haste would be a betrayal. They walked the length of the ranks together, talking in low tones, stooping to uncover a face here and there, very briefly, and at every assay the miller shook his head.

"It's been a while since I saw him last, but I'll know." He talked easily, inventing a kinsman not so far from the truth, not so close as to be an irreparable loss, or long or deeply lamented, but still having the claim of blood, and not to be abandoned. "Thirty year old, he'd be, blackavised, a good man of his hands with quarter-staff or bow. Not one for keeping out of trouble, neither. He'd be into the thick of it with the best."

They had arrived at the straw pallet on which Philip lay, so still and mute that Cadfael's heart misdoubted for a moment, and then caught gratefully at the sudden shudder and crepitation of breath. "He's here!"

The miller had recognized not the man, but the moment. He broke off on a word, stiffening and starting back a single step, and then as promptly stooped, with Cadfael's bulk to cover the deception, and made to draw back the linen from Philip's face, but without touching. He remained so, bending

over the body, a long moment, as if making quite sure, befor
rising again slowly, and saying clearly: "It is! This is ou
Nan's lad."

Still adroit, sounding almost as much exasperated a
grieved, and quick to resignation from long experience now
of a disordered land, where death came round corners unex
pectedly, and chose and took at his pleasure. "I might hav
known he'd never make old bones. Never one to turn awa
from where the fire was hottest. Well, what can a man do
There's no bringing them back."

The nearest of the grave-diggers had straightened his bac
to get a moment's relief and turned a sympathetic face.

"Hard on a man to come on his own blood kin so. You'
be wanting to have him away to lie with his forebears? The
might allow it. Better than being put in the ground among a
these, without even a name."

Their close, half-audible conference had caught the atten
tion of the guards. Their officer was looking that way, and i
a moment, Cadfael judged, might come striding towards ther
Better to forestall him by bearing down upon him with th
whole tale ready.

"I'll ask," he offered, "if that's your will. It would be
Christian act to take the poor soul in care." And he led th
way back towards the gate at a purposeful pace, with th
miller hard on his heels. Seeing this willing approach, th
officer halted and stood waiting.

"Sir," said Cadfael, "here's the miller of Winstone, ov
the river there, has found his kinsman, his sister's son, amon
our dead, and asks that he may take the lad's body away f
burial among his own people."

"Is that it?" The guard looked the petitioner up and dow
but in a very cursory examination, already losing interest
an incident nowadays so common. He considered for
moment, and shrugged.

"Why not? One more or less . . . As well if we could cle

the ground of them all at one deal. Yes, let him take the fellow. Here or wherever, he's never going to let blood or shed it again."

The miller of Winstone touched his forelock very respectfully, and gave fitting thanks. If there was an infinitesimal overtone of satire about his gratitude, it escaped notice. He went stolidly back to his cart and his charge. The long lad in sacking had drawn the cart closer. Between them they hoisted the pallet on which Philip lay, and in full and complacent view of the marshall's guards, settled it carefully in the cart. Cadfael, holding the horses meantime, looked up just once into the shadow of the sacking hood the young man wore, and deep into profound black eyes, golden round the pupils, that opened upon him in a blaze of affection and elation, promising success. There was no word said. Olivier sat down in the body of the cart, and cushioned the head of the thin straw pallet upon his knees. And the miller of Winstone clambered aboard and turned his team back towards the river, down the bleached green slope, never looking back, never hurrying, the picture of a decent man who had just assumed an unavoidable duty, and had nothing to account for to any man.

At noon FitzGilbert appeared before the gate with a company drawn up at his back, to watch the garrison march out and quit their possession of La Musarderie. They had mounted some of their wounded, who could ride but could not maintain a march for long, and put the rest into such carts as they had in store, and set these in the middle of their muster, to have fit men upon either flank in case of need. Cadfael had thought in time to establish his ownership of the fine young chestnut roan Hugh had lent him, and stayed within the stables to maintain his claim, in case it should be questioned. Hugh would lop me of my ears, he thought, if I should let him be commandeered from under my nose. So only late in the day, when the rearguard was passing stiffly by the watching and waiting victors, did he witness the withdrawal from La Musarderie.

Every rank as it passed was sharply scrutinized from either side, and the carts halted to search for concealed bows, swords and lances, but Camville, curling a lip at their distrust, watched without comment and protested only when some of the wounded were disturbed too roughly for his liking. When all was done, he led his garrison away eastward, over the river and through Winstone to the Roman road, heading, most likely, for Cricklade, which was secure from immediate threat, and the centre of a circle of other castles held by the king, Bampton, Faringdon, Purton and Malmesbury, among which safe harbours his fighting men and his wounded could be comfortably distributed. Olivier and the miller of Winstone had set off by the same way, but had not so far to go, a matter maybe of a dozen miles.

And now Cadfael had things yet to do here. He could not leave until a few other sufferers, too frail or sick to go with their fellows, were committed to responsible care under the marshall's wardship. Nor did Cadfael feel justified in leaving until the worst of the empress's rage had passed, and no one here was in peril of death in recompense for the death of which she had been cheated.

Minutes now, and all her main companies would be riding in, to fill the almost empty stables and living quarters, view their trophy of arms, and make themselves at home here. Cadfael slipped back into the ward ahead of them, and made his way cautiously into the shell of the broken tower. Stepping warily among the fallen ashlar and rubble from the filling of the wall, he found the folded cloak wedged into a gap in the stonework, where Olivier had thrust it the moment before he slipped out into the night among the besiegers. The imperial eagle badge was still pinned into the shoulder. Cadfael rolled it within, and took his prize away with him to his own cell.

Almost it seemed to him that a trace of the warmth of Olivier's body still clung to it.

They were all in before the light faded, all but the empress's personal household, and their forerunners were already busy with hangings and cushions making the least Spartan apartment fit for an imperial lady. The hall was again habitable, and looked much as it had always looked, and the cooks and servants turned to feeding and housing one garrison as philosophically as another. The damaged tower was shored up stoutly with seasoned timbers, and a watch placed on it to warn off any unwary soul from risking his head within.

And no one yet had opened the door to Philip's bedchamber, and found it empty. Nor had anyone had time to remark that the Benedictine guest who had been the last to sit in attendance on the wounded man had been at large about the ward and at the graveside for the past three hours, and so had the chaplain. Everyone had been far too preoccupied to wonder who, then, was keeping watch by the bedside during their absence. It was a point to which Cadfael had not given full consideration, and now that what was most urgent had been accomplished, it began to dawn upon him that he would have to make the discovery himself, in fairness to all the rest of Philip's remaining household. But preferably with a witness.

He went to the kitchens, almost an hour before Vespers, and asked for a measure of wine and a leather bucket of hot water for his patient, and enlisted the help of a scullion to carry the heavy bucket for him across the ward and into the keep.

"He was in fever," he said as they entered the corridor, "when I left him some hours ago to go out to the burial ground. We may manage to break it, if I bathe him now and try to get a drop of wine into him. Will you spare me a few minutes to help lift him and turn him?"

The scullion, a shock-headed young giant, his mouth firmly

shut and his face equally uncommunicative under this new and untested rule, slid a glance along his shoulder at Cadfael, made an intelligent estimate of what he saw there, and uttered through motionless lips but clearly: "Best let him go, brother, if you wish him well."

"As you do?" said Cadfael in a very similar fashion. It was a small skill, but useful on occasion.

No answer to that, but he neither expected nor needed one.

"Take heart! When the time comes, tell what you have seen."

They reached the door of the deserted bedchamber. Cadfael opened it, the wine flask in his hand. Even in the dimming light the bed showed disordered and empty, the covers tumbled every way, the room shadowy and stark. Cadfael was tempted to drop the flask in convincing astonishment and alarm, but reflected that by and large Benedictine brothers do not respond to sudden crises by dropping things, least of all flasks of wine, and further, that he had just as good as confided in this random companion, to remove all necessity for deception. There were certainly some among Philip's domestic household who would rejoice in his deliverance.

So neither of them exclaimed. On the contrary, they stood in mute and mutual content. The look they exchanged was eloquent, but ventured no words, in case of inconvenient ears passing too close.

"Come!" said Cadfael, springing to life. "We must report this. Bring the bucket," he added with authority. "It's the details that make the tale ring true."

He led the way at a run, the wine flask still gripped in his hand, and the scullion galloping after, splashing water overboard from his bucket at every step. At the hall door Cadfael rushed almost into the arms of one of Bohun's knights, and puffed out his news breathlessly.

"The lord marshall—is he within? I must speak to him.

We're just come from FitzRobert's chamber. He's not there. The bed's empty, and the man's gone."

Before the marshall, the steward and half a dozen earls and barons in the great hall it made an impressive story, and engendered a satisfying uproar of fury, exasperation and suspicion; satisfying because it was also helpless. Cadfael was voluble and dismayed, and the scullion had wit enough to present a picture of idiot consternation throughout.

"My lords, I left him before noon to go out and help the chaplain with the dead. I am here only by chance, having begged some nights' lodging, but I have some skills, and I was willing to nurse and medicine him as well as I could. When I left him he was still deep out of his senses, as he has been most of the time since he was hurt. I thought it safe to leave him. Well, my lord, you saw him yourself this morning . . . But when I went back to him . . ." He shook a disbelieving head. "But how could it happen? He was fathoms deep. I went to get wine from the buttery, and hot water to bathe him, and asked this lad to come and give me a hand to raise him. And he's gone! Impossible he should even lift himself upright, I swear. But he's gone! This man will tell you."

The scullion nodded his head so long and so vigorously that his shaggy hair shook wildly over his face. "God's truth, sirs! The bed's empty, the room's empty. He's clean gone."

"Send and see for yourself, my lord," said Cadfael. "There's no mistake."

"Gone!" exploded the marshall. "How can he be gone? Was not the door locked upon him when you left him? Or someone set to keep watch?"

"My lord, I knew no reason," said Cadfael, injured. "I tell you, he could not stir a hand or foot. And I am no servant in the household, and had no orders, my part was voluntary, and meant for healing."

"No one doubts it, brother," said the marshall shortly, "but there was surely something lacking in your care if he was left some hours alone. And with your skill as a physician, if you took so active a soul for mortally ill and unable to move."

"You may ask the chaplain," said Cadfael. "He will tell you the same. The man was out of his senses and likely to die."

"And you believe in miracles, no doubt," said Bohun scornfully.

"That I will not deny. And have had good cause. Your lordships might consider on that," agreed Cadfael helpfully.

"Go question the guard on the gate," the marshall ordered, rounding abruptly on some of his officers, "if any man resembling FitzRobert passed out among the wounded."

"None did," said Bohun with crisp certainty, but nevertheless waved out three of his men to confirm the strictness of the watch.

"And you, brother, come with me. Let's view this miracle." And he went striding out across the ward with a comet's tail of anxious subordinates at his heels, and after them Cadfael and the scullion, with his bucket now virtually empty.

The door stood wide open as they had left it, and the room was so sparse and plain that it was scarcely necessary to step over the threshold to know that there was no one within. The heap of discarded coverings disguised the fact that the straw pallet had been removed, and no one troubled to disturb the tumbled rugs, since plainly whatever lay beneath, it was not a man's body.

"He cannot be far," said the marshall, whirling about as fiercely as he had flown to the proof. "He must be still within, no one can have passed the guards. We'll have every rat out of every corner of this castle, but we'll find him." And in a very few minutes he had all those gathered about him dispersed in all directions. Cadfael and the scullion exchanged a glance which had its own eloquence, but did not venture on speech.

The scullion, wooden-faced outwardly but gratified inwardly, departed without haste to the kitchen, and Cadfael, released from tension into the languor of relief, remembered Vespers, and refuged in the chapel.

The search for Philip was pursued with all the vigour and thoroughness the marshall had threatened, and yet at the end of it all Cadfael could not fail to wonder whether FitzGilbert was not somewhat relieved himself by the prisoner's disappearance. Not out of sympathy for Philip, perhaps not even from disapproval of such a ferocious revenge, but because he had sense enough to realize that the act contemplated would have redoubled and prolonged the killing, and made the empress's cause anathema even to those who had served her best. The marshall went through the motions with energy, even with apparent conviction; and after the search ended in failure, an unexpected mercy, he would have to convey the news to his imperial lady this same evening, before ever she made her ceremonial entry into La Musarderie. The worst of her venom would be spent, on those even she dared not utterly humiliate and destroy, before she came among vulnerable poor souls expendable and at her mercy.

Philip's tired chaplain stumbled his way through Vespers, and Cadfael did his best to concentrate his mind on worship. Somewhere between here and Cirencester, perhaps by now even safe in the Augustinian abbey there, Olivier nursed and guarded his captor turned prisoner, friend turned enemy— call that relationship what you would, it remained ever more fixed and inviolable the more it turned about. As long as they remained in touch, each of them would be keeping the other's back against the world, even when they utterly failed to understand each other.

Neither do I understand, thought Cadfael, but there is no need that I should. I trust, I respect and I love. Yet I have abandoned and left behind me what most I trust, respect and love, and whether I can ever get back to it again is more than

I know. The assay is all. My son is free, whole, in the hand of God, I have delivered him, and he has delivered his friend, and what remains broken between them must mend. They have no need of me. And I have needs, oh, God, how dear, and my years are dwindling to a few, and my debt is grown from a hillock to a mountain, and my heart leans to home.

"May our fasts be acceptable to you, Lord, we entreat: and by expiating our sins make us worthy of your grace . . ."

Yes, amen! After all, the long journey here has been blessed. If the long journey home proves wearisome, and ends in rejection, shall I cavil at the price?

The empress entered La Musarderie the next day in sombre state and a vile temper, though by then she had herself in hand. Her blackly knotted brows even lightened a little as she surveyed the prize she had won, and reconciled herself grudgingly to writing off what was lost.

Cadfael watched her ride in, and conceded perforce that, mounted or afoot, she was a regal figure. Even in displeasure she had an enduring beauty, tall and commanding. When she chose to charm, she could be irresistible, as she had been to many a lad like Yves, until he felt the lash of her steel.

She came nobly mounted and magnificently attired, and with a company at her back, outriders on either side of herself and her women. Cadfael remembered the two gentlewomen who had attended her at Coventry, and had remained in attendance in Gloucester. The elder must be sixty, and long widowed, a tall, slender person with the remains of a youthful grace that had lasted well beyond its prime, but was now growing a little angular and lean, as her hair was silvering almost into white. The girl Isabeau, her niece, in spite of the many years between them, bore a strong likeness to her aunt, so strong that she probably presented a close picture of what Jovetta de Montors had been in her girlhood. And a vital and attractive picture it was. A number of personable young men had admired it at Coventry.

The women halted in the courtyard, and FitzGilbert and half a dozen of his finest vied to help them down from the saddle and escort them to the apartments prepared for them. La Musarderie had a new chatelaine in place of its castellan.

And where was that castellan now, and how faring? If Philip had lived through the journey, surely he would live. And Olivier? While there was doubt, Olivier would not leave him.

Meantime, here was Yves lighting down and leading away his horse into the stables, and as soon as he was free he would be looking for Cadfael. There was news to be shared, and Yves must be hungry for it.

They sat together on the narrow bed in Cadfael's cell, as once before, sharing between them everything that had happened since they had parted beside the crabbed branches of the vine, with the guard pacing not twenty yards away.

"I heard yesterday, of course," said Yves, flushed with wonder and excitement, "that Philip was gone, vanished away like mist. But how, how was it possible? If he was so gravely hurt, and could not stand . . .? She is saved from breaking with the earl, and . . . and worse . . . So much has been saved. But *how*?" He was somewhat incoherent in his gratitude for such mercies, but grave indeed the moment he came to speak of Olivier. "And, Cadfael, what has happened to Olivier? I thought to see him among the others in hall. I asked Bohun's steward after any prisoners, and he said what prisoners, there were none found here. So where can he be? Philip *told* us he was here."

"And Philip does not lie," said Cadfael, repeating what was evidently an article of faith with those who knew Philip, even among his enemies. "No, true enough, he does not lie. He told us truth. Olivier was here, deep under one of the towers.

As for where he is now, if all has gone well, as why should it not?—he has friends in these parts!—he should be now in Cirencester, at the abbey of the Augustinians."

"You helped him to break free, even before the surrender? But then, why go? Why should he leave when FitzGilbert and the empress were here at the gates? His own people?"

"I did not rescue him," said Cadfael patiently. "When he was wounded and knew he might die, Philip took thought for his garrison, and ordered Camville to get the best terms he could for them, at the least life and liberty, and surrender the castle."

"Knowing there would be no mercy for himself?" said Yves.

"Knowing what she had in mind for him, as you instructed me," said Cadfael, "and knowing she would let all others go, to get her hands on him. Yes. Moreover, he took thought also for Olivier. He gave me the keys, and sent me to set him free. And so I did, and together with Olivier I have, I trust, despatched Philip FitzRobert safely to the monks of Cirencester, where by God's grace I hope he may recover from his wounds."

"But how? How did you get him out of the gates, with her troops already on guard there? And he? Would he even consent?"

"He had no choice," said Cadfael. "He was in his right senses only long enough to dispose of his own life in a bargain for his men's lives. He was sunk deep out of them when I shrouded him, and carried him out among the dead. Oh, not Olivier, not then. It was one of the marshall's own men helped me carry him. Olivier had slipped out by night when the besiegers drew off, and gone to get a cart from the mill, and under the noses of the guards he and the miller from Winstone came to claim the body of a kinsman, and were given leave to take it freely."

"I wish I had been with you," said Yves reverently.

"Child, I was glad you were not. You had done your part, I thanked God there was one of you safe out of all this perilous play. No matter now, it's well done, and if I have sent Olivier away, I have you for this day, at least. The worst has been prevented. In this life that is often the best that can be said, and we must accept it as enough." He was suddenly very weary, even in this moment of release and content.

"Olivier will come back," said Yves, warm and eager against his shoulder, "and there is Ermina in Gloucester, waiting for him and for you. By now she will be near her time. There may be another godson for you." He did not know, not yet, that the child would be even closer than that, kin in the blood as well as the soul. "You have come so far already, you should come home with us, stay with us, where you are dearly valued. A few days borrowed—what sin is there in that?"

But Cadfael shook his head, reluctantly but resolutely.

"No, that I must not do. When I left Coventry on this quest I betrayed my vow of obedience to my abbot, who had already granted me generous grace. Now I have done what I discarded my vocation to accomplish, barring perhaps one small duty remaining, and if I delay longer still I am untrue to myself as I am already untrue to my Order, my abbot and my brothers. Some day, surely, we shall all meet again. But I have a reparation to make, and a penance to embrace. Tomorrow, Yves, whether the gates at Shrewsbury will open to me again or no, I am going home."

CHAPTER FIFTEEN

IN THE light of early morning Cadfael put his few possessions together, and went to present himself before the marshall. In a military establishment lately in dispute, it was well to give due notice of his departure, and to be able to quote the castellan's authority in case any should question.

"My lord, now that the way is open, I am bound to set off back to my abbey. I have here a horse, the grooms will bear witness to my right in him, though he belongs to the stables of Shrewsbury castle. Have I your leave to depart?"

"Freely," said the marshall. "And Godspeed along the way."

Armed with that permission, Cadfael paid his last visit to the chapel of La Musarderie. He had come a long way from the place where he longed to be, and there was no certainty he would live to enter there again, since no man can know the day or the hour when his life shall be required of him. And even if he reached it within his life, he might not be received. The thread of belonging, once stretched to breaking point, may not be easily joined again. Cadfael made his petition in humility, if not quite in resignation, and remained on his knees a while with closed eyes, remembering things done well and things done less well, but remembering with the greatest gratitude and content the image of his son in the guise of a rustic youth, as once before, nursing his enemy in his lap in the miller's cart. Blessed paradox, for they were

not enemies. They had done their worst to become so, and
could not maintain it. Better not to question the unquestion-
able.

He was rising from his knees, a little stiffly from the chill
of the air and the hardness of the flagstones, when a light
step sounded on the threshold, and the door was pushed a
little wider open. The presence of women in the castle had
already made some changes in the furnishings of the chapel, by
the provision of an embroidered altar-cloth, and the addition of
a green-cushioned prie-dieu for the empress's use. Now her
gentlewoman came in with a heavy silver candlestick in either
hand, and was crossing to the altar to install them when she
saw Cadfael. She gave him a gentle inclination of her head,
and smiled. Her hair was covered with a gauze net that cast
a shimmer of silver over a coronal already immaculate in its
own silver.

"Good morning, brother," said Jovetta de Montors, and
would have passed on, but halted instead, and looked more
closely. "I have seen you before, brother, have I not? You
were at the meeting in Coventry."

"I was, madam," said Cadfael.

"I remember," she said, and sighed. "A pity nothing came
of it. Was it some business consequent upon that meeting that
has brought you so far from home? For I believe I heard you
were of the abbey of Shrewsbury."

"In a sense," said Cadfael, "yes, it was."

"And have you sped?" She had moved to the altar, and set
her candlesticks one at either end, and was stooping to find
candles for them in a coffer beside the wall, and a sulphur
spill to light them from the small constant lamp that glowed
red before the central cross.

"In part," he said, "yes, I have sped."

"Only in part?"

"There was another matter, not solved, no, but of less
importance now than we thought it then. You will remember

the young man who was accused of murder, there in Coventry?"

He drew nearer to her, and she turned towards him a clear, pale face, and large, direct eyes of a deep blue. "Yes, I remember. He is cleared of that suspicion now. I talked with him when he came to Gloucester, and he told us that Philip FitzRobert was satisfied he was not the man, and had set him free. I was glad. I thought all was over when the empress brought him off safely, and I never knew until we were in Gloucester that Philip had seized him on the road. Then, days later, he came to raise the alarm over this castle. I knew," she said, "that there was no blame in him."

She set the candles in their sockets, and the candlesticks upon the altar, stepping back a little to match the distances, with her head tilted. The sulphur match sputtered in the little red flame, and burned up steadily, casting a bright light over her thin, veined left hand. Carefully she lit her candles, and stood watching the flames grow tall, with the match still in her hand. On the middle finger she wore a ring, deeply cut in intaglio. Small though the jet stone was, the incised design took the light brilliantly, in fine detail. The little salamander in its nest of stylized flames faced the opposite way, but was unmistakable once its positive complement had been seen.

Cadfael said never a word, but she was suddenly quite still, making no move to put the ring out of the light that burnished and irradiated it in every line. Then she turned to him, and her glance followed his, and again returned to his face.

"I knew," she said again, "there was no blame in him. I was in no doubt at all. Neither, I think, were you. But I had cause. What was it made *you* so sure, even then?"

He repeated, rehearsing them now with care, all the reasons why Brien de Soulis must have died at the hands of someone he knew and trusted, someone who could approach him closely without being in any way a suspect, as Yves Hugonin certainly could not, after his open hostility. Someone who could not possibly be a threat to him, a man wholly in his confidence.

"Or a woman," said Jovetta de Montors.

She said it quite gently and reasonably, as one propounding an obvious possibility, but without pressing it.

And he had never even thought of it. In that almost entirely masculine assembly, with only three women present, and all of them under the empress's canopy of inviolability, it had never entered his mind. True, the young one had certainly been willing to play a risky game with de Soulis, but with no intention of letting it go too far. Cadfael doubted if she would ever have made an assignation; and yet. . . .

"Oh, no," said Jovetta de Montors, "not Isabeau. She knows nothing. All she did was half promise him—enough to make it worth his while putting it to the test. She never intended meeting him. But there is not so much difference between an old woman and a young one, in twilight and a hooded cloak. I think," she said with sympathy, and smiled at him, "I am not telling you anything you do not know. But I would not have let the young man come to harm."

"I am learning this," said Cadfael, "only now, believe me. Only now, and by this seal of yours. The same seal that was set to the surrender of Faringdon, in the name of Geoffrey FitzClare. Who was already dead. And now de Soulis, who set it there, who killed him to set it there, is also dead, and Geoffrey FitzClare is avenged." And he thought, why stir the ashes back into life now?

"You do not ask me," she said, "what Geoffrey FitzClare was to me?"

Cadfael was silent.

"He was my son," she said. "My one sole child, outside a childless marriage, and lost to me as soon as born. It was long ago, after the old king had conquered and settled Normandy, until King Louis came to the French throne, and started the struggle all over again. King Henry spent two years and more over there defending his conquest, and Warrenne's forces were with him. My husband was Warrenne's man. Two years away! Love asks no leave, and I was lonely, and Richard de Clare was kind. When my time came, I was well served and secret, and Richard did well by his own. Aubrey never knew, nor did any other. Richard acknowledged my boy for his, and took him into his own family. But Richard was not living to do right by his son when most he was needed. It was left to me to take his place."

Her voice was calm, making neither boast nor defence of what she had done. And when she saw Cadfael's gaze still bent on the salamander in its restoring bath of fire, she smiled.

"That was all he ever had of me. It came from my father's forebears, but it had fallen almost into disuse. Few people would know it. I asked Richard to give it to him for his own device, and it was done. He did us both credit. His brother Earl Gilbert always thought well of him. Even though they took opposing sides in this sad dispute, they were good friends. The Clares have buried Geoffrey as one of their own, and valued. They do not know what I know of how he died. What you, I think, also know."

"Yes," said Cadfael, and looked her in the eyes, "I do know."

"Then there is no need to explain anything or excuse anything," she said simply, and turned to set one candle straighter in its sconce, and carry away with her tidily the extinguished sulphur match. "But if ever any man casts up that man's death against the boy, you may speak out."

"You said," Cadfael reminded her, "that no one else ever knew. Not even your son?"

She looked back for one moment on her way out of the chapel, and confronted him with the deep, drowning blue serenity of her eyes, and smiled. "He knows now," she said.

* * *

In the chapel of La Musarderie those two parted, who would surely never meet again.

Cadfael went out to the stable, and found a somewhat disconsolate Yves already saddling the chestnut roan, and insisting on coming out with his departing friend as far as the ford of the river. No need to fret over Yves, the darkest shadow had withdrawn from him, there remained only the mild disappointment of not being able to take Cadfael home with him, and the shock of disillusionment which would make him wary of the empress's favours for some time, but not divert his fierce loyalty from her cause. Not for this gallant simplicity the bruising complexities that trouble most human creatures. He walked beside the roan down the causeway and into the woodland that screened the ford, and talked of Ermina, and Olivier, and the child that was coming and minute by minute his mood brightened, thinking of the reunion still to come.

"He may be there already, even before I can get leave to go to her. And he really is well? He's come to no harm?"

"You'll find no change in him," Cadfael promised heartily. "He is as he always has been, and he'll look for no change in you, either. Between the lot of us," he said, comforting himself rather than the boy, "perhaps we have not done so badly, after all."

But it was a long, long journey home.

At the ford they parted. Yves reached up, inclining a smooth cheek, and Cadfael stooped to kiss him. "Go back now, and don't watch me go. There'll be another time."

Cadfael crossed the ford, climbed the green track up through the woods on the other side, and rode eastward through the village of Winstone towards the great highroad. But when he reached it he did not turn left towards Tewkesbury and the roads that led homeward, but right, towards Cirencester. He had one more small duty to perform; or perhaps he was simply clinging by the sleeve of hope to the conviction that out of his apostasy something good might emerge, beyond all reasonable expectation, to offer as justification for default.

All along the great road high on the Cotswold plateau he rode through intermittent showers of sleet, under a low, leaden sky, hardly conducive to cheerful thoughts. The colours of winter, bleached and faded and soiled, were setting in like a wash of grey mist over the landscape. There was small joy in travelling, and few fellow-creatures to greet along the way. Men and sheep alike preferred the shelter of cottage and fold.

It was late afternoon when he reached Cirencester, a town he did not know, except by reputation as a very old city, where the Romans had left their fabled traces, and a very sturdy and astute wool trade had continued independent and prosperous ever since. He had to stop and ask his way to the Augustinian abbey, but there was no mistaking it when he found it, and no doubt of its flourishing condition. The old King Henry had refounded it upon the remnant of an older house of secular canons, very poorly endowed and quietly mouldering, but the Augustinians had made a success of it, and the fine gatehouse, spacious court and splendid church spoke for their zeal and efficiency. This revived house was barely thirty years old, but bade fair to be the foremost of its order in the kingdom.

Cadfael dismounted at the gate and led his horse within, to the porter's lodge. This ordered calm came kindly on his spirit, after the uncontrollable chances of siege and the bleak loneliness of the roads. Here all things were ordained and regulated, here everyone had a purpose and a rule, and was in no doubt of his value, and every hour and every thing had a function, essential to the functioning of the whole. So it was at home, where his heart drew him.

"I am a brother of the Benedictine abbey of Saint Peter and Saint Paul at Shrewsbury," said Cadfael humbly, "and have been in these parts by reason of the fighting at Green-hamsted, where I was lodged when the castle fell under siege. May I speak with the infirmarer?"

The porter was a smooth, round elder with a cool, aloof eye, none too ready to welcome a Benedictine on first sight. He asked briskly: "Are you seeking lodging overnight, brother?"

"No," said Cadfael. "My errand here can be short, I am on my way home to my abbey. You need make no provision for me. But I sent here, in the guardianship of another, Philip FitzRobert, badly wounded at Greenhamsted, and in danger of his life. I should be glad of a word with the infirmarer as to how he does. Or," he said, suddenly shaken, "whether he still lives. I tended him there, I need to know."

The name of Philip FitzRobert had opened wide the reserved, chill grey eyes that had not warmed at mention of the Benedictine Order or the abbey of Shrewsbury. Whether he was loved here or hated, or simply suffered as an unavoidable complication, his father's hand was over him, and could open closed and guarded doors. Small blame to the house that kept a steely watch on its boundaries.

"I will call Brother Infirmarer," said the porter, and went to set about it within.

The infirmarer came bustling, a brisk, amiable man not much past thirty. He looked Cadfael up and down in one rapid glance, and nodded informed approval. "He said you might come. The young man described you well, brother, I should have known you among many. You are welcome here. He told us of the fate of La Musarderie, and what was threatened against this guest of ours."

"So they reached here in time," said Cadfael, and heaved a great sigh.

"In good time. A miller's cart brought them, but no miller drove it the last miles. A working man must see to his business and his family," said the infirmarer, "all the more if he has just risked more, perhaps, than was due from him. It seems there were no unseemly alarms. At any rate, the cart was returned, and all was quiet then."

"I trust it may remain so," said Cadfael fervently. "He is a good man."

"Thanks be to God, brother," said the infirmarer cheerfully, "there are still, as there always have been and always will be, more good men than evil in this world, and their cause will prevail."

"And Philip? He is alive?" He asked it with more constriction about his heart than he had expected, and held his breath.

"Alive and in his senses. Even mending, though that may be a slow recovery. But yes, he will live, he will be a whole man again. Come and see!"

Outside the partly drawn curtain that closed off one side cell from the infirmary ward sat a young canon of the order, very grave and dutiful, reading in a large book which lay open on his lap-desk. A hefty young man of mild countenance but impressive physique, whose head reared and whose eyes turned alertly at the sound of footsteps approaching. Beholding the infirmarer, with a second habited brother beside him, he immediately lowered his gaze again to his reading, his face impassive. Cadfael approved. The Augustinians were prepared to protect both their privileges and their patients.

"A mere precaution," said the infirmarer tranquilly. "Perhaps no longer necessary, but better to be certain."

"I doubt there'll be any pursuit now," said Cadfael.

"Nevertheless . . ." The infirmarer shrugged, and laid a hand to the curtain to draw it back. "Safe rather than sorry! Go in, brother. He is fully in his wits, he will know you."

Cadfael entered the cell, and the folds of the curtain swung closed behind him. The single bed in the narrow room had been raised, to make attendance on the patient in his helplessness easier. Philip lay propped with pillows, turned a little sidewise, sparing his broken ribs as they mended. His face, if paler and more drawn than in health, had a total and admirable serenity, eased of all tensions. Above the bandages that swathed his head wound, the black hair coiled and curved on his pillows as he turned his head to see who had entered. His eyes in their bluish hollows showed no surprise.

"Brother Cadfael!" His voice was quite strong and clear. "Yes, almost I expected you. But you had a dearer duty. Why are you not some miles on your way home? Was I worth the delay?"

To that Cadfael made no direct reply. He drew near the bed, and looked down with the glow of gratitude and content warming him. "Now that I see you man alive, I will make for home fast enough. They tell me you will mend as good as new."

"As good," agreed Philip with a wry smile. "No better! Father and son alike, you may have wasted your pains. Oh, never fear, I have no objection to being snatched out of a halter, even against my will. I shall not cry out against you, as he did: 'He has cheated me!' Sit by me, brother, now you are here. Some moments only. You see I shall do well enough, and your needs are elsewhere."

Cadfael sat down on the stool beside the bed. It brought their faces close, eye to eye in intent and searching study. "I see," said Cadfael, "that you know who brought you here."

"Once, just once and briefly, I opened my eyes on his face. In the cart, on the highroad. I was back in the dark before a word could be said, it may be he never knew. But yes, I know. Like father, like son. Well, you have taken seisin of my life between you. Now tell me what I am to do with it."

"It is still yours," said Cadfael. "Spend it as you see fit. I think you have as firm a grasp of it as most men."

"Ah, but this is not the life I had formerly. I consented to a death, you remember? What I have now is your gift, whether you like it or not, my friend. I have had time, these last days," said Philip quite gently, "to recall all that happened before I died. It was a hopeless cast," he said with deliberation, "to believe that turning from one nullity to the other could solve anything. Now that I have fought upon either side to no good end, I acknowledge my error. There is no salvation in either empress or king. So what have you in mind for me now, Brother Cadfael? Or what has Olivier de Bretagne in mind for me?"

"Or God, perhaps," said Cadfael.

"God, certainly! But he has his messengers among us, no doubt there will be omens for me to read." His smile was without irony. "I have exhausted my hopes of either side, here among princes. Where is there now for me to go?" He was not looking for an answer, not yet. Rising from this bed would be like birth to him; it would be time then to discover what to do with the gift. "Now, since there are other men in the world besides ourselves, tell me how things went, brother, after you had disposed of me."

And Cadfael composed himself comfortably on his stool, and told him how his garrison had fared, permitted to march out with their honour and their freedom, if not with their arms, and to take their wounded with them. Philip had bought back the lives of most of his men, even if the price, after all, had never been required of him. It had been offered in good faith.

Neither of them heard the flurry of hooves in the great court, or the ringing of harness, or rapid footsteps on the cobbles; the chamber was too deep within the enfolding walls for any forewarning to reach them. Not until the corridor without echoed hollowly to the tread of boots did Cadfael rear erect and break off in mid-sentence, momentarily alarmed. But no, the guardian outside the curtained doorway had not stirred. His view was clear to the end of the passage, and what he saw bearing down upon them gave him no disquiet. He simply rose to his feet and drew aside to give place to those who were approaching.

The curtain was abruptly swept back before the vigorous hand and glowing face of Olivier, Olivier with a shining, heraldic lustre upon him, that burned in silence and halted him on the threshold, his breath held in half elation and half dread at the bold thing he had undertaken. His eyes met Philip's, and clung in a hopeful stare, and a tentative smile curved his long mouth. He stepped aside, not entering the room, and drew the curtain fully back, and Philip looked beyond him.

For a moment it hung in the balance between triumph and repudiation, and then, though Philip lay still and silent, giving no sign, Olivier knew that he had not laboured in vain.

Cadfael rose and stepped back into the corner of the room as Robert, earl of Gloucester, came in. A quiet man always, squarely built, schooled to patience, even at this pass his face was composed and inexpressive as he approached the bed and looked down at his younger son. The capuchon hung in folds on his shoulders, and the dusting of grey in his thick brown hair and the twin streaks of silver in his short beard caught the remaining light in the room with a moist sheen of rain. He loosed the clasp of his cloak and shrugged it off, and drawing the stool closer to the bed, sat down as simply as if he had just come home to his own house, with no tensions or grievances to threaten his welcome.

"Sir," said Philip, with deliberate formality, his voice thin and distant, "your son and servant!"

The earl stooped, and kissed his son's cheek; nothing to disturb even the most fragile of calms, the simple kiss due between sire and son on greeting. And Cadfael, slipping silently past, walked out into the corridor and into his own son's exultant arms.

So now everything that had to be done here was completed. No man, nor even the empress, would dare touch what Robert of Gloucester had blessed. They drew each other away, content, into the court, and Cadfael reclaimed his horse from the stable, for in spite of the approaching dusk he felt himself bound to ride back some way before full darkness came, and find a simple lodging somewhere among the sheepfolds for the night hours.

"And I will ride with you," said Olivier, "for our ways are the same as far as Gloucester. We'll share the straw together in someone's loft. Or if we reach Winstone the miller will house us."

"I had thought," said Cadfael, marvelling, "that you were already in Gloucester with Ermina, as indeed you should be this moment."

"Oh, I did go to her—how could I not? I kissed her," said Olivier, "and she saw for herself I had come to no harm from any man, so she let me go where I was bound. I rode to find Robert at Hereford. And he came with me, as I knew he would come. Blood is blood, and there is no blood closer than theirs. And now it is done, and I can go home."

Two days they rode together, and two nights they slept close, rolled in their cloaks, the first night in a shepherd's hut near Bagendon, the second in the hospitable mill at Cowley; and the third day, early, they entered Gloucester. And in Gloucester they parted.

Yves would have reasoned and pleaded the good sense of resting here overnight and spending some precious hours with people who loved him. Olivier only looked at him, and awaited his judgement with resignation.

"No," said Cadfael, shaking his head ruefully, "for you home is here, yes, but not for me. I am already grossly in default. I dare not pile worse on bad. Do not ask me."

And Olivier did not ask. Instead, he rode with Cadfael to the northern edge of the city, where the road set off north-west for distant Leominster. There was a good half of the day

eft, and a placid grey sky with hardly a breath of wind. There
ould be a few miles gained before night.

"God forbid I should stand between you and what you need
or your heart's comfort," said Olivier, "even if it tears mine
o refrain. Only go safely, and fear nothing for me, ever. There
vill be a time. If you do not come to me, I shall come to
ou."

"If God please!" said Cadfael, and took his son's face
etween his hands, and kissed him. As how could God not
e pleased by such as Olivier? If, indeed, there were any more
uch to be found in this world.

They had dismounted to take their brief farewells. Olivier
eld the stirrup for Cadfael to remount, and clung for a
noment to the bridle. "Bless me to God, and go with God!"

Cadfael leaned down and marked a cross on the broad,
mooth forehead. "Send me word," he said, "when my grand-
on is born."

CHAPTER SIXTEEN

THE LONG road home unrolled laborious mile by mile, frus‐
trating hour after hour and day after day. For winter, which
had so far withheld its worst, with only a desultory veil of
snow, soon melted and lost, began to manifest itself in capri‐
cious alternations of blinding snow and torrential rains, and
roads flooded and fords ran too full to be passable without
peril. It took him three days to reach Leominster, so many
obstacles lay in the way and had to be negotiated, and there
he felt obliged to stay over two nights at the priory to rest
Hugh's horse.

From there things went somewhat more easily, if no more
happily, for if the snow and frost withdrew, a fine drizzling
rain persisted. Into the lands of Lacy and Mortimer, near
Ludlow, he rode on the fourth day, and outlines he knew rose
comfortingly before his eyes. But always the thread that drew
him homeward tightened and tore painfully at his heart, and
still there was no true faith in him that any place waited for
him, there where alone he could be at peace.

I have sinned, he told himself every night before he slept.
I have forsaken the house and the Order to which I swore
stability. I have repudiated the ordinance of the abbot to whom
I swore obedience. I have gone after my own desires, and no
matter if those desires were devoted all to the deliverance of
my son, it was sin to prefer them before the duty I had freely

nd gladly assumed as mine. And if it was all to do again, vould I do otherwise than I have done? No, I would do the ame. A thousand times over, I would do the same. And it vould still be sin.

In our various degrees, we are all sinners. To acknowledge nd accept that load is good. Perhaps even to acknowledge nd accept it and not entertain either shame or regret may lso be required of us. If we find we must still say: Yes, I vould do the same again, we are making a judgement others nay condemn. But how do we know that God will condemn t? His judgements are inscrutable. What will be said in the ast day of Jovetta de Montors, who also made her judgement vhen she killed to avenge her son, for want of a father living o lift that load from her? She, also, set the heart's passion for ts children before the law of the land or the commandments of he Church. And would she, too, say: I would do it again? Yes, surely she would. If the sin is one which, with all our vill to do right, we cannot regret, can it truly be a sin?

It was too deep for him. He wrestled with it night after ight until from very weariness sleep came. In the end there s nothing to be done but to state clearly what has been done, vithout shame or regret, and say: Here I am, and this is what am. Now deal with me as you see fit. That is your right. Mine is to stand by the act, and pay the price.

You do what you must do, and pay for it. So in the end all hings are simple.

On the fifth day of his penitential journey he came into country amiliar and dear, among the long hill ranges in the south and vest of the shire, and perhaps should have made one more tay for rest, but he could not bear to halt when he was drawing so near, and pushed on even into the darkness. When e reached Saint Giles it was well past midnight, but by hen his eyes were fully accustomed to the darkness, and the amiliar shapes of hospital and church showed clear against

the spacious field of the sky, free of clouds, hesitant on th
edge of frost. He had no way of knowing the precise hour
but the immense silence belonged only to dead of night. Wit
the cold of the small hours closing down, even the furtiv
creatures of the night had abandoned their nocturnal busines
to lie snug at home. He had the whole length of the Foregat
to himself, and every step of it he saluted reverently as h
passed.

Now, whether he himself had any rights remaining here o
not, for very charity they must take in Hugh's tired horse
and allow him the shelter of the stables until he could b
returned to the castle wards. If the broad doors opening from
the horse-fair into the burial ground had been unbarred, Cad
fael would have entered the precinct that way, to reach th
stables without having to ride round to the gatehouse, but h
knew they would be fast closed. No matter, he had the lengt
of the enclave wall to tell over pace by pace like beads, i
gratitude, from the corner of the horse-fair to the gates, wit
the beloved bulk of the church like a warmth in the winte
night on his left hand within the pale, a benediction all th
way.

The interior was silent, the choir darkened, or he would hav
been able to detect the reflected glow from upper windows. S
Matins and Lauds were past, and only the altar lamps lef
burning. The brothers must be all back in their beds, to slee
until they rose for Prime with the dawn. As well! He had tim
to prepare himself.

The silence and darkness of the gatehouse daunted hin
strangely, as if there would be no one within, and no mean
of entering, as though not only the gates, but the church, th
Order, the embattled household within had been closed agains
him. It cost him an effort to pull the bell and shatter th
cloistered quiet. He had to wait some minutes for the porte
to rouse, but the first faint shuffle of sandalled feet withi

d the rattle of the bolt in its socket were welcome music
him.

The wicket opened wide, and Brother Porter leaned into
e opening, peering to see what manner of traveller came
nging at this hour, his hair around the tonsure rumpled and
ected from the pillow, his right cheek creased from its folds
d his eyes dulled with sleep. Familiar, ordinary and benign,
earnest of the warmth of brotherhood within, if only the
uant could earn reentry here.

"You're late abroad, friend," said the porter, looking from
e shadow of a man to the shadow of a horse, breathing faint
ist into the cold air.

"Or early," said Cadfael. "Do you not know me, brother?"

Whether it was the voice that was known, or the shape and
e habit as vision cleared, the porter named him on the instant.
Cadfael? Is it truly you? We thought we had lost you. Well,
d now so suddenly here on the doorsill again! You were
t expected."

"I know it," said Cadfael ruefully. "We'll wait the lord
bbot's word on what's to become of me. But let me in at
ast to see to this poor beast I've overridden. He belongs at
e castle by rights, but if I may stable and tend him here for
e night, he can go gently home tomorrow, whatever is
ecreed for me. Never trouble beyond that, I need no bed.
pen the door and let me bring him in, and you go back to
ours."

"I'd no thought of shutting you out," said the porter roundly,
but it takes me a while to wake at this hour." He was fumbling
is key into the lock of the main gates, and hauling the half
f the barrier open. "You're welcome to a brychan within
ere, if you will, when you're done with the horse."

The tired chestnut roan trod in delicately on the cobbles
ith small, frosty, ringing sounds. The heavy gate closed
gain behind them, and the key turned in the lock.

"Go and sleep," said Cadfael. "I'll be a while with hi
Leave all else until morning. I have a word or so to say
God and Saint Winifred that will keep me occupied in tl
church the rest of the night." And he added, half against h
will: "Had they scored me out as a bad debt?"

"No!" said the porter strenuously. "No such thing!"

But they had not expected him back. From the time th
Hugh had returned from Coventry without him they mu
have said their goodbyes to him, those who were his friend
and shrugged him out of their lives, those who were le
close, or even no friends to him. Brother Winfrid must ha
felt himself abandoned and betrayed in the herb-garden.

"Then that was kind," said Cadfael with a sigh, and l
the weary horse away over the chiming cobbles to the stable

In the strawy warmth of the stall he made no haste. It wa
pleasant to be there with the eased and cossetted beast, ai
to be aware of the stirring of his contented neighbours in tl
other stalls. One creature at least returned here to a welcom
Cadfael went on grooming and polishing longer than thei
was any need, leaning his head against a burnished shoulde
Almost he fell asleep here, but sleep he could not afford ye
He left the living warmth of the horse's body reluctantly, ar
went out again into the cold, and crossed the court to tl
cloisters and the south door of the church.

If it was the sharp, clear cold of frost outside, it was tl
heavy, solemn cold of stone within the nave, near darknes
and utter silence. The similitude of death, but for the red-go
gleam of the constant lamp on the parish altar. Beyond, in tl
choir, two altar candles burned low. He stood in the solitude (
the nave and gazed within. In the night offices he had alwa
felt himself mysteriously enlarged to fill every corner, ever
crevice of the lofty vault where the lights could not reach, a
if the soul shed the confines of the body, this shell of a
ageing, no, an old man, subject to all the ills humanity inherit
Now he had no true right to mount the one shallow step th

would take him into the monastic paradise. His lower place was here, among the laity, but he had no quarrel with that; he had known, among the humblest, spirits excelling archbishops, and as absolute in honour as earls. Only the need for this particular communal peace and service ached in him like a death-wound.

He lay down on his face, close, close, his overlong hair brushing the shallow step up into the choir, his brow against the chill of the tiles, the absurd bristles of his unshaven tonsure prickly as thorns. His arms he spread wide, clasping the uneven edges of the patterned paving as drowning men hold fast to drifting weed. He prayed without coherent words, for all those caught between right and expedient, between duty and conscience, between the affections of earth and the abnegations of heaven: for Jovetta de Montors, for her son, murdered quite practically and coldly to clear the way for a coup, for Robert Bossu and all those labouring for peace through repeated waves of disillusion and despair, for the young who had no clear guidance where to go, and the old, who had tried and discarded everything; for Olivier and Yves and their like, who in their scornful and ruthless purity despised the manipulations of subtler souls; for Cadfael, once a brother of the Benedictine house of Saint Peter and Saint Paul, at Shrewsbury, who had done what he had to do, and now waited to pay for it.

He did not sleep; but something short of a dream came into his alert and wakeful mind some while before dawn, as though the sun was rising before its hour, a warmth like a May morning full of blown hawthorn blossoms, and a girl, primrose-fair and unshorn, walking barefoot through the meadow grass, and smiling. He could not, or would not, go to her in her own altar within the choir, unabsolved as he was, but for a moment he had the lovely illusion that she had risen and was coming to him. Her white foot was on the very step beside his head, and she was stooping to touch him with

her white hand, when the little bell in the dortoir rang to rouse
the brothers for Prime.

Abbot Radulfus, rising earlier than usual, was before his
household in entering the church. A cold but blood-red sun
had just hoisted its rim above the horizon to eastward, while
westward the sharp pricking of stars still lingered in a sky
shading from dove-grey below to blue-black in the zenith.
He entered by the south door, and found a habited monk lying
motionless like a cross before the threshold of the choir.

The abbot checked and stood at gaze for a long moment,
and then advanced to stand above the prone man and look
down at him with a still and sombre face. The brown hair
round the tonsure had grown longer than was quite seemly.
There might even, he thought, be more grey in it than when
last he had looked upon the face now so resolutely hidden
from him.

"You," he said, not exclaiming, simply acknowledging the
recognition, without implications of either acceptance or rejection. And after a moment: "You come late. News has been
before you. The world is still changing."

Cadfael turned his head, his cheek against the stone, and
said only: "Father!" asking nothing, promising nothing,
repenting nothing.

"Some who rode a day or so before you," said Radulfus
reflectively, "must have had better weather, and changes of
horses at will along the way. Such word as comes to the
castle Hugh brings also to me. The Earl of Gloucester and
his younger son are reconciled. There have been fighting men
at risk who have been spared. If we cannot yet have peace,
at least every such mercy is an earnest of grace." His voice
was low, measured and thoughtful. Cadfael had not looked
up, to see his face. "Philip FitzRobert on his sickbed," said
Radulfus, "has abjured the quarrels of kings and empresses,
and taken the cross."

Cadfael drew breath and remembered. A way to go, when he despaired of princes. Though he would still find the princes of this world handling and mishandling the cause of Christendom as they mishandled the cause of England. All the more to be desired was this order and tranquillity within the pale, where the battle of heaven and hell was fought without bloodshed, with the weapons of the mind and the soul.

"It is enough!" said Abbot Radulfus. "Get up now, and come with your brothers into the choir."

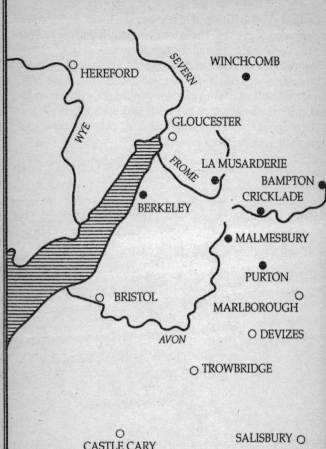

WINCHCOMB

HEREFORD

SEVERN

WYE

GLOUCESTER

FROME   LA MUSARDERIE

BAMPTON
CRICKLADE

BERKELEY

MALMESBURY

PURTON

BRISTOL

MARLBOROUGH

DEVIZES

AVON

TROWBRIDGE

SALISBURY

CASTLE CARY

SHERBORNE   SOUTHAMPTON

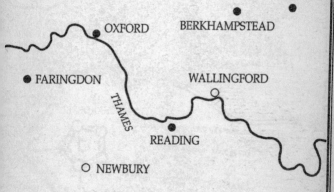

The Thames Valley, 1146

● Castles held by Stephen
○ Castles held by Empress Maud

DEDDINGTON
●

MIDDLETON
●

ST. ALBANS
●

OXFORD
●

BERKHAMPSTEAD
●

FARINGDON
●

WALLINGFORD
○

THAMES

READING
●

○ NEWBURY

GUILDFORD
●

FARNHAM
●

WINCHESTER
●

MERDON
●

BISHOP'S WALTHAM
●

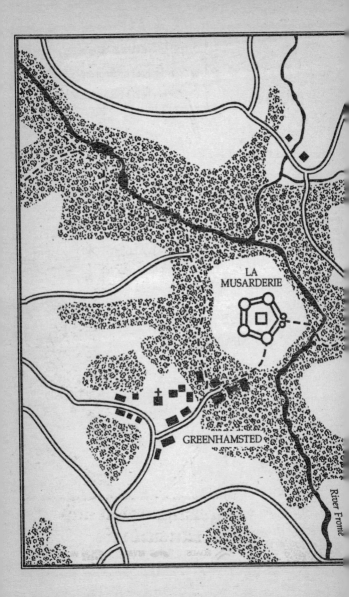

LA
MUSARDERIE

GREENHAMSTED

River Frome

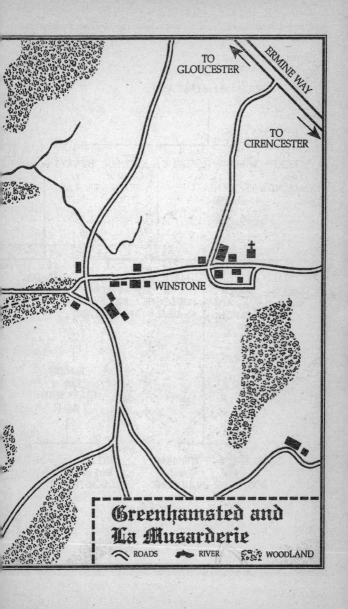

TO
GLOUCESTER

ERMINE WAY

TO
CIRENCESTER

WINSTONE

**Greenhamsted and
La Musarderie**

ROADS   RIVER   WOODLAND

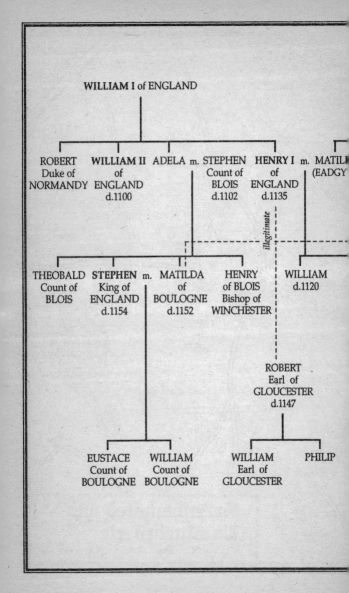

WILLIAM I of ENGLAND

ROBERT
Duke of
NORMANDY

WILLIAM II
of
ENGLAND
d.1100

ADELA m. STEPHEN
Count of
BLOIS
d.1102

HENRY I m. MATIL
of
ENGLAND
d.1135

(EADGY

illegitimate

THEOBALD
Count of
BLOIS

STEPHEN m.
King of
ENGLAND
d.1154

MATILDA
of
BOULOGNE
d.1152

HENRY
of BLOIS
Bishop of
WINCHESTER

WILLIAM
d.1120

ROBERT
Earl of
GLOUCESTER
d.1147

EUSTACE
Count of
BOULOGNE

WILLIAM
Count of
BOULOGNE

WILLIAM
Earl of
GLOUCESTER

PHILIP

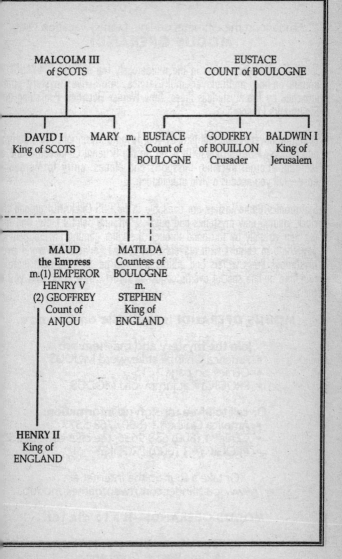

MALCOLM III
of SCOTS

EUSTACE
COUNT of BOULOGNE

DAVID I
King of SCOTS

MARY m. EUSTACE
Count of
BOULOGNE

GODFREY
of BOULLON
Crusader

BALDWIN I
King of
Jerusalem

MAUD
the Empress
m.(1) EMPEROR
HENRY V
(2) GEOFFREY
Count of
ANJOU

MATILDA
Countess of
BOULOGNE
m.
STEPHEN
King of
ENGLAND

HENRY II
King of
ENGLAND

Welcome to the Island of Morada—getting there is easy,
leaving . . . is murder.

Embark on the ultimate, on-line, fantasy vacation with
MODUS OPERANDI.

Join fellow mystery lovers in the murderously fun MODUS OPERANDI,
unique on-line, multi-player, multi-service, interactive, mystery game
launched by The Mysterious Press, Time Warner Electronic Publishing and
Simutronics Corporation.

Featuring never-ending foul play by your favorite Mysterious Press authors
and editors, MODUS OPERANDI is set on the fictional Caribbean island of
Morada. Forget packing, passports and planes, entry to Morada is
easy—all you need is a vivid imagination.

Simutronics GameMasters are available in MODUS OPERANDI around the
clock, adding new mysteries and puzzles, offering helpful hints, and taking you virtually by the hand through the killer gaming environment as
you come in contact with players from on-line services the world over.
Mysterious Press writers and editors will also be there to participate in
real-time on-line special events or just to throw a few back with you at
the pub.

MODUS OPERANDI is available on-line now.

Join the mystery and mayhem on:
- America Online® at keyword MODUS
- GEnie® on page 1615
- PRODIGY® at jumpword MODUS

Or call toll-free for sign-up information:
- America Online® 1 (800) 768-5577
- GEnie® 1 (800) 638-9636, use offer code DAF52
- PRODIGY® 1 (800) PRODIGY

Or take a tour on the Internet at
http://www. pathfinder.com/twep/games/modop.

MODUS OPERANDI—It's to die for.